Sisters by the Sea

4 Short Romances Set in the Sarasota, Florida, Amish Community

WANDA E. BRUNSTETTER

JEAN BRUNSTETTER
RICHELLE BRUNSTETTER &
LORINE BRUNSTETTER VAN CORBACH

Print ISBN 978-1-63609-660-5
Adobe Digital Edition (.epub) 978-1-63609-661-2

Model Photography: Richard Brunstetter III

Published by Barbour Publishing, Inc., 1810 Barbour Drive, Uhrichsville, Ohio 44683, www.barbourbooks.com

Our mission is to inspire the world with the life-changing message of the Bible.

Printed in the United States of America.

Sisters by the Sea

The Seashell Cake

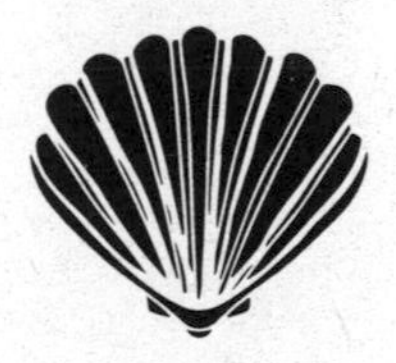

WANDA E. BRUNSTETTER

Prologue

Shipshewana, Indiana

"Are you sure you really want to do this?" Leora Lambright's mother asked as they huddled together outside of Yoder's Shopping Center, waiting for the Pioneer Trails charter bus to arrive. "It's not too late to change your mind."

Leora shivered against the cold winter wind blowing against her face and gave a quick nod of her head. At least there were no snowflakes tumbling down in a flurry today like there had been a few days ago. "The doctor said I should try living in a warm, sunny climate," she responded. "And since I've paid for my bus ticket and put money down for the rent on a house in Pinecraft, I can't back out now. Besides, the only way to know if I'll feel better in Florida is to spend an entire winter there."

"I suppose you're right, but you will surely be missed." Mom slipped her arm around Leora's waist. "Our home won't be the same without you."

"I shall miss all of you too. Maybe you and Dad, or my three sisters, can come visit me in Sarasota sometime soon."

"Since we all have jobs, we'll need to wait and see how it goes."

Soon the bus pulled in, and once everyone's luggage had been loaded, the group of forty-five people who would be heading south with Leora began to board. She turned to her mother and gave her a tearful hug. "I'll call and let you know as soon as I arrive."

"*Jah*, please do." Mom dabbed at a few tears that had spilled from her eyes. "We will all be praying that you have a safe trip."

"*Danki*." With a determined set of her jaw, Leora hoisted her purse and carry-on satchel over her shoulder and boarded the bus. After taking her seat next to an elderly Amish woman from their family's church district, Leora watched out the window until the bus pulled out of the parking lot and she could no longer see her mother waving goodbye. Leora felt a tingling sensation within her chest. While she was about to embark on a new adventure and felt eager to see what the future held for her in sunny Sarasota, Leora couldn't help wondering if her decision to leave Indiana was the right one.

She leaned firmly against the back of the seat cushion and closed her eyes. *Guess I'll know the answer to that question soon enough.*

Chapter 1

The village of Pinecraft in Sarasota, Florida

One year later

The sun's warmth felt welcoming as Leora lounged in a reclining chair on the lanai at the back of her long-term rental. The small, two-bedroom cottage was located on Kruppa Avenue in the village of Pinecraft, a community where Amish and Mennonite people came to vacation or stay during the winter months. A few folks, like the widow who lived in the house next door, resided in Pinecraft full-time.

Leora inhaled the sweet aroma drifting on the light breeze. It came from the lovely red flowering hibiscus planted close to the screened-in lanai.

She reached for her glass of iced tea and took a slow sip. The cool liquid felt refreshing as it trickled down her parched throat. This was Leora's day off from the bakery inside Der Dutchman Restaurant. Since Leora had been previously employed at Das Dutchman Essenhaus bakery in Middlebury, Indiana, she had no problem securing a position at the restaurant here. Leora liked her job, but she also looked forward to her days off, when she could relax at the house, ride her bike along the Legacy Trail, or catch the Scat bus for a trip to Lido or Siesta Keys Beach.

Some days Leora went with her friend Karen Schrock, who had come from Ohio to Sarasota a few months ago and stayed because she liked it here. Karen worked as a cashier at Der Dutchman. Leora and Karen enjoyed doing many of the same things—shopping, collecting shells at the beach, biking, and getting together to sing and play musical instruments with other friends. Karen had invited Leora to go shopping with her today, but Leora declined, saying she didn't need anything, and had decided to stay home and relax on her day off.

Leora yawned and repositioned the black scarf pinned to the back of her head. She rarely wore her stiff, white, cone-shaped, pleated-at-the-back covering unless she was at work, attending church, or going to some public place where she felt it was important to look her best. It was easier and more convenient to wear a scarf for most other activities.

It felt good to rest and do nothing. If the sunshine began to feel too hot, she would go inside, lie on the couch, and read the novel she'd picked up last week and hadn't had a chance to start. There was also the option of sitting out on the shaded front porch, but that would probably lead to visiting with people walking by who wanted to stop and talk awhile. Leora wasn't in the mood for conversation. She got enough of that during work hours at the bakery and at the frequent social events that took place at Pinecraft Park.

Leora's primary goal these days was to live as peacefully as possible. She had tried, without much success, to convince herself that she could be happy remaining single and didn't need to be married in order to feel fulfilled. But when she was honest with herself, she admitted that many times when she saw couples together on the beach, out shopping, or here in Pinecraft, she couldn't help feeling a bit envious. If she continued to live in sunny Florida, Leora would probably never get married, have children, and live the kind of life she used to dream about. *But at least that would be better than living someplace where I wouldn't be able to live a happy, fulfilled life*, she told herself.

She closed her eyes and tried to relax the tight muscles in her shoulders that hadn't been there a few moments ago. Thinking about her situation was no doubt the cause of the stress she now felt.

Leora's thoughts took her back to the day she was diagnosed with seasonal affective disorder, better known as SAD. This condition caused a person to feel sad or even deeply depressed throughout the dark, cold winter months. Additional symptoms included low energy, trouble coping, sleeping too much, losing interest in things one normally enjoyed, difficulty concentrating, and overeating due to certain food cravings. Leora remembered feeling hopeless, worthless, and guilty for not being able to function normally during the dark days of late fall, winter, and sometimes even early spring if the weather remained dreary. She'd always thought it was strange how she had been able to function like the rest of her family for just a few months, and never understood why she'd always dreaded the months when there was less sunlight and hadn't felt well once they arrived.

"What's the cause of this disorder?" Leora had asked her doctor back home after he'd given her his diagnosis.

"The lower level of sun in the fall and winter may disrupt your body's internal clock and lead to the symptoms you've been experiencing," Dr. Smithers had responded. "Also, reduced sunlight can cause a drop in a brain chemical called serotonin that may trigger depression. In addition, the change in the seasons can disrupt the balance of your body's level of melatonin, which plays a role in sleep patterns and mood."

"Is there anything I can do to manage my symptoms?" she'd questioned.

"Full spectrum lights inside your home could help, but since you don't use electricity, and your source of light is either battery operated or gas lanterns, it might not be a strong enough source of light for you. You can also surround yourself with healing colors, such as green, pink and red." He had patted Leora's hand and looked at her with sincerity. "Personally, my advice for you would be to relocate to a sunny place like Florida or one of the other southern states."

One of her neighbor's dogs began barking, and Leora's eyes snapped open. She sat up straight. The answer for her SAD was definitely here in Sarasota, because she felt much better than she had while living back home in Middlebury. The only problem was she missed her family and close friends. Even though she had invited all of them to visit her in Sarasota, so far no one had been able to come.

Before Leora's diagnosis, she'd believed that she wasn't pretty or interesting enough to attract a man. But after learning that she suffered with SAD, Leora had rationalized that she'd probably never been able to hold a boyfriend because of the depression hovering over her head like a dark cloud half the year. It made sense now, because Leora hadn't been a happy person when she'd lived where the weather was dreary and cold.

Leora had met a few single Amish men over the past year, but none lived in Sarasota full-time. They would come and go during the winter months, and most were either married or had steady girlfriends.

I must learn to be content to live here and find enjoyable and meaningful things to do on my own or with a friend, Leora reminded herself. *It's the only way I'll ever be truly happy.*

She looked up, shielding her eyes from the glare of the sun. *Lord, help me to be satisfied, and please give my life some special meaning.*

~

While working at a table behind a glass enclosure inside the bakery the following day, Leora had a hard time concentrating on her task. Yesterday's nap on the lanai had left her with a painful sunburn on her arms, legs, and face, but she had no one to blame but herself. She shouldn't have lain there as long as she did, and she couldn't allow the burning pain to stop her from doing her best work today.

Leora refocused, determined to put her full attention on adding the final touches to a wedding cake someone had ordered two days ago. She'd frosted all three layers of the cake with a pale blue frosting, and each layer was to be decorated with edible seashells. The candy shells weren't hard to make, and the molds she had used were shaped like different types of shells. Leora's favorites resembled a large starfish, some two-inch scallops, and a small Florida sand dollar. The nice thing about making the sugar seashells was that they could be done up ahead of time. Once hardened and removed from the mold, they would stay fresh at room temperature for up to a week. The ones she would put on this wedding cake had been made two days ago.

Leora pursed her lips as she took a step back and studied her creation. *If I were getting married, I'd want a lovely seashell cake like this one. The theme of the cake goes well with the life I live here in Florida, where I can go to the beach and look for shells on my days off from work.*

Her brows furrowed. *It's sad to think about, but as long as I choose to remain here in Sarasota, there will be no wedding cake for me, with or without seashells. Even if I moved back to Indiana, where I'd have to deal with SAD and the gray winter days again, it's doubtful that any man would choose me. After all, who would want a wife who struggles with depression when the seasons change and then feels hopeless and guilty?* Every family that came into the restaurant and walked past or came up to the checkout counter at the bakery was a reminder that Leora was a single Amish woman who most likely would never have a husband. It was hard to admit that during the years she'd lived in Indiana, she had never had a serious boyfriend.

A young mother, holding a baby, stepped up to the glass enclosure. "That is absolutely beautiful." The woman pointed to the seashell cake. "I wish I could have had something like that at my wedding reception two years ago." She smiled at Leora. "You're very talented to have created something so extraordinary."

"Thank you." Leora's warm cheeks grew hotter. She'd never been sure how to respond when receiving a compliment. She had been taught at an early age to be humble and not brag. Of course, Leora wasn't bragging right now; she just needed to learn how to accept a compliment graciously.

"You must enjoy cake decorating, because you certainly have a knack for it." The young woman shifted her infant so her other arm was carrying the weight of the child.

Oh, how she longed to have a child of her own. Leora pushed away the sudden feeling of jealousy. "How old is your baby?" she asked.

"She's one month today."

"What is her name?"

"Abigail. It was the name of my husband's grandmother."

"It's a beautiful name, and so is she." Leora could hardly take her eyes off the child.

"Guess I'd better move on," the woman said. "If I stand here much longer, I'll be tempted to order a cake, pie, or some doughnuts." She gave a light laugh. "I gained too much weight when I was carrying Abigail, so now I'm watching my sugar and carb intake."

Leora smiled. "It was nice talking with you. I hope you have a good rest of the day."

"You too."

Leora watched the woman walk away and then reminded herself to resume work on the cake. It wouldn't do to get behind on this, because she had a few other cakes to decorate yet today.

Leora's friend Karen stepped up to her and held out a credit card. "Did you by any chance see who laid this card on the counter over there?" She gestured to the section where doughnuts and other pastries were sold. "There are no customers over there now, but I found it a few seconds ago."

Leora shook her head. "My attention's been on decorating the seashell cake. Oh, and I visited for a bit with a young woman holding a baby. She seemed interested in the cake I was working on, but I'm sure I would have noticed if she'd laid a credit card down."

"Hmm. . ." Karen held the card up close to Leora and pointed. "If someone by the name of John Miller comes looking for it, would you please send him over to my checkout counter?"

Leora glanced at the card and nodded. "Sure thing. John Miller. I'll try to remember that name."

Chapter 2

John Miller took a seat in one of the wooden outdoor rocking chairs on the front porch of the Der Dutchman restaurant. With wallet in hand, he began thumbing through the separations, searching desperately for his credit card. *That's really strange. I thought I'd put it in here after paying for my doughnuts.* John rubbed his sweaty palm on his pant leg and took a few deep breaths in an effort to calm himself. The last thing he needed was for someone to get ahold of his card and start charging things. After John had eaten breakfast in the restaurant this morning, he'd gone over to the bakery section, eager to try some of the chocolate-covered doughnuts that were on sale today. Maybe in his eagerness he'd dropped the card.

He glanced at the box of pastries in his lap and frowned. The loss of his credit card had snatched John's appetite for doughnuts or anything else. *I need to go back inside*, he told himself, rising from the chair. *Maybe I left it on the checkout counter or lost the card on the floor. If so, someone may have picked it up.* If that should be the case, John hoped the person hadn't walked out of the restaurant with his card in their wallet.

When John entered the building, he turned to the right and headed straight for the bakery counter. As luck would have it, there were at least ten people in line ahead of him. He glanced around the floor where he stood but saw no sign of his credit card. He figured if he had dropped it, the card could have been somewhere between here and the counter.

He flexed his fingers repeatedly, then reached up with his free hand to rub the back of his neck. If there was one thing John disliked, it was waiting. Although he'd always been patient when it came to business matters, he'd never liked having to wait in line at the supermarket or any other place where there was a checkout counter.

John resisted the temptation to tap his foot as he gripped the box of doughnuts. He strained to see around the people in front of him, hoping for a glimpse of the counter where he'd paid for the treat. No such luck. There were too many people bobbing their heads this way and that as they spoke to those who were with them or told their children to stop asking for things.

John glanced to his left, where a sign that read CAKES had been suspended from the ceiling near a glass display case. He craned his head a bit and noticed a pretty Amish woman behind a table decorating a cake. He figured it must be a tedious job and took a lot of skill with a steady hand, not to mention patience. *Maybe once I'm able to talk to the woman at the cash register, I'll walk over there and see what kind of cake that Amish woman is working on. From where I stand, it looks like it's gonna be a nice one.*

John stood rigidly in line for several more minutes until the people in front of him finally dispersed and it became his turn. "Hello. My name is John Miller. I was here a while ago and bought some chocolate doughnuts," he said to the blond-haired Amish woman behind the cash register. "I paid with my credit card, but when I stepped outside, I realized that it wasn't in my wallet. I couldn't figure out what had happened to it, so I came back here, hoping I may have laid it on the counter and forgotten to put it back in my wallet." He placed the box of doughnuts on the counter, thinking the cashier might remember who he was.

She smiled and gave a nod. "Yes, John, I remember you, and I have the credit card you left on the counter. I was hoping you would come back for it."

He released a huge sigh when she handed him the card. "Thank you so much. I'm real glad you kept it here for me. I probably should have paid for the doughnuts with cash, but I use the card whenever I can because I acquire train points with it."

"Did you come here by train?"

"Just as far as Tampa, since passenger trains don't stop in Sarasota. When I arrived at the station in Tampa, a driver I'd hired was waiting to bring me here."

"Where are you from?" she asked.

"Clare, Michigan."

"You're a ways from home then. Did your family come with you?"

He shook his head. "I'm not married. It was actually my folks' idea that I come spend a few months here because I. . ." John stopped talking when he looked back and realized that another line had formed behind him. He slipped the credit card in his wallet, picked up the box of doughnuts, and said, "Thanks again," before walking away. With no thought of the cake he had wanted to look at, John headed out of the restaurant and hurried across the street when the light indicated it was safe for pedestrians to walk. John's appetite for something sweet returned as quickly as it had disappeared. Now the only thing on his mind was getting back to the house he'd rented in Pinecraft. He looked forward to sitting down with a glass of cold milk and one or two of those chocolate-covered doughnuts.

~

"John Miller came in, and I gave him his card," Karen said when she approached Leora before heading to a table in the restaurant for her lunch break.

Leora pulled her attention away from the cake she'd been putting last-minute details on. "Oh, you mean the man who lost his credit card?"

"Jah, and needless to say, he seemed quite relieved."

"I can imagine. I'd be relieved too if I'd lost my card and someone had found it."

"John seemed like a nice man. He's from Michigan, and he's not married."

"Were you hoping he might ask you out?" Leora gave her friend's arm a little poke.

Karen's cheeks reddened. "Of course not, silly. You know I've been seeing Ken Yoder. John looked to be about your age, though, so I was thinking maybe you might be interested in him."

Leora blinked rapidly, and her mouth slackened. "Jah, right. I don't even know the man, and I doubt he would be interested in someone like me, even if he were to come into the bakery again."

"Oh, he'll be back in, all right. That fellow has a thing for chocolate doughnuts, which I'm sure is why he'd bought a dozen of them."

"Be that as it may, even if he came to the bakery counter every single day, it's not likely he'd come over here by the cakes or take an interest in me."

"You never know." Karen grinned. "I didn't think Ken would be interested in me, either, but as you know, we've been going out regularly for the past month."

"Well, go enjoy your lunch," Leora said without commenting on her friend's last statement.

"What about you? Isn't it about time for your lunch break?"

"Not for another thirty minutes." Leora pointed to the seashell cake. "In the meantime, I need to finish up with this."

Karen gave a nod. "It sure is beautiful."

"I'm glad you like it. If I were ever to get married, I'd want my wedding cake to look just like this one." Leora's posture slackened a bit. "But that's never going to happen."

"Don't be so sure. You never know what God has planned for your life."

Leora gave a brief shrug. There was no point in talking about this or getting her hopes up about the possibility of getting married. She reminded herself once more to be content.

~

John entered the small house he had rented for the next two months, and set his box of doughnuts on the kitchen table. He'd arrived in Pinecraft yesterday afternoon and eaten supper at Yoder's Restaurant, located a few blocks from his rental on Estrada Street. Der Dutchman was a little farther from his place, but John hadn't minded the walk there. This afternoon he planned to rent a bike from one of several places right here in the village of Pinecraft. It would be a lot easier to get around, and he could go more places peddling a bicycle than on foot. Besides, he'd heard about the Legacy Trail that ran from Sarasota all the way to Venice, and he was eager to do some exploring. Perhaps he would stay local today and begin his adventures tomorrow.

"But not right now," John said aloud. "I'm gonna have one of those tasty-looking doughnuts and sit outside for a while to enjoy the warmth of the sun."

~

At four o'clock that afternoon, John left the bike shop on Kruppa Avenue, satisfied that he'd made a good choice with the ten-speed bicycle he had chosen to rent. There'd been many other choices, including three-wheelers and e-bikes, but he'd picked what he thought would work best for him. John figured the best part of riding a bike was the exercise it provided while pedaling. An electric bicycle might get him places sooner—some going as fast as thirty miles per hour, but he couldn't think of anywhere he needed to be that required getting there quickly. Besides, riding an electric bike had nothing to do with exercise and everything to do with speed. If John was going to see the sights in Sarasota during the time he would be here, he preferred to do it at a leisurely pace so he could enjoy some interesting scenery along the way.

Halfway up the street, John caught sight of an Amish woman walking at a brisk pace. He slowed his bike and took a second look. *Could that be the same woman I saw decorating a cake at Der Dutchman bakery this morning?* John had wanted to walk over to the cake section in the bakery and take a look, but after getting his credit card back, he'd forgotten all about his curiosity over what the cake she'd been decorating looked like.

John applied the brake and sat watching the petite woman as she approached a white house with maroon trim and slowed her steps. He was tempted to go across the street and ask if she worked at the bakery, but that would be too bold, and it wasn't the kind of thing John would normally do. He'd always been kind of shy around women he didn't know—especially if they had a pretty face. *Do I go on over there or keep riding in the direction of Estrada Street?* John asked himself. *If I stopped to talk to her and she's not the same woman who works at the bakery, I'd feel pretty foolish.* He clenched his handlebars and argued with himself. *Do I or don't I? And if I did go over there, what exactly would I say? Hello, my name's John Miller, and I was wondering if it was you I saw decorating a cake at the bakery this morning.*

Then another thought popped into John's head. *What if she's married and her husband came out of the house and saw me talking to her? It probably wouldn't go over too well—especially if he was the jealous type.*

A horn tooted from behind, and John nearly jumped off his bicycle seat. *Guess that's what I get for stoppin' in the middle of the road.* He moved his bike to one side and glanced across the street again, in time to see the Amish woman go into a house. John wasn't about to go over there and knock on her door, so he started pedaling again and soon turned off Kruppa Avenue. *Guess if I'm really that curious about whether she was the same person I saw decorating a cake, I'd better plan another trip to Der Dutchman. In fact, I think I'll go there for breakfast again tomorrow and stop over at the bakery after I finish eating.*

Chapter 3

John woke up the following morning to the sound of his cell phone ringing. He figured it might be important, so he got out of bed to answer the call. "Hello. John Miller here. How may I help you?" he answered with his usual business greeting and without looking at the screen.

"This is your mother, and you can help by letting me know if you got to your destination, which should have been yesterday."

John cringed. "Sorry, Mom. My phone battery was dead by the time I arrived, and I put it on the charger and forgot about it."

"Couldn't you have borrowed someone else's phone? Your *daed* said no news was good news, but I was worried about you."

"Sorry for causing you to worry. I didn't realize the battery had died until I got to my rental, and by that time my driver was gone. And since I don't know anyone here, I didn't feel right about asking to borrow some stranger's phone."

"It's okay. I'm not mad. Just relieved that you are there." There was a short pause. "You know, John, I wouldn't be surprised if you run into some people you do know while you're in Pinecraft. A lot of Amish folks from Michigan and Indiana visit there during the colder months. So you never know if someone you've done a roofing job for or have met somewhere else might be there now too."

John yawned as he lowered himself into a kitchen chair. "Maybe so."

"You sound tired. Bet I woke you, huh?"

"Jah, but it's okay. I needed to get up anyway."

"Have you gone shopping for food? The place where you're staying does have kitchen facilities, I hope."

"Yes, Mom, there's a stove, refrigerator, a kitchen table with four chairs, and even a dishwasher, which I'll probably never use. The cupboards and drawers are filled with dishes, silverware, glasses, and pans for cooking, so all I need to do is buy some food." *Although I don't plan to do much cooking*, he mentally added. *I'll probably eat out more than in.*

"I'd better let you go then so you can get to the store. I'll call again and check on you in a few days."

John wanted to tell her not to bother, that he was a thirty-year-old man, not a child, but he held his tongue. "It was nice talking to you, Mom. Please tell Dad I said hello."

"I will. Take care, Son, and I hope you get rested up. Oh, by all means, take every opportunity to get some sun, and enjoy your time in Sarasota."

"Sure thing. Bye for now."

When John clicked off, he remained at the table with his head bowed and eyes closed. *Lord, please give me more patience where my mother is concerned. She treats me like a child sometimes, and I don't want to be disrespectful, but it really gets on my nerves. At moments like this, I wish I wasn't an only child.*

~

"I see you're hard at work already. How long have you been here?" Karen asked when she popped into the bakery kitchen where Leora was busy mixing the ingredients for another cake she would soon decorate.

"I came in an hour sooner than usual so I could leave work earlier today," Leora responded. "I have some grocery shopping to do, and I'm way behind on my letter writing, so I thought the extra hour would help."

"I understand. There never seems to be enough hours in a day to get things done." Karen moved closer and sniffed the air. That batter sure smells good. Is it maple-flavored?"

"Butterscotch."

"Must be a special order then."

"Right. It's for an English man's eightieth birthday, and I was told that butterscotch is his favorite flavor."

"He's a man of good taste. I wouldn't mind a butterscotch cake for my birthday, or any other time, either." Karen chuckled and gave Leora's shoulder a tap. "Guess I'd best get out to the cash register before a line begins to form. As you know, it's strawberry season now, and folks will be wanting strawberry long johns and fresh strawberry pie."

Leora nodded. "And don't forget about strawberry cupcakes and cookies."

"Quit it now. You're making my mouth water, thinking about all those tasty treats. See you later, friend," Karen called over her shoulder as she left the room.

Leora lined up the two cake pans she'd gotten ready beforehand and poured the fragrant batter evenly into each one. She looked forward to decorating this cake and wished she could be at the man's birthday party to see his reaction.

~

John finished eating a hearty omelet with cheddar cheese, ham, and mushrooms, paid his bill, and headed for the bakery section near the front of the restaurant. He paused near the checkout counter to breathe in the delicious aroma of baked goods, then moved on to the display case filled with cookies in several flavors, including strawberry. It seemed strange that strawberries were in season in the middle of winter, but that was one of the many benefits of being in a warmer climate.

John debated about buying some of the strawberry long johns but talked himself out of it because he still had chocolate-covered doughnuts that needed to be eaten. Maybe tomorrow or the next day he would purchase some long johns or another kind of pastry. *Of course if Mom were here, she'd remind me not to eat too many sweets*, John told himself. He placed his hand firmly against his muscular chest. *I am not overweight, and I'm in pretty good shape, so I don't think a few bakery treats once in a while are going to make me gain weight.*

John moved on until he came to the glass display case for cakes. Although the woman he'd been curious about yesterday was not behind the table, he focused on the most unusual cake he'd ever seen sitting inside the glass case. Seashells, which he assumed had been made of frosting or some kind of candy, were scattered in various places on the three layers. He stood for several minutes, admiring the creation and wondering how long it must have taken to decorate the cake. Since there was no one behind the enclosure to ask, John figured he may as well go back to his rental for a while before he went grocery shopping. He was about to leave when the Amish woman he'd seen here before and again on Kruppa Avenue near the bike shop walked up and placed a cake on the table where she'd been working yesterday. This two-layered cake had been covered in a beige frosting, and it looked good enough to eat, even without any fancy decorations.

John smiled at the woman. "Sorry to bother you, but I couldn't help noticing this cake here and how it's decorated with shells." He pointed to the cake in question. "Did you make it?"

"Yes, I decorated it yesterday," she replied. "Sometime this morning it will be picked up to be taken to a couple's wedding reception."

"It's amazing! You must be real creative, because I'll bet it wasn't easy to create."

A visible flush swept across her cheeks. "It wasn't really that difficult, but maybe it's because I enjoy what I do." She gestured to some of the other cakes in the display case. "Are you interested in buying one of the cakes that are for sale?"

"Uh, no. . .not today. I just wanted to tell you that I was fascinated with your seashell cake."

John had trouble breaking eye contact with the pretty woman, but he didn't want to keep her by asking more questions. "Umm. . .guess I'd. . .uh. . .better. . .umm. . .be on my way." John's face warmed as he stumbled over his sentence. *I'd better get out of here before I make a complete fool of myself.* He said a quick goodbye and hurried away. *What's the matter with you, John? That woman who made you blush and become tongue tied could be married.*

~

The tall, muscular Amish man who'd asked Leora about the seashell cake had only been gone a few minutes when Karen rushed up to her. "I see you met John Miller."

Leora tipped her head. "Who?"

"John Miller. He's the man who left his credit card here yesterday and came back for it. Remember when I told you his name?"

"Oh. . .uh. . .yeah, I guess you did." Leora still felt the heat of her blush from the man's compliment.

"So what'd he say? He must not have been here to buy a cake, because he didn't come to the register with one."

Leora gave a quick shake of her head. "No, he just asked

me a couple of questions and made a few comments about the seashell cake."

"Did he like it?"

"Jah."

"Did he want to order one?"

"No." Leora glanced toward the cash register and motioned with her head. "Looks like there are some people waiting to check out."

Now it was Karen's turn to blush. "Oh, thanks for letting me know. I'd better go take care of them." She hurried off, and Leora felt relieved. The last thing she wanted to do was answer more of her friend's questions. John Miller was just a nice man who'd wanted to ask a few things about her cake, and there was nothing more to it. *Leave it to Karen to start plying me with questions.*

~

Leora rode into the grocery store's parking lot on North Beneva Road and secured her bicycle next to another bike that had only one basket. She was thankful that hers had both a front and back basket, because she had quite a few items to get.

Once she had gone into the store and gotten a cart, Leora's first stop was the produce aisle, where she picked out several avocados. After sitting a day or two on her kitchen counter, they would be ripe enough to make a batch of fresh guacamole. Her mouth watered at the thought of how good it would taste on a tangy taco salad or dolloped over a plate of scrambled eggs, which she often fixed for breakfast. Sometimes Leora ate sliced avocados with cottage cheese for lunch or breakfast.

She glanced at her grocery list and headed for the meat department to get three packages of frozen ground bison patties—another favorite of hers. From there she picked out two packages of cheese, one swiss and the other cheddar; a dozen organic, free-range eggs; and a carton of coconut-almond milk. She bypassed the baked-goods section. Being a baker, she made her own homemade bread and rolls but didn't indulge too often in order to keep her weight down.

The next aisle Leora headed for had a variety of canned goods on the shelves. She'd just turned down the aisle when she collided with an Amish man's cart. Leora let out a little gasp as her head jerked back. She was surprised to see that the man pushing the other cart was John Miller.

"Oh, I'm so sorry! Guess I wasn't watching where I was going." He quickly pulled his cart back. "You're the Amish woman I spoke to at the bakery this morning, right?"

Leora nodded.

"Are you okay?" His thick eyebrows drew together. "I didn't hurt you with my cart, I hope."

"No, I. . .I'm fine. How about you?"

"Other than being embarrassed, I'm fine and dandy."

"Good to hear. Do you shop at this store often?" she asked.

"No, this is my first time. I arrived in Sarasota yesterday."

"Where are you from?"

"Clare, Michigan, and my name is John Miller." He reached out his hand, and when she shook it, he said, "How about you? What's your name, where's your home state, and how long have you been in sunny Florida?"

"I'm Leora Lambright. I used to live in Middlebury, Indiana, and all of my family is there. I moved to Sarasota a little over a year ago."

"Oh, I see." John put both arms on the cart handle and leaned slightly forward. "You must like it here to have stayed that long."

Leora felt beads of sweat erupt on her forehead. She wasn't about to explain to a near stranger the reason she'd moved to

Sarasota or why she had continued to live here. Just as with everyone she didn't know well, Leora chose not to discuss her seasonal affective disorder. It would be embarrassing, plus John probably wouldn't understand, same as a few other people she'd told and who had made light of her condition, saying they'd never heard of such a thing.

John cleared his throat a few times. "You said that your family all live in Indiana. Does that mean you're a single woman living here by yourself?"

Leora was taken aback by his bold question, but she felt that it deserved an honest answer. "That's right. I'm not married, and I'm perfectly happy to be unattached." Her heart pounded like a drum beating an uneven rhythm. *I just told this man a lie. But he shouldn't have asked. My personal life is none of his business, and I wish John Miller would stop looking at me with those big blue-as-a-summer-sky eyes.*

Leora forced a smile and said, "It was nice seeing you again. Now, if you'll excuse me, I need to get the rest of my shopping done and head back to Pinecraft."

"Of course. I need to do the same." He gave her a brief nod and went on his way.

Leora pushed her cart up the aisle, wondering why her legs felt so wobbly. Surely it couldn't have anything to do with the encounter she'd had with John Miller. She pulled in a deep breath. *I won't give it another thought.*

Chapter 4

Lido Beach

Leora paid her driver, grabbed everything she'd brought with her, and stepped down from the van. The clear blue sky and bright sun overhead had created the perfect day for a trip to the beach. Leora couldn't think of a better way to spend her day off. Sometimes she came here on the bus; other times she rode her bike. Today, however, Leora had chosen to bring more beach things than usual, so she'd hired a driver who lived near Pinecraft to pick her up. Karen had planned to come with Leora, but at the last minute she'd been asked to fill in for someone at the bakery who had called in sick. Hearing that her friend wouldn't be joining her, Leora had decided to forget about the beach and find something else to do today that was closer to home. But after looking out the window this morning and seeing the beautiful weather, she'd changed her mind and packed up her things.

Leora headed down the short boardwalk toward the sandy beach, pulling a beach cart filled with everything she would need for the day. When her sandaled feet touched the sand, she paused and breathed in the briny sea air. Almost immediately Leora felt a release of tension from her body.

She moved on, tugging harder on the beach buggy's handle as she shuffled through the thick, white sand. It wasn't long before her sandals filled up with shifting sand, so she stopped to take them off. Walking barefoot worked better, and Leora continued on until she drew closer to the water. A sense of joy and awe welled in her soul as the crash of waves and fizz of foam swept ashore and spread across the sparkling beach.

Leora found a spot among other beachgoers' colorful towels, giant umbrellas, and a variety of beach chairs to make her own little campsite for the day. First, she pulled a reclining chair from the beach buggy and opened it up. Then she got out the big umbrella she'd bought recently and put the two pieces of the pole together. Next, she poked the sharp end of the pole into the sand and twisted the base of it several times until she felt sure the umbrella was secure. Her final step was to open the red-and-blue-striped umbrella by pushing it up until it was locked into place. She set her small cooler under the umbrella and placed a towel on the chair. After putting it into the reclining position, Leora took a seat and stretched out. Then she hitched her skirt up a bit and rolled up her dress sleeves.

It probably looks odd for an Amish woman to be wearing a dress and lying here with only her legs, arms, and face exposed, she thought, *but I'm not about to put on a swimsuit like most of the non-Amish women are wearing. In fact, I don't care what anyone thinks. I have always dressed modestly, and I'm not embarrassed of the clothing I wear.*

Leora reached into her tote bag, which she'd set next to her chair, and pulled out a tube of sunscreen. She slathered some on her face, arms, and legs, then closed her eyes and let the warmth of the sun penetrate her skin. Oh, how good it felt to be here on the beach where seagulls cried overhead and children squealed with delight as they frolicked in the water.

"Thanks for the ride. I'll call you when I've had enough sun and sand for the day," John told his driver, Arnie.

"No problem. I have a few errands to run this morning, but I'll be free the rest of the day."

John grabbed his backpack and shut the van door. Although he'd never been to Lido before, it didn't take him long to find a way out to the beach via one of the paths.

Snatches of people's conversations carried on the wind as he stepped around beach chairs and towels spread across the sand.

With all these people, maybe it won't be as peaceful as I'd hoped, but I'm here now, so I may as well make the best of it. John took his oversized towel from the backpack, spread it out, and then rolled up a smaller towel to use under his head. While lying in the sand wouldn't be the most comfortable position, John didn't own a beach chair, so this would have to do.

He was about to stretch out on the towel when a gust of wind came up, so strong that it blew sand in drifts and knocked several people's umbrellas over. One, several feet out in front of him, was lifted into the air and carried down the beach by the wind. An Amish woman John hadn't noticed before leaped out of her beach chair and stood shaking her head, as though in disbelief. Without giving it a second thought, John took off in hot pursuit of the umbrella, and the woman did too. They both reached out for the runaway object at the same time, crashing into each other. The next thing John knew, he was sprawled out on the sand, face-to-face with Leora Lambright.

Leora let go of the umbrella and clambered to her feet. John did the same. They stood staring at each other while repeating each other's names.

"I. . .I didn't realize the umbrella belonged to you," he stammered.

"And I didn't know you were here on Lido Beach." Leora looked down at her umbrella. "Thanks for your help in rescuing it."

"No problem. I'm glad I could help. Sorry about the collision, though. Are you all right?"

"Jah, I'm fine." She brushed some sand off her dress. "How about you?"

"I'm good."

Leora bent down to retrieve her umbrella, but John grabbed it first. "If you show me where you were sitting, I'll set it back up for you."

"Oh, you don't have to do that."

"I want to. It's not a problem."

"Okay, follow me." Leora released her grip on the umbrella and let him carry it. When they reached the area where her chair and beach buggy sat, she pointed to the spot where she had set up the umbrella. "That wind was either too strong for the umbrella to withstand or I didn't get it secured well enough. I'll have to try again or do without any shade."

"I'll make sure it's secure for you," John said.

She smiled. "That would be appreciated. I'm sure your grip is firmer than mine."

John positioned the end of the umbrella over the hole then knelt down and twisted the base until it was firmly in place. Leora marveled at how easy he made the job look. She felt sure that even if the wind whipped up again, the umbrella would hold in place.

"Well. . .umm. . .guess I should get back to my beach towel." John shuffled his bare feet in the sand a few times. "Unless you wouldn't mind if I brought my stuff over here by you. Being on the beach might be more pleasant if I had someone to talk with."

He gestured to her chair. "I assume you're here by yourself too?"

"Yes, that's right. I was planning to come with a friend, but she had to work today. So I'd be happy to have you join me."

A big grin spread across John's clean-shaven face. "That'd be great. I'll be right back." He walked up the beach a ways, and Leora stood watching him. Although she didn't know much about John, he seemed like a nice man. Leora wished she had another chair to offer him, but if all John had brought was a towel, maybe he'd be okay with that.

When John returned a few minutes later, he suggested they go look for shells and asked if she would mind if he put his things in her beach buggy.

"I don't mind at all," Leora replied. "And I like your idea of searching for shells. I'd planned to do that sometime today anyway." While John put his backpack and towels in her beach buggy, Leora reached into her tote bag and took out two zippered plastic bags and handed one to John. "While I've lived in Sarasota, I've collected a lot of unusual shells, many of them here on this beach."

"What do you do with them?" he asked.

"I mostly display the shells in jars or glass dishes, but I've also glued some on pieces of driftwood."

"Sounds like you're quite creative."

"Maybe with the cakes I decorate, but my sister Alana is an artist, and she has always been the most creative one in our family."

"I'm no shell expert," John said as they began walking toward the water, "and this is my first time on Lido Beach. So you're gonna have to show me what to look for."

"It's not too hard, really, because there are all kinds of shells on this beach. It's just a matter of picking up the ones that look the most interesting to you." Leora stopped and bent down to pick up a small shell. "This is called a kitten paw." She held it flat in the palm of her hand. "It's fairly common here in Florida, and if you'll notice, it has radial ribs that resemble a kitten's paw—hence the name."

John leaned close and studied the shell. "Well, for goodness' sake, that does look similar to a small cat's paw."

Leora pointed to another shell, this one lying close to John's bare feet. "That's a common cross-barred venus clamshell. It has a distinct cross-bar rib pattern, and it's often the most abundant shell on the beach."

John picked it up and rubbed his thumb over the surface a few times. "Mind if I keep this one?"

"Not at all. I have plenty of those, and I really don't need any more. In fact, feel free to take all the shells you want."

"Okay, thanks."

"Should we walk in the shallow water?" she asked. "We might find some good shells as they are washed ashore by the waves."

"Sure, sounds good." John leaned over and rolled his pant legs up to his knees. "Just in case I end up wading in deeper than I'd planned." He looked over at Leora and grinned.

She smiled and nodded. "I know what you mean. Sometimes the hem of my dress can get pretty wet when I wade in too deep. But out here, in the wind and warm sun, clothes dry quickly."

"Then I guess I won't have to worry about how wet I might get." John plodded into the water, almost up to his knees.

Leora stayed back a ways, watching this tall, muscular man prance around like a child enjoying his first taste of beach life and all that it had to offer. It was hard to believe this was the first time John had been to Sarasota or the beach.

She continued to watch until John beckoned to her with a backward wave. "Come on in! The water feels great!"

Feeling self-conscious all of a sudden, Leora went timidly into the water. This time she was spending with John almost felt like a date. *But that's ridiculous*, she told herself. *I hardly know the man.*

"*Kumme*. . .come look at this." John held up a shell and waved it around. "I found it right here in the water, but I have no idea what it's called."

Leora waded a little closer to him, where she could get a better look at the shell. "That's called a 'stiff pen.' " She gestured to the pointed end of the shell. "Oh, and look. . .there's a barnacle stuck to some of the wide ribs on the outer shell."

John opened his mouth, like he might comment, but before he could utter one word, a sizable wave rolled in unexpectedly, knocking them both off their feet.

Leora gasped as she went down and the water washed over her body. So much for trying to keep her skirt dry—every square inch of her dress was wet, not to mention her head. She reached up to grab the black scarf she was wearing and secured it firmly in place. Before Leora could manage to pull herself up, she felt John's strong arm slip around her waist, lifting her to dry sand. With water dripping down her face, Leora looked at John and stifled a giggle. His shirt and trousers were as wet as her dress, and a lock of dark hair hung over his forehead like a limp rag. To her surprise, he still held the stiff pen shell in one hand.

"Looks like we've had our baths for the day, jah?" John's grin stretched wide on his face.

Leora held her sides as uncontrolled laughter took over. She could only imagine what the two of them looked like, and she wondered what others on the beach must be saying about the Amish man and woman who couldn't stay on their feet when an unforeseen wave came up. Well, she didn't care. This was the most fun Leora had experienced since her arrival in Sarasota. She wished the day could last forever and wondered if there might be a chance of her seeing John Miller again. *Would it be wrong to hope for that?*

Chapter 5

Pinecraft

It had been three days since Leora spent time with John on the beach, and even though they'd exchanged phone numbers, he hadn't called. She didn't feel that it would be right for her to call him, so she'd waited patiently, hoping he would make the first move.

I don't know why I care whether John calls or not, Leora thought as she got ready for work that morning. *Even if he's interested in me, nothing will ever come of it anyway, since our homes are miles apart. And since he hasn't bothered to call, it probably means he isn't serious about the possibility of us getting together again.*

Leora moved over from the bed to stand at her bedroom window, where she looked out at the puffy white clouds feathered by the wind. It took her back to that enjoyable day when she'd met John on the beach and they'd spent a good portion of the day together. In addition to looking for shells, they'd sat under Leora's umbrella and visited about a variety of things as their wet clothes dried. Leora had learned that John was an only child, had his own roofing business in Clare, and had recently turned thirty. He'd also told her that the reason he'd come to Florida for an extended vacation was because he'd been suffering from burnout and needed time away to rest up. So he'd asked his friend Wayne Yoder, who worked for him, to oversee the business in his absence.

When John asked Leora why she had chosen to remain in Sarasota this long, she simply replied that after coming here a little over a year ago she had liked the weather and decided to stay. She'd seen no reason to tell him about her seasonal affective disorder, which he probably wouldn't have understood anyway.

"Why would he?" Leora murmured as she moved away from the window. "Hardly anyone else has."

Leora reflected on how nice it had been when John offered to buy her lunch from the snack shack at Lido. She'd thanked him and ordered a green salad with crab meat, and John had eaten a burger with fries. Later that afternoon, John called his driver for a ride back to Pinecraft and invited Leora to join him. John reasoned that since they were both going to the same place, it made sense for them to ride back there together. Leora had agreed and called her driver, saying she wouldn't need a ride after all.

On the trip to Pinecraft, Leora had given John the names of several interesting places he might want to visit while he was in Sarasota, and he'd said maybe she would like to go with him. They'd exchanged phone numbers before John's driver dropped her off, and John promised to call.

Leora bit the inside of her cheek. *But if he was going to call, surely he would have done so by now. Maybe John decided to see the places I mentioned by himself or with someone else. A man as friendly as John would no doubt have made a few new friends in Pinecraft by now, or maybe he'd met up with some people he knew from his hometown. There are certainly enough Amish folks from Pennsylvania, Indiana, Ohio, and Illinois, so why wouldn't there be some from Michigan too?*

Enough thinking about Mr. Miller, Leora told herself. *I need to get dressed for work, grab a bite of breakfast, and be on my way to Der Dutchman.*

~

John rummaged through his backpack for the umpteenth time, searching for Leora's phone number. He was sure he'd put it in his backpack after she'd given it to him, but it wasn't there. He had planned to call her yesterday, but he'd found a shuffleboard partner at Pinecraft Park and ended up playing the game for several hours. Following that, John had eaten a sandwich at the Postal 98 Café on Yoder Avenue, and then, on the spur of the moment, he'd decided to hop on the bike he'd rented and check out a portion of the Legacy Trail. John had ended up going farther than he'd planned, and by the time he got back, it was suppertime. In no mood to cook a full meal, he'd opened and heated a can of vegetable soup, then ate it with a few crackers.

After that, John had been too tired to do the dishes, so he'd soaked them in the sink and flaked out on the couch with a devotional book on the topic of worry that he had brought from home. He'd read a few pages and fallen asleep, then woke up the next morning and realized he was still on the couch, dressed in yesterday's clothes. After showering and changing into a clean shirt and trousers, John sat on the end of his bed, trying to remember where he could have put Leora's number.

"Here I go, worrying again." John thumped the side of his head. *If it isn't my business I'm worried about, it's something else. Losing Leora's phone number is not that big of a deal*, he told himself. *I just need to go over to Der Dutchman's bakery and talk to her in person. Maybe I'll speak to her first and then get some breakfast in the restaurant. A big meal this morning will make up for the lack of a hearty meal I didn't eat last evening.*

~

When John entered the bakery, the only person he saw was one cashier. He thought she might recognize him but then realized it was not the same woman who'd waited on him before. "Is Leora Lambright here?" John asked, stepping up to the counter.

"She's in the back mixing cake batter. May I help you with something?"

He shook his head. "I need to ask her a question. Can you go tell her that John Miller is here and would like to talk with her a few minutes?"

The woman gave a quick shake of her head. "Not unless it's an emergency." She gestured to the other cash register. "As you can see, I'm here by myself, and I can't leave my station."

John leaned a bit closer and spoke in a quiet voice. "I understand, but I really need to talk with Leora. Can you show me what room she's in? Maybe I can just poke my head in there and—"

"No one except for the restaurant manager and the bakery staff is allowed in that room. Leora will most likely be decorating a cake over there within the next hour or so." She motioned with her head to the cake display area.

John's shoulders drooped and his arms hung loosely at his sides. "I suppose I could go have some breakfast, but have you seen all those people waiting in line?"

She rolled her brown eyes. "Yes, I have, and since there are a lot of people waiting, the time it'll take to wait and then eat your meal will probably equal an hour or more. By then maybe Leora will be out here at her decorating table and you can speak to her then."

"Okay." John gave a reluctant nod and quickly made his way to the back of the line that was now nearly out the front door.

~

Leora had just begun decorating a cake shaped like a guitar when a familiar voice called, "Hello, Leora."

She looked up and was pleased to see John Miller on the other side of the glass case, smiling at her. "It's nice to see you, John. I heard you were here earlier looking for me."

"Yes, I was. I misplaced your phone number, or I would have called." He reached up and rubbed the back of his neck. "I was kinda thinking you might call me."

Leora's face warmed, and she glanced around, hoping no one was listening to their conversation. "Calling you seemed kind of forward, and I wasn't sure you would appreciate it."

"Why wouldn't I? We exchanged numbers so we could keep in touch, right?"

"Jah." Leora added some burgundy-colored frosting on one side of the cake. "I figured you might call me first."

He turned his hands palms up. "I would have if I hadn't lost your number."

Leora felt a sense of relief, knowing John had truly wanted to keep in touch. She'd convinced herself that he hadn't called because he hadn't enjoyed their time on the beach as much as she had.

"If you have something to write my number on, I'll give it to you now," she said, looking away from the cake and back at him.

"As a business owner, I almost always have paper and pen with me." He withdrew both items from the pocket in his trousers.

Leora told John her number and then resumed work on the cake. She had other cakes waiting to be decorated too and needed to get this one done soon. But it was hard to concentrate on her work with this dimpled Amish man smiling at her in such a way that it made her face, neck, and ears feel impossibly hot.

"I should get going and let you do your work," he said. "But before I leave, I do have a quick question."

She tipped her head. "Oh? What's that?"

"Do you have any plans for this evening? There's supposed to be a full moon, and I thought it would be nice to take a walk. I'd enjoy it more if you went with me."

A tingling sensation swept up the back of Leora's neck. The thought of walking in the moonlight with John would be ever so nice. Leora was about to say yes when she remembered about the plans she'd made to get together with Karen and some of their other friends for an evening of singing, snacking, and fellowship at Leora's place. With only a slight hesitation, she said, "A walk sounds nice, but I've already made plans for this evening. She explained to John what they were and said, "Would you like to join us?"

He gave a throaty laugh. "I sure would. Is it all right if I bring my *maularigel* along?"

"Of course. I'll have my guitar, and there might be a few other instruments as well, so the addition of a harmonica will be nice."

"Great! What time should I be there?"

"We'll probably begin around six thirty. Will that work for you?"

"Absolutely." His eyes seemed to sparkle as he offered Leora another wide grin. "I'd better go home now and practice up so I don't make a fool of myself tonight."

"I doubt that very much. Besides, none of us are professional musicians." She returned his smile and picked up her decorating knife again. "I'll see you later, John."

"Most definitely. And now I'll leave you alone to do the work you get paid for. Have a good rest of the day, Leora."

"You too."

As Leora watched John walk away, a sense of excitement welled in her chest. He'd clearly enjoyed spending time with her the other day, or else he wouldn't have asked her to go for a moonlit walk with him this evening. Maybe if they continued to see each other, they could take that walk some other time. Leora hoped that would be the case, because she felt like a young girl with a crush on one of the cute boys who attended her school. Leora could hardly wait for her shift to be over so she could go home and get things ready for this evening's gathering.

Chapter 6

Leora moved about the kitchen, getting all the snacks laid out for the evening's gathering. For those with a sweet tooth, she had brought home strawberry long johns, strawberry cookies, and chocolate-covered doughnuts. Karen had said she would bring potato chips, pretzels, and mixed nuts, so those items should satisfy anyone who had a craving for salt. Leora also had water, iced tea, lemonade, and grape juice to offer to drink. She figured no one would go away hungry or thirsty.

Leora hummed the tune to "Sweet By-and-By" while she got out paper plates, napkins, and plastic cups. She always looked forward to gathering with friends who liked to sing and play their musical instruments, but tonight she was even more eager. Although Leora had not said the words out loud, she knew in her heart that the reason for her enthusiasm was because John would be joining them. From the few times she'd been with him, Leora had found herself enjoying his company, and she felt fairly sure that he'd enjoyed his time with her too. She looked forward to introducing John to some of the friends she'd made in Pinecraft. It was too bad most only lived here part-time, but at least she had the opportunity to spend time with them a few weeks or months out of the year.

Of course, Leora reminded herself, *John's not a permanent resident here either. I need to accept that fact and not let my imagination carry me away. If I'm not careful, I might start believing I could establish a romantic and permanent relationship with a man—maybe John even.* She shook her head. *But that's impossible. No matter how much I'm attracted to John, I cannot allow myself to feel anything more for him than a casual friendship. It wouldn't be prudent to do otherwise.*

~

John had finished eating supper and was about to get his harmonica out when his cell phone rang. He picked it up, and seeing that it was his parents' number, he answered right away. "Hello."

"How are you doing, Son?" his mother asked. "I haven't heard from you in a while and thought I'd check and see how things are going."

"I've only been here a few days, Mom, and it hasn't been that long since your last phone call."

"I know, but I was in the phone shed checking messages, and after seeing the note here reminding me to pray for you every day, I thought I'd give you a call."

"I appreciate the prayers, Mom, but I don't have much time to talk right now." John glanced at the clock. If he didn't leave for Leora's now, he was going to be late.

"So are you doing okay?"

"Jah, I'm fine, but I—"

"How's the *wedder* there?" she questioned. "Is it nice and warm?"

"Jah, the weather has been quite warm. It was in the eighties today."

"You're fortunate. It never got any higher than twenty-five degrees here, I'm sorry to say."

"Then you probably shouldn't be out there in the phone shed where it's so cold."

"I admit, it is pretty chilly in here, but I bundled up real well before leaving the house."

"That's good." John looked at the clock again. "Sorry to cut this short, Mom, but there's someplace I need to go, so I have to hang up."

"Where are you going?"

"Someone I met the other day invited me to her house this evening for a time of fellowship and singing with some of her friends."

"Her? Who is she, John?"

"Just a nice woman who works at the bakery." John chose not to reveal any further information, because if he did, Mom would most likely ask a bunch more questions.

"What would make her invite you to the get-together?"

John drew a sharp intake of breath and blew it out. *Here we go with twenty questions. I really don't have time for this right now.*

"Son, did you hear what I asked?"

"Jah, but I didn't think it really mattered."

"You mean, my question?"

"It's not that. As I said, Leora's nice, and she. . ."

"You know her *naame*?"

"Well yes. All the employees at Der Dutchman wear a name tag." John rubbed the bridge of his nose. "I'm sorry to cut this short, Mom, but I am already late, and I need to go before it gets any later. We'll talk again soon, though, okay?"

"All right. I'll call you in a day or so. I'd like to know how your evening went, and I'm glad you're getting out and socializing. Even when you're here, you don't go out much or attend many functions, so it's good that you're doing it now."

John rolled his eyes as he lifted his gaze toward the ceiling. As far as he was concerned, his mother worried too much about him. He had his reasons for not socializing in his hometown, and he shouldn't have to be reminded of that.

"I've gotta go now, Mom. Please tell Dad I said hello."

"I will. Bye for now, Son."

When John clicked off his phone, he released a quiet moan. *If Mom knew I spent nearly a whole day on the beach with Leora, I can only imagine the questions she would throw at me.*

He picked up his harmonica, slapped a straw hat on his head, and hurried out the back door where his bike was parked. He'd planned to walk over to Leora's place, but given that he was now fifteen minutes later than he should be, riding the bike seemed like the best choice.

~

Leora jumped up from the couch when a knock sounded on the front door. Her heart pounded at the thought that it might be John and they could have a few moments alone to visit before the others arrived. Once everyone got here, it would be more difficult for any of them to carry on a one-on-one conversation.

She opened the door and saw that her first guests were Karen and her boyfriend, Ken. Karen held a paper sack in her hand, and Ken carried a portable keyboard with a stand.

"Welcome!" Leora opened the door wider for them. "You're the first ones here."

They exchanged greetings, and then Leora and Karen went to the kitchen to set out the salty snacks Karen had brought. Meanwhile, Ken headed for the living room, saying that he was going to set up the keyboard.

"Will your new friend John be joining us?" Karen asked as she poured potato chips into a plastic bowl.

"I believe so." Leora opened a bag of pretzels. "John said he would be here, anyway."

Karen smiled. "I'm sure he will be then. Based on the things you told me about the time you spent with him on the beach, I'm guessing you'll see a lot more of John before he goes back to Michigan."

"If I do, it would be nice, but if not, that's okay too." Leora shrugged her shoulders. "After all, with him living there and me staying here, there's no way we could ever develop a serious relationship. And I don't think either of us is looking for one either."

Karen bumped elbows with Leora. "You never know what might happen if you continue to see each other."

Leora gave no comment but continued to set things out for their snacks. She felt relief when someone knocked on the door again, because any possible relationship with John Miller was not a topic she wished to discuss.

"I'd better go see who's at the door." She hurried from the room. This time she discovered two Mennonite sisters: Kathryn, who everyone called Kass, and Miriam, who went by Mim. They both had brought their guitars, which they placed in the living room beside Leora's instrument.

Shortly after, two more people arrived—Aaron Byler and his cousin Charles. Aaron had brought his accordion, and Charles brought a banjo. What a nice variety they would have here this evening. Leora could hardly wait for things to get started. The only person who hadn't arrived was John. She wondered if he had changed his mind about coming. But if he had, surely he would have called to let her know. *Maybe John lost my number again*, she thought. *Would it be too forward if I called him?* Leora pursed her lips. *Maybe calling him would not be a good idea. If he changed his mind about coming, I wouldn't want to make him feel pressured or guilty about not showing up.*

"Should we get started now, Leora?" Aaron asked. "Some of us, like me, have to work in the morning, so we can't stay too late."

"Sure, of course." Leora hated to start without John, but since there was a chance that he wasn't coming, there was no point in waiting any longer.

"Why don't we pick a few songs and play awhile, and then take a break for snacks?" Karen suggested.

"Sounds good to me." Ken turned the keyboard on and played a few chords.

Since Karen was the only one who didn't play an instrument, she volunteered to be the song leader and passed out the songbooks. It wasn't long before the room came alive with music and song.

Although Leora played along, strumming her guitar, her heart wasn't in it this evening. After fifteen minutes of playing and singing, she took a break to bring some beverages into the living room, knowing it wouldn't be long before everyone became thirsty.

As she passed through the hallway, Leora thought she heard a faint knock on the door, but it was hard to tell with music coming from the living room. She opened the door in case someone was there and was pleasantly surprised to see John on the front porch. He smiled at her and said, "Am I too late to join the party?"

She shook her head. "Of course not. Come in, and I'll introduce you to everyone."

Leora took John's hat and hung it on the coat tree near the door, and he followed her into the next room and stood off to one side. When the last stanza of "I'll Fly Away" had been sung, Leora introduced John to everyone.

"It's nice to meet you," Ken said. "Do you play an instrument?"

John pulled his harmonica out of its case and held it up. "Sure do."

"That's great," Kass spoke up. "We need another instrument, and you're the only one here with a harmonica, so it's nice you could join us."

Leora offered John a chair, and as he was seating himself, she headed for the kitchen to get the beverages. When she returned to the living room, the music was in full swing. While the Amish never played instruments during their church services, singing only a cappella, it wasn't unusual to find some Amish communities using guitars, accordions, harmonicas, and a few other instruments at small gatherings such as this one. Of course, the more conservative ones frowned on the use of any musical instruments. Here in Pinecraft, however, Amish and Mennonite, and even many English folks, enjoyed concerts in the park or in the yards of people's homes, where musical instruments were accepted and enjoyed by all.

As Leora took a seat and picked up her guitar again, she was reminded of Psalm 150:3–6, verses she'd read during her time of devotions this morning. "Praise Him with the sound of the trumpet; praise Him with the lute and harp! Praise Him with the timbrel and dance; praise Him with stringed instruments and flutes! Praise Him with loud cymbals; praise him with clashing cymbals! Let everything that has breath praise the Lord. Praise the Lord!"

She strummed her guitar and sang loudly, "When the roll is called up yonder, I'll be there."

What a wonderful way to spend the evening—with good friends and the joy of singing praises to God. She looked forward to their next get-together, which would no doubt be held at someone else's house.

Leora looked over at John, blowing heartily on his harmonica. *And I hope John will be able to join us for that gathering too, for I will certainly make sure he receives an invitation.*

Chapter 7

Several days later, Leora's head was reeling from the wonderful evening she'd spent with John, and it was hard to concentrate on her work. They had gone to the upstairs dining room at Marina Jack Restaurant, which overlooked Sarasota Bay. John had made the reservations and hired a driver to take them there, although Leora thought they could have easily ridden their bikes, which wouldn't have cost him any money. He'd also asked for a table by the window, and they'd enjoyed a lovely view of the water.

The items on the menu were a bit pricey, but John had encouraged Leora to order whatever she wanted. She'd ended up getting shrimp scampi and a harbor salad, which was less expensive than the filet mignon with lobster John had ordered. Leora figured he must be doing pretty well with his roofing business to spend that kind of money on a single meal. She was used to pinching pennies, so ordering an expensive meal had been difficult for her, even though John had been so relaxed about the cost.

During the delicious meal, they'd seen several dolphins frolicking in the bay. Leora had also enjoyed watching pelicans swoop over and then dive into the water to catch their prey. "They have to eat too," John had said.

Leora continued to reflect on the pleasant evening they'd had, and how, as they'd waited for their driver to pick them up, John had taken hold of her hand. Even now her arm tingled, remembering how giddy she'd felt—like a teenage girl on her first date.

"Hey, are you zoning out? Do you realize how long you've been standing there with that bowl of frosting in your hands?"

Leora jerked her head. "Oh, umm. . .Karen, you startled me."

"I guess so. You looked like you were miles away. What were you thinking about?"

"It was nothing that can't wait. I'll tell you about it when we take our break."

Karen chuckled. "Okay. I'm going to hold you to that promise."

Leora grinned. "It wasn't a promise."

Her friend shrugged. "Doesn't matter. I'll insist that you tell me or I won't pay the bill the next time the two of us go out for lunch."

Leora wiggled her brows. "We'll have to see about that."

~

After work that afternoon, Leora went out on the lanai to relax and make a phone call. She hadn't called home for several days and figured if she didn't call soon, her mother would start to worry and check up on her. In fact, Leora was surprised Mom hadn't called already.

She took a seat in the chaise lounge and scrolled through her contacts until she came to her parents' number. It was doubtful that anyone would be in the phone shed right now, but at least she could leave a message.

The phone rang twice, and someone picked up. "Leora, is that you?"

"Jah, it's me. What are you doing in the phone shed, Violet?"

"I'm talkin' to you."

Leora gave a small laugh. "I'm aware of that. I just didn't expect you, or anyone else from the family to answer the phone."

"Mom asked me to come out and check for messages."

"I'm glad she did. It's much nicer to talk directly to someone than leave a message."

"How's it going, Leora?" Violet asked. "Are you still enjoying your life in Sarasota?"

"Yes, I am. Very much, in fact."

"You sound pretty upbeat. Is there something going on that you haven't shared with us?"

Leora reached for her glass of iced tea and took a drink before responding. "Umm. . .maybe."

"Well, don't keep me in suspense. What's the big something we don't know about?"

Leora moistened her lips. "I've been seeing someone here of late."

"Oh? Tell me more."

"His name is John Miller, and we've done a few things together since we met."

Violet gave a throaty laugh, then she hollered, "That's great, Sister! I had a feeling you would find a good man there in Sarasota."

"John does seem like a nice man. There's only one problem."

"What's that?"

"He's not from Sarasota. His home is in Clare, Michigan, and he's only here for an extended vacation."

"Well, you never know—he might like it there and decide to stay."

"It's doubtful, since he has his own business in Clare."

Leora heard a weird scratching noise, and she looked up. A squirrel hung part way up on the screened-in lanai, and it seemed to be looking right at her. Still holding the phone, she got up and went over to shoo it away. "Go! Get off there!" She moved her hand back and forth, thinking it would go, but the silly critter remained firmly in place.

"Who are you talking to, Leora?"

"No one, Violet. Just a persistent squirrel. He's hanging on my screened-in lanai, and with his sharp claws, I'm afraid he might tear a hole in the screen if he doesn't get off. Hang on a minute, would you?"

"Okay."

Leora set the phone down, walked over to the screen, and clapped her hands. Instead of scampering off, like she'd expected, the determined little creature started scratching even more.

She groaned. This was not going well at all. She picked up the phone again and said, "I'd better go, Violet. Tell Mom, Dad, and the rest of the family I said hello. Take care, and think about coming down here to visit me sometime soon, okay?"

"Jah, I will. Bye for now, Sister."

After Leora clicked off, she ran into the house, grabbed a metal bowl, as well as a large spoon, hoping the noise she planned to make would scare the critter off. Then she raced back to the lanai. Leora felt relief when she saw that the squirrel was gone, but her heart sank when she noticed a huge tear in the screen.

"Now what am I going to do?" Leora moaned. She needed to get this fixed as soon as possible but didn't know who to call.

~

John rifled through the cupboards and refrigerator, trying to decide what to fix himself for supper, but there wasn't much to choose from, and he had no ambition for cooking.

Maybe I'll stop by Leora's place and see if she'd like to join me for supper at Yoder's Restaurant. Since it's right here in Pinecraft, we won't have far to go.

He scratched his head. *Or maybe I should give her a call instead of dropping by without notice. That would definitely be the polite thing to do.*

John pulled his cell phone from his pocket and was about to tap on Leora's number when the phone rang. Seeing that it was his parents' number, he decided to let it go to voice mail. No doubt it was his mother again, and John didn't want to take the time to answer all the questions she'd most likely want to ask him. He had changed his mind about calling Leora, and if he didn't head over to her place now, she might start supper or make other plans, so he'd decided just to show up and hope for the best.

John shoved the phone back in his pocket, grabbed his hat, and headed out the door to get his bike. It would get him there faster than walking.

A short time later, John rode up the driveway to Leora's rented home and locked up his bike. He'd heard that several bicycles had been stolen within the last few days, so he wasn't about to take chances by leaving the rented bike unlocked.

John stepped onto the porch and knocked on the door. A few seconds later, Leora opened it and greeted him with a pained expression.

"What's wrong?" he asked, feeling concern. "Are you *grank*?"

"No, I'm not sick, and I am sorry for the less-than-friendly greeting. Something happened out on my lanai." She opened the door wider. "Would you like to come in? Maybe you can help me figure out who I should call about it."

"I'll help in any way I can. What's going on with your lanai?"

"One of my screens is torn, and it's all because of some irritating *eechhaus*."

"What'd the squirrel do?"

John listened as Leora explained what had happened while she'd been talking on the phone to one of her sisters. "Let me take a look at it. Maybe it's something simple I can patch."

Leora shook her head. "I think it's going to need more than a patch, but I would appreciate you looking at it."

John followed Leora out the sliding glass door at the back of the house. When they stepped into the enclosed lanai, she pointed to one of the screens on the left side.

John went over and inspected the hole. "The critter did a number on it all right. The whole panel needs to be replaced."

Leora heaved a sigh. "I was afraid of that. I'll have to see if I can find someone who can fix it."

"Won't your landlord take care of it?"

"She's out of the area right now, and I don't want to bother her with it."

"I'm sure I can replace the screen. Is there a hardware store nearby?"

"I'm not sure. In the time I've been here, I have had no need to go to a hardware store for anything."

"I bet the man I rented my bike from would know where the closest one is."

Leora gave a nod. "He probably would."

"I'll head over there right now," John said. "And when I get back, I'll replace the screen. After that, would you like to join me for supper at Yoder's?"

Leora didn't hesitate and responded with a smile. "I'd like that very much."

~

Leora sat across from John at a table in Yoder's Restaurant. It was a popular place, and they had waited in line outside the building for forty-five minutes to be seated. She didn't mind, though, because it had given them time to visit with each other, as well as with several people Leora knew from the area. She enjoyed introducing them to John. Though the restaurant was small, the food was good and definitely worth the wait.

She smiled, watching John dig into his smoked barbecued chicken. He had a hearty appetite, but apparently it didn't seem to affect his weight. He was probably one of the lucky ones who could eat anything and never put on a pound. *Of course*, Leora reminded herself, *I've always been slender, but then I don't overeat, and for the most part, I strive to maintain a healthy diet.*

"How's your meat loaf?" John asked, pulling Leora's thoughts aside.

Using her napkin, Leora dabbed at her lips. "It's *appeditlich*."

"Glad to hear it. My food's delicious too." He glanced around. "I can see why this is such a popular place."

"The Amish, Mennonites, and others who come here to visit like Yoders and Der Dutchman. Even the Postal 98 Café, which is a lot smaller than Yoder's, is a nice place to eat breakfast or lunch. The building used to be a small post office here in Pinecraft," Leora added.

"I've been there once. I had Dave's Special, and I while I ate, I talked politics with some Amish men who were there." John chuckled. "Some folks think that just because most Amish don't vote in government elections, we have no interest in what's going on politically, but it isn't true. We are very interested and often vote on our knees."

"Jah." Leora nodded. "The very least we can do is pray for our country and its leaders."

"So true. That's something we all need to remember."

"Would you like some dessert?" John asked when they'd finished their meal.

Leora placed both hands against her stomach. "I'd better not. I'm much too full. But you go ahead if you want to."

"Naw, that's okay. I'm fine without it. Not every meal needs to end with a piece of pie, ice cream, cake, or cookies." John pulled out his wallet to pay the bill. "I have an idea that's much better than dessert."

"Such as?"

He gestured toward the closest window. "It's nearly dark, and there's bound to be a bright moon shining tonight. We can take a moonlit walk back to your house and enjoy each other's company awhile longer before I head back to my place."

Leora remembered that John had mentioned wanting to take a moonlit walk with her previously, but so far they had not done it. "That sounds nice," she said, fussing with the ties on her head covering.

"All right then. I'll pay the bill, and we can be on our way."

The twinkle in John's blue eyes and the sincere-looking smile on his face caused Leora to tremble a bit.

~

The inky sky offset by millions of twinkling stars and a bright moon made the walk back to Leora's house lovely. Impulsively, John reached over and took her hand. He felt relieved when she didn't resist. When he stepped on her porch, prepared to tell Leora goodnight, John fought the urge to kiss her. *Do I dare? What would she think? How would she respond?* John stood there several seconds, weighing his choices. He could ask to see her again, thank her for joining him for supper, or say a simple goodbye. But, oh, his arms ached to hold Leora, and his lips yearned to kiss hers. John had never felt this way about a woman before—especially one he hadn't known very long. But what if Leora didn't feel the same way about him?

"Danki for fixing the screen on my lanai," Leora said, breaking the silence between them. "And also for taking me out to supper."

"You're welcome. It was my pleasure." John took a step closer, until he felt her warm breath on his face. Then, with his heart hammering in his chest until he thought it might burst, he leaned down and brushed his lips across hers. She didn't pull away, and he deepened the kiss. Leora responded to it, and John's pulse raced faster than his horse, Lightning, could trot.

Leora pulled away first, then drew a sharp intake of breath. "I. . .uh. . .had better get inside. *Gut nacht*, John."

"Good night, Leora. I'll talk to you again soon." John turned, leaped off the porch, and fumbled with the lock on his bike. When he heard Leora's front door open and shut, he paused to collect his thoughts. *Could I be falling in love with Leora after such a short time of knowing her? And what does she really think about me?*

Chapter 8

"How are things going with you and John?" Karen asked Leora during their lunch break. "Are you still seeing him every day?"

"Almost, but sometimes we both have other things to do."

"Does he call you on those days?" Karen grabbed the saltshaker and sprinkled some salt into her bowl of vegetable soup.

"Yes, we talk to each other nearly every day," Leora responded.

Karen ate some soup, sprinkled on a bit more salt, then leaned closer to Leora. "That means things must be getting serious."

"We're just friends." Leora forked some salad into her mouth. She wished her friend hadn't brought up the subject of John. The truth was, Leora liked him more than she was willing to admit. She'd even fantasized about what it would be like if she was his wife. *But that's ridiculous*, she told herself. *If John knew about my seasonal affective disorder, he'd probably run the other way. What man would want to be married to a woman who sank into depression every time fall crept in? It's a miracle I could even hold a job when I was living in Indiana. And if by some chance John would ever propose marriage, I'm certain that he'd expect me to move to Michigan, which I could never do.*

Leora thought about how difficult it had been to fight the waves of depression she'd had while living in Indiana during the dark, cold days of winter and how she'd tried to cover up her feelings of despair by forcing herself to make conversation when she just wanted to be left alone.

"Ken and I are going to see a ventriloquist this evening. Why don't you and John join us?"

Karen's question cut into Leora's thoughts. She drank some of her iced tea. "Is it that Christian entertainer I've heard so much about?"

"Yes, and he's excellent at what he does. Have you ever seen him perform?"

Leora shook her head.

"Well, you should go then. I promise you won't be disappointed. His lips don't move; what he makes his puppets say is funny; and he always includes a good spiritual message in his routines. Ken and I are planning to ride our bikes out to the church where the ventriloquist will be performing. It would be nice if you and John joined us."

"I suppose I could call him and see if he'd be interested. If not, I guess I could go without John. I'll need to get used to having him gone anyway because he will be going back to his home in Michigan next month, and we'll probably never see each other again." Leora slouched in her chair. "I'm sure going to miss him."

"Don't look so discouraged." Karen reached over and touched Leora's hand. "I'm sure John will keep in touch through phone calls, and maybe he'll come back to visit you."

Leora heaved a sigh. "Maybe so, but a long-distance relationship is not ideal, and after a time, our friendship would most likely dwindle."

"He could decide to move here permanently."

Leora folded her arms. "That's not likely to happen. He has a business in Clare, remember?"

"Good point." Karen picked up the saltshaker, then set it back down. "Maybe you should go back to Indiana during the summer months. At least you'd have a chance to see John during that time, since Michigan is a lot closer to your parents' home than Sarasota."

Leora didn't want to continue this conversation, because it was pointless. She glanced at her cell phone. "Our lunch break is almost over, so if I'm going to call John, I'd better do it now before he makes other plans for this evening."

~

"Be careful out here on your bikes," Ken hollered as he, Karen, John, and Leora turned onto Fruitville Road. "Part of this stretch of road leads to the interstate entrance, and it can get pretty crazy, especially during this time of the day when people are getting off work. So be sure to stay in the bicycle lane."

"Thanks for the warning," John called. "We'll be careful."

Leora's leg muscles twitched, and her stomach tightened. They weren't in the worst of the traffic yet, but already she felt nervous. Hopefully all the vehicles would stay where they should be, because the bicycle lane was too narrow for her liking.

They rode single file, with Ken in the lead, followed by Karen, then Leora. John brought up the rear. Leora wondered if the passengers in the trucks and cars passing them thought it was strange to see four Plain people on bikes way out here on this busy road. They could have hired a driver to take them to the church event, but Ken had told Karen he thought it would be an adventure, and she'd gone along with it.

As the traffic increased and vehicles switched from one lane to another, Leora decided this adventure was not so much fun. It wasn't that she was afraid to ride a bicycle—that had never been a problem for her in Sarasota or back home. She just wasn't used to this much traffic moving at a pretty good pace.

Please keep us safe, Lord, Leora prayed. *Be with those in their vehicles and us on our bikes.*

Always mindful to stay in the bicycle lane while keeping a safe distance from Karen, Leora clasped the handlebars tightly. Ken had told them that once they got past the turnoff for the interstate, the road would become two lanes on either side of the highway. Leora figured there would be less traffic by then too.

"Doin' okay up there, Leora?" John shouted.

All Leora could manage was a nod. She was not about to lose her concentration or glance quickly over her shoulder. Hearing John's voice gave her the courage to keep pedaling, though, while she continued to silently pray.

They had just passed the turnoff for the interstate when a pickup truck veered to the right and came partially into the bike lane, nearly sideswiping Ken.

Leora's breath came in bursts as she watched wide eyed, and she pushed down the urge to scream. Her lips parted, and she sighed with relief as Ken moved farther right and the driver of the truck caught himself in time and went back into his own lane.

Whew! That was close. Thank You, Lord, for watching over Ken and the rest of us too.

A few miles later, the road narrowed to one lane on each side, and then the church came into view. There was no traffic coming in the opposite direction, and Ken, followed by Karen, Leora, and John, turned into the parking lot.

Leora's legs felt like rubber when she got off her bicycle and secured it at the bike rack.

"Are you all right?" John asked, stepping up to Leora and putting his hand on her trembling shoulder.

"I. . .I'm fine. Just a little shook up from seeing what nearly happened to Ken. He could have been hit by that driver, who obviously wasn't watching what he was doing."

"I'm okay," Ken said. "But if that guy hadn't gotten back in his lane when he did, we all could have been hurt."

Karen's face was ashen, and she clasped Ken's arm with a shaky hand. "I'm so glad you're okay. It all happened quickly, and there was nothing I could do about it." She drew a couple of quick breaths. "If I'd had a horn on my bike, I would have honked it. But then due to all the traffic noise, the truck driver might not have heard me anyway."

"We're all safe, and God was watching over us." Ken gestured toward the church, where people had begun to enter the building. "Let's get inside so we can sit and relax. I'm sure once the program begins we'll have forgotten all about the near miss."

~

Leora and John followed Karen and Ken inside. Several people milled about the entryway, talking and looking at the table that had been set up with some CDs and small puppets for sale. Leora was tempted to buy one of the puppets, but since she had no use for it, she followed Karen down the hall to the women's restroom.

"I bet you were really frightened when that truck came so close to Ken," Leora said as they waited in line.

"That's for sure. I felt so helpless, and all I could do was pray."

"Same here. My legs were shaking, and by the time we got here, I wasn't sure I could even walk the short distance to the front door of the church," Leora responded. "It'll be dark by the time we leave here, and I hope everything goes okay on our way back to Pinecraft."

"All of our bikes are equipped with lights, and each of us has a reflective vest, so we should be noticeable to vehicle drivers. Also, there shouldn't be as much traffic going home as there was coming here."

Leora heard the reassurance in her friend's tone, and it helped to calm her anxiety. She would feel a whole lot better, however, once the four of them were safely home.

"Let's sit up close to the front," John suggested when the women joined him and Ken in the church sanctuary. "I'd like to get a good view of the ventriloquist so I can tell if his lips move when he's talking for one of his puppets."

"We can sit up there if you want to," Karen said, "but I've seen this ventriloquist before, and he didn't move his lips."

John shrugged. "Okay, but if nobody minds, I'd like to see for myself."

"I'm fine with it," Ken said.

"Me too," Karen agreed.

John turned to Leora. "Do you have any objections to sitting in the first or second row?"

She shook her head.

"That's great. Follow me." John led the way down the middle aisle, and they took seats in the second row, since the first row on both sides of the church were occupied by parents and their children. They didn't have to wait long before the ventriloquist stepped onto the platform, introduced himself, and brought a puppet with flaming red hair out of a suitcase. "This is my pal Barney, who some people refer to as a dummy."

Barney's eyes moved side to side and he said, "I ain't no dummy. I get straight As in school, and I can sing too. Can I sing something for ya now?"

"Sure, go ahead," the ventriloquist said. "I'm sure these good people would have no objections."

John leaned forward and watched the ventriloquist's lips as the puppet sang a silly little song. To John's astonishment, the man's lips didn't move at all. Then Barney the puppet told a few jokes and asked if any of the little girls would like to come up on the platform and give him a kiss. There were plenty of giggles from the front row, but not one child got out of their seat. Barney hung his head and sang, "Nobody likes me. Everyone hates me, and I'm goin' out and eat worms."

"Aw, come on, Barney," the ventriloquist said. "Don't be sad. You've got to understand that no one would want to kiss a dummy."

To that, the puppet said, "Why not? Your wife's been kissin' one for years!"

The audience laughed—John most of all. In fact, he laughed so loud, the people who sat close by stared at him. To make matters worse, the puppet's head turned in John's direction and he said, "The man with dark brown hair—the one wearing a white shirt and black suspenders—what's your name?"

John's face felt warmer than if he'd acquired a sunburn. "John," he said quietly.

"Could ya speak up? I didn't hear what you said."

"My name's John."

"I have a question for you, John. Has your wife ever kissed a dummy?"

John shook his head. "I'm not married."

The puppet looked at the ventriloquist and said, "I think I embarrassed the poor man. Can we move on to a different topic now?"

"Of course, Barney. Why don't you help me tell these nice people a Bible story?"

"Oh good. I love stories—especially the ones that come from the B-I-B-L-E. Those stories are the best 'cause they're all true."

At this point, John had quit watching the ventriloquist's lips and just relaxed and enjoyed himself. The banter between the ventriloquist and his puppet was funny, and the Bible story on the importance of loving one's neighbor was good. But what John enjoyed the most was when he looked over at Leora and noticed her relaxed expression. He'd been worried about her after that near mishap with Ken and the pickup truck. She'd been clearly shaken by it, and the truth was, it had upset John too. The thought that any of them might have been hit by some erratic driver didn't set well with him. He wished they had hired a driver to bring them here, because now they had the long ride back to Pinecraft in the dark, and he couldn't help feeling concerned.

Although it had only been a month since he'd first met Leora, John felt like he'd known her all of his life. He hoped that when he returned to Michigan next month, he and Leora would keep in touch. They could continue their relationship through letters and phone calls, and maybe someday, as their friendship deepened, he might ask her to marry him and move to Clare. It was definitely something to pray about, and that he would do.

Chapter 9

"Yes, Mom, I'm fine. Sorry for not returning your call, but I've been busy, and it slipped my mind."

"Busy doing what?" John's mother asked. "I thought you went to Sarasota to rest, and I don't see how you can do that if you're busy all the time."

John put his phone in speaker mode and placed it on the end table by the couch. "I am not busy all the time. I sleep well at night and have even taken a few naps. My energy has returned, and I'm no longer feeling so burned out."

"That's good to hear, Son. What about the woman you've mentioned a few times when we've talked? Are you still seeing her?"

John clenched his jaw until his teeth bit together in an audible click. *Here we go with Mom's questions again. I wish she wouldn't worry about me so much.*

"John, are you still there?"

"Jah, I'm here."

"You never answered my question. Are you still seeing Lenore?"

"Her name's not Lenore, Mom. It's Leora. And yes, we've been getting together quite often."

"What will you do when you leave Sarasota next month? Will you end your relationship with her or keep in touch through letters and phone calls?"

John's irritation increased. Why did his mother need to know every little thing he did or planned to do? Why must she be so controlling?

"Did you hear my question, John?"

"Jah, but I need to hang up now. Leora and I are supposed to play in a shuffleboard match at Pinecraft Park this afternoon, and I don't want to be late or we may have to forfeit the game."

"Can I call you later then?"

"No, Mom, we've made plans to eat supper together, and it'll probably be late by the time I get back to my rental."

"Guess I could wait to call until morning."

John's toes curled inside of his shoes. "Leora and I are going fishing in the morning, so I won't be free to talk with you then either."

"Oh, I see. Well, feel free to give me a call when you're not too busy."

"Jah, okay. Bye for now, Mom."

John hung up and pressed his palms against his closed eyes. He felt bad cutting his mother off like that, but it was time for her to realize that he was a grown man and had a life of his own. It wasn't fair for his mother to expect him to check in with her all the time. *The next time I talk to Dad, I'll bring up the topic of how Mom treats me like a child. Maybe he can get her to back off a bit.*

"That was some crazy game we played, wasn't it?" Leora used her apron to wipe the moisture from her forehead.

John wiggled his brows. "Jah, but we won, so it was worth the effort to play shuffleboard in this heat and humidity." He climbed on his bike. "But now, since I've made dinner plans for us, we need to go to our homes and take showers before my driver picks us up."

"Which restaurant did you choose this time?" she questioned.

"DaRuma. Have you ever been there?"

Leora shook her head. Where's it located?"

"There's one downtown and another on Fruitville. I made our seven o'clock reservations at the Fruitville location."

"What kind of food do they serve?" Leora asked as she got on her bike.

"It's a Japanese-style hibachi, and I've heard from some of the fellows here in Pinecraft who have been to that restaurant that it's a lot of fun."

"In what way?"

"You get to watch your food being cooked and see some of the fancy tricks the chef performs before and while he's cooking the meal."

"That does sound like fun. I'll make sure I'm ready for your driver to pick me up at six thirty."

They rode to Leora's home first since it was only a few blocks from the park. Before John pedaled off toward his place on Estrada, he hollered, "Goodbye, Leora. See you soon!"

Leora turned and waved, and after she rode into her yard, she got off the bike and put it in the storage shed out back. Then she hurried into the house to shower and change into one of the nicer dresses she'd made a few months ago. Each opportunity Leora had to be with John made her feel almost giddy. There was nothing she could do to stop him from leaving next month, so she was determined to enjoy every minute they could be together between now and then. Once John left, though, Leora knew she would feel as though there was big hole in her heart.

"I'm surprised you've never been here before," John commented as he and Leora took their seats at one end of the large table surrounding the hibachi grill. In addition to Leora and John, eight other people were seated at this table, but none of them were Amish. This wasn't the only hibachi table, either—several more were scattered around the restaurant, and all but a few were occupied with people.

"This must be a popular place to eat," Leora whispered to John.

"I would say so." He gestured to one of the tables not far from them. "Look how that chef over there is juggling those eggs. He's not only a cook but an entertainer too."

Leora watched in fascination as the man did a few other things before he broke the shells and mixed the raw eggs in with a large pile of rice he'd placed on the grill.

Soon a server came and took their beverage orders. She also gave everyone at the table a menu that included appetizers, as well as a list of the meat and fish choices that could be cooked on the grill, in addition to vegetables and fried rice. Leora chose chicken and shrimp, and John picked filet mignon and chicken. He also ordered spring rolls for him and Leora to share as an appetizer.

Leora was surprised at the high price of their meals and once again she wondered how John could afford to keep taking her out to expensive restaurants. *His roofing business must be doing well*, she thought, *even with him being away on an extended vacation*. On one of their dates, John had mentioned that a good friend of his was running the business in his absence. He'd also said there were several young Amish men working for him. Leora couldn't imagine running a business of her own, much less trying to stay up with things while away.

Soon after their appetizer came, the chef at their table squirted something on the grill, stacked onions he'd cut into rings, and lit a fire.

Leora gasped and jerked her head back. Although the flames he'd created went straight up and not out, she nonetheless felt the heat from the fire.

"You doin' okay?" John asked.

"I'm fine. It just startled me is all."

"Same here. Good thing I'm not married with a beard, or it may have gotten singed. If we ever come here again, we'll know what to expect and will make sure to lean away before he lights the fire."

Since John only had a few weeks left before he returned home, Leora figured this might be the only visit to DaRuma he would make. Of course, if he came back for a visit sometime and was still single, maybe he would invite her to eat here with him again. She felt sure, however, that a man as nice as John would probably establish a relationship with a woman in his hometown, if he hadn't already, and be growing a beard by this time next year. Although John was single and had spent time with Leora, for all she knew, he could have a girlfriend waiting for him in Clare, Michigan. That thought hurt, but Leora had no claim on John—especially since their homes were so far from one another.

~

The following morning, Leora found herself on a chartered fishing boat with John and four other people. She'd thought they would be staying in the calmer waters of Sarasota Bay, but the captain had taken the boat out into the Gulf of Mexico, where he said the fishing was better. And it was too, only the rougher water had taken away Leora's desire to fish. In fact, she wished the captain would turn the boat around and head for shore, because with every minute that passed, Leora felt worse. She knew the nausea and dizziness she felt was not a mild stomach upset or a simple loss of balance due to the waves that caused the boat to rock. Her symptoms were far from mild. At first she had felt a bit unsteady on her feet, and then she'd broken out in a cold sweat and noticed increased saliva. Then she'd become dizzy and felt nauseated. Now, after telling herself she would be all right, her stomach roiled, and her shoulders curled forward. She was going to throw up, and there was nothing she could do to stop it.

Embarrassed and miserable, Leora hung her head over the leeward side of the boat, facing downwind, and emptied her stomach. Afterward she tried to swallow the sour taste in her mouth, but it only made things worse. Her whole body trembled, and she could barely remain on her feet. In the past, she'd gone fishing in a boat on Lake Shipshewana and had never gotten sick, but that small lake was nothing compared to this vast body of water.

Leora closed her eyes and prayed. *Why did this have to happen to me now? Dear Lord, please help me to feel better.*

Leora's eyes popped open when she heard John's voice speaking calmly to her. She felt comforted when he came close and gently patted her back. But at the same time, she felt too embarrassed to look at him. If Leora had known she would get seasick, she never would have agreed to come on this trip. What a terrible way to spend her day off. She wished she and John had done something else today that would have kept them on dry land.

Guess that wouldn't have been fair to him, though, Leora told herself as she tried to regain her balance. *John has done plenty of nice things for me, and he's taken me to several places that might not have been his favorite thing to do. I had really wanted this day to go well for him since he's mentioned several times how much he enjoys fishing.*

"I have a few suggestions that might help your nausea go away," John said, leaning close to her ear. "Keep your focus on the distant horizon and not on the waves. I'll bring you a bottle of water to drink, because it's important that you don't become dehydrated. And take in several deep breaths. Oh, and one more thing"—John handed Leora a stick of gum—"if you chew this awhile, it might help too."

"Thank you," she murmured, resting her head against his strong shoulder. "Please don't worry about me, John. I don't want you to let my being seasick spoil your day. You came here to fish, and that's what you should do."

"Not to worry," John said. "The only way my day could be spoiled is if you weren't here with me. I enjoy spending time with you, Leora."

"I feel the same way about you." Leora put the gum in her mouth and chewed. The minty flavor tasted good and helped to squelch her nausea a bit. Hopefully she could make it through the rest of the day without getting sick again. Maybe if she followed John's instructions, she would feel better and might even be able to do a little fishing. If nothing else, it was nice to know that John cared about her well-being.

Leora blinked back unexpected tears. Oh, she would miss him when he was gone. She would have to find ways to keep busy and focus on other things besides John.

Chapter 10

Long Boat Key

"What do you think of the view?" John asked as he and Leora sat at a table inside the Chart House Restaurant.

"It's nice. A bit different from the view we had at Marina Jack, but it's interesting to see a different part of Sarasota Bay."

John pointed out the window and to his right. "This section of the bay is more like an inlet, leading directly to the Gulf. Can you see where it goes?"

Leora nodded. "There isn't a lot of boat action here like there is at Marina Jack, but I like the peacefulness of it." It was her turn to point. "Look over there, on that small sandbar where all those birds have gathered. I see pigeons, seagulls, as well as pelicans, and they all seem to be getting along with each other."

"Jah, not like some people I've read about in the paper, who can't, or won't, accept others who are from a different ethnic background."

"That's one thing I enjoy about living here in Sarasota, and in Pinecraft particularly," Leora said after she'd taken a drink of water. "The Amish, Mennonite, and other Plain folks who live there or come to visit accept and are even friends with English people who have homes in Pinecraft or come there as tourists."

"We're all equal in God's eyes," John said before taking a bite of his salad. "And I'm sure there are many people who know the Lord personally who'll be in heaven—not just one certain denomination."

"I agree. Even though every Christian-based denomination thinks a certain way or does some things differently than we Amish do, we're all part of the body of believers as long as we have accepted Christ as our Lord and Savior."

"I'm in complete agreement with that statement." John picked up his steak knife and cut into the prime rib he'd ordered, and Leora began eating her meal too.

The past two months had gone by way too fast, and it was hard to believe that this was their last evening together. During the past three weeks, Leora and John had seen each other every chance they'd gotten. They had gathered with Leora's friends a few more times to sing and fellowship. They'd visited the Sarasota Jungle Gardens and Mote Aquarium, and they'd made more trips to the beach to search for shells and relax in the sun. Leora had enjoyed their romantic moonlit walks, which always ended with a goodnight kiss. The times they'd spent on her lanai getting to know each other better had been wonderful too. Although Leora had told John many things about her home and family in Middlebury, she'd never once spoken about her seasonal affective disorder. Karen had reminded Leora several times that her diagnosis was nothing to be ashamed of, but Leora couldn't find the courage to discuss it with John. Since he would be leaving tomorrow, she saw no reason to bring the topic up now. It was doubtful that she would ever see him again, but she felt thankful and blessed for the time they'd had these past two months.

She looked across the table at him and smiled. "How's your

prime rib? Is it as good as it looks?"

He bobbed his head. "Definitely. Would you like a taste?"

"It's tempting, but I'd better not." She gestured to her plate. "I still have a lot of chicken left to eat."

"You can always ask for a box to take the leftovers in."

"True. Maybe I will have a small taste of your prime rib."

John forked a piece and fed it to Leora. She wasn't sure why, but the act made her feel closer to him. It was almost as if they were an engaged or a married couple. In a similar way, Leora had seen her parents feed each other when one of them wanted to taste something on the other's plate.

I need to stop letting my imagination run wild, Leora told herself. *John and I are not married or even betrothed. This special time we've had together will be over soon, and we'll both move on, living our lives the way we did before John came to Sarasota.*

Pinecraft

Leora's heart clenched as she stood in the parking lot of the Tourist Mennonite Church, waiting for the charter bus that would take John and several other Amish people to their towns up north. Goodbyes were always hard, and this one gripped Leora's heart as much as it had when she'd said goodbye to her family in Indiana. *Maybe more*, Leora chided herself, *because I foolishly allowed myself to fall in love with John. I should have stopped seeing him after our first date and before I knew what a wonderful man he was.*

As though sensing her discomfort, John put his hand on the small of her back and gave it a few gentle pats. "I'll call you when I get home tomorrow, and we'll keep in touch regularly. Maybe you can make a trip up to Michigan sometime this summer. I'd like you to meet my family, and it would be nice to show you around the town of Clare."

Leora swallowed hard. *I have to end this right now, before John gets any ideas that I might be willing to move there.* The thickening in her throat increased. "John, I don't think I'd be able to take enough time off work this summer to go anywhere. I used some of my vacation days so I could have more time to spend with you."

"Oh, I see." His voice was quieter and lower pitched than usual. "Well, maybe. . ."

Leora's mouth trembled as she spoke her next words. "I'm not the right woman for you, John, and we have no future together. You're a good friend, and I wish you well."

He blinked rapidly, and his eyes glazed over. "You can't mean that, Leora."

She opened her mouth to respond just as the bus pulled in. A flurry of excitement erupted around them, as those who would be traveling gathered up their luggage and moved toward the bus to make sure everything got put in the cargo area.

"You'd better go. You'll be boarding the bus soon," Leora said in a near whisper.

He continued to stare at her, as though in disbelief. "Isn't there something special between us, Leora? These last two months we've been drawing so close. I was sure that you felt it too."

"I. . .I did, but. . ." Tears filled her eyes and she tried to blink them away, but they dripped out and rolled down her cheeks.

When John reached out and wiped them away with his thumb, it was nearly Leora's undoing. She wanted to shout, *I love you, John, and I'd go anywhere to be with you.* But it wasn't possible. A short visit to Michigan might be okay, but she could never live there year-round. Her SAD would stand in the way of their happiness, and John deserved a stable, happy wife.

"I have to go now, John." She glanced toward the road. "My

shift at Der Dutchman starts in twenty minutes, and I don't want to be late." She gave him a hug, then quickly pulled away. "I'll be praying that you have a safe trip, and"—Leora paused for a breath—"I would appreciate a phone call to let me know that you got home okay." Before John could respond, Leora got on her bike and quickly rode out of the parking lot. It was better this way. It would have broken her heart to watch him get on that bus and see it pull out with John and the other passengers on board.

~

With a heavy heart, John stared out the bus window. He couldn't believe Leora had said she wasn't the right woman for him and that they had no future together. Was there someone or something keeping her here in Florida? Did Leora enjoy her job at the bakery so much that she felt compelled to remain in Florida? Could there be another love interest for her that she hadn't told John about? Maybe she had a boyfriend back home in Indiana.

He closed his eyes and lowered his head. *Why did You allow me to meet Leora and fall in love with her if she doesn't want to be with me, Lord? I wish now I'd stayed in Michigan and never gone on a vacation. I would have just kept working hard like I did before.*

~

Leora entered the bakery area and put on her apron. Without a doubt, today she would have a hard time keeping her mind on the cakes that needed decorating. One look in the hand mirror she kept in her purse let Leora know that her eyes were red and swollen from crying. She didn't want anyone to see her like this. No doubt there would be questions from someone—probably Karen.

Was it wrong to let John go without telling him much I love him? Leora blinked against a fresh set of tears. *Should I have explained about my seasonal affective disorder? Would he have understood? So many people don't, so why would John be any different?*

"Hey, how'd it go with seeing John off today?" Karen stepped up to Leora and shook her head when she looked at her. "From the look of your red-rimmed, puffy eyes, I'm guessing not so well."

Leora sniffed deeply and blotted her eyes with the back of her hand. Then she told her friend what she'd said to John before he boarded the bus.

Karen gave a slow shake of her head. "Oh, Leora, why didn't you tell him the truth?"

"I wanted to, but I was afraid of his reaction. Most people, at least those back home, have not understood any of my symptoms. I'm sure some of them believe that I made it all up just so I could move to sunny Sarasota."

"I think you worry too much about what others think, Leora. Wouldn't it be better to give them the benefit of the doubt? Better yet, just stop focusing on other people's opinions."

Leora sighed and turned aside. "I need to get busy now. There are four cakes waiting to be decorated."

Chapter 11

Clare, Michigan

"I wish you would eat a little more." John's mother gestured to his half-eaten plate of scrambled eggs. "You haven't had much appetite since you returned from Florida a month ago, and you'll waste away if you don't eat more."

"Can't make myself feel hungry if I'm not," John mumbled. He'd seen his mother's wrinkled brows and heard her tone, heavy with concern. John's mother loved him, but sometimes she pressed John too hard about certain things—especially when it came to taking better care of himself.

"But you work hard every day, and it seems like you've become more of a workaholic than you were before you went to Sarasota."

It was hard these days, dealing with what he thought were his failed attempts at his and Leora's relationship. John couldn't help how deeply his heart ached for her. He truly missed seeing her and thought often about the two of them together, talking and having some quality time. *I wish Mom would try to understand how frustrating it is when you want to be with a special person and it doesn't happen the way you'd hoped. I'm a mess internally and need a solution to the problem I'm going through. If only I knew what I had said or done wrong when I was with Leora that made her pull away.*

John shrugged at his mother's last comment.

"If you keep pushing the way you have been, you'll need another extended vacation," she persisted.

"Maybe so, but it won't be another trip to Sarasota." John drank the rest of his coffee and set the mug down.

"Will you be joining your daed and me at the bishop's house for supper this evening?" Mom asked. "Several others from our church district will be there too, including Ellen Yoder."

Not tonight. Even if I was free to attend, I would not be up for games, visiting or seeing people happily engaging socially with one another. Nope, that would only make me feel worse for not having a special someone in my own life, and I've never been interested in Ellen, so I wish Mom would stop pushing. John had searched his heart, which felt empty these days without Leora. He would rather stay at home every evening or spend extra time on a job. Besides, John was through listening to his mother fuss over his lack of eating anything more for breakfast. *I need to have peace and quiet to reflect on things.*

He looked at his mother and shook his head. "I can't go to the bishop's place with you and Dad tonight. I have a business to run, and . . ."

"You're still thinking about that young woman you met in Sarasota, aren't you?" This question came from John's father, who up until now had been quiet.

John nodded. "I think about Leora a lot and miss her more than I ever thought possible."

"Have you called or written to her?"

"Jah, Dad. I've done both, but she hasn't responded to any of my letters, and whenever I have called, it always goes to her voice mail, and she never calls me back." He drew in a deep breath and released it with a noisy huff. "I thought we had established a close relationship that might even lead to something permanent, but I was clearly wrong about that. Leora obviously doesn't have the same kind of feelings toward me as I have about her." John pushed away from the table and carried his dishes over to the sink. "I need to get going. My crew and I have a new roof to put on at one of the businesses in Shipshewana, and we need to get on the road."

"So you won't be home in time for supper?" Mom inquired.

John turned to face her and shook his head. "It'll take us at least a couple of days to complete the job, so I made a reservation for me and the crew to stay at a hotel in Shipshewana."

John couldn't miss the look of disappointment on his mother's face. Or maybe it was worry. She'd never liked it when he worked out of town; especially if it meant traveling a distance from home.

"Please let us know when you get there, okay, Son?" Dad asked.

John gave a nod. "Sure thing." He walked back to the table and gave his mother a kiss on the cheek. "Try not to fret. If things go well, I'll be back home by tomorrow night. I will let you know when we get there today, and if for some reason we end up having to stay a second night, I'll keep you informed about that as well."

John said goodbye to his parents, grabbed the things he'd set by the back door, and stepped outside. The March wind that had begun whipping through the yard caused Mom's colorful garden flag to flap more than usual, and several birds gathered in a frenzy around the feeders, eating as if it were their last meal.

John pulled his jacket collar tightly around his neck. He didn't have a shred of doubt that an early spring in Clare, Michigan, was a lot colder than it would be in Sarasota, Florida.

As he stepped around the side of the house to wait for the English man who'd be driving the truck full of supplies and transporting the crew, an image of Leora popped into John's head. *I wonder what she's doing right now. If the temperatures are warm and balmy and Leora doesn't have to work, I bet she'll make a trip to the beach before this day is out.* He swallowed around the constriction in his throat. *Oh, Leora, I sure wish we could be together right now.*

John took a seat at the picnic table and bowed his head. *Wherever Leora is and whatever she's doing, please guide and protect her. If it be Your will for us to carry on our friendship, please prompt Leora to answer the phone the next time I call her.*

Pinecraft

Leora put a slice of homemade raisin bread in the toaster and pushed the lever down. This was her day off, so there had been no reason to get up so early. She could have slept till noon if she'd wanted. Waking up early had become a habit, though, and today it would allow her to get a few things done before she and Karen headed for the beach on their bikes.

When the toast popped, Leora cut it in half and buttered both slices. She slathered them with strawberry jam and took a seat at the table. She then bowed her head and prayed, thanking God for the food and asking Him to watch over her family back home. She also prayed for her and Karen's safety as they biked out to Lido Beach in a few hours.

John came to mind, so she prayed for him too. Even though they couldn't be together, Leora still cared about him and hoped he was doing well. Knowing she could not live full-time in Michigan, or even Indiana, made having seasonal affective disorder seem even worse.

Leora slumped in the chair as a few tears slipped out of her eyes, splashing onto her cheeks. *Why can't I be like other people who are able to enjoy all four seasons and don't slip into depression during the colder, less sunny days and months? It doesn't seem fair.*

Knowing that if she wasn't careful, she could easily slip into depression, despite the warm day she'd awakened to, Leora reached for the new devotional book she had purchased recently. She'd found it on one of the racks at Der Dutchman the other day. Today's reading was on the topic of receiving the desires of one's heart and quoted Psalm 37:4–5. "Delight yourself also in the Lord, and He shall give you the desires of your heart. Commit your way to the Lord, trust also in Him, and He shall bring it to pass."

Leora sat up straight as she reflected on the verse. *God wants me to delight in Him, and that is what I should do because He is my Savior and Lord. God wants me to put my trust in Him no matter what trials or sorrows come my way.*

Leora got up from the table and began packing the things she would need for the beach into a tote bag. Today she would focus on the many beautiful things God had created and leave all negative and sad thoughts behind.

Shipshewana

Marie Lambright climbed down from her carriage and secured her horse, Belle, to the hitching rail. She had come to Shipshewana to do some shopping, and her first stop was Yoder's Department Store, where she would buy some fabric. Afterward she hoped to pick up a few things at the hardware store across the hall.

Once Marie's horse was taken care of, she headed for the back door of Yoder's. Hearing some serious pounding from above, she looked up and saw four Amish men on the roof of the building. Then she noticed a work truck parked nearby with the name John Miller's Quality Roofing painted on the side. Underneath that was a phone number and a Clare, Michigan, address.

She stood staring at it for several seconds. *Could that be the same John Miller Leora told me about—the one she'd been going out with for two months? Leora did mention that John was from Clare, Michigan, and I believe she said he was a roofer.* She shook her head. *But no, that would surely be too much of a coincidence.*

As Marie stood there, trying to put the pieces together, a tall, dark-haired Amish man came out of the building and headed for the truck. He had no beard, so she knew he wasn't married. She couldn't remember if Leora had ever said anything about the color of John's hair, but she was fairly sure that Leora had mentioned something about him being quite tall and muscular.

"Excuse me," Marie said, boldly walking over to him after he'd taken some supplies from the truck. "Are you John Miller?"

"Why, yes, I am. Have we met before?"

"No, but I think you might know my daughter. Her name is Leora, and she lives in Sarasota."

John's eyes opened wide. "Leora Lambright?"

Marie nodded. "Jah, that's right."

"And you're her *mudder*?"

"Yes."

He pulled his fingers down the side of his clean-shaven face. "Well, for goodness' sake. Such a small world we live in, jah?"

"Definitely."

"How is Leora doing? I've tried to contact her several times since I returned to Clare, but she's never responded." He lowered his gaze. "I figured she must not want anything to do with me."

"That's not true. My daughter broke things off with you because of her illness."

"Illness?" His head flinched back slightly. "I. . .I didn't know Leora was sick. Is it serious?"

Shaking her head, Marie saw the concern on John's face. To

her, it was an indication of how much he cared for Leora. "My daughter has seasonal affective disorder. Some people refer to it as SAD, for short."

He scratched his head. "I believe I've heard of it but never knew anyone who had it. What I don't understand, though, is why Leora never told me about it. Did she think I wouldn't understand?"

"Leora thought continuing to communicate with you would be an impossible situation since she needs to live in Florida where it's sunny and warm. There's also the fact that your business and family are in Michigan, so you would want to live there." Marie crossed her arms. "Do you understand now why she thought it best to break things off?"

One hand covered the front of John's shirt where his heart was, as he gave a slow nod. "I'm relieved to know that it wasn't because she didn't care for me or that I had done something to offend her."

"No, it was neither of those things. It's just a situation that was out of your control, and Leora is trying to make the best of things." Marie teared up. "I never thought I would say this, but moving to Sarasota was the best thing Leora could have done. She's been much happier since she relocated to a warmer climate."

"Danki for sharing all of this with me. At least now I can stop blaming myself, thinking I'd done something to upset Leora." John reached out and shook Marie's hand. "The next time you talk to Leora, please tell her I said hello and that I'm praying for her."

Chapter 12

Sarasota

"Are you excited about your birthday coming up in a few days?" Karen asked when Leora arrived at the bakery one morning in April.

She shrugged. "Not really. It's just another day, and I'll be another year older—twenty-nine, to be exact."

"We should go out to celebrate by having supper at one of the nice restaurants overlooking the water."

Leora slipped an apron on over her dress. "I don't feel much like celebrating." She gave a frustrated shake of her head. "I was hoping my folks or one of my sisters might come to Sarasota to spend my birthday with me, but it's the same old story—they're all busy with their jobs, and no one can get the time off right now."

Karen slipped her arm around Leora's waist. "You have me, dear friend."

Leora managed a brief smile. "I appreciate that, but I really don't want to go anywhere for my birthday."

"Why don't I plan a little get-together at my house? I'll invite several of our friends who like to sing and play instruments, and we'll have lots of good snacks. I'm sure that would help cheer you up."

Leora's hands hung loosely at her sides. "I doubt it."

"You're still pining for John, aren't you? I can see the look of longing on your face."

"It wouldn't do any good if I was." Leora's voice dropped to a near whisper. "I was foolish to allow myself to get involved with him. I knew going into it that things couldn't last. I just let my feelings for John take over and didn't use common sense."

"Maybe things would have worked out if you had told him the truth."

"I don't see how. I can't move to Michigan, and John can't move here. It was an impossible situation from the moment we first met." She turned aside with a deep sigh. "We'd better both get to work, or we might lose our jobs."

"Okay, friend. We'll talk again during our lunch break."

Karen moved over to the cash register, and Leora went to get the cakes she had baked yesterday that needed decorating.

Leora brought four cakes from the back room where she'd done the baking, and set them on a table behind the enclosed counter to decorate. She had to admit that the sweet scents of vanilla and chocolate mingling made her mouth water. The first special-order cake would have several colorful roses made from candy molds on it. Some were red, a few were white, and the rest were pink. The cake would look cheerful, and she hoped when it was finished it might brighten her mood.

With her back toward the counter, she'd just set the first two roses in place and secured them with frosting when a familiar voice said, "Excuse me, Miss, but I'd like to see about ordering a birthday cake for someone special."

Leora whirled around and emitted a little gasp. "John!

Wh–what are you doing here?" She could hardly believe her eyes.

"I came to see you and help celebrate your birthday."

Feeling flushed and somewhat giddy, Leora said, "It's three days from now."

He smiled. "I know. I got my information from a reliable source."

She tipped her head. "You talked with Karen?"

"Nope. Your *mamm* told me."

"My mom? When did you speak to her?"

"Met her in Shipshewana when my crew was doing a roofing job there. We spent some time talking about you. I won't go into everything she said right now—we can talk about that later, after you get off work." John pointed to the cakes on the table. "Now, about that birthday cake. . ."

Leora was speechless. This didn't seem real, yet here stood John on the other side of the counter, smiling at her and wanting to order a cake.

Leora gently bit down on her bottom lip. *I can't believe John would come all this way just to help celebrate my birthday.*

"So how about it, Leora? Can I put in an order for a birthday cake?" John's question cut into her thoughts.

"Well, yes, but you do realize that I'm the only person here who bakes and decorates the cakes. So it will be me making my own birthday cake."

John's smile grew wider. "I'm aware of that, and I think you're the best person to make the cake, because who knows better than you exactly what kind of cake you would like?"

"True, but I've never made my own cake before."

"Guess I could go someplace else and get a cake, but I'm sure it wouldn't look or taste as good as any you could make."

The heat of a blush spread across her face. "Where are you staying, and how long will you be here?"

"I got a room at the Carlisle Inn, and I'd better go there now so you can get back to work. What time do you get off today?"

"Four thirty."

"How about I get a pizza from Emma's and bring it over to your place around six o'clock? We can sit out on your lanai and talk privately. Would that work for you?"

"That sounds nice. It'll be good to catch up."

"All right then, I'll see you at six."

Feeling as though she were in a daze, Leora watched John walk out of the restaurant. *Did he really come all this way to spend my birthday with me, or does John have some other reason for being here? Will he ask me to leave Sarasota and move back home so we can see each other more often? If so, I need to be prepared to tell him the truth about my disorder.*

~

That evening, promptly at six, a knock sounded on the door of Leora's cottage. Her heart skipped a beat. John was here, and she worried about what he would say to her. If he brought up the idea of her moving back to Indiana, Leora would have to say no and tell him about her SAD. If he had only come here to celebrate her birthday, she would explain that a long-distance relationship was not going to work for them and suggest that he forget about her and move on with his life. Either option hurt, but she had no other choice. Leora glanced at her reflection in the bathroom mirror and checked her *kapp*, making sure it was straight. She'd changed out of her work dress earlier into something nicer after freshening up. *I hope I look presentable.* She moved from the sink toward the hallway.

The knocking continued, and Leora hurried to open the door. John stood on the porch, holding a box of pizza and wearing a smile that stretched wide. "Are you *hungerich*?" he asked.

She nodded, although at the moment her mind wasn't on food. "I'll get some paper plates, napkins, and bottled water. Why don't you take the pizza out to the table on the lanai?"

"Sounds good. After I set it down, I'll come back in and help you bring out the rest of the stuff."

"No, that's okay. I can manage. Just have a seat and relax. You must be tired from your trip."

"Naw, I'm fine. After I left Der Dutchman this afternoon, I went back to the hotel and took a nap."

"Oh, okay. Would you like something other than water? There's some lemonade and orange juice in the refrigerator, if you'd prefer either of those."

"Water's fine for me." John glanced at the stack of paper plates on the counter and picked up two. "Now you have two less things to carry." He grinned and sauntered out the door leading to the lanai.

Leora drew in a few quick breaths and tried to relax. Being with John again was wonderful, but she also felt apprehensive. When he left for Michigan again—and she felt sure that he would—she would grieve all over again.

Leora joined John a few minutes later. Once she was seated, they bowed their heads for silent prayer. Leora prayed that she would have the strength to tell John the truth about her disorder and that their time together would be meaningful.

They both took a piece of pizza and ate a few bites. Then John set his slice down and reached for Leora's hand. "I've missed you, Leora, and the love I feel for you has only grown stronger."

Unable to look directly at him for fear that he would see tears forming in her eyes, Leora lowered her head. "I feel the same way about you, John, but there's something you need to know about me."

"Is it concerning your seasonal affective disorder?"

Her head came up. "You—you know about that?"

"Jah. Your mamm gave me the details."

"So you must understand why I can't move back north where the weather makes me feel worse for all but a few months during the summer."

He nodded. "But you don't have to worry about that, Leora, because I have made the decision to move here."

Her eyes widened, and she blinked several times. "Seriously?"

"Jah."

"But your business is in Michigan."

"One of my workers will be in charge of the roofing jobs, and I'll run the business end of things from here—at least until I get my license to open my own business in Sarasota and the surrounding area. Once I get that going well, I may sell the business in Clare."

"You would do that in order for us to be together?" Leora could hardly believe her ears.

"Absolutely."

"What about your parents? How do they feel about you moving so far away?"

"Dad accepts it, and Mom understands how much I love you, but it may take a while for her to fully come around to the idea of me leaving home."

John stroked his thumb gently across Leora's hand. "Although we haven't known each other very long, I'm convinced that God brought us together." He paused a moment and looked lovingly into her eyes. "I'm equally sure that you're the woman He wants me to marry. I hope you feel the same way about me."

Tears coursed down Leora's cheeks, and John reached up and wiped them away. "I do, John, but it's too soon to be talking about marriage—especially since your mother doesn't approve."

"It's not you she doesn't approve of, Leora. She just hasn't totally accepted the idea of me moving so far away. But she will. I'm sure of it. We need to be patient and give her some time. In the meanwhile, I'll be busy trying to get a new roofing business established here, and you, my love, will keep busy with a wedding to plan and a cake to bake." He winked at her. "How about that seashell cake you told me about before? Wouldn't it be nice to serve a special cake like that to our wedding guests?"

Leora nodded with joyful tears. She could hardly wait to become Mrs. John Miller.

Epilogue

Middlebury
One year later

"You did a beautiful job on our wedding cake." John reached over and took Leora's hand as they sat together at the bride and groom's table during the meal that followed the service uniting them in marriage. Both of their families were here, as well as a few of the friends they had made while living in Sarasota.

Leora smiled and gave her husband's fingers a tender squeeze. "I've made several wedding cakes decorated with candy seashells, but I never thought I would make one for my own wedding someday. In fact, I didn't think I'd ever get married, much less to a wonderful man like you."

"Aw, I'm nothing special." John leaned close to her ear. "I'm just a man in love with a special woman who, for some reason, agreed to be my *fraa*."

"And I'm just a woman in love with a special man," she murmured. "You gave up so much in order to move to Sarasota to be with me, and I'm grateful." Leora glanced at the table where John's mother and father sat visiting with her parents. "I'm glad your mother doesn't resent me for taking her son away. She shared before the wedding that she's happy to have me as her daughter-in-law."

"I know. Mom told me that too." John fiddled with the napkin beside his plate. "Your folks seem to be okay that you chose me."

"Of course they are, and you've made an impression on my sisters, as well. Now, if I could just get one or all of them to visit us in Sarasota sometime soon. I'm sure they would enjoy the beautiful city, with its glorious, white sandy beaches."

"Well, at least we can all be together right now," he said. "See that table over there. . . if I'm not mistaken, that's Violet, Francine, and Alana."

Leora chuckled and bumped his arm. "Of course, dear husband. I just want them to come stay with us at our new house and be there longer than a few days."

"And once they've been to sunny Florida, I'm sure they'll want to come back. And who knows—one of 'em might actually like it so much that she'll decide to make Sarasota her home too."

"That would make me very happy." She looked over at John and smiled. "Do you think it would be wrong to pray for that?"

He shook his head. "Not at all. The main thing is that we should pray the Lord's will for our future and all three of your sisters."

Leora smiled. "You're absolutely right. All prayer should be ended with 'May the Lord's will be done.' "

Edible Seashells

Ingredients

2 cups sugar
½ cup water
¼ cup corn syrup
¼ teaspoon cinnamon extract (Vanilla or almond extract may be substituted.)
Gel food coloring

Boil sugar, water, and corn syrup in small saucepan over medium-high heat. Heat mixture to 300 degrees, using a candy thermometer to check temperature regularly. Remove sugar mixture from heat, add extract, and mix well. Add 2 to 4 drops of food coloring to sugar mixture. Use rubber spatula to thoroughly mix in coloring.

Carefully transfer mixture from saucepan into liquid measuring cup. Allow bubbles to settle for about 15 seconds. Use caution when transferring, as sugar mixture will be hot.

Carefully pour sugar mixture into shell-shaped candy molds. Allow sugar to harden at room temperature for 30 minutes. Once hardened, carefully remove sugar seashells from candy molds. If desired, spray seashells with color mist to add a shiny coating. Edible glitter adds a nice touch to shells as well.

New York Times bestselling and award-winning author **Wanda E. Brunstetter** is one of the founders of the Amish fiction genre. She has written over one hundred books translated into different languages. With over 12 million copies sold, Wanda's stories consistently earn spots on the nation's most prestigious bestseller lists and have received numerous awards.

Wanda's ancestors were part of the Anabaptist faith, and her novels are based on personal research intended to accurately portray the Amish way of life. Her books are well read and trusted by many Amish, who credit her with giving readers a deeper understanding of the Amish people and their customs.

When Wanda visits her Amish friends, she finds herself drawn to their peaceful lifestyle, sincerity, and close family ties. Wanda enjoys photography, ventriloquism, gardening, bird-watching, beachcombing, and spending time with her family. She and her husband, Richard, have been blessed with two grown children, six grandchildren, and two great-grandchildren.

To learn more about Wanda and her books,
visit her website at www.wandabrunstetter.com.

The Beach Ball

Jean Brunstetter

Chapter 1

Sarasota, Florida

Violet Lambright walked barefoot along the sidewalk to the mailbox on this fall day. Living for over a month in sunny Florida had its perks. Unlike being in the country back in Middlebury, Leora and John lived in a smoothly paved neighborhood. Back home, Violet had to walk down her parents' rough gravel driveway, trying to avoid stepping in horse droppings. Even though many other Amish lived here in Sarasota, none of them used horses and buggies for transportation, as they were not allowed on the roads.

After opening the mailbox, Violet thumbed through the mail. Most were addressed to her sister and husband, but Violet spotted a letter in the mix addressed to her. She clenched the envelope. *It's from Mom. I don't really want to read it—especially when she brings up that I need to come back home.*

The last time Violet spoke on the phone with her parents, they'd pressed her on the issue of her staying true to her Amish roots. She had listened to Mom and Dad express their desires for her life, but her own heart didn't line up with their intentions.

Coming back into the house, she set the mail on the kitchen

table and went to the refrigerator for a bottle of water. It was wonderful living with her sister and brother-in-law. They were both easy to get along with, their home was nice, and it was just a few blocks from the village of Pinecraft. Violet had her own room, and she had a new job at a restaurant that was affiliated with the one back home where she'd worked previously.

Getting to the restaurant each day appealed to her, just like back home. Violet had driven her car from Middlebury to her sister's place in a couple of days. Her parents weren't happy about her driving by herself and had tried to talk Violet out of it. But she stood strong in her decision to go it alone and follow the path she'd chosen. She had her cell phone to use, which she'd gotten while living at home. Violet reassured her folks that she'd leave messages on their answering machine, updating them on the progress of the trip. She'd had an uneventful time driving to Florida, and that was fine with Violet. Her compact car had done well, and she was able to carry most of the items she had wanted to bring from home to live with her sister.

Since moving to Florida, Violet had worn more English attire and put her Amish dresses in the back of the closet. It felt nice to wear shorts and a cute shirt, like most of the Floridians did.

Leora was patient with her, and she appreciated it. Violet enjoyed the freedom of trying out new things, like painting her fingernails and wearing makeup. She had thought about getting her long hair redone into a short new style. Violet made an appointment, but she just had the split ends removed and then had the stylist add some subtle highlights. She enjoyed her fresh, new look, and Leora said she thought it looked nice too.

Today was her day off from work, and the weather was gorgeous. It was easy to take all of this nice, warm sunshine for granted. Back home, the weather was cold, and they'd get good rains this time of the year. Violet didn't miss that weather at all. It was hard to beat living here.

She had been helping her sister with washing the clothes and setting the clean, damp loads in a laundry basket for Leora. Her sister was out back hanging up the laundry Violet had washed. She would be coming in soon to see the mail on the table. And since she knew the situation between her parents and Violet, Leora would probably urge her to read the one from Mom.

Violet thought back to when she'd dated a fellow in Middlebury who wasn't Amish. When her mother and father found out, the relationship was discouraged. So Violet broke up with him and dated one of the Plain boys. But she craved her independence and not having to be told how her future should be.

She set the water bottle down and stared at Mom's letter. *I'd like to live my life the way I want and experience the freedom to choose.*

Leora came in with the laundry basket and looked toward the table. "I see we've gotten some mail."

"We did, and one is from Mom."

"Is it to you or me?"

"It's for me." She frowned. "I have a feeling she'll start up again about my life choices."

Leora hurried to the laundry room, then returned without the basket. "She loves you and only wants what's best for you. Just open the letter, and you'll know what Mom has to say."

Violet watched her sister head out of the room. *I know Leora is right, but it doesn't make this any easier.*

Violet sighed, reluctantly opened the letter, and took a seat on the sofa.

~

Dear Violet,

I hope you, Leora, and John are doing well. We're all

doing fine here. Are you enjoying your new job? I hope you're not working too hard. What have you been up to? I'd like to know what's new. Dad and I miss you. The last time we talked, things seemed a little strained. We wish you'd reconsider and come back home. There are some real nice Amish fellows here and in the nearby communities. We wish you'd give joining the church more thought.

I'll try to change the topic now. I've been sewing a couple of new dresses and can't wait to wear them. Your daed is busy working at the machine shop and seems to never run out of work, which is a blessing. When he's home having some downtime, he's often out on the front porch watching the birds in our yard.

We got a new kitten. It's cute, has tiger stripes, and is a blackish-gray color. She came from a litter of the neighbor's cat down the road. Since we could use a new barn cat around here, it seemed fitting.

Your sisters are doing well and keeping busy. They asked me to say hi and said that you need to stay in touch with them.

Take care, and please give what I've said about coming back home and joining the church some thought.

Love,
Mom

Violet held the letter, not saying a word. *Mom's not done with expressing her feelings about how I should live my life.*

Leora came in and took a seat across from her. "Did Mom have much to say from home?"

"Not a lot. She brought up the topic of me coming home again, and dating some of the Amish boys there. She's still urging me to join the church."

"I can tell by the tone of your voice that you're not happy about her views."

"I'm not. It really bothers me that she doesn't understand how I feel. Our mother got to choose her path in life, and you have also chosen yours. Now it's my turn to go out and pursue my dreams."

"I see your point, and in time, our *mamm* will also. Just be patient with her and dad. When you've laid out your priorities and accomplished them, we will all understand and acknowledge them."

Violet smiled. "I hope so, Sister. It's nice to have you in my corner."

"No problem." Leora looked at the clock hanging on the wall. "Since you are not working today and will be here for supper. . ."

"I'll help prepare the meal. What are we having this evening?"

Leora shifted in the chair. "Thought we could make something easy. How about a chicken-and-rice casserole?"

"That sounds tasty." Violet glanced at the letter. "There's a guy I'm interested in whose sister works at the restaurant. It's Anne Yoder's brother. He's about my age.

Leora's brows shot up. "Really?"

"I know you're surprised that I'm thinking about dating an Amish fellow, but it's only for fun."

"Mom will be pleased to hear about that. She may even think you'll change your mind about straying from the faith."

Violet smiled. "I'm going to take this one day at a time and see how things go."

"Now, let's go into the kitchen and get the food ready for supper." Leora rose from the chair.

"I'll be there in a minute." Violet got up and gave her sister a hug, then took the letter to her room, placing it in the top drawer of the dresser. She would have to decide whether to respond to

Mom with a note or give her a call. It would be less stressful to write a quick letter than to speak to her directly.

~

Violet sat at the dinner table with Leora and John, enjoying the meal. John looked content eating what they'd made. Besides the casserole, there were seasoned green beans, homemade biscuits, and pickled beets.

John raked his fingers through his brown beard. "That was a tasty meal, *Fraa,* and I can't wait for dessert."

"I'm glad you enjoyed it," his wife replied.

John turned to Violet. "Your sister says you heard from your mother today in a letter. How are things there?"

"Mom says everyone is fine."

He smiled. "That's good."

"They have a new addition, a barn cat. Mom sounded happy about that."

"That's one thing we don't need around here is a barn *katz.*"

"I agree." She looked at Leora. "There's an apple pie for dessert if everyone is ready."

"I could handle a slice after we get some of this put away."

"That does sound good." John gave a nod. "And maybe a hot cup of *kaffe* to go with it."

"After we clear the dishes and get things cleaned up, I'll brew the coffee to go with dessert." Leora placed her napkin on the plate.

Violet stood and began clearing the dishes. There was plenty of casserole left over for tomorrow night. She sat the heavy dish on the stove top to let it continue to cool before putting it in the refrigerator. Leora soon joined her, and John headed to the living room to relax.

Violet thought about Levi Yoder. He was cute, and she'd seen him riding on his motorcycle, which intrigued her. Anne, from the restaurant, was Levi's sister, and she had told her all about him. Violet thought it would be fun to give this fellow a try and see what would happen. She wished she could keep her dating Levi a secret so her folks wouldn't find out about it. Leora's comment about Mom seemed spot-on. Violet was sure their mother would be quick to hope that her dating an Amish boy could mean they'd get their way. At least Leora wouldn't be trying to push Violet into a relationship with him just because he was Plain. She was ever so grateful that she lived with her sister and not back at home at this point. Tomorrow, if Anne was working during her shift, she would ask her about the possibility of going on a date with Levi.

~

The restaurant had been busy at lunch, and it was full for supper too. Violet waited on her assigned tables, taking orders and bringing out the guests' food. If anyone needed a way to get exercise, this job would fit the bill. Violet had even noticed that she slept better on her workdays due to keeping so busy.

During her break, Anne came over to where Violet sat. "How's it going?"

"Not bad. I'm glad it's my break time. My feet are appreciating that I'm sitting right now."

Anne laughed. "I'll be happy for my break in a half hour."

Violet wasn't sure how to approach the topic of dating Anne's brother. She felt awkward, and her body tensed up at the idea of asking about meeting Levi. *Come on, Violet. It's easy. Just like ripping off a Band-Aid.*

Anne tilted her head. "By the way, my brother would still like to meet you. Would you be available after work to see him?"

Feeling a sense of relief, Violet nodded vigorously. "Sure, that would be fine."

"Okay, I'll give Levi a call during my break and let him know to come by," Anne said before heading back to work.

Violet was a little nervous about meeting Levi but figured it might be fun. She wondered how things would play out. Well, in just a few hours, she would know.

Chapter 2

It won't be long and I'll be meeting Levi. Violet finished her shift and headed off to freshen up in the ladies' room. Once inside, a glance at the mirror showed her shiny face and creased eye shadow could use some attention. Violet rummaged through her big purse for the pink flamingo cosmetic bag and a brush. Once she'd dug them out, it didn't take long to refresh her look and fix the long, brown ponytail she sported.

I hope I look okay. Violet checked the time on her smartphone, wondering when Levi would arrive. Her muscles twitched at the thought of meeting Levi for the first time. It was one thing to casually chat about him with Anne, but entirely another thing to be seeing and talking to him in person.

Violet stepped back from the mirror, gave a quick check of her clothes, and took off her name tag, setting it inside her handbag. *I suppose I'm ready now.* She slid the big bag onto her shoulder. *It's time for me to head out.*

Violet exited the ladies' room, hurrying back over to the restaurant. She saw Anne standing by one of the tables with her cute blond brother. Violet had seen him come in before to visit with his sister. She joined them and stood quietly, rubbing her arm.

Anne turned to Violet and smiled. "Let me introduce you

two. Violet, this is my brother, Levi Yoder, and Levi, this is my coworker, Violet Lambright."

"Nice to meet you." Levi grinned, revealing a pair of cute dimples.

"It's nice to meet you too." Violet's face warmed.

"Since I still have a few tables to clean, why don't you two sit and visit for a while?"

They looked at each other and then back at Anne. Violet spoke first. "That would be fine."

Levi gave a nod. "Sounds good to me."

Anne hurried off to clean tables. Levi grabbed a chair across from Violet and took a seat. "My sister said you're Amish."

She sat. "Yes, I am, but as you can see, I'm enjoying the English world." Violet gestured to the blouse and maxi skirt she wore.

"Me too, and it's been great just wearing T-shirts and jeans. I've been living here since the spring and found a job at the hotel near this restaurant. It's good work, but I'll be looking forward to going back home, probably by next spring. How 'bout you?"

Violet shook her head. "I'm not in any hurry to go back to Indiana. In fact, I am planning to stay here in sunny Florida."

"Really?" His brows lowered. "It's okay here, but it's not like being in Goshen. Besides, my real future awaits me there. I'm planning to join the church sometime next year. My father wants me to work at his shop back home along with my older brother. And I'm sure *Daed* will want one of us to take over his business someday."

"That sounds like a good plan." She fiddled with her purse strap. "I like working at this restaurant because it's a lot like the one back home. It's been a good fit for me. To be honest, I was ready to leave Middlebury and start a new adventure. Even driving myself here shows how much I wanted to get started with something different."

He nodded while rubbing his chin. "I had a car for a short time back home, but I like having the motorcycle here to get around on. It's a lot more fun. Sometimes my sister lets me drive her car when she's not using it."

Violet tilted her head. "Does Anne plan on staying here after you've gone back home to Indiana?"

"She's not sure yet, but I have a feeling she'll end up coming back to Goshen." Levi paused. "If Anne stayed here, she'd miss the four seasons. I would especially miss the fall, with all the intense colors the trees offer."

"They are pretty, but the downside is all the raking. That isn't my favorite thing to do."

They continued to visit, sharing about their families and the communities they were from. It didn't take long to become familiar with each other's Amish roots. Sometimes though, as he spoke, Levi would throw in some Pennsylvania Dutch words or even full sentences. Violet wasn't thrilled with that aspect because she was determined to be English. She continued to speak strictly English and wondered if he was just goofing around. If so, she hoped he would quit doing that.

~

When Violet returned to her sister's house that evening, she went to her room and put her things away. Her first meeting with Levi had gone well, and in a couple of days, they'd be going out on a date. Violet looked forward to that. He would be coming by the house to pick her up after work. Since she wasn't as familiar with the area as Levi, maybe he'd show her some new places.

Her stomach growled. It was after suppertime, and she needed to eat something. Walking into the kitchen, she saw John and Leora at the table chatting.

"How was your day, Violet?" her sister questioned.

"It was good. And I met Levi after work."

John smiled. "Just curious, is he English or Amish?"

Leora tapped him on the shoulder. "You are going to embarrass Violet."

Violet shrugged. "I don't mind saying." She opened the refrigerator. "He's actually Amish."

He gave a brief nod, then glanced at his wife. "Okay, so changing the subject, is there something sweet to nibble on for dessert?"

"There are some doughnuts from the bakery in that box on the counter." Leora pointed.

"Sounds good to me." He got up and put one on a plate.

"I'm going to fix myself a peanut butter and jelly sandwich." Violet looked at the doughnuts John had picked out. "Maybe I'll have one of those after I eat my sandwich."

Violet stood at the counter and grabbed two slices of bread. She watched John leave the room with his snack, heading for the living area. A nice breeze drifted through the open kitchen window. The warmth of the day had cooled off, and it felt nice. Although they had air conditioning in the house, they usually chose to cool off by opening the windows in the evenings. John and Leora also owned a couple of battery-operated fans that were used in different rooms to help move the air around when it got too warm, so that helped too.

Leora turned to Violet and said, "How did it go, meeting the young Amish fellow?"

Violet spread the peanut butter and jelly on her bread before responding. "I was nervous to begin with, but as we visited awhile, I began to relax."

"That's good. Can you tell me about him?"

She took a seat at the table with her sandwich and a glass of milk. "Levi's cute and seems pretty sure of himself. His family is from Goshen, and he's planning to go back there in the spring to work for his dad."

"Sounds like he has made his plans."

"I have to agree." Violet prayed silently and then took a drink of her milk. "Levi owns a motorcycle, so I'll be able to go for a ride with him."

Leora played with the napkin in front of her. "I have never ridden on a motorcycle. Those things look kind of tipsy to me. I'd be afraid to ride on one myself."

John stepped back into the room. "I can honestly say I've never ridden one either, but I have had the pleasure of riding on the back of a horse, and that's what I call real horse power."

Leora chuckled. "That's true."

Violet took a bite of her sandwich and listened to John talk fondly about growing up on the farm. Violet could tell Leora was happy being married to John. They got along well. She hoped one day that a nice guy like her brother-in-law would come into her life. But for the moment, Violet was only looking for some fun.

~

On Sunday, John, Leora, and Violet prepared for church. Sometimes they would walk or ride bikes to the church house for service.

This morning Violet went to her closet and sighed. *I still need to buy a couple more skirts for work or church. I guess I'm stuck wearing my* kapp *and one of my Amish dresses this morning.* She picked out one in blue and took out a new head covering. It was hard to put these items back on after being used to wearing English clothes during the other six days of the week. It almost seemed as though she lived two different lives.

A knock sounded on Violet's bedroom door. "We'll be ready to go in forty-five minutes," Leora called from the other side. "How about you?"

"I should be ready in time." Violet opened her bedroom door to let Leora in.

Her sister stepped into the room. "Do you think Levi will be at church?"

She shrugged. "I have no clue. In fact, we never discussed church."

Leora took a seat on the unmade bed. "Just wondering, have you written Mom back yet?"

"No, I haven't, but I need to."

"Will you be bringing up Levi in your letter?"

She sat on a little stool in front of the vanity, brushing her long hair. "Why?"

"I was going to write Mom too, and I didn't want to say something that you wanted to keep quiet."

"For now, I'm not going to say anything. It's just a casual relationship. No sense in getting Mom thinking or hoping that I'm going to get serious about an Amish guy."

"I'm sure our mother would do just that if she knew what you were up to."

"Well, his family is living in Goshen, and ours is in Middlebury. So it might go undetected."

"Maybe, but the grapevine is alive and well. Didn't you mention that his sister works with you and has a cell phone?"

"Yep, she does. I suppose the word could get around back home." Violet released a sigh. "But I'll take my chances and say nothing."

"Okay, then I won't mention it. I'll leave that up to you. On that note, I need to finish getting ready, and I'll let you do the same."

Violet looked in the mirror and began putting her hair up in a bun. *I don't need to tell our parents everything. What I decide to do is my business. If they find out from someone else, then so be it. Besides, a little fun with a cute guy on wheels can't hurt.*

Chapter 3

Violet finished up her shift and hurried out of the restaurant. She made a beeline to her car. *I can't wait to see Levi soon and go for a motorcycle ride for the first time.* On one hand, Violet was thrilled, but on the other hand, her palms sweated with an uneasy feeling. *Maybe I'm a little nervous, but it will be fun.*

It didn't take long for her to arrive home, and after she'd pulled in, Violet brought up the garbage can next to the house. It was one of the jobs she did to earn her room and board. She also did several other chores and paid rent each month to help out with her sister's and brother-in-law's bills. It was a nice arrangement, and she didn't mind contributing at all.

When Violet entered the house, the air smelled of fried chicken. Coming from the kitchen, Violet heard Leora humming a happy melody. She found her sister preparing supper. John hadn't arrived home yet, but sometimes, depending on his schedule, he arrived later, and Leora would keep the meal warm for them.

Violet came into the kitchen, sniffing the air. "It sure smells good in here."

Leora turned and smiled. "Thank you. Just making John's favorite meal. I'm about ready to start mashing the potatoes."

Violet glanced at the battery-operated clock on the wall. "I'd like to help you out, Sister, if I had more time, but I need to hurry and get ready for my first date with Levi. He'll be here in half an hour."

She nodded. "No problem."

Violet headed down the hall to her room. She needed to figure out what to wear to make a good impression, and she hoped they'd have fun together.

After some time had passed, Leora called from the hall, "Violet, he's here."

Hurrying, Violet grabbed her little cross-body purse and threw it on. The blaring sound of Levi's motorbike drifted in through the open window. It was definitely a noise that was hard to miss. Violet stopped to look in the mirror attached to the outside door of the restroom. *These new peach capris and my yellow hooded T-shirt look nice.* She looked at her white tennis shoes. *These should be comfortable enough for riding on the bike.*

Violet headed for the front door and turned in time to say goodbye to John and her sister. "I won't stay out very late because I've got work in the morning."

John stood by the entrance leading into the kitchen, holding a glass of water. "Okay, have a nice time."

"See you in a while, and have fun." Leora stepped out into the living room. Her eyes flitted to the front room window.

Violet wondered what her sister thought as she stared out. *She's probably glad not to be the one riding on that noisy motorbike, and maybe she's a bit worried about me.* She saw Levi wearing his helmet. When he took it off, his hair was a little disheveled, but he still looked cute.

After coming out of the house and closing the door, Violet walked up to him and smiled.

He'd set the kickstand and turned off his motorcycle. "Hello."

"Hi, it's sure a nice evening." She watched him climb off the bike.

"I agree." He undid the holder for the other head gear. "Here's a helmet for you. You'll need to put it on, and I'll help you with the chin strap."

Violet took the bulky item and slipped it over her head. "This is weird."

"Yeah, they take a little getting used to, but it's good to wear some protection." He helped fasten the chin strap. "How does that feel? I hope it's okay."

"It's good." She fingered it and nodded.

He slipped his own helmet back on and cleared his throat. "Just some basic tips when you ride with me. First, you'll need to hang on to me when we're rolling. And second, when I lean turning left or right, you need to lean with me. It'll make for a smoother and more balanced ride for both of us."

Violet smiled. "That doesn't sound too difficult. Almost like riding a horse."

"Jah, but this is far faster to ride." He got on first. "Climb on behind me."

This wasn't the time for her to be shy. She had to share the seat with Levi and sit close enough to him that she could put both arms around his waist. Levi started up the loud engine. It would be a lot harder to talk to him with the noisy two-wheeled vehicle under them. She wondered where they would go and what place he had in mind to get a bite to eat later.

"Okay, are you ready to go?" he called.

"I am." Violet put her arms around his midsection. It felt strange doing that to someone who was pretty much a stranger, but she didn't want to lose her balance and fall off the bike. She smelled his mild-fragranced cologne but there was also the smell of cigarettes. *Maybe he's a little wilder than me.*

Levi twisted the handle, giving the bike forward momentum, and they swiftly headed down the road. The air blew at her shirt and the legs of her capris. It was an awesome feeling, almost like flying. When Levi went around a corner, she would lean just like he did. Violet enjoyed the motorcycle and thought it was great.

After they'd driven through town and got out on the highway, Levi sped down the road. Violet felt the air swishing past her frame, and it was such a new feeling for her. The bike was much quicker than the cars. Levi switched lanes often with little problem since the bike was smaller than most of the vehicles on the road.

Along the way, Violet's nose began to itch and she wanted to scratch it. She let go of Levi with one hand and was almost able to touch it when the bike hit a bump in the road. Violet grabbed him harder to compensate and keep herself from falling off the bike. *That was thrilling, but I still have a very itchy nose.* Being desperate to lessen the itch, she leaned close to Levi's back and swiped her nose a couple of times against his shirt. *Aw, now that feels better.*

Levi turned his head toward her for a moment but then fixed his gaze on the road again.

~

When they exited the highway, Levi pulled over and gave Violet a couple of options as to where they might go to eat. Violet said she didn't care which place they went to, so Levi took them to a pizza place.

Inside the restaurant, a waiter seated them at a table by the window. Savory, tantalizing aromas of baking pizzas made her mouth water in anticipation.

The waiter left menus for them to peruse. Violet sat there deciding what to drink. She noticed that Levi wasn't looking in the same place for his beverage.

He pointed at the alcohol list. "If only I was twenty-one, I'd order a beer instead of a soft drink."

"I don't mind having a soda." She paused and spoke quietly. "I've had a taste of beer before."

"Only a taste?" His brows rose. "I've tried different beers since living here. A friend of mine bought some and shared with me."

"Really?" Violet noticed their waiter returning.

The man took their drink orders and left again. Levi looked at her and smiled. "Why don't we share a pizza?"

"Sounds good to me."

"What do you like for toppings?"

Violet looked at the menu and pointed at the choices. "I like pretty much any of these except the hot peppers."

"There's a supreme pizza that has a good number of toppings on it. We could probably eat a medium, no problem."

"That should work. I know I'm hungry."

"Me too." He sat back as the waiter set down their beverages and took their order.

Levi spoke once their waiter had walked away. "There's one thing I've noticed about riding the bike like we did this evening."

"What was that?"

"The forced air we've breathed seems to tire us out. You'll probably sleep good tonight."

"I suppose that makes sense. I've been out on a boat with the wind blowing into my face. It had that same effect with the forced air thing."

"In Indiana, did you like to fish or just like riding around on the water?"

"Either one is fine with me. How about you?" she asked.

"I like both. I've caught some fish on the lake and have enjoyed a good many fish suppers."

"Fish is good. We've even cooked them on sticks over an open fire."

"I haven't done that," he said. "Usually, when we catch fish, Mom coats and fries them in a pan. We always have other things along with the fish, like Mom's potato salad and her homemade baked beans."

"That's making me hungrier, talking about food." Violet took a drink of her root beer.

Levi sipped on his cola and leaned back again, this time speaking in Pennsylvania Dutch. "What would make you change your mind about staying here rather than moving back to Indiana?"

Violet tried not to appear shocked by his question and to overlook his using more Dutch words. "I can't think of anything right now. And since I haven't been in Sarasota that long yet, I don't really know."

"I was just curious is all." He gave a sweet dimpled smile.

They visited until their pizza came to the table. Violet was famished but waited as they bowed their heads in silent prayer before enjoying their meal. Then they both dived right in.

Levi ate through his first slice of pizza pretty fast and went for another. "What do you think of the pizza?" he asked.

"It's good." Violet took another bite.

"I noticed you kind of let go of me on the bike for a few seconds."

She swallowed her food. "My nose itched, and I tried to scratch it. But we hit the bump, and I didn't want to fall off."

"I was wondering what you were doing behind my back when I felt a nuzzle through my shirt."

Violet's face warmed. "I'm sorry about that. I was desperate because my nose itched so bad."

He waved his hand. "Don't give it another thought. I just wondered what you were up to is all." He winked at her and took a sip of his soda.

Violet took another bite, peering out the window for a moment. The food tamed her hunger and the forced air from earlier had made her feel relaxed. She stared out at the steady traffic flowing by, but her attention was soon back on Levi.

He leaned closer. "We should plan another date."

"I'd like that."

"I'm glad." Levi nodded. "I live with two roommates where I'm staying. One guy is Amish and the other fella is English. We all work at the same hotel, so we see each other quite a bit. Once in a while, we trade shifts if one of us needs a day off or has an appointment."

"That sounds like a good arrangement." She wiped her hand on a napkin.

"It is."

Levi expressed how he enjoyed hanging out with his roommates sometimes and they'd share a few beers. The English guy was twenty-one and could go out and buy the alcohol. The other roommate was around Levi's age and would be going back to Ohio sometime this winter.

Violet listened to Levi talk about his work schedule and when they could go out again. She looked forward to hanging out with him and thought it was interesting to find out about his living arrangements. She didn't have any roommates, except for Leora and John, so she had no strangers to deal with. Levi seemed to be content with his circumstances, but Violet was content living with her sister and brother-in-law. Regardless, she decided to focus on their date.

"This pizza is really good. Did you discover this place yourself?" She tilted her head.

"No, one of my roommates told me about it. I can't take any credit for that." He took a drink of his cola. "I should have gotten a side salad. Maybe next time."

Violet looked toward a nearby table. "I can see one of them there; it looks like a pretty nice-sized salad. I don't think I could eat all of that and help you eat this pizza."

"If we don't finish it, that's okay. It would be a little hard to bring back a box of leftovers on my motorcycle."

"I suppose that's one drawback to traveling on a two-wheeler." She smiled.

Violet thought Levi was so cute and charming. They visited longer until Levi mentioned that he'd have to get back to his place to be up early for work. Violet felt the same way. She needed her rest as well. Even though Levi was a little on the wild side, Violet couldn't help her attraction to him. She was eager to find out where he would take her when they went out again.

Chapter 4

The last few weeks at work and at Leora's home had gone smoothly for Violet. She had set aside some time to write and send a nice letter back home to her folks, telling them how well things were going and sharing about the new places she'd been able to see so far. But Violet had left out the fact that she had been dating Levi. The truth was that things were not going well with him. He had a bad habit of dropping by unannounced. He'd show up after her shift and want to hang out. And when she told him she had other plans, he became defensive and even rude.

Levi had invited Violet to his apartment to meet his roommates. When she'd finally accepted the invitation and driven herself there, she couldn't get over how Levi just wanted to sit and enjoy having beers with his friends. She was not that into drinking and wasn't amused listening to him boast about how great he had things. Violet had wanted to leave and go explore new places on his bike.

To make matters worse, he'd lit up a cigarette and blown out that annoying smoke while she sat beside him. It reminded her of the stories she had read about dragons. The more Levi drank, the more he began speaking Pennsylvania Dutch. He had even said that it would be best if Violet moved back home to Indiana and settled down with him.

Levi was no doubt showing his true colors. She was hurt and tired of his actions. It was apparent that he didn't care for her decision not to join the church. In fact, Levi had gone on to say, "I'm just having fun like you for now, but then we need to get serious about our future."

Our future? I'm not interested in settling down yet. And Levi isn't the right fellow for me. He needs to grow up and stop acting so immature.

Violet stood in front of the bathroom mirror, applying makeup. She thought of her sister, Alana, while looking at herself. *I don't have a single freckle on my nose. Yet Alana has a smattering of them. I've always thought they made her look naturally pretty.*

She was at home by herself, enjoying some free time since today was her day off. Leora and John had gone to work already this morning. Having the house to herself was peaceful, but she wanted to get out and explore. She had an idea to go shopping at some of the gift stores. Her room was decorated in warm colors, which she liked. She wanted to add a beach theme to it since she chose to live in Florida. Hopefully, she'd be successful in finding some decor that suited her taste.

Recently the gas gauge in Violet's car had begun to act up. It wasn't showing the true amount of fuel the tank held. So she had to make sure she topped off the tank before going very far. It wouldn't be fun to run out of gas and be left stranded. That would make for a bad day, and Violet wanted to have a nice time without it being ruined by unpleasant surprises.

~

St. Armand Circle

Violet had finally found a place to park at Armand Circle. It was busy, but she couldn't wait to do some exploring. After paying for her parking, Violet walked with a crowd of people and noticed a group taking pictures by the statues. With the number of them wearing shirts reading FLORIDA, Violet couldn't help wondering if some of those people were tourists.

Different shops outlined the streets. Some sold clothing, while others featured sunglasses, shoes, and souvenirs. There were also a lot of restaurants.

Violet spotted a gift store and went right in. She browsed the aisles and took her time looking through the selections. She had walked through most of the store before she noticed an area with some traditional beach things. Sun hats, bucket sets with shovels, water toys, and blow-up toys filled the shelves.

Nearby, a handsome young man with blond hair shopped too. He came closer to her and looked in the same direction. Violet found something she'd like to buy. A colorful beach ball sat on the shelf, and it was the last one there. It seemed like the perfect accessory for a fun day out on the sand.

They both reached for it at the same time. "Oh, I'm sorry. You can have it." His tenor voice was soothing to her ears.

She felt her face warm. "Are you sure?" She noticed how tall he was, and his shiny blond hair and tan skin were striking.

"I'm fine with you having it." He smiled. "I'm from Sarasota, and I can come back anytime to get another one of these."

"Thank you very much." Violet smiled too. "I've been living here a couple of months, and I'm working at a restaurant in Sarasota." *He's sure handsome.* Violet tried not to stare at him.

His brows shot up. "I—I thought you might be a tourist. Are you liking this tropical place?"

"I am." She could see that another fellow was waiting for him not far from where they stood.

He looked away at his friend for a moment. "I should get going. It was nice talking to you. Maybe we'll see each other again sometime."

"Who knows," she replied with a smile.

Sarasota

Arriving back at the house after a busy day, Violet grabbed her shopping bags from the trunk of her car and carried them into the living room. Leora was sitting on the sofa reading a book. "Did you have a nice day?" she asked.

"I did." Violet sat down on the couch and opened one of the bags. "I saw this in that big gift store in Armand Circle and thought it would look pretty in my room."

Leora set aside her book and glanced at it. "That's a nice, light green bottle."

"I'll probably put some dried flowers inside to dress it up. I will set this on my dresser near the window."

"That would be the perfect spot."

Violet pulled a pair of Sarasota mugs from the same bag. "I know how much our sisters like to drink their favorite teas. I couldn't help myself. They made me think of Frannie and Alana the moment I laid eyes on them."

"I see what you mean. They'll make nice gifts." She handed the mugs back to Violet. "I can tell you miss our sisters, and so do I." Leora leaned closer to her. "What else did you buy?"

"At a different store, I found this pillow with seashells on it." She withdrew it from the bag.

Leora nodded. "That's nice. I'm sure it'll spruce up the room you're staying in."

"Thank you. It will either set on my chair or on the bed. I'll have to decide, but I still have one more thing I picked up."

"Where is it?"

"I left it out in the car. I'll go get it now." Violet sprang from her seat. "There's actually a tiny story that goes with it."

She hurried from the room and returned with the colorful beach ball. "How about this? Catch!" Violet tossed the ball to her sister.

After Leora caught it, she lifted it up with a perplexed expression. "This is a cute beach ball. When are you going to use this?"

Violet shrugged. "Not sure, but I have a story to share about that ball."

"Okay, I'm all ears."

Violet joined her sister on the couch. "I had been hoping to find this kind of ball to take to the beach. And finally, I spotted the one you're holding and headed for it, but there was another shopper nearby." She paused for a breath. "We both reached out for it at the same time, and he let me have the beach ball. He was so polite to me. It was unforgettable."

"Sounds like he was a nice fellow." Leora patted Violet's arm playfully. "It seems he may have made an impression on you."

"Yes, and we even visited a little. He said that he lives here in Sarasota." She smiled. "I'd mentioned that I had moved here and was working at a restaurant."

"Did you say much more to each other?" Leora questioned.

"Not really. He was with a friend, so we just said our goodbyes."

"Even though Sarasota is a big area, maybe you'll see him around sometime."

"That would be nice, but it's probably doubtful." Violet frowned. "All I'm sure about is that I'm done with Levi."

"I know from what you've told me that he's been getting on your nerves. And it's not that great having him just showing up here unannounced. It's like he's checking up on you or something."

"I've voiced that to Levi, and he just does what he wants. I'm going to be the one to have to call off this relationship. The next time he shows up, I'm going to let him know that I'm done." Violet gathered her items back into the bags. "I should go put these away and help you start supper."

"That would be nice. We can talk more when you've come back out to help me in the kitchen."

Violet brought her things into the room and plopped on the bed. Just sitting there staring into nothing for a moment allowed her mind to imagine the way she'd tell Levi they were done. This guy was not the one for her, and she needed to break it off with him soon. Was it wrong to rehearse what she would say to end their relationship? Violet didn't want to go another day being his girlfriend. She was ready to move on and hopefully find someone new.

Violet couldn't help envisioning this mystery fellow and how nice he had been. Even though they'd only crossed paths briefly, he'd piqued Violet's interest. *Seeing him again would be like finding a needle in a haystack. I'd mentioned that I worked at a restaurant in Sarasota, but I didn't say which one.*

She took the new pillow from the bag and laid it on the comforter. It added a modern touch, blending with the blanket's gold hue perfectly. Violet then rose from the bed and took out the glass bottle. Setting it on the dresser, she played with its position. She wanted to have plenty of light shining through the bottle from the nearby window. It looked nice, and the sea-glass-green color it gave off created a beachy look. Now she'd have to find some dried flowers for it.

Violet imagined how much fun it would be to one day have a beach-themed bedroom of her own that was painted and furnished.

At her sister's place, she wouldn't do something like that. It wasn't Violet's house, and Leora had already done all the themes and colors in each of the rooms. Violet respected her sister's choices and would only do minimal things to make her surroundings beach-themed while staying here.

Looking at the wooden floor of the guest room, she considered buying a little throw rug. Maybe something that would go with the pillow on the bed. Violet tapped her cheek. *If I could find a light green rug with something beachy, that would be perfect.*

Violet put the rest of her purchases in the closet. She needed to get to the kitchen and help her sister with supper. She left the room and was on her way but stopped in her tracks when the sound of a motorcycle blared through the open window. *That's Levi, and now's not the time for him to drop in. I'm going to let him know right now that we're through.*

Violet took a couple of deep breaths and walked out of the house. As soon as Levi spotted her, he turned off the bike. She was not happy seeing him and didn't even try to be polite.

"This isn't a good time to drop by."

Levi raised his hands defensively "I just wanted to see how my girl was doing."

"You were here just yesterday."

"I can't help that I want to see you. That's what a boyfriend is supposed to do, right?"

The hair on the back of Violet's neck raised. She drew in a gulp of air before speaking. "I can't see you anymore, Levi."

His brows shot up. "What? What do you mean?"

"It's not working for us. I'm done going out with you."

"Look, you are just being a little headstrong is all. I can tell you'll calm down in a while and want to continue dating me." He gave a deceivingly sweet grin, revealing his dimples.

"That would have worked on me in the beginning, but your charm is not enough anymore."

He laughed. "We aren't over, Violet."

"I'm done dating you, Levi. It just isn't working out between us." She turned to head back into the house. "Please, don't come by anymore," she called over her shoulder.

"Violet, you're just being stubborn. Mark my words, you have not seen the last of me. You can count on that!" He started his motorcycle and shot out of the driveway.

It was a relief to tell him that she was done. Now Violet could move on without any problems.

Chapter 5

With the back of her hand, Violet wiped the perspiration from her forehead. The breakfast rush had been a hectic start to the workday, and it didn't seem like things would settle down much for lunch. At least every employee was present. Having fewer bodies would put more strain on those who were already there on such a busy day.

She noticed a line forming again outside the restaurant's entrance. Lunch was just starting, so Violet picked up the pace while heading to place four more orders from one of her tables. The cook chatted briefly with her and took the orders.

Violet looked off into another section of the restaurant and noticed a familiar face. It was the handsome blond fellow she'd crossed paths with at Armand Circle. Seeing him again made her heart quicken. He sat across from another young man.

I can't believe he's here. She lowered her gaze to her moistened hands. *I'd really like to say hi to him before he finishes and leaves.*

Her thoughts were interrupted when Anna's voice broke through. "How's it going, Violet?"

Violet turned her attention to her friend. "Good, and keeping busy."

"It looks like we'll be continuing to stay busy for a while." She motioned toward the line of customers.

"Yes, I see what you mean." Violet tucked a loose strand of hair behind her ear.

Anne's voice lowered as she leaned in close. "By the way, I was told by my brother that you two are having some problems."

Having problems? Violet didn't want to discuss Levi, but Anne seemed concerned over their relationship. Keeping her voice close to a whisper, Violet responded. "We aren't having problems. I broke up with Levi."

Anne's brows drew together. "He didn't mention that you had broken things off with him."

Violet looked around, wondering if they were keeping quiet enough. "That's odd, but it is true. Things weren't working out between us."

"I'm sorry to hear that, but I hope we can still remain good friends." Anne brought her arm around briefly Violet's shoulder.

"I would like that, Anne."

"Well, Violet, I'd better let you get back to work. We'll have more time to talk later."

Violet watched Anne head off. It was a relief that Levi's sister wasn't offended by the break-up. It would've been hard to work together if there had been hurt feelings over this. She was unsure why Levi had kept the break-up a secret. It seemed as though a gray, cloud-like presence loomed over her. But it couldn't be that big of a deal, could it? Violet tried to shake off the odd feeling and headed toward the two fellows to say hello.

~

The young man grinned at her as she approached the table. "Well, hello. So we meet again."

Violet smiled. "Yes, and welcome to Der Dutchman. I'm surprised you remember me from the other day."

His blue eyes glinted, complementing his tanned skin. "Of course. And I think it would be a good idea to introduce myself this time. I'm Dan Hunter, and this is my friend Steve."

I like the smooth tenor voice of his, Violet thought. It seemed to make the negativity from earlier fade away. "I'm Violet Lambright, and it's nice to meet you both."

Dan's eyes remained fixed on her. "This restaurant is sure a popular place for the residents, as well as many tourists."

"I have to agree. The customers keep all of us here on our toes." Violet wanted to stay and continue visiting with Dan. She looked toward her section, then back at him. "I should get back to waiting on tables now. I hope we can have more time to chat some other time."

"No problem. Maybe we'll see each other again soon. I come here to eat fairly often."

She nodded and returned to her tables. *If only I'd been on my break, I could've hung around and chatted with Dan.*

Violet was glad she'd been able to see him again, even if she didn't have much time to linger. But it was important to get back to her customers because problems would arise if they had to wait a long time for good service, especially when they were hungry.

She walked up to the first table, where two older women sat. "Good afternoon. Are you two ladies ready for me to take your drink orders?" Violet took out her pad and pencil.

One of the gray-haired women with curls spoke up. "Yes, I'd like a coffee with cream."

The other woman tugged at her polka-dot scarf. "I would like an iced tea with lemon."

"All right, I'll get those and be right back." Violet went to the drink station, got the two beverages, and brought them back.

After briefly speaking with Dan, the day seemed better to

Violet. It was fun to catch a glimpse of him when she took orders to the back where the cooks were, but she hoped he wouldn't think she was staring at him. That would be embarrassing.

Violet moved on to the next table, where four Amish men sat. They all wanted coffees to start with and said they wished they'd arrived sooner to enjoy breakfast. They settled for having something for lunch instead. Violet took their orders, and as she went to the back to turn them in, she noticed Dan and his friend were getting up to leave. Violet paused a minute to watch them head out, wishing she could leave her assigned area and follow them outside to see what kind of vehicle he was driving. It would be hard to get Dan out of her mind, but she had work to do and needed to stay focused. Maybe, just maybe, she would see him again.

~

After getting home, Violet changed into some comfortable clothes and headed into the kitchen to help Leora with supper. She grabbed a bottle of water and took a drink. *I wonder what Leora has brought home today. In the bakery where Leora works, there's always a nice variety of pies, doughnuts, cakes, and cookies. I can only imagine what my sister has brought home for us to enjoy.*

Violet looked down at her bare feet, which were aching after a long day of standing and walking. They felt a bit better against the coolness of the hardwood floor. Today had been busy at the restaurant, but the highlight of her day was seeing Dan's genuine-looking smile.

Her sister stood at the sink washing her hands. "I sure like that 'Legend of the Sand Dollar' picture hanging there."

"Yeah, I like it too." Violet drank some more water.

Leora dried her hands while looking out the window. "That's odd."

"What's odd, Sister?" Violet stepped next to her and peered out the window.

"The lid was off our garbage can out back, and I saw something poke its head up. I wonder if it was the neighbor's *katz*?"

They both stood by the window, staring at the can. The thing lifted its head again, and Violet saw a light-colored animal.

"Oh no, that's not a cat. Its nose is too long." Leora pointed. "I believe it's a possum, and I bet the critter's trying to hide out in there until it gets dark."

Violet scratched her head. "That's crazy. I suppose if we needed to go outside, the poor thing wouldn't do anything to us but continue trying to stay hid."

"That's true. We'll just keep an eye on it." Leora brushed her apron. "But if the possum decides to stick around our place, we might need to call someone to have it removed."

"I'm sure the poor possum will disappear as soon as it gets the chance." Violet leaned against the sink. "I'd like to take my phone outside and get a picture of it."

"That would be something to remember this day." Leora smiled. "We best get back to getting supper on the table."

Violet set the water aside and prodded the potatoes boiling on the stove. "These are about ready to mash."

"The meat loaf's done, and I've turned down the temperature. I think we are almost ready to have supper." Leora set the pot holder aside.

"I noticed in the refrigerator that you brought home something for dessert this evening." Violet carried the pan of potatoes to the sink and poured off the water.

"Jah. I wanted to surprise you, Violet. There's a chocolate cream pie inside of that container."

"Oh, Sister, that's a nice surprise." Violet licked her lips as her mouth watered.

"I knew you'd be happy about it." Leora brought the dish of carrots and celery sticks to the table, along with some ranch dip.

Violet returned the pan to the stove, adding butter and warmed milk to the potatoes. "I had a busy day at the restaurant. I'm sure you were busy at the bakery too."

"Yes, we were. In fact, the chocolate cream pies were so popular, I had to make sure to buy that one and mark the box with my name on it."

"Thank you for thinking of me." She grinned. "I can't wait to sample a piece of it after our meal."

"You're welcome." Leora checked the green beans warming on the cooktop. "I'll put on some coffee before we serve the pie after supper, and we can heat up the kettle for tea if that appeals."

"That does sound good. I might have a cup of mint tea to go with my dessert." Violet continued mashing the steaming potatoes.

Not long after, John came in the door from work. "Hello, ladies." He gave Leora a kiss on the cheek. "How was your day, dear Fraa?"

"It was good." Leora pointed toward the kitchen window. "We have a guest out in our garbage can, though."

"We do?" He peered through the glass a few seconds. "I don't see anything."

"It's a possum." Violet and Leora spoke in unison.

"Well that's something else! When did you notice it?"

"It hasn't been long, but Leora discovered it," Violet replied. "I wasn't sure what I was seeing at first."

Leora stepped beside him. "When I saw its long snout and white fur, I knew what it was."

John lingered at the window and then set his lunch container aside. "I'll go outside and take a look at our possum friend."

"Supper's ready, so don't take long out there," she responded.

"Do you want to get a picture of it? I have my phone." Violet motioned to her cell on the counter.

John pulled the phone out of his lunch container. "Nope, but if I get a decent picture I'll send it to you."

"Okay!" She smiled.

John went out the back door while Violet and Leora peeked out the window for a moment, watching him. He walked cautiously toward the can. John then raised his hand high over the top of where the possum was and took some pictures of it. He turned and headed back into the house.

"I think I've got some good pictures of our guest." He showed his phone to them as they readied supper.

"How about your day?" Leora poured the hot green beans into a bowl and added a spoon.

John groaned and took a seat at the table. "We were busy at that job near the park—the one that needed the roof replaced after a fire." He took off his work boots and set them aside. "I'm glad it's about finished, because we've got another project that is waiting to get started. It's nice to be catching up so I can have next Saturday off. There are a few things around the house I'd like to get done."

"What were you thinking of doing next Saturday?" Leora rinsed out the empty pan at the sink.

"I'd like to repair the leaky valve out by the garage, and I want to add some more pavers along the patio."

Leora brought over the meat loaf and some sliced bread. "That would be nice."

Violet carried the mashed potatoes to the table and went back for the green beans.

At each place setting, glasses were filled to the brim with iced water. Violet enjoyed listening to their friendly banter. It reminded her of Mom and Dad back home. She missed being with them at times, but not enough to move back to Indiana permanently. Violet was determined to remain in Florida and hoped that the Lord would someday provide the right man in her life as he'd done for Leora.

John went to the sink and washed his hands. "Supper sure smells good. I can't wait to have your homemade meat loaf and some mashed potatoes. I know they'll be good."

"Thank you, John," Leora replied. "We're all set to eat."

Violet sat down at the table and waited for her sister and John to join her. She couldn't wait to share about her day. She could picture Dan's face and how his voice sounded so mellow when he spoke. *Dan Hunter—what a nice name for such a good-looking fellow. He has the shiniest golden hair I've ever seen.* She tapped her chin. *I truly hope he doesn't have a girlfriend.*

Her thoughts were interrupted by John's voice. "Are we ready for silent prayer?"

Violet nodded, lowering her head in prayer. *Father, I hope that Dan will come by the restaurant again. I also hope he might like to be my friend and that he isn't dating someone else and will take an interest in me.*

When they'd finished praying, her sister passed the meat loaf to John, and he set the platter near Violet. She helped herself to everything offered on the table. Her appetite was good this evening, and she couldn't wait a second longer to share about her day.

"Remember when I went to Armand Circle a while back?" She took a sip of water.

"Of course. You had a good day shopping and you met a young man." Leora poked a fork into her meat loaf.

"He was at the restaurant today with a friend."

"Was the friend a she or a he?" John questioned.

"His name is Dan Hunter, and his friend is Steve. We were

able to introduce ourselves, which was nice."

"Do you think you'll see him again?" Leora questioned.

"I'm hoping so." She poked her fork into the mashed potatoes on the plate. "Also, I'm hoping he doesn't have a girlfriend already."

Leora gave her spouse a glance but didn't comment. Violet wasn't sure what either of them would say about her concern, but she waited, hoping for reassurance over her worry.

John finished his bite of food, then took a drink of water. In a comforting tone, he spoke. "Time will tell in the days to come if this fellow is dating anyone or not, but I hope things work out the way you're hoping they do."

Leora smiled. "I agree."

Violet felt better having her family's support, but she couldn't help wondering about Dan and whether he was free to date. For the time being, though, all she could do was wait, and if she did meet him again, she'd keep her Amish roots to herself. She wasn't embarrassed about it, but Violet wanted to keep being as English as she could for now. She took a bite of her mashed potatoes and thought about Anne's comment concerning Levi. It didn't set well with Violet, and it didn't make any sense that Levi hadn't mentioned their break-up to his sister. Violet gripped her fork. *I told Levi the other day that we were through because things weren't working out. Why would he hide that from his sister? What is he up to anyhow?*

Chapter 6

A couple of days had gone by, and the workweek had begun for Violet. Due to the pleasant weather, Leora rode her bicycle to work that morning. Violet had thought about riding too, but it was more convenient to take her car. John had left before the ladies, and since Violet was the last to depart, she'd locked up the house before leaving.

The morning commuters heading to work caused heavy traffic, but thankfully the drive to the restaurant didn't take more than a few minutes. Violet came to a complete stop at a red light and waited for it to turn green. Dan Hunter flashed through her mind as she sat there.

I can't help but be drawn to him. He seemed so polite, and his voice was engaging. I want to get to know Dan better, so I hope I'll see him again soon.

A blaring horn sounded, bringing Violet out of her musing. "Not the time to think about Dan. I need to focus on driving." She shifted her foot from the brake to the accelerator, continuing on to the restaurant.

~

Waiting on tables had kept Violet busy all morning. Anne had the day off and would be back tomorrow. Lunch had begun, and the hostess seated guests for the meal. Violet had come back from a quick break and began taking her customers' orders.

When the hostess seated Dan in Violet's section, she was pleasantly surprised. Even before Violet tried to approach him, her palms began to sweat and her heart picked up speed.

I can't wait to talk with Dan again. She took out her pad and pencil as soon as she arrived at his table. "Good afternoon."

Dan smiled up at her. "It's nice to see you again, Violet. The weather we're having is perfect today, isn't it?"

"Yeah. If I didn't have to work, I'd like to be out in it myself."

"To be honest, I'm here for two reasons. First, I was wondering if you'd be free to go out with me to the beach later today."

Violet's face warmed. "That would be nice. I'd like to go with you after I'm done working."

"Great, what time would I need to come by to pick you up?"

"I should be done about four thirty."

"Okay, I'll be here right around that time." He gazed at her with his enchanting blue eyes. "And the second reason I'm here is to grab some lunch."

She grinned. "Of course. What would you like to drink?"

"I'll have a root beer."

"Would you like to order off the menu, or do you prefer going over to the buffet for lunch?"

"I'll have the buffet. I'm pretty hungry right now." Dan handed her the menu.

"All right, you can get your food anytime. I'll bring your drink back here in a little bit."

Thanking Violet, he slid out of the booth and headed for the buffet area. She tried not to stare as his form disappeared behind the partition. She was pleased that Dan had come here today, and even more so because he'd invited her to go to the beach with him. Violet felt like she could walk on clouds. She wanted to keep pinching herself to make sure this wasn't a dream.

What a nice surprise this turned out to be. I can't believe Dan asked me out. I do have to get through my hours here, but overall, this will be an exciting day for me.

~

After work, Violet had gone to the bakery, letting Leora know what her and Dan's plans were. Her sister seemed happy over her good news about the date. Violet's hands felt clammy as she waited inside, near the restaurant's entrance.

She fiddled with her ponytail. *I should be fine wearing my work clothes on the beach.*

"Hi, Violet. Are you ready to go?" Dan asked when he walked through the doorway.

"Yes, but if you don't mind, I'd like you to follow me in your car to my sister's place so I can drop off my vehicle." *I'll just hurry there before Leora and John get home so Dan doesn't see them and catch on that I'm from an Amish family*, she added mentally.

"No problem. I'll follow you."

They went out to the parking lot, and Violet's excitement grew when she saw his red convertible. She'd never ridden in one and figured it would be a fun experience. They both got into their cars, and Dan followed her to John and Leora's place.

Violet parked her car in the driveway while the convertible pulled up to the curb. When she got out, Dan followed suit.

Violet called to him, "I need to go into the house and grab my flip-flops and tote for the beach."

"Okay." Dan leaned against his car.

Violet returned with her tote bag and rushed over to Dan. "Do you remember this?" She dug out the semi-deflated beach ball.

Dan chuckled. "I sure do. That's the toy we both wanted from the gift store."

She gave him a thumbs-up. "We can enjoy using this on the beach."

Dan came around to open her door. "I hope you're okay with riding in a convertible. We can always drive separately if you're not."

"Are you kidding? I'm looking forward to riding in it." Violet climbed in and buckled her seat belt.

After shutting her door, Dan came around and got in. He stowed her tote behind the front seats. "I stopped by the gas station before coming to the restaurant, so we're ready to go."

"This is a really nice car, Dan. Have you had it long?"

"About a year now. It's been a pretty good vehicle."

"I like the color. Actually, red is my favorite color."

"It is?" His thick brows rose as he started the engine. "It's my favorite too." Dan drove away from the house. "Would you be okay with going to Lido Beach?"

"That would be fine." She reclined in the seat as her long ponytail blew in the breeze. Riding in his cute little car was great.

Lido Beach

After Dan found a place to park, they grabbed what they wanted to take with them. As they strolled on the sidewalk, a small courtyard with round tables came into view, but only a few people were seated there. The concession stand was still open, and the familiar smells of hot dogs and fries drifted from the little establishment. Violet wondered if they'd get a bite to eat right now.

She looked at him. "Are you hungry?"

"I feel a little bit empty, but I could wait to eat. How about you?"

"I can wait, but won't this place be closed soon?" Violet questioned.

He stretched his arms above his head. "There are some nice sit-down restaurants back at Armand Circle we could go to."

Violet liked that idea more than eating a quick bite at the concession stand. "I'm fine with waiting until we're done on the beach."

Dan pulled off his sandals as they headed onto the white sandy beach. "I like to go barefoot."

"I'll join you." Violet slipped off her flip-flops and placed them inside the bag she carried.

They walked side by side across the sand. The beach this evening had a good number of people, but Violet's focus was mostly on Dan and the excitement of being with him. She felt drawn to him. Something about him made her feel relaxed. It seemed funny to Violet how comfortable she was around him, since this was their first date.

Along the shore, she spotted a reddish scalloped shell and reached down to get it. It reminded her of their favorite color. *I'm going to save this one to remember this day.* Violet slid it into the pocket of the sizable bag she carried, which held the beach ball. They stopped together, watching a large cabin cruiser go by.

"I would like to have a boat to go out on the water with someday. Something like that one would be nice, but I'm sure it'd be real expensive." Dan turned to Violet. "Have you been out on the water before?"

"Yes, I've been on a lake back home in Indiana." She ran a thumb over the strap of her bag. "Have you ever been there?"

"No. What town did you live in?"

"Middlebury. It's a more rural setting than Florida. Lots of green pastures, wide-open spaces, and a good share of farms." Violet was careful not to say anything about being Amish. She wasn't sure how Dan would react to her not being English like him.

"Do you miss Indiana? I mean, would you change your mind

and want to move back there?" Dan's gaze seemed focused on her.

"I like Florida a lot, and I'm staying for now at my sister and her husband's place."

"It's good that you've got close family living here. Especially if you choose to stay permanently."

"It's a nice place with all of its tropical feel and the great weather—at least most of the time."

"I assume you get all four seasons in Indiana?"

"Yes, and the winters can get pretty cold." She looked away. *Especially riding in our buggies being pulled slowly by a horse.* "I'm glad to be here and only have to deal with two seasons."

"Do you have any other siblings beside the one sister living near Pinecraft?" His head tilted.

"Yes, I have three sisters, and I'm the youngest, making four daughters in my family."

"No brothers?"

"Nope." She paused. "How about you? Do you have any brothers or sisters?"

"I do. One brother and one sister. I'm the youngest in the family too. We also have a dog."

She laughed. "What's its name?"

He grinned. "We call her Sassy."

"That's a cute name, Dan. What breed is she?"

"A golden retriever, and she's a big baby. Do you have any pets?"

"No, but a dog would be fun."

Dan pointed to a vacant area near the shoreline. "Hey, how about we toss the beach ball to each other?"

"Okay." She followed him to an open place and got out the ball. Since it needed some air, she blew until it was fully inflated.

He shifted out of the way, facing Violet. "I'm ready."

She held it in one hand and gave it a hit, lofting it up into the air toward him. He returned with a good fist shot. The beach ball went back and forth for a while until Violet missed.

"That was fun." She wiped her forehead, then retrieved the toy.

"Let's play a little more," he called.

They kept going for a while and then decided to watch the sunset. It was beautiful as the sky's colors shifted from orange to pink hues. Violet and Dan sat on the sand, watching the sun descending on the horizon.

He pulled out his phone and took a few photos of the sunset. "Would you mind if I took a few pictures of us?"

Violet smiled, bringing out her cell phone. "Not at all. I'd like to do the same with my phone."

Dan leaned closer to her, and they took turns taking photos. Then they continued to watch the sun disappear. *It's so nice spending time with Dan. I don't want the day to end.* Violet peeked over at him. *I wonder if he is enjoying our time together like I am.*

~

Armand Circle

After Dan had parked the car, they headed for the Crab and Fin restaurant, a nice seafood place with outdoor and indoor seating. They chose to eat outside and were seated at one of the tables. Soon a waitress came over, gave them menus, and took their drink orders. It was a pleasantly warm evening, and the restaurant bustled with activity.

Dan sat back, looking over his menu. "How would you like to work here close by the beach?"

"It's nice, but it's a ways from home. I think I'd rather stay where I'm at for now." She browsed the menu to see what the eatery offered.

"Where I'm working, I don't have to drive far to get to the shop. But depending on where the customer lives, it can dictate how much driving I need to do."

"What kind of work do you do, Dan?" Violet asked.

"I'm an electrician."

"Do you like that kind of work?"

"It's a good-paying trade, and I get to do commercial work sometimes, but usually residential. Most of our customers are nice, and a few have even fed us on the job." He paused. "And in my kind of work, I'm up and down ladders most days. So I get plenty of exercise."

Violet nodded. *I don't know much about electrical work, but he seems to enjoy what he does for a living.*

~

As Dan drove Violet back to her sister and brother-in-law's place, he sneaked glances at her. He couldn't resist his attraction to her. She had pretty, long brown hair and the deepest brown eyes he'd ever seen. He also liked the sound of her laughter. Dan had definitely enjoyed their time together and hoped she'd had a good time being with him. He wanted to go out with Violet again and get to know her better.

There's something genuine about her. Maybe it's . . . He put on the blinker and made the turn onto Violet's street. *She said she lived in Indiana. I wonder if she knew any Amish while living there.* Dan pulled near the driveway, and as they remained in his convertible, they talked about their time together on the beach and the fun they'd had with the beach ball. Dan was caught off guard when a bellowing motorcycle drove up behind them.

The guy riding it propped his bike and stood up. "Hey Violet, would you like to go for a ride with your boyfriend?"

Dan looked at Violet. "Boyfriend?"

"I broke up with Levi. He is not my boyfriend anymore, and I have no idea why he's here."

Dan's stomach tightened as he sat staring at her in disbelief. This was not a good way to end the evening.

Chapter 7

Violet hadn't been in this kind of situation before, and it frustrated her. Those she'd dated in the past had moved on after breaking up. But Levi was back and intruding on her new relationship with Dan.

Despite Levi showing up, Dan had politely sat and listened to Violet explain that she'd broken up with the man.

"Well, if he isn't your boyfriend, I'd like to go out with you again." Dan's blue eyes seemed to twinkle under the moonlight.

Violet reached for the door handle and grinned back at him. "I would like that. I had a nice time this evening on our date." She climbed out of the convertible and grabbed her things, walking toward the house.

Levi shut off his bike and rushed over to Violet's side. As he followed her, he wrapped his arm around Violet's waist and drew her in close. "I've missed seeing my girl. I've bet you missed me too."

"What are you doing?" She attempted to push Levi away.

Dan drove away from the parking strip, squealing his tires, without even a wave goodbye. Violet was shocked and couldn't believe Levi's actions, and she pulled away from him. "You need to leave. We are not going out together anymore!"

Levi laughed. "You're not really interested in that guy in the fancy car, I hope. I'll come by again when you have had time to cool off."

Not saying anything in response, Violet rushed into the house and slammed the door behind her.

Once inside, she set her things down and took a seat on the couch. Leora came over and sat next to her.

"What's going on, Violet? I heard a motorcycle pull in. Was that Levi?"

Violet grimaced. "Yep, showing up unannounced right after my date with Dan."

"I'm sorry to hear that." She patted her arm. "I also heard squealing of tires out there."

"That was Dan leaving after Levi put his grubby arm around my waist."

"That wasn't right of Levi," Leora replied. "Dan should be able to figure out what Levi is trying to do."

"What is Levi's problem?" Violet shook her head. "Why can't he take no for an answer?"

"He must be hoping you'll change your mind and choose him."

"Not happening. I've moved on, and Dan is far nicer and much more polite to me." She looked at her sister. "I'm worried though. I can't help wondering if Dan thinks Levi is back in my life. I told him I'd broken up with Levi, but with the way Dan left here, he might think I'm lying to him."

John came in from the garage. "Hello, ladies. What was all that ruckus outside?"

"Levi was here." Leora shifted her feet.

"I thought Violet was done dating him." John went to the kitchen and returned with a bottle of water.

Violet fixed her gaze on him. "I did break things off with Levi, but he doesn't seem to care about that."

He took a sip of his water. "He must be hoping to win you back."

"That's what I'm thinking too," her sister chimed in. "How about a change in topics, and tell me how your date with Dan went this evening."

"I'll let you two visit while I go back out to the garage to do some work." He yanked on the strap of his suspenders and walked out of the room.

"A change in topics would be nice right now." Violet slid a decorative throw pillow behind her back and nestled into it. "To start with, Dan and I rode from here down to Lido Beach. It was sure fun riding in his red convertible. That was something I'd never done before, and it was thrilling."

"Kind of like riding in an open buggy back home, except a lot faster and minus the horse." Leora laughed.

Violet continued to tell Leora about her date. At least that was a way to end the evening on a pleasant note.

~

Levi dropped by Leora's house after work two days later. Violet was in her room sitting on the bed when there was a knock on the guest bedroom door.

"Come in." Violet smiled at her sister.

"Levi's outside waiting to talk to you." Leora came over by the bed.

Violet grimaced. "Not again. It's only been a couple of days since he came by here and messed things up between me and Dan. I don't want to visit with him. You could've told him that I was too busy to talk with him." Violet released a lingering sigh. "But it's not your place to lie for me or to get involved in this mess."

"I'm sorry Levi is putting you through this. It's tempting for me to go outside and say something to him, but you're right—it's not my place." She patted Violet's arm and left the bedroom.

Violet leaned back on her pillow and mumbled, "If I don't go speak to him, he'll probably just come back later."

Violet hadn't heard from Dan so far, and she'd checked her phone several times. She longed to talk to Dan but didn't want to call him since he'd been pretty upset after Levi had shown up the other night.

Despite Levi's bad habits, he had mentioned on their first date that when he returned home in the spring, he would go to work for his dad. He'd also said that he'd be joining the church sometime that same year. *Guess I'll go out and see what Levi wants this time.* She rose from the bed, grabbed her phone, and headed to the front door.

In the living room, Leora got Violet's attention. "You're going to have to hold your ground with him. Don't allow Levi to wear you down."

Violet tapped her chin. "Don't worry. I have no intention of changing my mind."

Though in a way, it was kind of flattering to have a young man that determined to hold on to a relationship with her. But the reality was that she didn't want to stay Amish, nor did she want an immature boyfriend. If she were to cave into Levi's wishes, she would be miserable, and sooner or later, Levi would be unhappy with their relationship too. Since Violet would have regrets about not following through on her desire to be more independent, she had to stand her ground no matter what. She had no choice at this point, even if it meant she would end up losing both young men.

As she stepped outside, Levi looked up from his phone. He flashed her a deceptively charming smile. Violet figured this guy was hoping to wear her down. *If I were weak, that could happen, but I am holding my ground.*

"Violet, I was wondering if you'd like to hang out with me this evening."

She shook her head.

"Oh, come on. . .please. You know you want to."

Violet couldn't believe how hard Levi tried to persuade her to be with him. He seemed bound and determined to get what he wanted. She didn't want it at all, though. The thought of whether Levi was still smoking and drinking with his roommates also crossed her mind. It was funny how being around Levi a few minutes brought back her concern for him. But this fellow wasn't her problem anymore. He needed to figure things out on his own and grow up, like Violet had been doing lately.

"Look, I'm not interested in—" Her phone vibrated, so she checked the screen. It was Dan calling her. Violet was overjoyed and answered it immediately. "Hello."

"Hi, Violet. I was hoping to talk to you." The inflection of Dan's voice reassured her.

"You're talking to that guy from the other night, aren't you?" Levi scoffed and pointed to her phone.

Violet turned her back on Levi. "It's good to hear your voice, Dan, but now's not a good time for me to talk."

"Violet and I are going out on a date!" Levi shouted.

Violet's face grew hot like a boiler in flames. "Levi is lying. He dropped by unexpectedly."

Levi grabbed her phone. "Hey, Dan. I'm in love with Violet, so don't bother calling her again." And then he ended the call.

Violet stood, stunned. "What have you done?"

Levi handed Violet her phone. "See, Violet? I've fixed the problem. Now you're free to go out with me."

"You need to go!" She was furious, and her jaw ached from clenching her teeth. "I can't believe you did that! I've told you before—several times in fact—that I am not going out with you anymore."

"He's not your type. You and I are both Amish, and you oughta see that we are better suited. If you give it more thought, I'm sure you'll see things my way, Violet." He winked, flashed her a smile, got on his bike, and drove off.

~

Dan blinked rapidly, holding his phone tightly in his grasp. "I can't believe this."

He was both shocked and hurt by this turn of events, as well as quite upset. Levi had made it clear about his feelings for Violet. The question was, did she feel the same way about him?

He set his phone down and walked over to the couch, taking a seat. The family dog, Sassy, came up to him and planted herself against his knee.

"You are looking for some attention, aren't you, girl?" He scratched the dog behind her ears. Sassy leaned in, seeming to enjoy it.

Dan hoped to do a little catching up to see how Violet was doing. He'd come home from work, had a shower, and changed into some clean clothes. He had been feeling optimistic, but after that phone call, he was at a loss for words.

While sitting there on the couch, his mind went back to Violet. *I was hoping to ask her out again, but I'm going to hold off. I need some time to process all of this.*

He rose and headed for the kitchen. "Come on, Sassy, it's time for your food."

The dog followed on his heels as though she understood what he'd said. She looked up at him and wagged her tail.

Dan turned on the oven and then opened the dog's food, pouring it into the dish on the floor. It felt nice to have at least the dog's company.

"How was your day, girl?" He crouched by her, giving the dog a few gentle pats. "I've had a long day, and I can't wait to have my food when it's cooked." Dan went to the freezer and pulled out some frozen fries and chicken strips.

He lived at home with his parents, and it was nice and convenient for him. Being twenty and having a full-time job as an apprentice electrician was great. Some of his acquaintances were out living with friends, being more independent, but Dan liked being around his family, and he wanted to leave when the time was right.

While working, he had been setting money aside for his future. His parents were good people and had a love for the Lord. His background was Mennonite, and he liked attending church. Living at home with his folks had been a blessing, especially during the time he was with the last girl he'd gone out with. She was into herself and controlling, and that had been hard for him to deal with. Dan could remember seeing her perfectly combed hair and made-up face frowning at him when she said, "Why don't you move out and live on your own?" He was happy with his family and appreciated their help. Religion didn't appeal to the girl either, which was another downside to their relationship.

Thankfully, things ended with her not long after that evening when she'd suggested he leave his family. Dan wanted a girlfriend who was a believer in the Lord. His parents had a genuine bond that was strong, and he longed for such a thing. Being with Violet had struck an inner chord with him. Something about her seemed to keep his interest going.

He checked the oven and noticed that the light had gone off. It was time to get his supper going, so Dan got out a baking sheet and dumped some fries and chicken strips on it. Afterward, he placed the remaining food back into the freezer. Dan then put his meal in the oven and set the timer. Glancing up at the clock, he was tempted to give Steve a call. He would be home by now and might have time to talk. But then he figured maybe he could wait for his folks to get back from visiting with their friends. Sara, his sister, could show up at any time. She also lived at home, but unlike Dan, she'd found someone and had become engaged a few months ago. Even though Sara was two years older than him, they both looked the same age. His brother, Paul, was married and lived close to St. Petersburg, near his wife's family. Dan and Paul didn't see each other as often as they used to because his brother was married, working, and living a distance away.

Dan got out a plate and fork and set them on the kitchen table. He heard the familiar sound of the front door opening and closing.

"Hello, I'm home!" Sara's tone sounded cheery.

"Hi," he called, taking a seat at the table.

She stepped in with two bags of groceries. "I made a side trip to the store on my way home from work. I bought some things for me and a few to help out around here—a bottle of laundry soap, a case of water that is out in my car, and these cereals we like." She set the bags on the counter and looked back at her brother. "You look pretty bummed out. What's up?"

"After I got home from work today, I hoped to talk to Violet and catch up with her."

"You weren't able to reach her?" Sara's brows knitted together.

"Yes, I did reach her. . ." Dan told his sister all about the call and how he felt about the whole thing. Sara was sympathetic and offered her thoughts. But Dan wasn't sure if Levi could sway Violet back to him. If he could, what was the use of pursuing a relationship with Violet?

Chapter 8

Violet woke up from a good night's sleep. She glanced at the battery-operated clock on the nightstand.

Normally I'd have to get up and get ready for work, she mused.

But today was different, because Anne had asked Violet if she could trade days off so that she could get a necessary dental procedure. Violet had taken Anne's shift earlier in the week, and Anne was now working her shift that morning. She was glad to come to Anne's aid.

While lounging in the guest room, she heard Leora and John getting ready for work. The smell of breakfast food and their muffled voices carried through the house.

Violet stretched, then closed her eyes with a yawn. It was nice being able to stay in her pajamas considering how she would spend her day off.

Yesterday had been the church's off Sunday, so they'd attended the Mennonite service. Afterward, Violet had driven John and Leora to a Mennonite friend's home to visit. They planned to have lunch there too, but instead of joining them, Violet chose to come back home and fend for herself. It had given her some time alone to do what she wanted in the quiet house.

After returning to Leora's home and changing out of her

church clothes, Violet had reflected on the sermon on Paul's letter to the church of the Thessalonians. Paul had mentioned to the people, in 1 Thessalonians 4:9–12, not only to show love for one another but to live quietly and to mind their own business, because by doing so their everyday lives could win the respect of outsiders.

I really liked that advice the pastor preached yesterday, but can I apply it to my own life? Violet wondered. *It would be great if Levi took that advice.*

She picked up her phone from the nightstand, checking to see if Dan had tried to call, but there was nothing. It hurt that he had seemed to pull away from her.

I've blown it with Dan, and for all I know, he could be moving on to someone else. Maybe this is what I get for keeping my Amish roots hidden from him. Violet set the cell phone down and rolled onto her side to look out the window. *Oh, Violet, you worry too much.*

Violet lingered in the warm bedding until her phone vibrated on the nightstand, and she quickly grabbed it. *Could this be Dan calling me?*

But Dan's name wasn't displayed on the screen. It was from home, so Violet assumed it was her mom calling. Even though she'd hoped Dan was calling, she was happy to speak with Mom. She pressed the TALK button. "Good morning, Mamm."

Mom greeted her in a chipper tone. "Good morning, Violet. How are you doing this lovely Monday?"

"I'm good, and I've got time to talk because this is my day off."

"I timed that just right then." Her mother paused. "I was thinking about you and thought I'd give you a quick call in case you were going to work."

"I'm glad you did, and you sound happy, so I guess you're doing well."

"Jah, I'm fine."

"How's Dad doing?"

"Your father is busy, but he's doing well. Oh, your sisters said to say hello."

"Tell them hi back when you get the chance." Violet sat up in bed, leaning against the headboard. "I miss you all very much."

Mom began talking about Grandma's painful sinuses and her visit to the doctor on Friday. She'd been given a different prescription to help with the pressure and pain.

Violet shifted under the sheets. "I hope Grandma will feel better soon."

"Yes, we do too. Oh, and your grandpa is fine. He's been busy trimming some shrubbery in his yard. He's sprucing up the place nicely."

"Yard work is something he enjoys. He likes to keep his and Grandma's place looking good."

Mom seemed to breeze through the topic of how her sisters and dad were doing. She brought up Francine and Matthew going out to eat Saturday night and briefly mentioned Ben coming to the house. It wasn't long into the conversation about relationships when the topic was directed toward Violet. "I've heard through the grapevine that a certain young man and a certain young lady have been dating."

"Who are you talking about, Mom?"

"I heard Levi Yoder and you have been dating. Is this true?"

Violet twisted her ponytail. "We were dating, but I broke up with him."

The phone seemed to go dead. Not a word was said for several seconds.

"Mom, are you there?"

"Yes, I'm here." Mom let out a small sigh. "Why would you

break up with a nice young Amish man?"

Violet didn't want to tell Mom that Levi had been smoking and drinking with his roommates while she'd been dating him or that he'd been boastful and pushy. The last time Levi had stopped by, Violet had told him she would pray for him. Expressing her concern for his bad habits, she had urged him to stop before it got worse. Violet wanted Levi to understand that even though they wouldn't be dating anymore, how he cared for himself was still important. But Levi, being stubborn, seemed to spin what she'd said. With a wink, he had said, "See? Your worrying about me means you want to be with me."

Violet told her mother that the two of them didn't get along and that their personalities weren't good together. Of course, Violet wasn't sure Mom was truly satisfied with the explanation, but she hoped it would be enough.

"Maybe you'll find another Amish young man there to date."

"There are different fellows that do come down here from Pennsylvania, Ohio, and Indiana." Violet paused. "But usually they don't intend to stay in Florida."

"I see." Her mother coughed. "Off topic, I know you don't like cauliflower, but hear me out on this. I've found a recipe that you've got to try. It's simple to make, and it barely tastes like plain cauliflower."

Violet was relieved that Mom had taken the conversation in another direction. She needed a change in topics and this one worked for her.

"I'd be willing to give it a try."

"Okay, sounds good. If you can write it down, I'll read the ingredients from the recipe to you."

"All right, Mom. Let me find a notepad and something to write with." Violet rose from the bed and opened the drawer of the nightstand, removing a notepad and pencil. "Okay, I'm ready."

Violet placed it on the nightstand and began scribbling down the ingredients and instructions as Mom read them to her. There weren't many ingredients or much preparation involved in making the dish, which was nice.

"You're right about it being simple. This sounds pretty easy, and I'll let you know when we've tasted it."

"I hope you'll like it as much as we have. You could make it for supper and share it with Leora and John."

"Sure, they'd probably like to try this." Violet's stomach gurgled. "Maybe this evening."

"Oh, before I hang up, can I ask a quick question? Were there many at church yesterday?"

"Yes, there was a good number of people."

Violet liked attending the non-Amish church. It was different in many ways. For example, the sermons and songs were all spoken in English. Amish church was three hours long on backless benches versus an hour or so sitting on a pew in the Mennonite church. Plus, Violet didn't have to wear Plain clothes. She wore her printed skirts and embellished blouses.

Violet set the writing pad aside and visited a bit longer with Mom, catching up on some other things happening back home. It was great hearing that everyone was in good health. Besides, talking to her mother and shedding the yoke of hiding her past relationship with Levi helped too.

After ending their conversation, Violet thought back to earlier in the phone call. It was evident that Mom had been thrilled about her dating Levi. Her mother hadn't let go of the thought of Violet finding a suitable mate.

"As long as he's Amish," she mumbled. Violet wondered if her father felt the same way as Mom.

She got out of bed and put on her robe. Breakfast was on Violet's mind now, as well as seeing her family before they left for work.

Stepping into the kitchen, she found Leora and John finishing up their hot cereal. "Good morning."

They answered, "*Guder mariye*," in unison.

"You're welcome to finish what's left of the hot cereal." Leora added a few more fresh blueberries from the bowl sitting on the table.

"*Danki*." Violet grabbed a small dish from the cupboard and a spoon from the drawer. "I plan on doing some shopping later. Would there be anything from the store we need for supper?"

"I'd like to barbecue this evening," John replied.

"I've pulled out some frozen beef patties to thaw in the refrigerator. Otherwise, we have the rolls and vegetables needed to put on them. We could make fries too," Leora put in.

"That sounds good. If I come up with any other ideas to add to our meal, I'll pick up the food while I'm out." Violet dished the oatmeal into her bowl.

After breakfast I'll go out to the store and buy the ingredients to make that cauliflower recipe. Maybe I'll go to the mall later and look for some new skirts and tops too.

Opening the fridge, Violet grabbed the orange juice and poured a full glass. Then she sat down with her food at the table by her sister and silently prayed.

John excused himself to finish getting ready for work, and Leora soon got up from the table.

"I best get going myself." Leora offered Violet a smile. "I hope you enjoy your day off."

Violet held up a spoonful of oatmeal. "Thank you for the yummy hot cereal this morning."

"No problem." Leora left the kitchen.

While eating, Violet speculated on whether Dan would call her back and when. Or was it already too late for them? What if he had decided to move on? She yearned for the chance to see him again. If she knew where he lived, would driving by his house help her feel better?

Violet tried not to blame Levi completely for this situation. If she hadn't gone out with him to begin with, she wouldn't be in this mess right now. But she did go out with him, selfishly seeking to have fun. Where did it get her? Violet hadn't made a good choice, and now she was stuck with it.

~

Later that evening, Violet, Leora, and John finished praying silently before their evening supper. Violet's mouth watered at the enticing grilled hamburgers. She and Leora had prepared homemade fries to accompany the burgers, and the new recipe of broiled cauliflower was there too.

Violet dished up her plate with all the good food. She went for the new recipe from Mom and forked a bite of the glistening, browned vegetable. The floret was tender, and the seasoning complemented it well.

"Hey, this tastes great." Violet smiled. "I'll have to thank Mom for finding this recipe and having me try it out."

Leora took a bite. "Yep, this is real good."

"I like cauliflower any old way." John bit into a floret and wiggled his brows. "But I've got to admit, this is quite tasty."

They all chuckled and started eating again. During the rest of the meal, Violet shared about her shopping excursion at the mall, and her sister talked about their visit with friends. It was nice to have a good meal and pleasant time with her family. Even so, Violet couldn't help thinking about her situation with Dan. *If only I could fix the mess I managed to put myself into with Levi. Maybe then I'd have a chance with Dan.*

Chapter 9

Three weeks had passed. Early on Friday, Violet was at the restaurant. Her alarm clock hadn't gone off this morning, so she dashed out the door to get to work on time. She hadn't had time to eat breakfast, so she couldn't help but notice how good the food smelled. At least Leora had come knocking on her bedroom door so Violet could arrive at work on time.

Violet made an effort between serving tables to grab a plastic cup and fill it with water. She took a few gulps before resuming her duties.

Anne came over, carrying an empty tray. "I just took my table their order." Anne grinned. "How's it going?"

"Good. I'm just trying to fill the void in my stomach, that's all." Violet took another swig of water.

"You didn't have breakfast before coming in, huh?"

"No, I overslept."

"You got here on time, so you did good." Anne patted her shoulder. "When your break comes up, you should probably get yourself something to eat. It's not good working on an empty stomach."

Violet smiled. "Yep, I'm looking forward to that."

"I need to get back to my tables. See you later, Violet." Anne headed off toward the tables by the salad bar.

After throwing her cup in the waste bin, Violet went right back to waiting on customers.

~

During her lunch hour, Violet ordered a grilled hamburger with everything on it and fries. She took a seat at one of the tables tucked away in the back.

As Violet sat at her table eating, she thought about Dan. She still hadn't heard a word from him or even seen him in passing. The hope she'd had of them getting back together didn't seem likely. She made an effort to cope with that reality and keep herself busy.

Violet had done some things with her family during that time. They had gone on a picnic at the park in Pinecraft. John, Leora, and Violet had enjoyed their time outdoors, soaking up the warm weather. Another day they biked on the Legacy Trail and then went to a restaurant on the water for supper. Recently Violet had invited John and Leora to go to the beach with her, and they had a nice time out on the sand for a couple of hours. Afterward, Violet drove them to Armand Circle to have lunch at one of the restaurants. She had parked in the lot across the street from the Tommy Bahama Restaurant. It had been their first time trying out the place, and they all enjoyed the meal.

One day, Levi had again popped by John and Leora's place, trying to ask her out. He had even tried to kiss Violet, but she'd pushed him away. Violet worried that, despite her protests, he would continue with his possessive behavior.

After eating her meal and freshening up in the bathroom, Violet was ready to get back to work, feeling satisfied after having eaten good food and gaining energy to tackle the rest of her shift. The restaurant had a steady group of customers filing in. Violet could only guess why it had become so busy today. Perhaps a tourist bus had come in and dropped off travelers for a meal. Quite often, Amish people from different communities arrived in Pinecraft and came into the restaurant with others from their group. Regardless, she needed to take care of the guests, no matter how many had entered the establishment.

As Violet waited on a young couple, she was surprised to see Dan coming into the restaurant. Her heart seemed to pick up its pace when she saw him. He hadn't looked her way yet, but he was seated near her section. Violet hoped for the chance to speak with him. It would be tricky since she'd already had her break.

It wasn't long before they made eye contact. Dan's hand came up, and he waved at her in a friendly manner.

Violet smiled in his direction. *At least he's smiling back at me. I really need a moment with him.*

She finished up a customer's order and headed to the kitchen first, then went over to Dan's table.

"Hello, Violet. How have you been?"

I've been missing you, she wanted to say. "I've been doing okay."

"I was hoping to see you today." Dan paused. "Are you still seeing Levi?"

"No, I'm not. Like I had told you before, Levi and I are not dating anymore."

When he tilted his head, the light above shimmered on his blond hair. "Seriously?"

She gave a nod. "I would really like to visit with you, but I'm a little busy right now."

"Okay. How about when you're done working?"

"That would be fine. I'll be finished here at four today."

Dan rolled up his gray cotton sleeve, revealing his watch. "That's not too long from now. I'll come back about then."

"Good. I'll see you later, Dan."

She headed back to her customers. *I have another chance to get together with Dan.* Violet's heart swelled with hope. *Thank You, God. I'll do my best to make it work this time.*

~

The restaurant was still open, but Violet's shift was done. She had gathered her things and now sat off to the side, waiting for Dan to show up. *He said he would come by so we could talk, and I need to be patient. I hope Dan and I can have a fresh start on our relationship.* Violet looked at her phone to check for messages. But there weren't any, so she scrolled through some apps to pass the time. Soon she spotted Dan wandering in and waved him over. "I'm glad you came back, Dan."

He took a seat across from Violet. "It was good to see you today. And I was surprised to hear that you and Levi aren't dating. When I came through the parking lot, I saw Levi out there."

Violet grimaced. *I hope Levi doesn't come around and try to bother me here. Why can't he get a clue and move on?*

"Violet, did you hear what I said?" Dan reached across the table and put his hand on hers.

"Could you repeat that?" Violet's face warmed, and she had to admit it felt nice having Dan's attention.

"After what had happened with calling you the last time and what Levi had said, it made me wonder if you two were still going out. I wanted to be sure that you are free to date me."

"I am, Dan, and I'd like to go out with you again." Violet hoped her tone was reassuring.

"Good to hear." Dan gave her hand a gentle squeeze before letting it go.

They had only visited a few moments, when Levi strolled up to them. "Hi, Violet, how's my best girl doing?" He flashed his charming grin at her, practically ignoring Dan.

"Levi, for the last time, we are through."

Dan looked at him with a stern expression. "You heard her."

Levi grabbed Violet's wrist to pull her up. "Come on, Violet. You can't pick this loser over me."

Dan, being taller than him, stood up from his seat. "You heard what she said."

Levi pulled away from Violet. She wondered if he might be intimidated by Dan's height. "Fine, have it your way!" Levi turned and sauntered off.

Violet gasped. "That's the first time he's ever given up that easily."

"Maybe he won't bother you anymore."

"I'd like that very much." Violet hoped that was the case since she wasn't sure if this new relationship could handle much more of Levi. Even though Dan was still new in her life, she was drawn to him.

~

Violet was so happy to be home. She couldn't help it. Seeing Dan and working things out had made her day much better. She hummed a hymn as she headed into the kitchen. Leora was in the middle of putting away the dishes from this morning.

"Somebody sounds happy." Leora opened an upper cabinet, placing a mug inside.

"I am." Violet grinned. She explained to her sister what had taken place after work with Dan. She also mentioned Levi showing up at their table and how everything went with that situation.

Leora gave her a hug. "I'm glad you and Dan are giving your relationship another try." She pointed at the counter. "By the way, you have a letter here."

Violet picked it up. "Oh, it's from Francine." She ripped open the envelope and began to read it.

Hello, Violet,

How are things in sunny Florida? I hope you all are doing fine and keeping busy.

We are well here and having plenty of cold weather in Middlebury. The fireplace is a good spot to warm up by, that's for sure. Alana and I do have to compete for room, but we try to share or walk away when we've gotten warm enough.

I hate to pry, and I know it's not my business, so if you don't feel like telling me, I'll understand. I was wondering why you ended your relationship with Levi. Mom had said it was because you and he didn't get along. But I can't help feeling that there was a more serious reason. Just curious—if you and Levi had continued going out and he'd asked you to marry him, would you have wanted to move back to Indiana?

I'm bombarding you with questions, but it's hard being so far away from you. We used to be able to talk regularly, and it's not easy to write what I'm thinking. I hope you can understand.

Mom was in high spirits when she'd found out that you were dating Levi. But after your break-up from him, she seemed a little bummed. I tried to convey how difficult it is to find love in today' s world and that it's not good to settle. I know you'll meet the ideal partner to start your life with someday.

I hope you'll write back soon, Violet. I prefer writing to phone calls, but if you need to talk, you can always call me. I'm looking forward to hearing from you.

Love,
Francine

~

Violet folded the letter and slid it back into the envelope. It was good to hear from her second oldest sister and nice to know that her family back home was doing well.

"How is everyone?" Leora leaned against the counter.

Violet sat at the table. "Francine mentioned that they were all doing fine."

"That's always good to hear. Any other news from home?"

"The weather is cold, and they're using the fireplace." She paused. "Remember how not too long ago we were taking turns absorbing that wonderful bone-warming heat to stay comfy?"

Leora nodded as she looked off across the room. "I do recall those days, but I'm happier here with John and my little sister."

"Thank you, Leora. I have to agree. I have fond memories of home, but even so, I look forward to new things yet to come." She set the letter on the table.

When John arrived home, Violet shared the story again during supper. She was pleased that Dan had chosen to stop at the restaurant to see how she was doing. And it was a relief that Levi had finally given up. Violet felt unburdened and completely free again to pursue her life.

After they had eaten their meal and the kitchen had been put back in order, Violet talked Leora into going out to the grocery store for ice cream. While there, the idea of making banana splits came up. They purchased ice cream, chocolate syrup, and bananas before returning to the house.

Back home, they enjoyed the yummy treat. John thanked Leora and Violet for the great idea they'd come up with for dessert.

As Violet sat in the living room eating her ice cream, Dan came to mind. The soothing coolness from the treat glided down her throat. *It's too bad he can't be here with us right now.* Violet took another bite of banana. *But I've been hiding my family background, and if he finds out I'm Amish and not English, he could choose to break up with me. I don't believe an English man would want to date an Amish woman.*

Chapter 10

Violet went over to her closet and put on a burgundy short-sleeved dress in preparation for another date with Dan. She slipped on a pair of black, low-heeled dressy sandals, then used her butane curling iron to add a few subtle curls to her brown hair. She thought back to a few days ago when she'd chatted with Dan over the phone for a while. He'd asked if she wanted to go out to a Thai restaurant for supper. Violet told him that it would be fun to try something new. It was great catching up with Dan and hearing his voice again.

After that phone call, Violet made an appointment to get her hair trimmed just below the shoulders. She missed the longer hair she'd sported since childhood, but the shorter length was easier to take care of.

Violet stepped out of the guest room holding her smartphone. She wanted to use the full-length mirror in the hallway to see how her outfit looked.

"You look pretty," Leora said as she came up to her.

"Would you mind getting the zipper?" Violet asked, turning so her back faced Leora. "I can't reach it."

"No problem." She went over and zipped her up. "Maybe one of these days we'll get to meet your new boyfriend. With you putting yourself together like this, he appears to be someone very special."

Violet didn't respond. *I'm not ready to let Dan know of my Amish heritage. That's why I arranged to meet him at the restaurant.*

Hoping to change the topic, Violet looked up the Thai place on her phone and waited for it to load the information about the restaurant's menu. "I'm curious about the kind of food they serve."

"Me too." Leora moved closer to Violet to look over her shoulder. "Some of the choices seem pretty good."

"I agree." Violet kept scrolling through the menu. "There's plenty to choose from."

"I should probably let you figure out what you'll be ordering. I hope you have a good time on your date tonight."

"Thank you, Leora." She gave her sister a hug. Violet felt confident she would enjoy her time with Dan that evening.

~

While Dan waited in the car, his eyes scanned the parking lot, but he didn't see Violet's vehicle. He'd made reservations the other day and had cleaned his car yesterday. A few minutes went by, and he saw her car pulling into the lot.

Dan glanced in his rearview mirror, seeing if his hair looked okay. *Maybe it doesn't matter how my hair looks. I'm driving a convertible, after all.*

He wanted to appear presentable for his date and had anticipated going out with Violet since their last conversation. He planned to invite her to City Island if she was interested. He'd thought it would be fun for her to see the Mote Aquarium.

Dan got out of his car to greet Violet. He couldn't help noticing how lovely she looked and that her hair appeared shorter. "Did you get a haircut?"

"I did. What do you think?" Violet turned her head from side to side.

"I think it looks cute on you, and your outfit looks pretty too."

"Thanks. You look nice as well."

Dan motioned toward the restaurant and led the way, opening the door for her. Since he liked eating there, he hoped Violet would too. The restaurant was furnished in a Thai style, and the cuisine was consistently good.

A hostess greeted them, asking for Dan's name, and led the two to a booth with menus in hand. It wasn't long before a waitress came over with two iced waters and asked to take their drink orders.

"Think I'll stick with water," Dan responded.

"I will too." Violet glanced up at the waitress and then continued to scan the menu.

"I'll come back in a few minutes to take your orders." The waitress walked away from their table.

Dan set the menu aside. "I am going to have the Bangkok broccoli with beef. It's a go-to for me."

Violet scratched her head. "There's a lot to choose from on this menu. But I'm leaning toward the Bangkok cashew nut with chicken."

"Sounds good. Have you looked at their dessert section yet?"

She flipped the page. "Those are different. Like the ice cream, for instance."

"If you like coconut, the ice cream here is fantastic. I've had it many times." He took a sip of his iced water.

"It must be good, especially with the way you're smiling. I might be willing to try it if I have any room left after my meal." She set down the menu.

"I've heard it said that after you eat this kind of food, you don't feel full for very long."

"I'll have to see about that," Violet replied.

After a few minutes, their waitress returned and took their

orders, then headed off. Dan tried not to stare at Violet's pretty brown hair that complemented the color of her eyes. The burgundy outfit she wore stood out against her fair complexion. He was glad to be out with Violet again. He'd missed being with her. They continued catching up on their days until their meals came.

After they finished their savory entrées, they ordered coconut ice cream for dessert. Violet understood why Dan had chosen that flavor often. It was delicious.

Once outside, Dan offered Violet a ride in his car. She accepted, and he helped her into the convertible. The sun was about to set, so he offered to drive them over toward the bay to watch it.

While admiring the sunset, Dan looked over at her. "Would you be interested in coming with me down to City Island?"

"Where is that?"

"It's not very far from Armand Circle." He paused. "I was thinking this Sunday."

"Sure. I think that would be fun."

"Unless you already have plans with your family."

"No, I could be free to go with you."

Dan's dimples were pronounced. "I could come by and get you."

"After church would work. I can give you a call when I'm ready."

"All right." He tapped the steering wheel. "So how would you like to take my convertible for a spin?"

Violet's eyes widened. "Really?"

"Why not? You've expressed how much you enjoy riding in it, and I trust you."

After they watched the sunset, Dan offered her the driver's seat. Violet couldn't wait to take the red sports car out for a joyride. Once she was settled in the driver's seat and both she and Dan were buckled up, they were off.

"This is fun!" She maintained steady control of the steering wheel.

"I agree, Violet. This car is always fun to drive!"

But on the straightaway, Violet's wild side kicked in. She drove faster than she should have. When a car pulled out in front of them, she nearly collided with it.

"Watch out!" Dan shouted.

Violet slammed on the brakes to avoid hitting the vehicle. Her heart pounded while she gripped the steering wheel. "Are you okay?"

"I'm fine, but that was too close." His brows furrowed.

"I'm sorry, Dan. I shouldn't have been so irresponsible, and I won't do it again." Violet drove on with the flow of traffic. "I'll pull over now and let you take over."

"If you like."

"You should take over. I don't feel right because of what I did back there."

Looking over at her, Dan expelled a breath. "You did tell me that you won't do it again. So I believe you'll keep your word."

Violet felt relieved that they hadn't gotten hurt and Dan had forgiven her reckless driving. "Okay, I would like to drive a little more before giving you back the wheel again."

She drove carefully the rest of the time. After experiencing that wake-up call, Violet realized she needed to stop being reckless and foolish.

~

That evening, in the privacy of her room, Violet prayed, asking God for His direction in her life.

I still need to prioritize God in my life even if I stay in Florida and choose not to join the Amish community.

After reading some scripture, Violet acknowledged that she

needed to tame her actions and start living as a Christian. She must also rely on God for His strength.

~~~

On Sunday, Violet arrived home from church and changed from her Amish dress to her English clothing. Leora and John had plans to go out with their friends. Violet hoped they'd be on their way before Dan arrived to pick her up. She checked the time from the battery-operated clock on the wall. There was still time before he showed up.

While waiting, she thought about the call she'd made to Francine the day before. They didn't get to chat long due to the weather being so chilly in Middlebury. The phone shed didn't give much protection from the elements. Violet wondered why Francine had given up her smartphone. Perhaps she was too traditional to understand how to use one.

Violet told her sister more about dating Levi and said that she wasn't looking for a long-term commitment. She also mentioned her date with Dan and how well it had gone.

Francine talked about the young people's get-together at Allison Yoder's place. They'd all been dressed for the cold and sat around a bonfire, singing and chatting with one another. The food had been good too.

John and Leora said goodbye before leaving to join up with friends. Violet glanced at her cell for the time, knowing it wouldn't be long before Dan showed up.

Violet headed to the guest room to get her purse and the tote bag she used for souvenirs. After grabbing what she needed, she looked in the mirror one last time. She wore a pair of aqua capris and a floral T-shirt. She brushed her hair and touched up her lip color before leaving the room.
~~~

City Island

Violet came out of the house with her tote and handbag. Dan thought she looked stunning and couldn't wait to start their date. He looked forward to taking her to City Island.

When they arrived, he hunted for a parking place and found a spot. Dan had brought them to the Mote Aquarium, thinking it would be a fun place to visit. He could see from the grin on Violet's face that he'd made a good choice.

"This was a great idea." Violet removed her sunglasses and put them in her tote.

"I'm glad you like my choice."

They got out and headed to the entrance. Dan handed the tickets he'd purchased online to the clerk.

They headed in to check out the different displays, and Dan wandered along with Violet, looking over the exhibits.

He leaned in close for a brief moment. "It's a good thing you brought your tote bag because there's a gift store right here before you leave the aquarium."

"I can't wait to peruse what they offer."

They came upon a jellyfish tank, and Violet stood watching the jellyfish with interest. "It's something how they propel themselves through the water."

"Yeah, it's kind of cool." He couldn't help but smile.

"It's mesmerizing. I almost want to stay here all day and watch them."

Dan chuckled. "There's a lot more to see, and they close at five." He paused. "When we're done here, we can go across the street to the Old Salty Dog for a bite to eat if you'd like."

"Another new place. That sounds like fun." Violet held her hands close to her heart. "Thank you, Dan, for taking me here."

Dan's stomach fluttered at the thought of pleasing Violet. He was glad he'd planned this date with her.

~

Violet eyed the front of the house as they pulled up to the curb. The blinds were open, and she saw her family inside. Violet hoped they wouldn't come out to greet her.

She'd enjoyed the aquarium and had bought some trinkets to give to her sisters and parents. It was fun to try out a new place, and she also enjoyed dining at the Old Salty Dog with Dan.

"I sure had a good time today." Dan shifted his gaze to Violet. "How about you?"

"I had fun observing all the sea creatures there. They have plenty of exhibits to take in and there's so much information to absorb. Oh, and thank you for the meal as well."

He put his hand on hers. "You're welcome. I enjoyed being with you today." Then he leaned in and gave her a tender kiss on the lips.

Warmth radiated through Violet's body, and she soaked in the moment, wishing to continue being with Dan. He made her feel special.

"I'd like to go out again. Maybe we could try going to church with each other."

Violet turned toward the house and noticed her sister peeking out the front window. She moved away from Dan. "I should probably get inside. I've got work early in the morning." She grabbed her purse, opened the car door, and closed it behind her. "I'll text you so we can figure out when to see each other again. Have a good evening, Dan."

"Good night, Violet." Dan waved as he backed away from the curb.

Violet headed for the house. She rubbed her sweaty hand over the front of her shirt as her stomach began to churn. *How long can I keep my Amish heritage hidden from Dan?*

Chapter 11

Sarasota

The next morning, Dan went out to his car to head for work and noticed that Violet's tote bag lay behind the passenger seat. *I'll need to run that bag to her after work today.* He picked up the tote and locked it inside his trunk. He wished he had noticed her leaving it behind when she went into the house. He got back into his convertible and turned the key. *It was a little strange though. She seemed to be in a hurry to head inside.*

Still, this gave him another chance to see Violet, and he looked forward to it. He wasn't sure if he would arrive before or after she was done working at the restaurant.

Violet had gotten home from work and was in the kitchen helping prepare supper. Leora went outside to check on John, who'd gone up on the roof to do some repairs. There had been a little storm that came through with some gusts of wind that damaged the roof. Violet could hear him walking above her as she set the table.

Leora came into the kitchen. "He found a loose *schindel* and will be replacing it."

"It's good that you're married to a roofer and John can repair the loose shingle."

"I sometimes worry about him up on roofs, but it doesn't help me any to do that."

"That's true. John is good at what he does, so he'll be careful." Violet patted her sister's shoulder as they continued getting supper ready.

~

Dan left work and headed to where Violet lived. He couldn't wait to return her tote bag, but mostly he was eager to see her.

Dan drove up the block and pulled his car up to the curb across the street. He did a double take when he saw an Amish man up on the roof and an Amish woman standing in the front yard talking to him.

"What? Why are there Amish here?" he muttered. "Hold on a minute, this is starting to make sense now. Violet has been trying to keep me from knowing that she's Amish." He was taken aback by this revelation and wondered if he should wait until she confessed on her own or ask questions later about her heritage.

Before pulling away, he watched the Amish woman go back into the house. Dan reasoned that he would let Violet come clean on the topic.

I'll give her a call and see if she's free to hang out with me tomorrow.

~

Violet waited outside the next day for Dan to come by and pick her up. She looked forward to spending time with him and wondered what they would be doing this evening. Violet wiped the sweat from her hands, waiting for him to arrive. It wasn't long before he pulled into their driveway.

Violet hurried to the car. "Hello, Dan. It's good to see you."

"It's nice seeing you too." He motioned to the back seat. "I have your tote here from our last date."

"I can't believe I forgot it. Thank you."

"No problem." He smiled. "I thought we could run by and grab some fast food to go. Interested?"

She tilted her head "Where would you like to go?"

"Do burgers and fries appeal to you?" He backed out of the driveway.

"Sure, I wouldn't mind that for supper."

Dan drove to a fast-food place, and they ordered their selections at the speaker in front of the menu board.

"Would you mind if we went back to where I live to eat our meal?" he asked.

"That's fine with me."

"My dad will be there, but my mom is at a friend's, and my sister is out with her fiancé." Dan handed the cash to the employee at the drive-through window.

Soon the employee passed out their drinks and the bag of food. Violet took the bag and set it on the floor in front of her.

I wonder where Dan lives. He mentioned living with his parents and sister. She sat back and enjoyed the little jaunt to his parents' place.

When they arrived, she noticed that their home was a white, two-story house in a nice neighborhood.

"Here we are. I'll take the bag of food." He held out his hand, waiting for Violet to pass it to him.

After giving him the bag, she opened her door and slid out of the passenger seat. *I'll leave the tote in the car. It'll be safe in here.*

Violet carried the drinks while following Dan up to the house. When they entered, she saw that the inside was clean and modestly decorated with overstuffed furniture. It didn't take long for her to notice some scripture plaques on the wall and a Bible on one of the end tables. *Are Dan's family Christians?* she thought. *I wonder what denomination they're from.*

Dan motioned to the dining room table. "Let's take our seats."

Violet set down her purse and pulled out a chair. "This is a nice place you have here."

"Thank you." A voice spoke from behind them.

When Violet turned, an older man with a lengthy beard but no mustache stood before them.

Dan chuckled. "This is my dad."

"Hello, Dan's dad."

"You can call me Marvin." He held out his hand.

Violet reached out and shook his hand. "It's nice to meet you, Marvin."

"My wife, Shawna, is out this evening, but hopefully you'll meet her the next time you're by."

Violet nodded. "I'll look forward to that."

Dan opened the bag and began to remove their food. "Here's your burger."

"I'll let you kids pray and start eating. I have some reading to do in the living room." Marvin turned and headed in that direction.

Violet couldn't help noticing his gentle spirit and kind eyes. Marvin reminded Violet of her own father. She didn't know why, but it felt comforting to be in their home.

They visited while they ate, and she enjoyed getting to see where Dan lived. Violet thought it was funny how Marvin had no mustache. She couldn't help wondering why he wore it that way since he was English. She thought it best to wait to ask about this until they were alone and heading back to John and Leora's place.

~

After they'd finished eating, Dan asked if she wanted to go for a ride before heading home. Violet agreed to that, and they said goodbye to his father. They got into his sports car, and Dan took them out onto the main road.

I can't help thinking about what I noticed at his parents' place. Violet tapped her leg to the rhythm of the music playing on the radio. "I've got a question." She looked at Dan.

"Go ahead and ask me anything." He glanced her way briefly, then turned down the radio volume.

"Are you and your parents Christians?"

"Yes, we are."

"I had a feeling by what I saw in your parents' house, with the scripture on the plaques and the Bible sitting on the table."

Dan sat quietly as he drove along, listening to the music.

"I was wondering about your dad's missing mustache."

"Really?" He grinned. "He has always worn it that way."

"I see." Violet's palms grew sweaty. "I need to tell you something I've been keeping from you. And I hope you won't get mad."

"This sounds serious. I'll find us a place to park." Dan pulled off into a nearby shopping center.

She cleared her throat. "I've been trying to hide the fact that I'm not English."

"Go on." He looked at her directly.

Violet took in a deep breath and released it slowly. "The truth is that I'm Amish."

"Is that all?"

"What do you mean? Did you already know I was?"

"I put two and two together yesterday when I stopped by to return your bag and saw your Amish family outside. One on the roof and the other in the yard."

She nudged his arm. "Even so, I'm relieved to have confessed to you."

"I'm glad you feel better." He leaned back into his driver's seat.

"You mentioned my father's missing mustache, right?"

"I did."

"That's because he's Mennonite. My family attends a Mennonite church." He gave a sheepish grin. "I guess we both didn't tell one another about our home lives. Sorry about that." Dan paused. "And my offer still stands if you'd like to come to church with me."

"I would like that." She looked at him. "When you drop me off, I'd like you to come in with me before you go. I met your father, so it's only fair that you meet my family."

"That would be nice. But honestly, I'm a little nervous."

"You have nothing to worry about, Dan. I know they'll like you."

He scraped a hand through his thick hair. "I sure hope so."

Chapter 12

Violet walked out of one of the department stores in the mall after doing some shopping. She had put her bag into her car and headed out of the mall parking lot. Her car began to stammer and sputter, which was weird. Then it quit running, but the radio was still playing. *Uh oh. I forgot to put gas in my tank.*

She got out of the car and looked around for the nearest station. Violet couldn't see one from where she stood. Taking her phone, she looked up gas stations nearby. A couple appeared, but they were a little too far for Violet to push the car to either place. She then made a call to John. He was at work but said he would come. She desperately waited for him to pick her up.

Violet had told John roughly where she was parked at the mall. At least she wasn't blocking traffic. She was relieved that John was able to come to her rescue, but this would be the first and last time Violet would put her brother-in-law through this. She didn't feel right taking him away from his business to help her out. This was all the more reason Violet would be taking her car in as soon as possible to get the fuel gauge fixed, no matter what the cost.

Violet climbed into the warm car and waited patiently for John to arrive. *Here I thought I'd take a little time away this morning on my day off and do some quick shopping and then go back to the house and get some cleaning done.* She grimaced and looked over at the big bag lying on the passenger seat.

"I need to get my priorities straight. I like to go shopping, but I should've done better." Violet opened her car door to let in some fresh air. Since she had no air conditioning running at this time, the car quickly became warm inside. She would have to make do until she was able to start up her vehicle again. No doubt John would be arriving as soon as he could with the gas can. Then Violet could drive to the station and fill up her tank the rest of the way

Violet pulled up to the curb at John and Leora's place and shut off the engine. After a stressful morning at the mall on her day off, she was happy to be back home. *I can't wait to tell my sister about what happened today.* Violet unlocked the door and headed inside. She was glad that her brother-in-law wasn't upset about having to leave work to help her. Violet appreciated how nice Leora's husband truly was.

Taking her bag to the guest room, she set it on the bed and took a seat. Violet had finally found some pretty dried flowers to put inside her light green glass bottle. She took the package carefully from the big bag, unwrapped the flowers, and put them in the bottle. Violet fiddled with the arrangement a few moments until it looked just right to her. She went back to the bag and drew out of it a nice throw rug she'd spotted to put next to her bed. It wasn't very beach themed, but it was the perfect sea-glass-green color she had been looking for. Violet laid out the fluffy rug on the floor and pulled off her sandals to try it out. The little carpet was nice and soft under her feet. She also liked the way it looked next to the warm gold comforter on the bed. Violet stepped off the carpet and moved toward the door. *I told Leora I would do some cleaning for her, and I've used up enough time already on other things. I need to get busy.*

~

Violet had wiped down all the kitchen cabinets and counters with warm soapy water. It looked much nicer, and they shined from all her work. She turned to the sink and removed the stopper to let the used soapy water drain out. She looked out the window in front of her and saw the trash can. She mused about the day the possum was in it. The next morning, John had checked for it before going to work, but the critter was gone, and they hadn't seen it since.

Violet reached under the sink and grabbed the dusting spray and a new rag. As she got ready to begin another task, she wondered how Dan's day was going. She'd been thinking of him more often these days, with the two of them dating regularly.

As Violet headed out into the living room and applied the oily spray onto one of the tables, the sound of a familiar motorcycle told her Levi had pulled in.

She set the cleaning tools aside and peered out the window. Levi was getting off his bike. Violet had no way of knowing why he'd chosen to come by today, and although hesitant, she headed outside to find out the reason.

Levi came up the walk and met her. "Hi Violet. How have you been?"

"I'm doing all right." Violet shuffled her feet. "What are you doing here?" She noticed Levi's demeanor seemed a bit different, and his tone and features appeared softer too.

Levi rubbed a hand on his shirt. "I've got something to say to you that needs to be said. I wanted to come here in person to apologize for acting rude and to say I'm sorry for the crummy way I've treated you."

Violet blinked, trying to take in what Levi had said. "Really?"

"I wasn't doing the right thing. I crossed your boundaries, and I found it enjoyable to do so. Guess it was kind of like a challenge to see if I could win you over. But I regret what I did because it was wrong. It was really messed up, and I'm very sorry. Will you forgive me, Violet?"

"I accept your apology, Levi. Thank you for coming by."

He let out a long breath. "While I'm here, I wanted you to know that I've quit drinking and smoking because I came to realize that it's not for me anymore."

"Wow, that's good to hear. I've been praying and hoping you could give up those bad habits."

"I appreciate you doing that for me, Violet." His tone was cheerful. "I won't keep you any longer, and I really should be getting back to the apartment."

"Okay, I guess I'll see you around. Most likely at the restaurant."

"For sure. Talk to you later." He walked back to his bike and started it up.

Violet waved and headed back inside to resume her dusting. She was pleased to hear Levi's apology. Violet was glad he had given up those bad habits. At first, Violet had been concerned that he had only apologized in the hopes of reuniting, but that was clearly not the case.

~

Violet, Dan, Leora, and John rode their bikes on the Legacy Trail one Sunday afternoon after Violet had enjoyed going to the Mennonite church Dan and his family attended.

She had met Shawna, Dan's mother, and his sister, Sara. Violet was able to introduce her family to his family since she'd brought Leora and John with her to check out the church. It worked out because it was their Amish church's off Sunday.

The weather was beautiful, with clear blue skies, sunshine, and a gentle breeze. Violet felt good that she wasn't hiding anything from Dan anymore, and she appreciated Levi's unexpected apology. Now she could move on and enjoy spending time with Dan and having fun together.

It was easy to reflect while on their bike ride. Violet thought back to the day she'd first met Dan when they both reached for the beach ball in the gift shop. Even though she wouldn't be joining the Amish church, her parents and family had accepted her interest in a Mennonite boy. Violet's parents had said they were happy Dan was a believer and his other family members were too. They expressed their understanding of her decision not to return home. Violet had definite plans to remain in Florida and attend the Mennonite church with Dan.

I'm grateful to have found Dan and thankful that he's a follower of Christ. I can't wait to see where our relationship is heading, but for now I have found a keeper. I have a feeling that the prayers from my sisters, parents, and Dan helped me realize that I need to become a responsible person. I know that I can only do that by living a life pleasing to the Lord.

Dan pedaled alongside Violet. "Do you want to race me to the bridge?"

"Sure. I'll see you there." Violet shifted her weight onto the pedals, causing the wheels to spin quickly.

They pushed ahead of the group, riding side by side to the bridge over Deer Prairie Creek. Violet could not have been happier at this moment, and she was glad she'd made the decision to leave her Middlebury community and move into her sister's home in Sarasota. She couldn't wait to find out what her life would be like in the days ahead.

Roasted Cauliflower

(Egg-free, gluten-free, low carb, nut-free, and sugar-free)

Ingredients

3 tablespoons olive oil
½ teaspoon paprika
1 teaspoon garlic powder
¼ teaspoon salt
½ teaspoon pepper
1 large head cauliflower
¼ cup grated Parmesan cheese
2 tablespoons fresh parsley flakes

Toss olive oil, paprika, garlic powder, salt, and pepper with cauliflower. Spread on baking sheet covered with silicone or parchment paper. Sprinkle with Parmesan cheese and parsley. Bake at 425 degrees for 15 minutes or until browned.

Jean Brunstetter became fascinated with the Amish when she first went to Pennsylvania to visit her father-in-law's family. Since that time, Jean has become friends with several Amish families and enjoys writing about their way of life. She also likes to put some of the simple practices followed by the Amish into her daily routine. Jean lives in Washington State with her husband, Richard Brunstetter Jr., and their three children but takes every opportunity to visit Amish communities in several states. In addition to writing, Jean enjoys boating, gardening, and spending time on the beach. Visit Jean's website at www.jeanbrunstetter.com.

Fragments of a Sand Dollar

Richelle Brunstetter

Prologue

Middlebury, Indiana

Francine Lambright shivered as snowflakes found their way into Matthew Bontrager's buggy. Heavy snowfall had made an appearance on New Year's Eve, and she inched closer to her date—not to keep warm but to be near him. After spending a fun evening with a bunch of their close friends, Francine and her boyfriend were headed to her parents' house. She had a wonderful time with Matthew, as she always had over the two years of their relationship.

After they arrived in her parents' driveway, Francine hopped down from the buggy and secured Matthew's horse at the hitching rail. Hand-in-hand, they trudged to the front porch, and Francine tapped the toes of her boots to knock off the chunks of snow clumped on the bottoms. She yearned to gaze at Matthew's dark brown eyes, but she couldn't see his face well on the unlit porch. She felt her insides constrict as he leaned toward her.

"This evening was great, Matthew." Francine grazed the sleeve of his jacket. "I had a fun time at the gathering."

"So did I. We made a pretty *gut* team during the game playing too." Matthew reached out for Francine, bringing her a smidge closer. "I'm sorry, but this isn't easy. I know you're set on joining the church, but"—he puffed out a breath, gently grasping Francine's arm—"I don't want to lose you."

"I don't want to lose you either. But I understand you'll be able to reach many people by becoming a missionary. As much as we don't want our relationship to end, we can't keep each other from what's set in our hearts."

"You're right. And I can't thank you enough for agreeing to go out with me this one last time."

Francine could no longer fight the urge to tilt her head toward Matthew's face. His quavering voice caused her to choke up. Francine's breath hitched as she rested her head on Matthew's chest. She did her best to muster her next words. "I'll miss you so much. You know that, right?"

Matthew hugged Francine and placed a tender kiss on her forehead. "I'll miss you too," he responded with a hushed tone.

Of all the break-ups I've had, this one cuts the deepest. Because neither of us wants our relationship to end. I love Matthew with all my being, and I wish this night never had a morning. Francine burrowed further into his embrace. She absorbed Matthew's essence, gentleness, and nurturing temperament one final time. *I thought Matthew would stay Amish. Why did it have to turn out this way?*

Chapter 1

Francine stretched toward the end of the shelf, pushing the books to make room for the ones stacked up on the floor. The bookstore she worked in was quaint, with the shelves making the space narrow like a maze.

"Let's see here," Francine muttered to herself. She lowered the glasses resting on top of her head and squinted through her lenses at the spine of the books. "With the addition of new novels, I'll need to rearrange these shelves again."

She began shuffling them, reaching down to place one of the new books with the rest. Then she pushed her glasses back up, brushing the dust from her palms onto her apron. The door's bell chimed, and Francine peered past the shelf. Two customers who appeared to be in their twenties strolled in.

"Hello, welcome!" Francine greeted, then went up to them with a grin. Seeing people come in brought excitement since business had been stagnant.

"Oh, hi!" One of the customers exclaimed. "You're Amish, aren't you?"

Francine nodded, gesturing to the bookshelves behind her. "There's plenty to browse through, and if you need help with anything, I'll be happy to assist."

Francine was minding the bookstore while the owner, Geneva, was out running some errands. Francine had been working there for more than a few years, so Geneva trusted her to manage the store on her own. Rodney, another employee, had worked at the store for a year, and Francine alternated days with him. Having more employees, along with a handful of customers, would make for a tight squeeze.

The customer's necklaces jostled like wind chimes as she turned to Francine. "Do you have a section on traveling? Specifically, Europe?"

"Yes, I'll show you where you can find it." Francine led the way to the travel section at the back of the bookstore. "Are you planning a trip to Europe?"

"It will be my first time there, and I'll be seeing plenty. The Louvre, Amsterdam, and Dona Ana Beach. I'm ecstatic to see it all with my own eyes."

"Sounds like you'll have a great time." Francine moved out of the way so the two women could skim the shelf.

"Do the Amish travel?" the other girl questioned.

"Some of my friends have traveled while on rumspringa. Even outside the country." Allowing a yawn to escape, Francine continued. "I've only been out of state to visit my sisters on occasion. A lot of Amish vacation in Sarasota during the spring, even after joining the church."

"Interesting. On reality shows, they make it seem like you guys don't fly by plane."

Francine snickered. "Normally, we don't, but there are exceptions. Family emergencies are one of them. When we do take trips, our transportation is usually by bus, train, or a hired driver."

"You said something about joining the church. Have you done that? I mean, you look our age, yet you're wearing the bonnet and dress—"

The girl with the necklaces bumped her friend's head with the book. "Forgive her for asking all these questions. She's overly curious about the Amish."

"It's all right. I don't mind. I planned to join last year, but. . ." Francine sighed, clenching her fist.

The bell from the door jingled, so Francine peeked over to see who had entered. "Geneva! *Gut* to see you back!"

"Hello, Fran." Geneva carried a box over to the reception counter. "I have some stuff in the back of the van to bring in. Help me out, would you?"

"Sure thing." She turned back to the two young women. "Whenever you're ready, I'll meet you at the register." Francine waved to them and hurried out of the bookstore, thankful for Geneva's return. The conversation had stirred up emotions Francine didn't want to experience while working.

After loading the boxes from the van and ringing up the books chosen by the two girls, the space in the store was vacant. Geneva sorted the supplies from one of the boxes, which contained flyers used to advertise the novels they carried in the store. Francine tried to pay no mind to it, but as she unraveled rolls of change and sorted them in the register, she caught sight of Geneva's darting gaze every now and then.

"You're still hung up on that boy, huh?" Geneva tapped her manicured nail on the cardboard flap of the box. "The one who came in to visit you most days."

"I don't know where you're getting that from. It's all done. Water under the bridge."

"Fran, even when you seem upbeat and are working with what is in front of you, there are times when you are not here."

Francine bit the inside of her cheek. "I suppose I'm still coming to terms with the break-up. But it's out of my hands, and I can only manage what's in my grasp."

"Well, spring break is approaching, and you rarely use your vacation days. It would do you some good to take time off."

Tilting her head, Francine prepared to rip the paper off another roll in a swift motion. "For how long?"

"How about a month?"

Francine jerked her hand. "A month?!" The coins spilled out and clattered onto the wooden floor. Heat traversed her ears as she bent down, picking up the change. Francine attempted to keep her composure as she put the coins in the columns of the register drawer. "You must be pulling my leg."

"No leg pulling here. I'm being serious."

"That's way too many days. I can't leave the bookstore knowing that."

"I insist, dear. You've been gloomy for a month, and a month of fun would be a good remedy. You can take the entire month or a week. It's up to you, so just let me know." Geneva winked. "Besides, you are letting Rodney off too easily with all your hard work. Not leaving him with much to do."

Francine stood alone behind the register after Geneva walked out of sight to her office. She brought her hands together, fixating on a flickering fluorescent bulb.

What would I even begin to do with all that free time? There are the singings, but then again, I might bump into Matthew like last time, and it was way too awkward. I could barely look at him, let alone have a conversation. Her stomach fluttered. *Wait, I can hang out with my friends. They may be free next month too, so I'll see if we can all do something fun together.*

Pressing her fingers to her mouth, she couldn't help but grin while squeezing her eyes shut. "I'll make the most of my time off, and it'll be the most memorable spring break yet. I'm sure of it."

Francine sat in Grace Rivera's car, getting a lift home from work. Francine's neighbor Grace hadn't grown up Amish, but she had been Francine's close friend for many years. Allison Yoder, Francine's other close friend, sat in the back seat, also having finished her shift at a small health food store. They had all bought some goodies from the store before heading home. Allison was also Amish, and like Francine, she was likely not to stray away from her Amish upbringing.

Pulling into the driveway of Francine's family home, Grace jerked the vehicle as she stepped abruptly on the brake. "Here you are, Fran. Home, sweet home."

"*Danki,* Grace." Francine grabbed the container in the cup holder, lifted it up, and took a sip of the fruity liquid. "And thank you again for making me this yummy smoothie."

Grace beamed as she swept her curly hair over her shoulder. "No problem."

"See you at church, Frannie!" Allison exclaimed, waving her hand like a swaying branch.

Francine looped the grocery bag over her arm as she got out of Grace's car. When Grace drove off the property, Francine peered down at her black shoes, shaking her head. "I should've known they would both be busy this upcoming month."

As she approached the house, Francine spotted her father sitting in the rocker on the porch. He looked toward the bird feeders dangling in the yard.

"*Guter owed, Daed.*" Francine wandered over to him. "What birds have you seen this evening?"

His eyes, the color of the summer sky, flickered to Francine, then back to the yard. "Saw a couple of chickadees chasing one another through the arborvitae."

A brisk evening breeze swept her frame. Francine wrapped an arm around her torso, gripping her drink container tighter. "It's a little chilly out here, with it still being the last week of February. Don't you want to be surrounded by the comforts of home?"

"In a minute. Could see some more birds fly on by before the sun sets."

She nodded, patting her father's shoulder. "Just come in before the chill of the night takes you."

Francine beelined to her room. Setting down her belongings, she flopped belly-first onto her mattress. "*Ach.*" She groaned. Her limbs weighed her down like blocks of lead. "Would it be wrong to lie here for the rest of the evening?"

She raised her head, then reached for her Bible on the nightstand. Donning her reading glasses, Francine opened the bookmarked page and began reading Matthew 19:10–11.

" 'His disciples said to Him, "If such is the case of the man with his wife, it is better not to marry." But He said to them, "All cannot accept this saying, but only those to whom it has been given." ' " She plopped the Bible on her pillow.

"Leora had her struggles, but she ended up with the man she loves. Same with Violet, and I never would have guessed she would marry someone who's grounded in his faith. And Alana is afraid of her own shadow, yet she's dating that guy, Ben." Francine laughed to release the tension in her throat. "I thought Matthew was the one I'd be spending the rest of my life with, but maybe marriage is not what's meant for me. Why else did all my relationships end because the guy didn't want to stay in the community?"

Francine thought about how her older and younger sisters were doing in Sarasota. It had been over a year since her last visit to Florida to see Leora and Violet. Francine was somewhat of a homebody, but she made an exception by traveling to Sarasota to visit her two sisters living there. When she stayed at Leora's, it felt similar to home. That, and Francine always had a great time searching for shells on the beach. Since Leora and Francine preferred to communicate through letters, the last time they spoke on the phone was soon after Francine's break-up.

I should call John's cell phone and see if I can talk with Leora. She crawled to the foot of her bed and grabbed her purse, sliding out her flip phone from the outer pocket. She opened the cover and dialed. The phone rang for a moment, then someone picked up.

"Francine?" Leora answered.

"Evening, Leora. I'm sorry for calling you all of a sudden."

"It's all right. You're always allowed to call me," Leora responded.

"How are things in Sarasota? Was it a nice day for the most part?"

"It was pretty warm. In the high seventies, and now it's rather *kault* out. I'm surprised you called me. I wrote you back yesterday."

Exhaling, Francine pressed the phone closer to her ear. "To be honest, I'm still not doing well. I keep wondering if I made the right choice."

"With Matthew, right?"

"Jah. I mean, would it have been wrong of me to follow his decision not to join the Amish faith?"

"Is that what you wanted to do?"

"No. I always got that feeling in my stomach when I saw our childhood friends changing so rapidly. Even with Violet, I was worried for her when she strayed from the faith. As much as I admire Matthew's ambition, and I know that some people can be immersed in the world while remaining devoted, I'm not sure I could handle becoming English. I've never felt out of place within our church."

"I know what you mean, Francine. And I'm truly sorry things didn't work out for you and Matthew. But I'm sure you'll meet someone else who wants to live with Amish values as much as you do."

"Or maybe I'm not meant to be with anyone. I thought it would be better to join after finding someone, but some people our age do not want to stay Amish."

"Hmm. Don't you think you should let loose a little? If you allow yourself to try some things outside of your comfort zone, then you'll know for sure if you do want to commit to joining the church."

Francine was taken aback by Leora's suggestion. *I would expect that response from Violet, but not from my oldest sister who had no desire to be English.*

"I'm not saying go crazy. All I'm saying is, it's all right to consider other options first. Who knows? You could wind up Mennonite like Violet."

"No way." Francine chuckled, rising from the bed.

"Actually, I'm glad you decided to call. In my letter, I was asking if you would like to come visit next month. I know you're usually busy at the bookstore, but could you or Alana get some days off and come down to Florida?"

"Geneva gave me the whole month off if I want it. Grace is seeing family, and Allison is not able to get time off, so I may tell Geneva I'm working after all. And Alana mentioned she wanted to spend time with her boyfriend, so I don't think she'll go."

"Even if Alana can't come, why don't you take the opportunity to stay with me and John for the whole month?"

"A week I can do, but a whole month? I don't know."

"Please consider, Francine," Leora implored. "I barely get to see you. If anything, I think it'd be good for you to take a break and relax."

Francine gripped the hem of her apron. "I'll think about it."

She talked with Leora for a little longer, but it was nearing suppertime, so their conversation had to come to an end. Francine said goodbye to her sister, shutting the phone with a *clap*.

I'd like to see my sisters again, but can I leave Indiana for that long? Francine placed her phone on the nightstand. *Could taking that long of a break from Middlebury get me through these emotions or at least help me cope with them?* She maneuvered around her shoes strewn about the room. *If I were given some indication that I should go, then I would hop on a charter bus next month and hope for the best.*

Francine stumbled over the grocery bag from the health food store, nearly plummeting into her desk. Although she prevented herself from doing so, Francine caused the desk to quiver, knocking over a jar too close to the edge. She knelt down with a grimace. The jar was intact, but the contents had spilled out, and a good number of sand dollars she'd collected last year were now in pieces.

Francine pressed a palm to her temple. "It took me forever to find those on Lido Beach. Sand dollars are not an easy find." She tweezed one of the fragments with her fingertips, bringing it within her field of vision. It was a tiny piece in the shape of a dove.

Her lips curled as she cradled the dove in the palm of her hand. "I suppose I'll let Leora know I'm staying with her and John next month."

Chapter 2

Shipshewana, Indiana

Francine stood with her friends at one of the scheduled charter pickups at Yoder's Shopping Center. She held a flourishing umbrella above her for protection and parked her suitcase beside her. As they waited for the buses to arrive in the lot, the sun's rays pierced through the opaque cloud coverage in the sky. But the rain had not subsided, drizzling nonstop since they'd gotten there.

An hour later, the charter bus rolled in. Soon after it parked, the bus passengers flocked to it, preparing to load their luggage.

Is leaving Middlebury for a month really a good idea? Francine pondered as she raised her shoulder to keep her tote's strap from slithering off. *I could always ask Grace to drive me back home, but I did commit to this. I'm excited to see my oldest and youngest sisters again. And I won't have to worry about bumping into Matthew. He has never been to Sarasota, and I doubt he'll travel there anytime soon.* She eyed a nearby murky puddle. *I really do hope this experience will help me move forward in a healthy way.*

"You doing okay, Frannie?" Allison clasped Francine's arm. "You haven't uttered a word in the past ten minutes."

"I'm *naerfich.* Very nervous. Anything can happen on a long drive." Francine clenched the handle of her umbrella.

Grace nudged Francine with her denim-sleeved elbow. "You'll be fine. Besides, I'd do anything to be in your shoes right now. Flying to Georgia to see family who are practically strangers isn't my ideal spring vacation. You get to have your toes in the sand." Grace spread her arms out like a dove in midflight. "Kissed by the sun for approximately thirty days."

Francine thrust her hand past the shield of the umbrella. Steady droplets sprung off her skin. "Unless it rains there too. I can only pray for mostly sunny days."

Once Francine's luggage had been stowed with the rest of the load, she placed her tote on the ground and turned to Allison.

"Can you do me a favor and bring me back some shells like you did last year?" her friend asked. "It really spruced up the bare patches along the driveway, and it wouldn't hurt to have more."

"I plan to, Allison. Don't worry." Francine smiled. She envisioned Lido's glistening shoreline and hues of pink and orange during sunset. *If anything, taking in those celestial sights while searching for shells will surely put my troubles at ease.*

With her russet eyes brimming with tears, Allison wrapped her arms around Francine. "*Sean dich widder.*"

"See you again soon too. Keep an eye on Alana for me, okay?"

"Will do, Frannie."

In an instant, Grace joined in on the hug. "Don't get into too much trouble. Only a tad bit of trouble." Grace stuck out her tongue.

"Ach. The most trouble I'll get into is getting sunburned." Francine gave her friends one final squeeze, then shook the umbrella and closed it. She had stepped onto the stairs of the charter bus, trying to avoid getting wet. Francine hadn't gone far when she heard Grace and Allison calling out to her.

They yelled in unison even louder. "Francine! Your tote bag!"

She peered over her shoulder. Sure enough, Grace had the bag held up heavenward. It got more and more soaked by the second. Her heart hammered at the sight. Not wanting to open her umbrella again, Francine hopped off the bus and ran over to snatch the tote from Grace. "I can't believe I almost forgot this. Thank you both for catching that." Francine gave a final wave to her dear friends before running back to the bus.

She grabbed the railing and hoisted herself with her belongings in tow. Francine was more than ready to sit down and unwind for the next day or so. She made her way through the middle section dividing the rows of bus seats. The space tapered, but Francine was used to that from the cramped spaces in the bookstore.

Once seated, Francine set the tote bag by her feet and buckled herself in. She turned her gaze to the window, briefly eyeing her reflection. *I do seem to be pretty out of it. It's no wonder Geneva recommended I take time off.* Forming a steeple with her hands, Francine closed her eyes and began to pray in silence. *Lord, please keep everyone on this bus protected while on the road to Sarasota. And please, by the end of this trip, let me know what Your will is for my future. I'll do my best to allow You to guide me so I'll know for certain I'm on the right path. I entrust my life to You, Lord. Amen.*

~

Sarasota, Florida

Francine awoke, stretching her limbs like a feline. The ride had been rough during the night. Sitting upright wasn't the most comfortable position to get some shut eye. The sound of people sawing logs had disrupted her sleep as well. And she struck the bus's wall with her shoulder when it veered during sharp turns.

Despite being drowsy, Francine perked up when she saw rows

of palm trees and the ocean through the window. She leaned on the armrest of her seat. Inside the bus, it felt like winter because of the air conditioning, yet Francine imagined how nice it must be outside. Giddiness swelled in her chest.

It wasn't long before the charter bus pulled into the parking lot behind a Tourist Mennonite church. Francine gathered up her tote, following the line of passengers to the front and out of the parted doors. The subtle, balmy wind caressed her bare arms as she waited to get her luggage. When she noticed her ride wasn't present, she dug for her phone. Violet was supposed to pick her up, as she had last year, but she was nowhere in the lot. Francine opened her phone and dialed her sister's number.

"Hey, Francine," Violet answered. "Sorry I'm not there yet. There was an accident on my way to get you, so the traffic is backed up and bumper to bumper where I'm at."

Adrenaline surged through Francine's body. "Goodness. How bad was it?"

"From what I could tell, no one was injured, but both vehicles were most likely totaled."

"I sure hope those who were involved are doing okay." Francine pinched the skin along her collarbone. "Wait, you're in the midst of traffic. Should you be talking with me right now?"

"First of all, you called me while I was driving. Second, I'm on speakerphone, so no need to get on my case."

Francine exhaled in an attempt to calm herself, then pressed the phone closer to her ear. "You're right, Violet. I'm sorry. I understand you won't be here for a while due to circumstances."

"It won't be too much longer. They're finishing up with towing, so I would say I'll be there in about fifteen minutes. By the way, how was the trip over?"

"Nothing exciting happened. The only problem was trying to

sleep. It's hard sitting straight up in the high-backed seat for hours and hours."

"I hear you, Frannie. I'm not a fan of those buses. I'd rather drive myself and stop at a nice hotel to rest. But I can say one thing: the passengers do make good time getting here."

"True." Francine paused. "Okay, I should probably let you go. We can talk more when I see you."

"Looking forward to it. Bye, Sister."

The line went silent. Francine shut her phone and slid it back in her tote. While having her hand submerged in the bag, she grabbed a bottle of water and took a huge gulp. Francine wiped her forehead as she basked in the Florida sun, waiting for Violet. *I have no idea how my little sister handles driving, especially in a busy place like this.* She hummed the first few notes of "Come Thou Fount," then placed her tote down, since it had grown heavy. *But I am thankful for her willingness to take me to John and Leora's home. It's funny—Violet depended on us three to help her learn how to navigate the world. She really has become her own person, and now I'm dependent on her at times. I'm proud of my sister's growth.*

~

Later that evening, after finishing supper with Leora and John, Francine stood at the sink, scrubbing the grimy dishes from their meal. Francine still had to unload her luggage, which had been stowed away in the guest room. But her first priority was to catch up with her sister and brother-in-law. Francine had a general idea of how Leora was doing, but only so much could be expressed in letters.

Leora approached from behind, giving Francine's shoulder a pinch. "Danki for helping me clean up." Leora set a damp sponge near the edge of the sink.

"It's no problem. I may have the month off, but you still have to work at the bakery, so I'm more than happy to lighten the load around here." Francine dried the last dish and brought it over to the cabinet, where she stacked it with the rest.

"So Fran, Violet convinced you to get your nails done with her this weekend. How was she able to do that? You seemed adamant about not doing it when she offered last year."

"Well, you did say to try something new. Colorful nails seem harmless enough." Giggling, Francine leaned against the counter. "May as well take advantage of not having joined the church yet, right?"

Leora slapped a hand against her oval-shaped face. "Oh my. Look at how rebellious you're becoming, and you just got here."

Both of them laughed.

Francine lightly elbowed her sister. "How are we only two years apart? You're married, and here I am starting my late rumspringa."

Leora's smile faltered. "Hey, every person is different. There isn't anything wrong with where you're at right now."

"I suppose. But"—Francine lowered her gaze to her bare feet—"a tad bit of guidance would do me some good. Like when I broke those sand dollars."

She strolled over to the kitchen wall. Hanging on to it was something that had resonated with Francine ever since she first laid eyes on it. " 'The Legend of the Sand Dollar.' When those sand dollars shattered on my bedroom floor, I knew I had to come here. That was my reassurance during a moment of uncertainty."

"Honestly, Fran, I know something good will come of your stay here." Leora grinned. "And John and I are glad to have you in our home again."

"Speaking of John, where did he go after supper?" Francine questioned.

Right on cue, the sound of what sounded like a pig snorting blared from the living room. They both peeked in, and John was on the couch with his mouth wide open like a guppy.

"Sounds similar to the snores I heard on the bus last night."

"John did say he had a rough day, so I don't blame him." Leora tapped Francine's shoulder. "Want to sit outside for a bit and talk more?"

"Sure, Leora. I'd love to."

Leora led the way to the lanai in the backyard. It was a smidge chilly, but not in comparison to how it had been in Middlebury. Admittedly, Francine did not clearly understand Leora's seasonal affective disorder. Though, in a way, Francine did feel more positive in warmer weather. So she empathized with Leora and her need to move someplace where the sun shone most days of the year. Tied to her roots, the notion of living in Sarasota seemed unrealistic to Francine. It was suitable for vacation but not for long-term living. If it weren't for her two sisters living in Florida, she never would have considered going.

Francine was curious about what awaited her over the next few weeks. She hoped to be content with what she had and to potentially gain from her time in Sarasota. While she wondered about the possibilities, she tried not to linger on them for too long.

Chapter 3

Pinecraft

"I can't believe I have paint on these now." Francine uncurled her fingers and stared at her light yellow nails. *I'm not trying to be proud, but my fingernails look great!*

Leora leaned over the table at the booth they were seated at. "They look nice, Fran."

"Danki. Violet said they're not supposed to chip easily. But I'm a hands-on kind of person, so we'll see." Francine took in the scents of the afternoon meals mingling throughout the restaurant. It caused her stomach to gurgle. She propped up a menu, getting out her glasses to peruse the selections. "I'm still unsure of what to order. Yoder's has plenty to choose from."

It wasn't long until the waitress came to the booth with their drinks on a tray. "Here's your iced tea, and I'll be out with your mug and some coffee." She set the iced tea by Leora, then tugged on the collar of her dress. Taking the empty tray under her arm, the waitress took out a notepad and pencil from the front pocket of her apron. "Are you both ready to order, or do you need more time to decide?"

"I know I'm ready. I would like the fresh spinach, mushroom, and swiss cheese omelet with a small glass of tomato juice," Leora answered. "But my sister still isn't sure what she wants—"

"I'll have the fresh veggie Benedict, please."

After the waitress left with their orders, Leora's brow arched like the rooftop of their family's barn. "Didn't you have the Benedict when we were here earlier this week?"

Shrugging, Francine slid her glasses to the top of her head. "It's my favorite meal on the menu. I've had the Southern grilled oatmeal too, but that was when I was here with Violet and Dan yesterday morning. Benedict is hard to resist."

The waitress came back and set an ivory mug by Francine's elbow, pouring the steaming brew to the brim. Francine thanked her before the waitress left the table again. "Besides, as delicious as the grilled oatmeal is, it's very sweet and has way too much sugar."

"Too much sugar? What about when I lived at home? I remember the time you ordered three slices of pie in one sitting. For dinner. Nothing else."

"Hey, I was having a hard time then." Francine grasped the handle of her mug and sipped. She recoiled when it scorched the tip of her tongue but continued to drink in spite of it being a tad bit hot.

Leora looped a finger around one of the ties of her *kapp*. "What about when you broke up with Matthew?"

"I had one slice—and I took three more to go." Heat flushed across Francine's nose and cheeks. "But I haven't felt the urge to indulge for weeks, especially here. This first week in Florida has lifted my spirits."

"Well, I may indulge in a slice of key lime after we eat breakfast." Leora's pale blue eyes narrowed. "So Fran, are you getting homesick?"

"I am a little, though not as much as I thought I'd be. It's nice to have more time to reconnect without feeling rushed." Francine took another sip of coffee. The heat of the brew trickling down her throat enveloped her body in a sense of comfort. "I am wondering how Alana is doing since we last spoke over the phone. She seemed to be doing well, but I have a hard time getting her to open up to me. Ever since you and Violet moved here, there's been less excitement than before, when we all lived under one roof. I've missed those times, and I'm sure Alana would like to be here right now to relive some of those fond moments together."

"I discussed it with Violet, and it would be good to see if our parents would be okay with us visiting Indiana soon."

Francine overheard someone in the booth behind her order a slice of Yoder's black raspberry pie. That was the pie Matthew ordered at Essenhaus in Indiana. It was his favorite flavor, and even though Francine didn't order dessert on their dates, Matthew would always offer some of his. He didn't want to exclude Francine from anything, even something as simple as sharing a slice of pie. She had always accepted and savored it. The smile that stretched to his ears made the effort worth it.

But Francine shut those thoughts out as fast as they materialized. "Regardless, I'm just happy I get to spend time with you, Leora. We have the entire day to ourselves, and I can't wait to get out on the beach. What could be better than sand between our toes and salty ocean air in our faces?"

Leora giggled. "We'll definitely try to make the most of it. Perfect way to spend a Saturday. I'm thankful I got time off from the bakery today."

"Me too."

When their meals arrived, Francine unwound the silverware from the napkin. Before she cut into the plump center of her Benedict, her gaze went to the wall hangings above their booth.

There was a quilt square with the Dresden pattern resembling a flower made from pieces of green and floral fabric. Above it hung a rectangle-shaped print, which Francine could read without her glasses. It read: "Never forget your hopes and dreams."

Francine was a firm believer that there were no coincidences in this world. As with everything else in her life, she knew there had to be some significance to where she was right now. God had a way of communicating with people. It was subtle and easy to miss at times, but Francine knew it was there.

She bowed her head and prayed in silence. *Thank You, Lord, for this meal and the reminder about my hopes and dreams. I pray You will show me that joining the church is the path You want for me.*

Lido Beach

Lucas Hayes dropped two quarters into the kids' hands. "Here you go, little man. And here's your hot dog and water. Have a great time out on the beach."

The youngster tipped his red baseball cap to Lucas before grabbing his food and running toward his parents. Lucas kept his pleasant demeanor when a group of young teens strolled by. Their exposed skin appeared as red as the kid's hat. As soon as no one was near the concession stand where Lucas worked, he dropped the act. His shoulders rolled forward, and he leaned his head against his hand. *Wish I could ditch this job and head over to St. Armand's Circle, but I've got rent to pay. Maybe tomorrow, considering I have Sunday off.*

Since no one else was in line at the moment, Lucas listened to the bustling music and voices resonating from the shore. His work wasn't strenuous, but it was mundane. The earnings barely kept him afloat. But Lucas had other means of earning money that supplied him with certain luxuries. He had his friend Barry to thank for that. Although Lucas did get an abundance of money at times, it wasn't enough to achieve what he desired.

Lucas reached into the front pocket of his jeans, pulled out his phone, and checked the time. "Less than a few hours left. I should text Barry to let him know I'll be driving to Tampa once I close up here." He skimmed his thumb along the screen and proceeded to type the message.

Lucas sent the text and then caught sight of two girls advancing to the concession area from the beach. He did a double take because they weren't the typical girls he saw at Lido. Both wore long, plain-colored dresses, with their hair covered in white cones.

Lucas knew straight away they were either Mennonite or Amish. He had seen some before at Lido, but it wasn't a common occurrence. The majority of those he'd seen were either part of families with small children or gray-haired couples wandering near the water. These two young women appeared to be around his age. One of them in particular caught his eye.

She placed a massive bag on a table, while the other girl beelined for the public restrooms. Attempting to be discreet, Lucas brought the phone to his face. He observed the girl at the table while pretending to use his phone. The sight of her caused his heart to beat faster, though he wasn't sure why. She was a sight to take in, but Lucas never thought he would find a Plain girl to be so alluring.

She dug into the bag. The lines on her forehead creased as she pulled out what appeared to be a wallet. The girl approached the concession counter. Lucas averted his gaze, not wanting her to know he'd been staring.

"Hello," she greeted. "I would like two bottles of water, please."

Lucas placed his phone face down on the counter and examined her hazel eyes speckled with brown. *Wow*, Lucas thought. *She's even cuter up close.* "Sure thing, Miss."

Her upper lip curved as she beamed. "The name's Francine."

"Francine. Nice to meet you." Lucas extended his hand to her, wondering if Francine would accept his offer of a handshake. "I'm Lucas."

Sure enough, she grasped his hand. In that moment, a jolt of energy shot up Lucas' arm. He felt the rhythm of his pulse speed up. After letting go of Francine's hand, his gaze trailed to the glossy paint on the tip of her fingers.

"Good handshake." He went to grab the water bottles, continuing to converse with her. "So you're either Mennonite or Amish, right?"

"I grew up in an Amish community in Indiana."

"What brings you to this lil' slice of paradise? Here for vacation?"

"Visiting my sisters. I'm staying with my oldest sister and her husband while I'm here. She should be back from the restroom soon. We just got done collecting shells."

Lucas couldn't help himself. He had to ask about her nails. "I didn't know Amish were allowed to paint their nails. Aren't you guys strict about that sort of thing?"

"Only if you've joined the church, which I haven't yet. The nail painting was my youngest sister's idea, and I figured it would be fun to try something I haven't done before."

"They look really nice." Lucas placed the bottles down, wiping the condensation onto his pant legs. He shuffled closer to the counter. "Especially on an adorable person like yourself."

Francine seemed undeterred by his compliment, except for her lip curving a little more and a patch of red spreading across her nose. "Thanks."

Since there was no other activity by the concessions, Lucas seized the opportunity to speak with Francine a bit longer. He wasn't normally invested in flirting, but something about Francine intrigued him. She was receptive to his questions. Lucas thought Francine had a slight interest in him and contemplated whether he should be bolder and try to get to know her.

~

After paying for the water and stowing the bottles in her tote, Francine continued to converse with the young English man behind the concession counter. While they were conversing, she took note of Leora returning to the table from the restroom. Francine had been set on wrapping things up, not wanting to keep her sister waiting. But it was as if there was a gravitational pull drawing her in and keeping her fascinated with Lucas.

"How long do you plan on staying?" Lucas asked.

"For the rest of the month. My boss was gracious and gave me a long vacation."

"Sounds like the golden opportunity to venture out and go to places you haven't been in Florida."

"I mostly want to stay close to Sarasota, but maybe it would be fun to go to Tampa. I'm trying to take it day by day, so I don't really have any definite plans."

Francine felt a tender squeeze on her shoulder from behind. "Fran, we should get on home." Leora yawned. "We don't need John worrying about where we are."

"You must be Leora, Francine's sister." Lucas held out his hand to her. "Good to meet you."

Leora shook his hand. "Nice to meet you too."

"Well, we both had a long day, and the sun is getting lower." Francine smiled, offering him a small wave. "It was nice chatting with you, Lucas. Maybe we'll cross paths again sometime."

Francine began to follow her sister to the table to collect what they'd hauled to the beach. But when Lucas called out to her, she whipped around like a pinwheel in the breeze.

"Wait, do you have a way for me to contact you? I can show you around Sarasota if you want."

Francine hitched a breath, pressing a hand against her collar bone. "Are you asking me on a date?"

"Sort of." His chin dipped down, no longer meeting Francine's gaze. "I mean, if you're okay with that."

Francine hesitated, her thoughts flowing like a surging stream. She had to admit that Lucas was undeniably attractive. His short, curly locks coiled like ribbons. The dimples forming from his grin caused a tremor in her chest. Francine had never dated anyone outside of her community before. The guys she'd gone out with were familiar because they lived in her community back home. Although they'd strayed from their Amish upbringing, they still had a hint of their heritage rooted in their mannerisms and values.

Despite that, something about Lucas kept her from declining his offer. Francine found her instantaneous attraction to him to be peculiar. Beyond a physical attraction, she felt the urge to give Lucas her number. *As long as it stays casual, I guess going on a date with him wouldn't be a bad thing.*

Exhaling, she returned to the concession and drummed her fingers along the counter's edge. "All right, Lucas. If it's a date you want, then it's a date you'll get." Francine winked. She sauntered to the table and got out her phone, then went back over to Lucas to exchange numbers.

"A flip phone?" His eyes expanded at the sight of it. "I haven't seen one of those since the early 2000s. Kind of nostalgic."

She merely shrugged in response.

When they had finished entering each other's phone numbers,

Francine cast a glance at Leora. Francine bid Lucas goodbye one final time, her heart throbbing, and gathered her things. She followed behind Leora as they headed toward the parking lot.

As they waited for their driver to pick them up, Leora pulled Francine to the side. The foliage behind the concrete wall almost grazed their heads.

"Fran, are you sure giving a stranger your number is a good idea?" Leora's lips pressed together. "And he's English. The reason you and Matthew broke up was because he's choosing to become English."

"Lucas knows I'm only here for a month, so it wouldn't turn into anything serious. You did say to try something new, and I've never dated anyone outside of our community." Francine clutched the strap of her tote. "Better to have a brief relationship with a person from that life than marry into it."

It's especially preferable to not knowing what to expect when living an English lifestyle and then regretting it later. Francine cupped the side of her cheek, and her skin heated. *Everything happens for a reason, and for whatever reason, God had me meet Lucas. He seems nice enough. How bad can dating a concession worker from Lido be?*

Chapter 4

Tampa, Florida

After issuing his voucher, Lucas moved through the casino's throng of patrons. The trills and alarms blaring from the slots enticed Lucas in certain regards. It took him back to his childhood visits to the arcade, minus the cigarette smog and the adults throwing temper tantrums instead of children.

Lucas reached the bar where his group of friends were gathered. Massive monitors broadcast baseball's spring training above the glistening countertops. An empty stool awaited him, and Lucas slid onto the showy upholstered seat.

"Hey, Louie." Marvin, who sat to the right of Lucas, passed him an opened beer bottle. "What was tonight's payout?"

"Thank you kindly." Lucas took his first swig of the chilled, pungent liquid. "It was 20 percent above my budget. Not too shabby, if I do say so myself."

Barry, who sat adjacent to Lucas on the left, shook his head. "You should have wagered my recommended limit. You're not going to see results the way you're holding back."

"Rather not risk emptying my pockets, Barry. Last time I listened to you, I was in a bind with my landlord. I can't afford not to pay her on time again."

"Just means you'll reach your dream later than sooner, so if that's dandy for you, then fine." Barry pointed to himself, a cunning expression unfurling from his face. "I earned close to 35 percent above my set budget, and it was from not holding back."

Marvin groaned. "It took you forever to make up what you lost." His gaze darted to Lucas, with his thick eyebrows pinched together. "Barry wanted to keep hitting. I had to pry him away from the tables with brute force."

Leaning over the counter, Barry's eyes narrowed in Marvin's direction. "If I wasn't making peanuts for a paycheck at work, I wouldn't be desperate to make a profit in this place."

Lucas toasted with his beer bottle toward Barry. "Hear, hear."

"You ever considered the lottery, Barry?" Their friend Jim, who was seated the farthest from Lucas, called out.

Dismissing Jim's remark, Barry waved his hand as if a gnat buzzed near his ear. "Anyways, Lucas texted me something interesting earlier. Isn't that right, Lucas?"

All eyes from their group directed to Lucas, like they expected him to divulge the details.

Of course, Barry would draw attention away from himself. He placed the bottle down, clenching his hands together. "I may have given my phone number to a cutie near the end of my shift."

"That's not the best part, Lucas. The kicker is she's a Mennonite."

"Amish," Lucas corrected as he reached for his drink again, rubbing his thumb on the condensation remaining on the neck of the bottle before taking another sip.

"Like there's a difference. They all have a sheltered upbringing. Completely naive to the world around them." Barry fiddled with the collar of his polo shirt. "I know you're not usually forward when it comes to flirting. Is that why you went for it with the Amish?"

"Her name is Francine, and she seems to carry herself fine from what I could tell." Lucas leaned against the back of the stool as he dug out his phone from his pocket. After finding the desired image, he placed the phone on the bar for his buddies to see. "Plus, look at her. I took this when she was leaving the beach."

As Marvin scooted to take a gander at the screen, the scent of dense cologne flooded Lucas' nose. "I have to admit, for a Plain girl, she's a beauty."

"Too bad for that traffic cone on her head." Barry snickered, finishing off his fourth beer.

The conversation pivoted away from Francine, which brought Lucas some ease. He didn't need his friends forming their brazen opinions of her, especially since he didn't know Francine well enough yet. All Lucas knew was he found her to be attractive, and if that was from his first impression of Francine, Lucas wanted to uncover more of who she was.

Lucas kept talking with his friends, sipping from the mouth of the bottle. As the liquor dwindled, Lucas felt slightly lightheaded and loosened up. His friends had poked fun at him before for being a lightweight, especially after the night of his twenty-second birthday. Thanks to his friends buying him drinks one after another, Lucas had gotten blackout drunk that evening, accompanied by a grueling hangover the morning after. It was not an enjoyable experience, which is why Lucas had stuck to a single beer or two ever since.

Barry patted Lucas on the back, leaning closer, his voice barely audible. "You know, I have a hunch you haven't thought things through about going out with an Amish girl. What if she tries to make you one of them?"

Lucas cocked his head. "I haven't even gotten in touch with Francine to ask her out, and you're saying that? She's only visiting

Florida for the rest of the month."

"You never know. What if you end up liking her and it gets serious? Don't you want to be prepared for when or if that happens?"

"Might be overthinking it, my friend." Tilting the bottle toward his mouth, Lucas swallowed the rest of his drink.

"It wouldn't be a concern if you got her to leave. In fact, you could be doing her a favor by getting her out of that life. I've seen those reality shows about the Amish. My ex was invested in those shows, and from what I saw, it sounded like their home lives weren't so great. Consider how liberating it would be for her to gain some perspective on how we live."

"I don't know, Barry. That's really none of my business."

"I'm sure I can make it worth your while. How about a bet? If you can persuade her to leave before she returns home, I'll give you my casino winnings for the rest of the month. Of course, you have to wager vice versa, giving me your earnings if you're unsuccessful. Do you accept?"

Lucas was reluctant to respond. His eyes trailed to the dangling light fixtures above them, contemplating his friend's offer. *Suppose I could be doing Francine some good by getting her to leave that life behind. Francine does have a cell phone, albeit a flip phone. And her fingernails were painted, so she could be wanting to leave anyways. Barry may be giving me a quick buck while I help out Francine.*

With a heavy sigh, Lucas turned to Barry, who had a broad grin resembling a string of pearls. "All right, Barry. I'll think about it."

Sarasota

The early morning sun burned Francine's brow as she reached for another soaked garment from the woven basket. She wrung out the dress until it no longer dripped and slid a clothespin along the line. Francine clipped the shoulder seam to hold the damp fabric in place.

Since Leora and John were at their respective jobs, Francine had her sister's house all to herself. The seclusion was troublesome. There wasn't enough for Francine to be entertained with on her own. Solitaire was the only card game she could play, and playing with friends and family was more fun. She kept herself busy most of the morning by doing household chores.

I can't call Grace or Allison right now. They're both busy. Francine tugged out a buttoned shirt and waved it like a fluttering flag. *I wanted to tell them about the guy I met at Lido, but I haven't even heard back from him.*

She had left Lucas a message the day before, hoping he would call her so they could arrange their date. Although disappointed he hadn't responded, part of Francine felt relieved. She willingly carried out what had happened at the concession, but on reflection, Francine recognized that exchanging numbers with Lucas had been a hasty decision.

Lucas could have thought it over afterward too. That may be the reason he hasn't called me back.

After hanging up the last piece of clothing, Francine scooped the basket up and headed into the house. She set the basket down in the utility room, her bare feet sticking to the wooden floors with each step.

It's probably for the best. Why would I go out with an Englisher when I'm planning to join the church when I return home? What was I thinking? Francine took in a deep breath, and the pit in her stomach felt like soil being tilled deep into the ground. *I'm starting to believe Leora was right, and here I sounded so sure of my choice before.*

Francine figured it would be good to rest a little after her hard work, so she made her way to the guest room. Her suitcase lay open in the middle of the floor. She'd been using it as a dresser for the past week, yet there was a vacant closet and dresser in the room. If it weren't for her getting around to washing her own clothes, the dresses she wore last week would still be strewn about the guest room.

Stepping over the suitcase, Francine sprung onto the bed and grabbed her Bible and glasses from the nightstand. The nice part of having the home to herself was enjoying peace and quiet while reading from the Word. She had to make time to read back home, between working at the bookstore and hanging out with her friends. Francine turned to 1 John 5 and read verse 14 aloud, dragging her pinkie underneath the words: " 'Now this is the confidence that we have in Him, that if we ask anything according to His will, He hears us.' " Francine brought her hands together with the pads of her fingers meeting to form the shape of a steeple.

Even after their break-up, Francine had speculated on how Matthew was doing. It was natural to continue caring for someone even if you weren't close with them anymore. She wondered if he thought about her too. Matthew could be pressing on just fine, and she understood if that was the case. Francine prayed every chance she had to get back on track and be optimistic about whatever lay ahead.

Her phone hummed from across the room. Slapping the Bible shut, Francine bounded for her purse and began searching for the phone. When she found it, the phone continued to pulsate, and the tiny screen displayed the caller's name.

"It's him!" Francine nearly squealed. "It's Lucas. Oh no. I need to answer, right?" She flipped the phone open and pressed it to her ear. "Lucas, hello."

"Hey, Francine. I got your message, and I'm glad to hear you haven't forgotten about meeting me the other day."

"Seems like you haven't forgotten about me either." She chuckled.

"Yeah, I'm sorry I didn't get back to you sooner. I did come up with where we can go for our date."

Francine knelt to the floor. "Really? Where did you have in mind?"

"Well, I was stuck behind a counter as you were wandering the shoreline of Lido. How about we walk along the beach later this evening? Then we can grab a bite to eat afterward." As though he might be stalling, Lucas chuckled. "If you're busy tonight, we can try a different time this week."

"No, no. Tonight sounds great, Lucas. I'm free as can be." She wiped her suddenly sweaty hand across her dress in an attempt to dry it off.

"Okay, then. Would you be comfortable with me picking you up, or do you want to meet at Lido and go from there?"

"It is our first date, so I think I'll meet you over there."

"Are you saying there will be a second date?"

Francine couldn't help but smirk at his joke. "Let's see how tonight goes before answering that question."

"That's fair." Lucas cleared his throat. "Wish I could chat a little longer, but there are some hungry-looking faces approaching. I'll call you when I'm about done working so you'll know when to meet me."

"I'll let you go then. See you tonight."

"You too. Bye, Francine."

The line went silent, and Francine squirmed as her legs grew sore from resting on them. Her frame trembled as she rose from the floor.

"This is actually happening." The onset of nervousness

churned in her core.

Although anxious about going out with a stranger, Francine was also excited about the prospect of new experiences. She thought of herself as a homebody, yet it was undeniable she had always adored bustling environments. Francine was eager to get out and try something new.

For now I'm going to push aside my worries and follow through with this date. I need to make sure I'm prepared for tonight.

Chapter 5

Lido Beach

Lucas trailed behind Francine as she strolled upon the white sand close to the sea's edge. The foam from the crashing waves trickled in the nooks of the shells washed up on the beach. Francine had brought along a couple of net bags, intending to collect shells with him. Since Lucas wouldn't know what to do with them, he wasn't interested in participating. He merely wanted to talk to Francine as they ambled over the salty landscape. Though, Lucas had to admit, it was endearing to see her beam whenever she discovered a shell that wasn't fractured. His chest fluttered at the upward curl of her plum-colored lips.

Keeping in mind what Barry had said about the Amish last Saturday, Lucas made an effort to ask Francine questions as casually as he could. He didn't want to be too intrusive, but if he wanted to win Barry's bet, he needed to know how to go about getting her to leave her faith.

"Just out of curiosity—and don't get me wrong, you do look nice—but didn't you wear the same dress when we first met?" He scratched his chin.

Francine's brow lowered as she wiped her hands on the fabric.

"Our dresses look alike, but they have distinct shapes and cuts, and the sleeve lengths vary according to the season."

"So you're not stuck wearing the same one?"

"My friend wears a denim jacket most days, but it's not always the same one." Her bonnet's ties flittered in the gentle wind.

Lucas tilted his head. "I'm guessing your friend isn't Amish."

"Grace is my friend from childhood, and her home is close to mine, but she isn't Amish." She slipped the net bag into the opening of the bigger bag strung on her shoulder.

"Your parents are fine with you being around someone who isn't Amish?"

"Of course. She isn't a stranger. Grace is trustworthy and has always been there for me." As Francine gathered her ties, Lucas noticed her nails were still coated yellow.

"Has your friend suggested you shouldn't stay Amish?"

"Not Grace, but someone else hoped I wouldn't join the church." Her face reddened. "I wasn't compelled to leave. But part of me wanted to, so then I wouldn't be left feeling confused—"

She tripped, and Lucas grabbed Francine's hand and helped her up. To see what she had tripped over, Lucas peered down and saw a piece of lumber jutting out of the sand.

"Thanks, Lucas. I nearly took a tumble there." Stepping away from him, Francine formed a steeple with her hands and brought them to the base of her neck. "We just met, and I'd rather not unload my personal stuff on you. I don't think that is anyone's idea of a pleasant first date."

"I'm sorry. I know we barely know each other, but I'm just concerned is all. If you need to unload, I'll help you carry it."

Francine's eyes, resembling a summer leaf changing to autumn colors, glistened as she locked her gaze on him. She walked away from Lucas, pulling the bag of shells back out, and continued walking along the shoreline.

The grains of sand rubbed against Lucas' heels as he shuffled his feet. *So much for being subtle. I should have asked Barry more about what goes on in their homes. I can tell something is eating away at her. Francine said part of her wanted to leave. Now, for whatever reason, she's putting on a brave face.*

Francine retrieved an ivory, saucer-shaped shell from the wet sand and handed it to him. "Look, Lucas. Another sand dollar. Can you believe it? It's also completely undamaged."

"You really admire sand dollars, huh?" He examined the shell before returning it to Francine.

"I broke the ones I found on the beach last year, and they're not easy to come by. I used to believe shells were merely homes for snails and mollusks. I was shocked to learn they're exoskeletons from those animals, and that sand dollars were once living sea urchins."

"I've seen the live ones on the cusp of the shore before. Everyone on the sand flocked over to them like a bunch of seagulls. It was certainly a sight."

The remainder of their walk went without incident. Lucas assumed it would be simple to get Francine to open up on her own, but he wondered if he would need to take a different approach. For the time being, Lucas preferred to be himself and enjoy spending the rest of the date with Francine. There was no rush because he had the rest of March to win Barry's wager.

"Getting hungry, Francine?" Lucas inquired as he pulled out his phone to check the time. "It's almost six thirty."

"A little. You want to make us a couple of hot dogs at the concession?" She gave Lucas a delicate elbow nudge.

"I wouldn't want to eat there for our first date, especially if I was working right now. What I'm thinking about is some savory grub at St. Armand's Circle. Do you mind riding over there with me? Or we could walk—whichever you prefer."

"I wouldn't mind the car ride. We did plenty of walking this evening."

He stuffed the phone back into his jeans' pocket. "All right, then. Let's get going."

St. Armand's Circle

They left Café L'Europe, and Francine found it interesting that Lucas had chosen that restaurant over the others. The brick structure's arches and antique ornamentation gave it a European flair. She remembered the two young women in the bookstore and wondered if the restaurants in Europe looked similar.

The sky was lit with hues of purple and blue, and the lights from the storefronts and lampposts illuminated the palm trees surrounding the area. Francine, walking alongside Lucas, moved in step with the crowd. Many tourists had dispersed along the brick pavement, some of whom were glancing over at Francine. She was used to it back home as well, but like Middlebury, Sarasota locals were accustomed to Plain folks going about their daily lives.

Speaking of which, Francine relaxed when Lucas stopped asking questions about her being Amish. Francine wasn't opposed to sharing, but it appeared he wanted to learn more intimate details about her life in a short period of time.

Maybe it's common for the English to be upfront about their lives on the first date. I understand he's curious, but it was still odd. Francine wrapped an arm around her stomach. *There's a twinge of that bad feeling inside of me, and I'm not sure if another date with Lucas would be a good idea.*

"So, Francine, got any ideas of what else you want to do? Or is it getting late for you?"

"It's not too late. Do you want to go into the shops and look around?"

"Sure, but before we peruse the knickknacks, there's something I need to get out of my car." Lucas offered his hand to her as the gentle glow of the lights accentuated his squared jawline.

Once Francine rested her hand in the crease of his broad palm, Lucas took hold and whisked her through the stream of people. They had to travel quite a distance to where he had parked.

When they arrived, she grabbed the opportunity to take some deep breaths. Lucas opened the trunk of his vehicle, and she saw a black case propped against the left side. He flipped the case over and unfastened the flap, revealing what was inside.

"You play the violin?" To get a better look, she rolled onto the tips of her toes.

"Yep, and I come here to perform for the people after my long hours at Lido." After resealing the case, Lucas set it down on the sidewalk and locked his car.

Francine followed behind Lucas with his violin case in tow. They were heading back in the direction of the eatery along the side of the street. She kept her gaze fixed on the violin case the entire way there.

Lucas chuckled as he appeared to notice her lingering stare. "I'm guessing you don't see instruments often."

She shook her head. "A lot of people in our community play instruments. Guitar, harmonica, and sometimes a battery-powered keyboard. We play them for family and young people's gatherings, but instruments are never used in church."

"Well, I'll be." He leaned forward to open the case as he sat down on a green bench. He pulled out a container and the bow. Then he rubbed the contents of the container against the bow's hairs. "Do you play any instruments?"

"No. I do hum to music, but I don't have the best singing voice, so I only sing hymns at church. Allison, one of my friends, plays the guitar, and all her siblings do as well. I hum along with them when Allison's family jams and sings during gatherings at their house. Despite not being able to play an instrument, I still adore listening to music."

Lucas rested his chin on the end of the violin. "You'll surely adore this then. Hang on to your cone-shaped hat." He danced his fingers across the four strings while swinging his bow back and forth.

"Create in Me a Clean Heart." How does Lucas know that hymn? She took in the music while Lucas continued to play. Francine felt a wave of joy wash over her. Even in the low light, she could see a smile developing on his face. The words formed in Francine's thoughts as she hummed along with the music. *"Restore unto me the joy of Thy salvation and renew a right spirit within me."*

Taken aback, Francine glanced around St. Armand's Circle. Most people walked by them without pausing to notice the sound of his instrument. Lucas' violin pierced through the jumble of voices and the rumble of passing cars. How could so many people rush by without stopping to listen to the moving melody?

After Lucas played his concluding note, Francine heard a few claps and spun around to see a family with two small children. The father handed one of the kids a dollar, and her ponytail bounced as she dashed up to the case to put it in. Lucas thanked them, tipping his invisible hat to the family as they waved goodbye.

Francine went up to him. "You were right. I did enjoy that very much. How did you come across that song?"

"Funny you mentioned singing in church. That's where I first got inspired to play the violin. There was a violinist on the worship team at the church my family used to attend. I was entranced by the sounds this instrument was capable of." Lucas made a swift motion with his bow on the strings to emphasize his point. "My school had an orchestra program, so I had a good excuse to start learning. Of course, the violin I had back then was a rental, whereas the one I have now is a student violin. I bought this as soon as I moved out of my parents' home. It's my dream to one day own, at the very least, a Di Matteo violin. The higher quality violins are very expensive but way easier to handle. Smooth as silk. Still got a way to go, unfortunately."

Captivated by his vulnerability, Francine's breath became trapped in her chest. Finding out that Lucas had grown up discovering his passion in church made her tremble.

"I'm pretty sure I just bored you with my woeful backstory."

"Not at all. In fact, you should perform for us sometime. My family would love to hear you play. You're very talented."

Lucas sagged against the bench. "Shucks. Thanks, Francine." With a shaky laugh, he extended the instrument to her. "Want to give it a try? It's a cheap old thing. Now, if this were my dream violin, I'd only let you look at it." He extended it closer to her, his dark eyes reflecting the bulb from a nearby streetlamp. "Come on, give it a whirl."

She took the instrument from Lucas and did her best to hold the violin like he did. Francine gazed at him as she slid it under her chin. She placed a finger on the first string after receiving a thumbs up from Lucas, then raised the bow.

The sound the strings produced resembled a piglet squealing for feed. Francine's eardrums recoiled, but she kept skidding the bow on the strings.

"Not an easy instrument to play. You have to hold the bow with a little slack, but not too much, or you won't produce any sound."

Lucas made an effort to demonstrate by feigning a violin. "Relax your wrist a bit."

Listening to Lucas' critiques, Francine tried to lessen the stiffness in her wrist. Even though she was just sounding out one note and not a complete melody, it sounded a little better. Her muscles started to ache, so she drew the bow-wielding hand down to her side.

"My upper body hurts, yet I work on the farm and carry books back home." She bit her lower lip. "I don't think I'm cut out for the violin. You make it seem effortless, like anyone could pick it up and begin playing."

"Got to give you props for trying. None of my friends went for it. It's refreshing to be around someone who enjoys music for a change." Lucas held out his hands to reclaim his violin. "Unless you wish to browse the shops, I still have more to share tonight."

"I want to listen for a while longer." Francine handed it back to him, lacing her fingers behind her back.

Nodding, Lucas proceeded to play another tune. This one was unfamiliar to Francine. More people congregated, implying it was likely a popular song heard on the radio. Whatever the case, it was good to see more admirers of Lucas' performance. Francine understood he was passionate. She couldn't believe that his friends weren't impressed by his musical abilities.

I'm going to give Lucas the benefit of the doubt. I believe he asked me so many questions earlier because he prefers to be more personal. I suppose I ought to give Lucas a chance to learn more about me. I might not feel comfortable sharing things now, but as I get to know Lucas, perhaps I'll begin to understand why I'm drawn to him.

Francine reached into her tote for the bag of shells after Lucas finished the song. She opened the net bag, walked over to the violin case, and placed the sand dollar on the velvet lining.

With a smirk, Lucas squinted up at her. "Very funny, Francine. But that's not going to cut it for my rent this month."

"Keep it. It's my gift to you for our first date."

His mouth slacked a smidge, but his dimples were prominent. "So there's going to be a second date after all?"

"Yes, Lucas. I'm looking forward to another date." Francine's heartbeat sped up, hoping she wouldn't come to regret saying those words.

Chapter 6

Sarasota

"*Jah, Ich habe gewonnen*!" Violet tossed the last card she had in her hand onto the card pile.

"You sure did. Congratulations on finally winning a game." Francine winked at her younger sister.

"I know you're being sarcastic, but I'll still take the compliment." Violet swept her hand along the floral-patterned fabric of her dress. "Is anyone opposed to playing another round of four up and four down?"

John raised a fork to his bearded face, finishing the slice of chocolate cake Leora had brought home from the bakery. "One more game would be enough. It's getting pretty late."

Violet stood up from her chair. "I'll have another piece of Leora's delightful dessert."

"I'll have another one too." Dan grinned and extended his paper plate.

She came over and took it from him. "It's no surprise that my husband would want another slice of this rich, moist cake. It is, after all, Dan's favorite dessert."

"It sure is, and while I'm waiting for my last piece to enjoy tonight, I'll deal the cards this time." Violet's husband extended his hand to the center of the dining room table.

As Dan began shuffling the playing cards, Francine rose from her seat, holding her empty plate. She hurried to the kitchen and scooped up more potato salad left over from supper. Since the only snack available was the cake, the salad was the healthiest option for Francine.

"That was some delicious potato salad, Francine. You definitely made plenty for all of us," Violet remarked as she strolled over to the kitchen island. "I've never had potato salad with avocado instead of egg before, but it works."

"Danki. I'm glad you liked it. Avocados are a good substitute until they oxidize. Regular potato salad can be stored in the refrigerator for a while. That's something I can't do with avocados." Francine put the salad on the plate after scooping it up. "So, I have to eat up what's left before I go to bed."

Violet pointed to the cake. "Are you sure you don't want any before Dan and I take the rest home? It's really yummy. Hard to resist."

Francine raised a palm. "Violet, I'm good. Thank you."

"Okay, but you're missing out." She cut herself another slice. "Just curious, Francine, but why didn't you invite that fellow over?"

"I considered it, but this is the first time we've all been together since I arrived in Sarasota. I didn't want to make Lucas uncomfortable either. I did suggest for our next date that we go to where you and Leora work so that it may be less intimidating."

Violet's slim features slanted. "Does he not like us Plain folk?"

"I'm not sure how he feels, but I'm trying not to pass judgment on Lucas. He's never dated someone Amish before, and I've never dated anyone from outside of our community. I understand his curiosity, and this is new territory for both of us."

"I'll keep an eye on him if I end up waiting on your table tomorrow. I never pictured you dating an English guy in a million years. I'm even surprised you're dating so soon after ending a long-term relationship." With her scarlet nails glistening in the illumination of the space, Violet brushed a strand of hair away from her ivory skin. "But I hope everything works out for you, because a shift like this could be what you need in your life."

Violet reentered the living room. Leora was nudging John, who was attempting to "rest his eyes." Violet encircled Dan with an arm while pecking his cheek like a finch at a bird feeder. Francine couldn't help but think back to last year. During Christmas, Matthew had been at her parents' place, sitting by Francine in the living room. She had a vivid memory of him moving near to her on the couch and her fingers entwining with his. It was as though her body was being crushed by a recollection that had once made her feel weightless.

It's stressful not to get caught up in the present moment, visualizing what could have been. I'm at this point now, and while I'm not sure where it's going, this could be exactly what I need without even knowing it. Just like Violet said. Francine averted her gaze to the wall-mounted print of the "Legend of the Sand Dollar." *Let it be Your will, Lord. I can't see what's ahead, so please direct me. I'm in the place You led me to be at, Lord. So please let me know why You've called me here.*

~

The cheerful hostess led Lucas and Francine to an open booth near the salad bar. He placed the menus on opposite sides of the slender table.

As Lucas slid onto the wooden bench, he observed the restaurant. Most of the tables were occupied by the Amish. A group of young Amish lads sat at one of the rectangular wooden tables. They seemed to be a bit older than Lucas and Francine, and their hair appeared to have been cut with a bowl on their head.

A waitress approached their table, asking Francine what she wanted to drink. She ordered a club soda, which is what she'd had at the restaurant in St. Armands. Lucas stuck with cola. The European restaurant had offered beer, but Lucas didn't think it was appropriate for their first date. He never felt the need to drink unless he was with his pals. It was more enjoyable to eat and socialize while sober.

When the waitress brought them their drinks, they decided to order from the menu rather than peruse the buffet. He saw a couple of Amish women leaving a booth, but their bonnets weren't cone-shaped like Francine's. Lucas had seen those hats worn on Lido Beach before and wondered why they were shaped differently.

"Is there a reason for the variety of hat styles Plain women wear, Francine? Like the ones with heart shapes."

"The Lancaster communities in Pennsylvania wear those." Francine hadn't removed the paper wrapping from her straw before placing it in her cup, so she retrieved the straw and peeled away the waterlogged wrapping.

Lucas chuckled. "Got a lot on your mind?"

"In a way. At times my thoughts flood in at once." Francine's smile faded, and her demeanor became solemn. "Why did you ask me out? Did you want to get to know me better, or was it solely because I'm Amish?"

I should've seen that coming given that I kept asking her about the Amish. He considered Francine's questions while twiddling his thumbs beneath the table. "Honestly, it's both. I've seen Amish throughout Sarasota, but I don't know much about your customs and beliefs. Anything I've heard is hearsay. And it's hard to ignore the clothing the Amish wear. Aren't you on that thing Amish do—to go out and see what the world is like?"

"It's called *rumspringa*. Plenty of young Amish partake in it, but how common or accepted rumspringa is depends on where you live." She curled her shoulders forward. "Joining the church is an option, but in some homes, it's expected. Expectations also depend on the household."

"So not all communities and parents are strict?"

"No, and strict ones are often the ones outsiders think of when they hear the word *Amish*. Those communities still exist, but they aren't as common as they once were."

If she's not expected to join the church in her community, then Francine must be somewhat interested in leaving. She did agree to date me, after all. But it's possible her parents expect her to stay.

He pricked the skin under his chin. "Do your parents approve of you making your own decisions?"

"Lucas, how did your parents feel about you getting an apartment and living on your own?"

"Yeah, I suppose all young people face expectations from their parents."

"Most parents, including mine, want their kids to stay. Fortunately, my folks will support whatever choice we make. My youngest sister isn't Amish, but she is Mennonite. They're like us in many ways, except they drive cars, whereas we travel mostly with horses and buggies." With a wave, Francine cast a glance beyond Lucas.

Lucas turned his head, seeing one of the waitresses waving back. Promptly, she went back to serving tables. "I'm guessing that's your other sister."

"Both of my sisters have jobs here. Violet works in the serving area, and Leora works in the bakery."

A server approached the table and presented Lucas and

Francine with their meals. Puzzled by Francine's bent head, Lucas soon realized she was praying. He sipped from his straw while waiting for her to finish. Francine's lashes flitted as she opened her eyes, resembling the wings of a hummingbird ceasing flight.

"How about you, Francine? Sure, I put myself out there, but you could've turned me down. Why did you agree to exchange numbers?"

"As you put it, to go and see what the world is like." Francine motioned to their steaming plates on the table. "Now you're getting a taste of my life. Literally."

He didn't think twice before slicing into the chopped sirloin on his plate. When Lucas placed a chunk on his tongue, the juicy, tender flavors enthralled his taste buds. *This is definitely homestyle cooking at its finest.*

Lucas quickly started slicing another piece. "What about your flip phone? Are you not allowed to use smartphones in your community?"

"It's a personal choice. Grace tried to introduce me to social media when I owned a smartphone for a little over a year. Let's just say it was too much for me. Now I use a phone strictly for communication." She sunk her teeth into the veggie burger. Setting it back on her plate, Francine dabbed her mouth with a napkin. "We don't use smartphones after joining the church, but some of us, like my brother-in-law, have phones or computers for business purposes. But again, that's usually in progressive communities."

"Wow, you guys are far more advanced than I imagined. Given the rate of technological change, I suppose you have to be." Setting down his utensils, Lucas nibbled on the crispy end of a french fry after dipping it in ranch dressing. "Did you have misconceptions about how I live my life?"

"I had no idea you loved music as much as you do. Knowing

you had a spiritual background surprised me as well."

"About that, I love playing the hymns I grew up hearing in church. My belief, on the other hand, has shifted over time. I haven't attended church since my early school days."

Francine's eyes broke contact with him as she sagged against the booth's back cushion. "I'm sorry to hear that."

"But hey, I don't want to discourage you. If you want to share anything spiritual with me, I'm not opposed to it. I'm willing to listen." *Francine may dress simple, but I'm thinking there's a complexity about her. Maybe I could use some good words from her faith.*

After they had finished eating, their waitress came over to the table. "Will that be all for you two?" she asked, gathering their empty platters.

"I wouldn't mind having dessert." Lucas peered down at the menu, dragging his finger down the dessert list. He discovered his favorite pie flavor while browsing the selection. "Why don't we split a slice of pie? Does black raspberry pie sound good?"

Francine remained silent. When Lucas looked up, she stared at him with her mouth agape.

"Something wrong, Francine?"

"N–nothing." The tip of her nose crinkled like an accordion. "Sure, I'll have some."

The pie was brought to them, along with two forks. Francine did take a bite, though she didn't engage much in conversation. She didn't seem as enthusiastic as usual—as if her mind was elsewhere.

Dipping his fork into the pie, Lucas couldn't shake the dullness in his body. He was still curious about what was going on with Francine. But he didn't want to press her any further for the time being. *Francine seems to be contemplating whether to remain Amish, so there's a chance I can persuade her to leave. I know where to take Francine on our next date.*

Chapter 7

Francine stretched her arms as she rose from the mattress, having awoken from what seemed to be a dreamless sleep. She was drawn to the exterior light shining on the drapes, which resembled patches of embers attempting to burn through. Stifled by the lethargy of waking up on a Saturday morning, she crawled out of bed holding her phone.

Hope Grace is awake and not busy with her family right now. I keep thinking about what I should do, but I'm stuck. She dialed Grace's number while on the way to the bathroom. She hadn't had the best night's sleep with what weighed on her mind. She needed encouragement and someone to confide in.

Francine held the phone to her ear as it continued to ring. She stared into the mirror mounted above the sink. Her hair was frizzy and tangled from rolling around all night, and she had swelling under her eyes. She'd had a pleasant time with Lucas on the first few dates. However, after their last date at Der Dutchman, Lucas brought up Francine's interest in sightseeing in Tampa. He asked if he could drive her there tonight. Despite her desire to see a new place, Francine was now out of her comfort zone.

"Frannie, hi!" Grace answered. "It's been a while. How are things going in sunny Sarasota?"

"Hello, Grace. It's going well, I guess." Preferring some privacy, Francine shut the bathroom door. "Okay, the truth is, I'm stressed about something and need some advice, and you were the first person who came to mind. Lucas is driving me to Tampa for supper. I trust Lucas enough to ride with him, but he's keeping our venue a secret. There aren't many Amish people strolling about Tampa, so I'm feeling a bit self-conscious."

"Francine, wear whatever makes you feel comfortable. If it's out of concern for what Lucas may think, then I wouldn't recommend wearing anything other than your own clothing."

"Lucas didn't suggest my Amish clothes are a problem, but I'm still unsure what to do. I don't really know who Lucas is, and sometimes I wonder if I'm potentially playing with fire." Francine shifted her stance along the floor tiles as her legs began to tremble. "I keep questioning why I'm going along with this. Do I truly feel compelled to interact with him, or am I just deluding myself?"

"It could be both of those things. Whether we choose to get into situations or they are brought to us, God allows us to go through them for a purpose. Whatever happens, I have no doubt He'll provide you with answers, and you will come to terms with your reasons soon. Continue concentrating on the present. If you don't expect Lucas to change, you shouldn't worry about changing for him. You two agreed that this was only a casual relationship, so do your best not to be anxious, all right?"

Francine sighed as she leaned against the sink. "You were the right person to talk to. Thank you, Grace."

"You can always count on me, Frannie. Even when we're hours and miles apart." A squeak from a young child could be heard in the background. "I have to go. My niece is right at my hip and wants me to play with her after breakfast. Hope it goes well for you tonight."

"Thank you again, Grace. Have a good time with your family."

"No problem. And remember, don't act on anything until you hear Him." The line went silent after Grace said goodbye.

Next to the faucet, Francine pumped out some lotion and applied it to her hands. *I know how I can feel comfortable. I'll keep my hair down and wear one of my favorite traditional Amish dresses. That way I won't completely stick out in a crowd. The perfect compromise.*

Her fingers slipped off the doorknob as she tried to grab it. Francine clenched the knob and twisted her wrist, but despite her effort, she was unable to rotate it.

"Why didn't I open the door first before putting lotion on my hands?" She turned on the faucet and pressed her palm on the spout. "It riles me so."

Then, feeling the need for a cup of coffee, she hurried to the kitchen. She had until the evening before Lucas would pick her up. For the time being, Francine wanted to unwind and savor the peaceful morning. Before removing the jar of coffee from the upper cabinet, she glanced at the sand dollar legend.

Her hands quivered as she reached for a mug. *Lord, please keep me safe when I'm out tonight. Give me the strength to not be fretful.*

Tampa, Florida

Once Lucas found a parking space, they got out of the car. Francine's eyes locked on the view from above. The skyline was gray with a white background and sporadic charcoal blotches of fluff. It dawned on her where they were. The street's glitzy billboard revealed it.

"C–casino?" Francine flinched. "Why a casino?"

"My pals and I hang out here Saturday evenings, and I thought it would be great for you to meet them."

"I see." Something gnawed at Francine's stomach. "Look,

Lucas, I don't think this is a good idea. I've never been to a casino, and I never had any intentions of going to one either."

"Do you not trust the people I hang out with?"

"Well, I haven't met them yet."

"Then you won't know until you do. In the meantime, you can put your trust in me." He held a hand out to her. "It'll be fine, Francine. I promise."

Gathering the courage to do so, she took Lucas' hand. *I guess it'll be okay. I can find ways to enjoy my time here if I'm not doing anything I'm uncomfortable with.*

As they drew near the entrance, the doors swished open, accompanied by the banter of people in the foyer. Francine rummaged through her tote for her wallet as she approached the casino's threshold. Providing her state identification wasn't the norm for Francine. She hadn't learned to drive, nor did she show her identification card often.

Lucas proceeded after showing his license, and Francine followed suit. She had a lot to take in at that moment. As they walked by, people were playing at tables. One brunette lady released the dice, but they sailed past the table and landed on the geometrically patterned carpet.

They navigated through slot machines to a bar lined with padded stools. A group of young men sat in the middle of the bar, and one of them waved in their direction.

"Hey, look who it is!" the person who waved hollered out. "And he brought someone with him. Who's your friend, Louie?"

"Wait a minute—isn't that the Amish girl? The dress is a dead giveaway," one of the other friends remarked, pushing up the sunglasses he wore on his head.

Lucas motioned to her. "Guys, this is Francine. Francine, this is Marvin, Barry, and Jim."

"Nice to meet you all." She shook hands with two of them, but the one wearing the sunglasses didn't offer. "You all seem to know a little bit about me already."

"Lucas has mentioned you. He likes you a lot." Jim poked Lucas as he snickered.

"The night is young, but it won't be for long. Let's get a round of beers going." Marvin slapped a hand on a nearby stool, implying that they should sit down.

Francine shook her head. "A club soda is fine for me. I'm not too keen on drinking."

Barry, who didn't shake her hand, let out an unruly laugh. "Because of your Amish background, I bet. I heard some of you let loose on that rumspringa thing, so why not do the same?"

"Enough, Barry," Lucas interjected. "If she doesn't want to drink, then that's the end of it."

"Of course, a lightweight like you would say that." Barry lowered his glasses and crossed his arms.

They all groaned in response, and Francine took a seat at the bar next to Lucas. After ordering drinks, Lucas' friends had no trouble striking up a conversation with Francine. They, like Lucas, were intrigued by her Amish heritage but were mostly respectful in their questions. Compared to when she first entered the space, she was more at ease.

Francine mentioned she would be in Florida for a couple more weeks and was eager to return to Indiana. That was true, and she especially wondered how Geneva was doing with Rodney at the bookstore. Francine also considered Alana, curious to know how her time with Ben was going, and realized she hadn't spoken with her parents since the first week in Sarasota. Her thoughts changed direction as she briefly remembered the date at Der Dutchman and how Lucas' favorite pie was the same as Matthew's.

Francine began to miss home and was relieved when Lucas took over the interaction. Some of what they were saying was muffled by raucous cheering and laughter, but Francine didn't mind.

This entire situation is daunting. But Lucas' friends are nice and easy to talk to. Except for the one guy. Francine eyed Barry swigging from the glass bottle's narrow neck. *I have a hunch he's the reason why Lucas asked those questions during our dates. But I should give Barry a chance. Perhaps he's one of those people who takes time to warm up to.*

~

Francine chatted with Marvin and Jim at the bar while Lucas stood with Barry out of earshot.

Lucas was ecstatic that Francine seemed to be getting along with his buddies. He would catch her brushing her light brown hair behind her shoulders. Francine gave off the impression that she could easily fit into his lifestyle. Barry, though, vehemently disagreed.

"You may as well hand over your money tonight, Lucas."

"I don't think so. Francine told me her community is not like how it's portrayed on TV. Makes sense, since reality shows are exaggerated." Backing up on his heels, Lucas swayed. "Her community isn't strict, but I still think she will choose to leave. Francine says her parents would support whatever decision she made."

Barry huffed. "Her upbringing has taken refuge in her head. Look at her. She wore the clothes, didn't drink, and went on and on about how excited she was to go home. Her hair and nails don't fool me, Lucas. I had a hunch someone like her wouldn't change."

"Is that why you were set on that bet? Not because you cared about her circumstances?"

"Don't get the wrong impression. I care, but I knew this bet would be a breeze. I'm sorry to break it to you, but she'll never come to terms with how much better our lives are."

Lucas pinched the bridge of his nose, then dragged his fingers to the tip. "Maybe we should call it off then. Honestly, it was a stupid bet to make."

"Hey, you must hold true to your part of the deal. If you want to end this, then cough up your wager." Barry brushed his oily dark hair away from his face.

Lucas' shoulders shuddered. He wanted to retaliate, but the bet was what kept him from doing so. Lucas would be out a significant sum of money, and he knew having Barry's casino earnings would put him ahead.

He turned from Barry, then beelined toward Francine, nudging her. "Hey, Francine. Can I talk to you for a second?"

Francine rose from the stool without hesitation. She followed him away from the bar, and Lucas came to a halt once they were out of sight of his friends.

Her forehead lines accentuated. "What's wrong, Lucas?"

"You said before you were curious about my life, right?" He positioned himself in front of one of the slot machines. "Try this out; then you'll gain a better understanding."

"You want me to gamble?"

"We're at a casino. What were you expecting? Come on, Francine. Just try it."

"Lucas, I was fine with meeting your friends, but pressuring me to gamble is taking it too far."

"What's the big deal? The whole point of being at a casino is to gamble. You can't walk into this place and not play something."

"The 'big deal' is I don't want to. I told you I had no interest in going to a casino. You said I could trust you, and now you're stepping over a line."

"Wow, Barry's right. You are well entrenched in your simplistic outlook, Francine."

Lucas spoke without thinking, and Francine's response to his words made the hairs on his neck stand on end.

She clenched the center of her dress, and her mauve lips formed a straight line. "I want to leave. If you won't drive me back to Sarasota, I'll phone Violet for a ride, and you can carry on playing the slots."

He stuffed his hands into his jeans pockets, circling his key ring with one finger. "No, I'll take you back to your sister's house."

And with that, the evening came to an end. Lucas didn't say goodbye to his friends, didn't take Francine's soft-skinned hand in his, and couldn't think of anything else to say to her. Silence hung between them. As they approached Lucas' vehicle, they felt the crisp air of dusk.

The car ride back was uneventful, but Francine's silence was out of character. Lucas could sense that her discomfort came from a belief that what he'd done that evening was unacceptable. As they neared the exit to Sarasota on the freeway, Lucas deliberated while gripping the steering wheel.

I should not have tried to persuade Francine to play the slot machines. All this for a bet, and now I might have put my future relationship with her in jeopardy.

When he came to a stop at a red light, he gave her a brief glance. Francine had her head tilted toward the window, and the lights from nearby buildings cascaded on her.

I'll give her some space tomorrow. I want to go on another date with Francine, but I get it if she doesn't want to see me anymore.

Chapter 8

Lido Beach

Lucas still reeled from what had happened at the casino last night. He didn't try to get ahold of Francine but wanted to, which was why he was surprised when Francine called him later in the day. It was during his shift, but there was a lull in the flow of people approaching the concession, so Francine's phone call didn't interfere with his work. She asked if they could talk in person after Lucas finished working.

As the day drew to a close, he started to feel anxious. Lucas wasn't looking forward to Francine breaking things off with him, but he expected it. She'd been upset with him after the way he had urged her to sit at a slot machine, although he wasn't sure why exactly. Perhaps the Amish were not allowed to gamble, and Francine was concerned about what her family would think if they found out.

It didn't help that Barry incentivized me. I can't believe I let him get to me. He noted the food products needing to be resupplied. *Whatever the reason, I didn't need to be so forceful in my approach.*

Lucas jerked out from behind the concession stand as soon as he caught sight of Francine. She wore her hair tied back but without her usual cone-shaped hat. The dark red fabric of her Amish dress highlighted her freckled skin.

"Francine, about what happened, I—"

"Lucas, before you say anything, I need to get something off my chest." She sidestepped away from the counter but kept her gaze on him. "Let's sit on the beach. That way, we'll have a good view of the sun setting while we talk."

He gripped the neckline of his shirt. "Sounds good to me."

After closing the concession stand, Lucas collected his possessions, which he could fit in the pocket of his jeans. He wandered along with Francine but held a respectful distance. To reach the sandy grounds, they crossed through the gap where the shrubs parted. Dispersed around the beach were groups of people seated either in folding chairs or on the sand. They made their way over to a spot that was midway from the water's edge.

Francine bent down to the white grains of sand, setting down her massive bag next to her hip. She motioned for him to take a seat beside her, and as soon as he did, Lucas turned his attention to the horizon as the sun started to set below the ocean. For some time, they sat in silence as the sky gradually shifted from turquoise to peach tones. Finally, Francine nudged his arm and her voice broke the hush.

"Remember at Der Dutchman when you asked me why I agreed to date you? I was attempting to move on and didn't want to discuss it because it hurt so much." Francine folded her arms. "The truth is, I had just gotten out of a two-year relationship."

Lucas went slack-jawed at the revelation. "Two years?"

She nodded. "We ended our relationship in January."

"Wow, that's pretty soon after a break-up." He stifled a gasp. "Hold on a second—you're not telling me that I was a rebound, are you?"

She hunched her shoulders. "Admittedly, yes. You were a way to keep my mind from dwelling on my pain."

"Spending two years with someone is a long time. Why did you break up after being together for so long?" Lucas asked.

"I thought Matthew and I were going to get married and join the church together. It seemed like that's what he wanted too. He did want to marry me, but. . ." Francine grimaced, giving her head a small shake. "Matthew felt led to become a missionary and understood that remaining Amish would restrict his ability to minister. When he asked me to accompany him, it didn't sit well at the time. I believed staying in my community was the right decision for me."

"But why did you agree to go out with me if you don't want to leave your community?"

"I had doubts that breaking up with Matthew was the right choice. I wanted to see what the English life was like without the commitment. After last night, I may have gotten my answer." She lifted her arms briefly, then lowered them onto her lap. "I didn't want to gamble because I know how addictive it can be, to the point of enticing others to join you. As with any addiction, it's difficult to pull away from it once you've had a taste."

His chest swelled with the sensation of a kerosene heater. Francine, despite her curiosity, had no intention of leaving her Indiana community. That meant his casino winnings for the month would be thrown out the window. And what did she mean by saying gambling was an addiction? Gambling could be risky at times, but he believed it could also be beneficial. Still, it had gotten him into trouble before, and this situation was evidence of that.

Francine's lips quivered. "I'm sorry for not being upfront with you earlier, Lucas."

Being angry with her for not divulging something so private

would be foolish, and Francine was unaware of the bet he had made with Barry. Besides, Lucas wasn't mad about Francine wanting to stay Amish. He thought it was commendable that she stayed loyal to her beliefs.

"We met a few weeks ago, so who you were with before wasn't really my business. It was personal, and now I understand why you didn't like it when I questioned you too much. I'm sorry for what I said last night and for pressuring you to gamble."

She gave him a weightless stare with her eyes half closed. "Thank you, Lucas. I'm glad we can both be honest with one another."

Those words pricked him to the core. "Yeah, me too. You know what they say—honesty is the best policy." He cleared his throat. "I made it sound horrible last night, but nonetheless, I'm interested. How do you keep your behavior on such a firm base, Francine?"

"Whenever I have a gut feeling about something, I know that feeling of conviction comes from the Lord." Francine plucked a sand dollar from the bag of shells. "There's a reason why sand dollars resonate with me. I keep a little version of the 'Legend of the Sand Dollar' in my bag, but I'll quickly summarize what a sand dollar represents." She traced a finger along one of the edge holes. "These four holes represent when Jesus was affixed to the cross. The middle hole reflects the spear wound inflicted by a Roman soldier. Then, there's the doves." She presented the tiny birds in the crook of her hand after breaking the shell into fragments. "Within this shell, when broken, are five doves that emphasize peace and love. I recall the legend each time I find a sand dollar. It makes me think of Jesus' sacrifice, and that reminds me to depend on Him."

Lucas mulled over Francine's words, fixing his gaze on the doves resting in the center of her hand. He knew the story of Jesus and had played hymns on his violin countless times. Perhaps it was Francine's evident vulnerability that affected him. He'd never met anyone who seemed to be deeply reliant on their faith before.

She slid the sand dollar pieces back into the shell collection. "I know you don't go to church anymore, so I don't want to press you to listen to any of this."

"No, like I said before, I'm all ears. You've certainly piqued my curiosity with that sand dollar legend."

"We've both seemed to have piqued the other's curiosity, haven't we?" Francine smirked. "Well, I have something else that may answer more of your questions." She reached into her bag and pulled out a small but dense book, handing it to him. "Here's a pocket version of the New Testament. I want you to have it. It's helped me when I've needed it most."

Lucas thanked Francine and tucked the Bible into the front pocket of his jeans. His eyes trailed back to the water. The remaining sunlight shimmered on the ocean's surface. The brilliance of the day had given way to the freshness of the night.

In that moment, he took a chance and stroked his palm along the sand, brushing Francine's knuckles. She twisted her head to him wide eyed, but her smile was unwavering. She entwined his fingers in hers and rested her head on his shoulder. Her hair gave off a subtle scent of lavender. His heart rate increased, and he trembled a bit. But the frigid air kept him from becoming too engrossed in the moment.

"So, you okay if we continue where we left off?"

"You're sure you want to, Lucas? I talked your ear off for a while."

"Oh, is that why you did that? You can't get rid of me that easily." Lucas snickered. "I'm sure. You're leaving soon, right? I'd like to enjoy your company before you head back to Indiana."

Francine snuggled against his shoulder and sighed. "Likewise."

The sun descended, and the ocean's waves beating on the shore were all that remained.

Sarasota

Lucas unlocked the door to his apartment around ten o'clock that night. The entire living area was enveloped in darkness.

He slipped out his phone and used the light from it to make his way through the pitch-black room. Fortunately, there wasn't much Lucas could collide with. Aside from his room, the furniture in his flat was a tiny bookcase next to a solitary lounge chair in the living area.

As he entered his bedroom, Lucas kicked off his sandals and collapsed face-first onto the mattress. Between working at the concession stand and Francine expressing her situation to him, the day had done a number on him. Lucas wanted to unwind for the time being because there was a lot of information to take in. He rolled onto his back, staring toward the ceiling. He attempted to concentrate his thoughts on getting up early tomorrow for another day of work, but moments of his conversation with Francine lingered in his mind.

He had been resting on the pocket Bible Francine gave him, so he pulled it out of his pocket and held it up, barely able to see it in the dark. Lucas wasn't sure if he should read it. Granted, his family had attended church when he was a young child, so he didn't have any hard feelings against it. His parents stopped attending soon after his grandfather died, and Lucas did the same. Lucas had given some thought to attending services again now that he was living alone, but he had always shelved the idea. Too much was on his plate for him to find time for it.

He placed the book on the pillow near his head. The memory

of the bet he made with Barry wormed its way into his thoughts. He pressed his fingers against his temples.

I figured it would be no hassle to make Francine give up on being Amish. Lucas' throat thickened. *Why did I agree to that stupid bet? How could I even think of doing that to her?*

He murmured, "I wonder if this guilt toward trying to change Francine is my 'gut feeling.' "

Out of curiosity, Lucas flipped open the pocket Bible, then took out his phone to illuminate the tiny print on the pages. He read several passages, but eventually a wave of fatigue washed over him, and he drifted to sleep.

Chapter 9

For dinner the following weekend, Francine invited Lucas to have supper at her sister's home. Dan and Violet brought pizza from a nearby restaurant and placed the boxes on the kitchen counter. The relaxed atmosphere surprised Lucas, but it also quelled his nerves. He was out of his element, but it was fair, given that Lucas had taken Francine to a casino. Being around her family wasn't anything like hanging out with his friends.

Francine said her family would enjoy hearing him play the violin, so he brought it along to perform once they had finished eating. Accustomed to performing in front of strangers, Lucas was not at all nervous.

"Someone once stole the money from my case as I was playing along the streets of St. Armand's Circle. It was a respectable amount too, but I kept on going and made back at least half of what was taken." Lucas bit into a slice of margarita pizza. The cheese stretched out, so he severed the mozzarella string with his front teeth.

Dan leaned forward, wiping his hand on a napkin. "People are unbelievable at times. It's incredible how some can act on compulsive ideas without taking the situation personally. Why treat someone else like that if you don't want to be treated that way yourself?"

Violet nodded. "It's sad when someone covets enough to take what they haven't worked for."

Dan's words caused Lucas to cringe inwardly, and he thought about the bet that was still on with Barry. Lucas eyed Francine with his peripheral vision, knowing full well he had done something horrible in connection to her, and she knew nothing of it.

Lucas kept the conversation going for the time being, saying he was relieved to have his violin with him. Even though it was a student violin, it was the first one he'd owned. The strings Lucas had removed when he first purchased new strings remained in the case. Lucas even shared about times when he was heckled at St. Armand's Circle, admitting they happened more often than he'd prefer. Despite this, he received favorable feedback and particularly liked it when people approached him with delight or curiosity. The streets were hectic, but that didn't stop him from driving over there every week and performing.

They sat in the living room after everyone had finished eating. Lucas moved his bow across the strings, accompanied by the steady rain pattering against the window. His pant pocket buzzed against his leg. It had been vibrating intermittently all evening. He had sent a message to his buddies informing them that he wouldn't be driving to the casino that night. Lucas was met with understanding responses—except for one recipient.

He's been a real thorn in my side. Lucas thought. *You can keep texting and calling me all night, Barry, but I'm not leaving to drive to Tampa. I haven't had this much fun since I performed my first solo in high school orchestra.*

Lucas reached the end of the song and positioned his instrument by his side. As Francine's family applauded him, he leaned forward for a bow.

John, on the other hand, stood up from the couch, fumbling

with a pen cradled in his right suspender. "Classical playing is nice and all, but can you fiddle with that violin?"

Lucas smirked and shifted the instrument back under his chin. With a bent neck, he clamped down on the head rest, which pressed against his left collar bone. "You'd better believe I can."

He began stomping his foot on the wooden floor of the living room, and Francine's family followed suit, clapping their hands to the beat. The next song Lucas played was "I Saw the Light." When the violinist at Lucas' previous church played the song, the joyful gospel tune became one of his favorites to listen to on a Sunday morning. His hand muscles cramped up from vigorous playing, but he kept smiling and swaying his head. It was well worth it for him to be able to produce such high-quality notes from his modest instrument.

Straightaway, when he heard a voice puncturing through his music, Lucas locked eyes with Francine. He hadn't heard her sing before. Francine's voice was a smidge higher in volume than the violin, and each word before a breath had a subtle vibrato. He was in awe, but it didn't stop his motion. It heightened it.

The cheers of Francine's family burst through the music as they continued to clap in time with Lucas' set rhythm. He was no longer solely fiddling. Driven by the tremendous positive vibrations encircling him, his limbs flowed seamlessly. It was as if gravity was nonexistent. Even his playing-related discomfort wasn't at the forefront anymore. Francine's vocals were the only thing present, and he accompanied her voice. For the first time, Lucas took in each word.

With one more vibrato formed by his shuddering finger, Lucas raised his bow from the strings. When he glanced over at Francine, she rose to her feet. She beamed as she brought up her hands to form a steeple. Her eyes gleamed like a cave of aventurine stones.

He slid his instrument back into its case before pressing his hand to the center of his chest. Exhaustion from playing finally took hold. *Before, those words had no impact, but now the lyrics are stirring something in me. I'm beginning to wonder if I'm finally seeing the light. And Francine is helping me welcome it in.*

Sarasota

It was the brink of a new day by the time Lucas got back to his apartment. He shuffled into his room, kicking off his sandals before settling into his bed. It was like any other night—except that it wasn't.

He rolled over to the nightstand and snatched one of the sand dollars Francine had given him. It was the one she'd placed in his violin case. What Lucas felt now reminded him of the night Francine let down her guard and expressed more of herself. She now seemed self-assured enough to sing along with him. Affected by her, Lucas couldn't brush his feelings aside.

There's no doubt in my mind that I have feelings for Francine. My life has improved in the short time I've known her, but am I meant to be with Francine for the rest of my life? Lucas ran his finger along the shell's edge. *If so, would it mean asking her to leave the Amish faith? She's not set on it right now, but maybe later? Either that, or I'd have to become Amish, which would not be easy.* His eyes lingered on the ceiling as he exhaled. *Yet everyone knew how to have fun this evening. It was the most incredible evening, from conversing during dinner to playing for them. Most people are overly invested in superficial forms of entertainment. It's not common to meet someone who embraces the simplicity of things. Being Amish may not be so bad. It could even be the change I've been searching for in my life.* He chuckled. *I can only be sure if I keep getting to know Francine. That feels right, like the gut instinct she described.*

The sound of pounding shattered Lucas' peaceful contemplation. It resonated from the confines of his bedroom.

He put the sand dollar on his pillow before rushing to the door. *It's one o'clock in the morning. Who would be banging on my door at this hour?* Lucas peered through the peephole. *Oh, great. It's Barry.* Reluctantly, Lucas unbolted the door.

"Lucas, why weren't you at the casino with the rest of us?" Without being invited in, Barry stepped by Lucas and collided with his shoulder.

"Please, come on in, I guess." Lucas rubbed his sore shoulder and shut the door. "I told you why I wasn't going to be there tonight."

"You're still trying to convince that Amish girl to leave? Since we both know that's not going to happen, I won the bet. How am I supposed to reap the benefits when you're not putting in the full month?"

"Yikes, Barry. You're really desperate for money, aren't you?"

"Big talk for someone living in a dinky apartment." Barry's hand jerked toward the living area. "You're not exactly living it up in a penthouse while sipping mai tais by the pool. You don't even have any furniture here. It's pathetic."

Lucas' insides constricted, and an adrenaline rush swept across his upper body. "Frankly, I didn't want to gamble to begin with. You were the one who talked me into it, even after I told you I wasn't interested."

Barry grunted. "Nobody can force you into something you don't want to do. You kept gambling because you said it helped pay your rent."

"I'll admit that gambling did help keep me going. It took what I made on the street and turned it into something much more. But it also caused me to dip into what I earned at work." Lucas cuffed his shirt sleeves. "We don't need to get slammed and waste time every weekend trying to make a profit, Barry."

Barry's sneer contorted into something more primal. His nostrils flared, and he let out a snarling yell before kicking his sneaker against the door. It left muddy scuff marks behind.

Lucas' brow vein strained. "Hey now, I intend to get my security deposit back when I decide to find a new place."

"You won't be moving out of here at this rate." He halted his door kicking and met Lucas' eyes. "What about that fancy-schmancy violin you wanted? Kissing that goodbye too?"

"People value my abilities with what I already have, so I can postpone purchasing my ideal violin."

"That Amish girl is to blame for your change of heart. So what are you going to do? Move to Amish land? Sell your car and luxuries for horses and oil lamps? You're being ridiculous." Barry swept his hair away from his face. Lucas was unable to determine if Barry's black strands were glossy because of the rain or his hair gel.

"Maybe I am. But like you said, nobody can force you to do something you don't want to do."

Barry resembled a boiling teakettle with steam seeping out of the spout. He flicked his hand in the air. "Do what you want. I could care less as long as you pay me."

"It's 'couldn't care less,' and I'm not giving you that money."

"What?" Barry hissed.

"I said it at the casino. It was a dumb bet. Trying to earn money at someone else's expense is tainted. So no, I'm not rewarding that kind of behavior."

Barry raised his finger and pointed at Lucas. "I warned you about this. I knew she would do this to you."

"Really, Barry?" Lucas' internal temperature rose. He took a step closer to Barry, purposefully bursting his personal bubble.

"Since you knew how this would pan out, it was stupid for you to make that bet then, wasn't it?"

"You'll regret this. Mark my words." Barry turned away and took his leave, but not before taking one more kick at the entry.

"Yeah, well, don't let my banged-up door hit you on the way out."

The apartment's walls quaked as it slammed. Lucas hoped that none of his neighbors would complain about the commotion to their landlord. He could picture her showing up at his place at daybreak and grilling him.

Come on, Barry. You can't go around pretending to be a mafia member. Lucas squeezed his hands together behind his back. *But I'm glad I finally gathered the courage to speak my mind. This whole time, I didn't want to deal with his temper. At this point, I don't care. Barry needs to learn to stop dragging others down with him.*

Chapter 10

St. Armand's Circle

Lucas had driven Francine back to Lido Beach, where they spent a couple of hours searching for more sand dollars along the shore. They returned to Café L'Europe, the restaurant where they had their first date. It was almost a replication of that night, except Francine was less nervous. Why would she be when she had grown so fond of the person she had met a month ago?

Like they had before, Lucas got his violin case out of his vehicle, brought it over to the storefronts, and began performing the night away. This time, Lucas played exclusively hymns and gospel music. Even as he played, Lucas waved Francine over and encouraged her to join him. Francine wasn't sure, but when Lucas strode over to her, moving his bow and fingers methodically on the strings, she couldn't refuse. Although it was nerve racking to sing in front of people, seeing them around her with pleasant faces helped Francine loosen up.

After a while, Francine's vocal cords strained, so she stopped and went to sit on a nearby bench. She listened to Lucas' music, humming and swaying her dangling legs to the beat.

Once Lucas finished, he shut his case and carried it over to where Francine was seated. He put his violin case down by the bench, opened it, and nestled his bow and violin on the velvet.

"That's about all the playing I can muster tonight." He wiped off the sheen of sweat on his forehead. "I'm beat."

"I don't blame you, Lucas. You were putting on quite a performance. It may have been the best one I've seen from you."

"Actually, the performance I gave at your sister's place was the best I've given in a while."

Francine moistened her lips. "Really?"

"Yeah, that sure was a fun time with your family. I may not have known them long, but they seem like good company."

"I think you won them over with your fiddling. I know how much you want an expensive violin, but you play the one you have wonderfully. It's the person holding the instrument that makes the instrument valuable."

Lucas scooted forward, his hand resting on his knee. "Now I'm getting all flustered. What about you? You said you don't sing, But that beautiful voice of yours disproves that."

"Our community has singing groups, and I sing in church, so I have some experience. I just mentioned that I don't have the best singing voice."

"It's fine to take a compliment every now and then." He nudged her arm with his elbow.

The arch of Francine's nose heated up. "I'm working hard not to be boastful because it can lead to pride, which leads to a lack of gratitude. But thank you for your kind words."

"You see, that's one of the reasons I admire you, Francine. You stay true to yourself regardless of what's directed at you. Personally, I would like to do that as well. I need to work on understanding how my actions and words may affect those around me."

His sentiments caused Francine's heart to skip a little. She had been moved by Lucas' candor, and her first impression of him had undoubtedly changed.

"But I will admit, it was hard to get up the next day after visiting with your family. I wasn't expecting us to chat past twelve. You Amish know how to hold a conversation."

"Amish and Mennonite, Lucas." She stifled a giggle. "I'm glad you had fun. Honestly, I wish we had more time together before I head home. This month went by much faster than I expected."

"We still have one week, so if things go well, we might be able to make this work. We can stay in touch, and I could even pay you a visit sometime soon." He slung his arm over her shoulder. "I'll bring my violin along with me, and I can perform for your friends and relatives back home. What do you think, Francine?"

She gave the bench leg a tap with her heel. "I've had a good time with you, and I really want to see what the future holds for us, but it feels like I should wait and not make any hasty decisions. But I wouldn't mind keeping in contact, so we'll see."

Lucas didn't pull his arm away, but he did relieve the pressure on the back of her neck. "No, I get it. We can ease into this, so don't worry."

Francine straightened out a crease in her dress. *I feel at ease with him during moments like these, but I'm still unsure about a lot of things. That gravitational pull to him is prevalent, and I don't want to stop talking to him, but am I really meant to be with Lucas? Whatever the reason, I know Lucas was placed in my life with purpose. Until I have an answer as to why, I want to savor this moment and the last week with him.*

"Hey, Lucas."

Francine recognized the voice straight away. She looked up and saw one of Lucas' friends she had met at the casino. The shadows of dusk underlined his angular facial features. His teeth were the same tone of ivory as the crescent moon overhead.

Lucas stood up from the bench, his arms folded. "Fancy seeing you here, Barry. You don't usually come over to Lido."

"Siesta's parking lot was packed, and I know you're here in the evening, so I thought I'd swing by." Barry slapped Lucas on the back. "By the way, buddy, you haven't paid me for our bet."

Lucas kneaded his T-shirt neckline. "I told you, Barry. I'm not paying you."

"You two made a bet?" Francine asked.

"Didn't Lucas tell you? That makes sense. It was a terrible bet to agree to."

Lucas scowled. "Shut your mouth, Barry."

"It's not my fault you weren't honest with her." Tsking, Barry turned to face Francine with a wide grin. "Lucas agreed to a wager to make you leave your Amish community."

A sharp chill swept through Francine. She had trouble comprehending what Barry had said as her breaths grew shallow. *Did I hear that correctly?*

"And all for a pricey instrument. Can you believe that guy?"

"Is this true, Lucas?" She twiddled with her kapp's ties.

Lucas dipped his chin. "It's true."

Many questions materialized in Francine's mind at once, and she longed to ask more. She tried to suppress her instant reaction before deciding what to say. Unfortunately, there wasn't enough time to do so.

"Well, since you won't pay me. . ." Barry snagged the violin case by the handle. "I'll take this as compensation."

"Hey—" Barry shoved Lucas, knocking him to the ground.

"Lucas!" Francine crouched down next to him. "Are you all right?"

He winced. "I'm fine, but Francine, I need to clear some things up."

"We can talk later. We need to get your violin back from that *dummkopp*." Francine extended her hand to help Lucas stand.

He sprang up while grasping her hand, and his rust-colored curls bounced along with him. Lucas didn't hesitate; he took off at full speed, and Francine followed.

Barry weaved his way through the crowd. Due to the awkward shape of the case, he pinballed to and fro whenever he bumped into anyone. It slowed him down, but once Lucas was on his tail, Barry picked up the pace.

"Barry, this isn't funny!" Lucas hollered.

"What's not funny is you backing out of our deal!"

While Barry was preoccupied with Lucas, Francine pushed against the concrete with all her might, matching Barry's stride. She tried to grasp the case but was unable to get a good hold of it.

Barry snorted. "Lucas wagered against you. Why help him?"

"What he did was wrong, but you played a part. And what you're doing now is also wrong."

Francine made another attempt to take the case, but Barry wasn't above playing dirty. He thrust the case into her midsection and she tumbled to the curb. The roadway stones scratched her skin. Lost in her surroundings, Francine heard Lucas shout her name and saw him standing by her.

"Are you badly hurt?" Lucas grasped her arm and gently pulled her up.

"I'm fine, Lucas. Just scuffed my ankle is all."

They turned to face Barry, who had stopped running and had begun taunting them with his gestures.

"You vindictive little—" Lucas muttered. "You made a big mistake by stopping."

Barry advanced past the column of statues as they carried on after him. Granted, Barry didn't get far before whacking the case against the streetlight's base. The case unhinged, and the violin spilled out. *Berkring!* The hollow instrument resonated as it made contact with the pavement.

Francine brought a hand up to her mouth, shocked by what she'd seen and heard. Francine sensed Lucas was distraught. He ran full force toward Barry.

"I was going to sell it to make some money, but I guess this will suffice. You've taken my winnings, and I've taken your violin. We're now even."

Lucas huddled on the pavement, scrounging up his violin's dismantled pieces. "We're done, Barry." His voice wavered. "I no longer want anything to do with you."

Barry scoffed but didn't utter another word. He whirled around and sprinted away until he was no longer visible in the midst of the crowd.

"I'm so sorry," Francine said under her breath.

"I'll just have to go to the music store and buy another violin." Lucas situated the instrument's pieces in the case and sighed as he closed it.

As her thoughts settled, Francine's heartbeat seemed to slow down. "You should be able to since you didn't give Barry his money."

"Francine, about that bet, Barry coaxed me into it by telling me how hard life is for Amish people, so I figured I'd be helping you while—"

"It doesn't matter how you came to that decision, Lucas. What matters is you did." Francine drew her arms in, with elbows pressing against her ribs on both sides. "And to hear it from Barry. Even if you hadn't kept that from me, I would be disappointed, but I would respect you more for being truthful."

"I know what I did was wrong, but that's why I called it quits and refused to pay him."

Her shoulders trembled. "Is that why you showed interest in my faith? Because of the bet?"

"No, Francine. That wager was made after I asked you out. When I first met you, I was drawn to you for reasons I couldn't explain. Now I know why, and I remain interested."

"Okay, so it wasn't because of the bet, but are you sure it's not because of us dating? Do you want to please your curiosity for me or for yourself?"

Lucas' mouth opened, but no words formed. Although it was dark, the moonlight was bright. His face had become slack, and his eyes looked toward the bustling streets.

"We both have a lot of thinking to do before we decide on moving forward." Her vision became hazy. "I'll call Violet to come get me."

She started to leave him, but Lucas called her name. Francine lingered, anticipating his response.

"For what it's worth, thank you for trying to get my violin back from Barry."

Francine couldn't reply without losing her composure. She kept on walking down the sidewalk, digging her phone out of her tote and flipping it open.

Sarasota

Upon entering his apartment, Lucas peeled off his sandals. He set the violin case on the floor, shuddering at the reality of his violin split in half.

Lucas sank into the cushion of his living room chair. He reached into his pocket and pulled out a sand dollar he had found on the beach with Francine. Lucas raised his other hand and applied pressure with both thumbs on the shell. With a smidge of force, the shell snapped like a delicate piece of china.

This was mostly Barry's fault, but I didn't have to agree to the bet, and I should have told Francine about it. I thought it didn't matter because I called it off, but Barry used that against me. If I had been honest with her, then it wouldn't have turned out this way. Francine took a chance by telling me about her previous relationship, and I could have come clean with her too.

As he clasped the dove-shaped pieces, Lucas was brought back to the moment Francine had told him the sand dollar legend. Lucas thought it was odd the teeth of sand dollars resembled, of all things, doves. He leaned toward the small table beside him. Setting aside the sand dollar shell, he placed the doves on the surface.

"Within this shell, when broken, are five doves that emphasize peace and love." Gingerly, Lucas arranged the five doves into a star.

He focused his attention on the window, which was obscured by the curtain. He rose from the chair and parted the drapes. The sky was void of clouds. Clusters of stars lit the navy blue sky. At that moment, Lucas was hit with a feeling of weightlessness. The sensation was out of body, as if he were no longer present on earth. He covered his eyes, allowing his emotions to flow.

Please, God. Let me know where to go from here. I am willing to follow You, so I will do my best to lean on You from this moment forward. You've always been present in my life, and I'm glad I can finally feel Your presence.

Chapter 11

Lido Beach

Francine got out of Violet's vehicle on the passenger side. It had been a couple days since the events at St. Armand's Circle. She'd spent those days sorting through her clothes in the guest room closet and stowing away the seashells she found on Lido.

While placing the shells in bags, Francine picked out a sand dollar and wondered about Lucas. She was aware they needed to have a resolution and shouldn't leave their final exchange as it was. The following day, Lucas contacted her, and Francine suggested they meet. They arranged to talk things over on Lido's shoreline.

"I pray for the best outcome for you both, Francine," Violet said while adjusting the air conditioning in her car.

"Me too, Violet. Thank you."

As Violet drove off, Francine inhaled oxygen into her lungs and raised her gaze to the heavens. The clouds resembled a snowbank, with pale gray crevasses creasing the surface. Francine referred to Philippians 4:6, which had been the subject of her recent prayers. "Be anxious for nothing, but in everything by prayer and supplication, with thanksgiving, let your requests be made known to God." *Being anxious is a natural part of being human*, she thought. *But I cannot allow it to sway me from what needs to be done. I know this is the right decision, and I need to follow through.*

She moved toward the seating area near the concessions but saw no sign of Lucas behind the counter.

Where is he? Lucas should be working here today.

As she turned to face the building where the restrooms were, she felt a tap on her shoulder.

"Boo."

Francine jolted, and it felt like her stomach did a somersault as she whirled around to face the culprit. Sure enough, it was Lucas, smirking at his success.

"Looks like I got you."

"Not funny, Lucas."

"You're smiling, so it must be funny."

"I'm smiling out of disgust." Francine's snickers gave way to laughter.

He laughed along with her, but when it dwindled, his mouth drew a line. "I guess we should talk. I've got time."

"That's why I'm here."

"Well, and to soak up the rest of the daylight." Lucas looked to where Francine clutched the strap of her tote. "Hey, your nail polish is gone."

"Yeah, it was not easy to remove. I went back to the nail technician and had my fingers covered in foil. It's a lengthy process."

They carried on their small talk as they walked to the beach. People no longer cluttered the sandy terrain, which made sense given that spring break was over. Lucas glanced at his feet, submerged in seafoam, as they stood at the water's edge. He raised his gaze to meet Francine's.

"Francine, I should have told you about the bet. I wish I hadn't agreed to it in the first place. I held back from telling you because

I was embarrassed and afraid you wouldn't want to see me anymore. I reasoned with myself that ending the bet would've been enough, but I knew better. I hid it from you to cover my hide. I'm sorry for agreeing to that bet and for not telling you. I'm sorry for everything."

"I forgive you, Lucas," Francine replied in a low-pitched voice. "When I was with Matthew, I thought it was good I didn't venture out before joining the church. While part of me believes that to be true, I'm glad I did. Now that I'm clearheaded, I have no reservations about formally joining my Amish community."

Along with a stern lip twist, Lucas tousled his hair. "So that means we're done."

"I'm sorry. I don't want you to change for me. That should be on your own accord, and I don't want to pressure you into becoming Amish because of my decision." She gulped as the back of her throat began to ache. "And I realized that getting married is not necessary for me to be committed. If marriage is meant for me, it will happen. I'm not sure whether you agree with this, but if you want to stay friends, that's fine with me. I've enjoyed having you in my life, Lucas, even if only for a little while."

He rubbed his stubble and raised his chin toward the amber hue of the sky above them. "I'm not going to lie. I was worried you'd say that. Although my outlook on religion has shifted, I'm not committed to it yet. So I get your intention of ending things. It's ironic that I agreed to persuade you to change your ways, but it was my life that changed. You've taught me how to value simplicity. And because of your love and dedication to your faith, you paved the way for me to find Christ. I'm not sure I could have done it without you."

Tears streamed down her cheeks. Francine knew in her

heart that his words were sincere, and she couldn't have been happier for him.

He spread his arms. "No hard feelings, Francine."

She walked over to Lucas after wiping her cheek with the sleeve of her dress and embraced him. For a split second, she thought how similar it was to ending her relationship with Matthew. Yet this experience was filled with relief rather than sorrow.

Lucas patted her back. "I do kind of wish I could be Amish. I'm sure it's easier to stay committed with your kind of life."

With a headshake, Francine pulled away. "It makes no difference where you come from. We all have baggage, and it can influence us to make decisions that affect people for better or worse."

"You're right. Thanks, Francine. Would you mind aiding me on my spiritual journey for the remainder of your vacation?"

"I'd be delighted to."

She and Lucas rested on the sand and watched the horizon. Francine delved inside her tote for some tissues to properly wipe her face.

I now know why I was led to come to Sarasota. I wasn't drawn to Lucas to be with him, but to point him to You.

"Fran?"

Lucas assumed that one of Francine's in-laws stood behind them. When Lucas turned to face the voice, he didn't recognize him. The young man wore a button-up shirt, suspenders, and slacks. It all clicked when Francine said his name.

"Matthew?" She leapt to her feet and wiped the sand off her dress. "What are you doing here?"

"I came to see you. I would've called, but I needed to talk with you in person. Leora told me you would be at Lido, so I got a ride over here." Matthew fixed his eyes on Lucas, his shoulders curving. "I suppose what Allison said was true. You really are seeing someone else."

"No, no. Matthew, is it? We're just friends. I mean, we were dating, but it was only on a casual basis," Lucas spoke up.

"And you are?" Matthew stood up straight and wrapped his thumb around a suspender.

"Lucas. Lucas Hayes." He gave Matthew a firm handshake. "I've been able to improve my life thanks to Francine. She has been sharing things from the Bible with me and helping me give my life to Jesus." With a wink, Lucas turned to face Francine. "That and sand dollars."

After breaking off the handshake, Matthew looked at her. "We should talk privately."

Matthew started to leave, but Francine didn't budge. Her hazel eyes trailed to Lucas.

"Go on ahead, Francine. It's okay."

With a nod, Francine's lips formed into a "thank you," and she followed Matthew across the sand.

Because Lucas harbored romantic feelings for Francine, seeing her walk away was bittersweet. Yet he knew those feelings were fleeting. Beyond them, he felt a more profound emotion. He had an actual connection with Francine and didn't feel the need to suppress his interests in front of her. It made him wonder about Barry and how their disagreement would affect his relations with the rest of the group.

If they all side with Barry, it'll be okay. I can always find people who will get to know me on a personal level. Just like Francine.

Francine's light purple dress billowed in the breeze, fading farther from view.

I still need to work through my issues before pursuing another relationship. I'm hoping I can find someone who is as devout as Francine and that I'll be strong in my faith too.

~

Francine's mind raced miles a minute as she and Matthew wandered along the beach. She was at a loss for words, and Matthew was silent as well. Her heartbeat quickened, and she decided to end their awkward silence.

"This place is nice, isn't it? All this scenery to bask in, and most days sure are comfortable. It's breathtaking, even on rainy days." Francine pushed out a laugh, hoping not to sound uncomfortable.

"Jah, it's *schtraahllich*, almost out of a dream." He smiled and stroked his throat. "Fran, I came here to tell you that I've been thinking about certain decisions since February. And I wanted you to know that I'm not leaving Middlebury."

Francine halted, her jaw hanging open. "What about you becoming a missionary?"

"I believed that I had a calling to the ministry. Given that I'd led people before, it felt natural. But it seemed like I drifted further away from what was meant for my life during our time apart. I knew there was a reason our break-up didn't sit well. Now I regret ever doing it. I haven't stopped loving you, Francine. Even if you don't want to get back together, I would still stay in our community. I've realized that I belong in the Amish community and want to be a part of it."

"I never wanted you to feel obligated to stay because of me. If you feel compelled to minister, you should do so."

He shook his head. "I don't have to leave our community to minister to people. As long as I'm guiding someone to Christ, I'm doing what's intended for me." Matthew brought his hand to her upper arm. "I'm sorry for ruining our relationship by not recognizing all this sooner."

"Sometimes we have to get off the path to remember why we need to keep following it. Regardless of how hard it was to be apart, I'm grateful we had the chance to figure out exactly where we needed to go." Francine clasped Matthew's hand and intertwined her fingers with his. "I don't think our relationship is ruined, Matthew. It only needs to be stitched together."

"I'm glad. Very glad." As he leaned closer, his eyes shimmered.

Francine missed getting lost in his coffee-colored gaze. She felt Matthew's lips faintly brushing against hers. She closed the gap and instinctively wrapped her arms around him, her eyes closing in the intimacy of the moment.

Likewise, Matthew. That chilly evening, breaking up seemed wrong. But right now, this is everything I've ever wanted. Regardless of my decision to join the church without marrying, I have you again and have a greater sense that you are the person I am meant to be with. Tears trickled down, and Francine ran her fingers along the side of Matthew's face. *I'm grateful that God has given me this life. I'll make an effort to avoid taking it for granted.*

Chapter 12

Sarasota

Lucas awoke to his phone's alarm, realizing he had pressed the snooze button thirty minutes past when he needed to wake up. He sprang out of bed and grabbed his jeans from the floor. He hopped on one leg, attempting to worm his other leg inside the jeans.

Lucas prepared to drive over to the charter bus pickup in Pinecraft. Francine and Matthew were heading back to Indiana in the next hour or so, and he didn't want to miss saying goodbye.

After getting dressed, Lucas glanced at his brand-new violin, now perched on the violin stand in the bedroom corner. Even if his new instrument wasn't his ideal violin, he was nevertheless glad to have one. It was an extension of him, and without it he felt as if a piece of himself was missing.

He couldn't help thinking about the instrument and how he'd used it the previous weekend. Lucas attended a community church near his apartment complex, and after Sunday service, he asked if they needed a violinist on the worship team. They were thrilled to have him on board, and he made his debut with the team at evening practice. Lucas looked forward to playing with the group the upcoming weekend.

As for Francine and Matthew, they had spent the last few days together in Sarasota. During that time, Lucas gave them plenty of space, seeing them once at St. Armand's Circle. He was delighted to perform for Francine once more and hear her sing one last time.

He put on his sandals and patted his pockets to make sure he had his wallet and key ring. *Sure hope I'll make it to Pinecraft in time.* Twisting the doorknob, he hurried out of his apartment.

~

Francine stood with Matthew at the charter bus pickup spot, located at the Pinecraft Tourist Church parking lot. Their bus had arrived, and other passengers began getting their luggage loaded. Francine had said her goodbyes to her family at Leora and John's house. After a tearful goodbye, they had been dropped off at the church parking lot by Violet an hour ago.

It wasn't raining, unlike the day she'd left Middlebury. The temperature was expected to hit eighty degrees, and the humidity swirled along her skin. Francine wished she didn't have to return home yet. She did, however, anticipate seeing Grace and Allison and getting back to work with Geneva. Francine couldn't wait to tell her parents that she and Matthew would be taking classes to join the church.

While Francine waited for Lucas to show up, she pressed a hand over her sternum. The bus passengers were already boarding, and it was only a matter of time before the motor coach would depart from the parking lot. Thankfully, she heard a familiar voice shouting her name. She whirled toward the voice. Lucas was sprinting over to them.

"Sorry for getting here at the last minute." Lucas wiped the sweat from his brow.

"No worries, Lucas." Francine scuffed her sandal on the pavement as she dug around in her tote. "Before I leave, I made something for you."

Francine lifted something from her bag with care. It was a sand dollar, but it was strung up like a Christmas ornament. Glued on were six sand dollar doves, and the doves encircled some painted text. Francine had constructed the ornament a few days earlier to show her gratitude for Lucas' friendship.

"I wrote the 'Legend of the Sand Dollar' on it. I am not as good at crafts as my sister Alana, but I gave it my all."

"It's wonderful, Francine." He beamed. "Thank you."

Francine gave Lucas a big hug. "Goodbye, Lucas. I'm going to miss you. Thank you for making my time here an adventure."

"Me too. Feel free to visit me the next time you're in Sarasota."

"You are also welcome to come and see us." Before releasing him, she gave him one last squeeze. "I'll let you know when we arrive in Middlebury, all right?"

As Lucas smirked, his cheeks wrinkled. "Will do. I wish you both well and a safe trip home."

Francine waved to Lucas and stepped onto the stairs, but she continued to observe Matthew and Lucas at the bottom. She leaned forward a little to hear them.

Matthew cleared his throat. "I appreciate you keeping an eye on Francine during her stay."

"She may have been the one watching out for me." Lucas reached out and shook Matthew's hand. "You're with someone who is incredibly wonderful, so don't take it lightly."

"Bye, Lucas. And thank you." Matthew tipped his straw hat before removing it.

Francine ascended the stairs of the bus. The toe of her sandal caught on the step and she stumbled, but Matthew propped her up and prevented her from falling. Francine seized the railing and hoisted herself up, thanking Matthew for breaking her fall.

Once seated, Francine buckled her seat belt and placed the tote bag by her feet. She turned her attention to the window. Lucas stood outside, holding up the sand dollar ornament by the string. She offered another wave to Lucas as the bus rolled out of the church parking lot.

So this is it. I'll begin classes so that I can join the church, and I will be with the love of my life the entire way. Lucas found a church where he can express himself through music and is growing closer to God. Everything fell into place in the end. She leaned closer to Matthew. *Do our plans transpire the way we expect them to? Sometimes, but not always. Having things not go according to plan is terrifying. It's crucial that we put our trust in God to get us through when things don't go our way. I will keep on praying about what the Lord has given me as He continues to guide me.*

Matthew took hold of her hand. "Fran, I'm glad you're back in my life. I appreciate you giving me another chance."

She closed her eyes as her heartbeat picked up. Images of their two years together drifted through her mind. She absorbed Matthew's essence, gentleness, and nurturing temperament and was relieved that there was no longer any uncertainty. What rolled off her tongue came naturally and without hesitation.

"I love you, Matthew. I am fortunate to have you by my side with our future ahead of us."

Francine's Avocado Potato Salad

Ingredients

- 6 potatoes
- Sprinkle of salt
- 4 small avocados
- ½ cup egg-free mayonnaise
- 1 teaspoon Dijon mustard
- 6 dill pickles
- 4 slices diced shallot
- 2 cloves garlic, minced
- Pinch of salt
- Pinch of pepper
- 2 tablespoons dried dill
- Pinch of dried basil
- 1 tablespoon olive oil
- 1 tablespoon apple cider vinegar
- Pinch of Xylitol or other sweetener
- Paprika
- Chives

Peel potatoes and cut into small pieces. Bring salted water to a boil in large pan. Add potatoes to boiling water and turn burner down to medium heat. Cook potatoes 18 minutes or until soft. Strain potatoes and cool in refrigerator.

Cut avocados into small slices and place in medium bowl. Add mayonnaise and mustard and mix. Slice pickles and shallots and add to bowl. Add garlic, salt, pepper, dill, and basil. Remove potatoes from refrigerator and add to bowl. Add olive oil, apple cider vinegar, and Xylitol, then mix. Garnish with paprika and chives. Serves four to five people.

Richelle Brunstetter lives in the Pacific Northwest and developed a desire to write when she took creative writing in high school. After enrolling in college classes, her overall experience enticed her to become a writer, and she wants to implement what she has learned into her stories. Just starting her writing career, Richelle's first published story appears in *The Beloved Christmas Quilt* beside the writings of her grandmother, Wanda E. Brunstetter, and her mother, Jean. Richelle enjoys traveling, her favorite destination being Kauai, Hawaii.

A Sarasota Sunset

Lorine Brunstetter Van Corbach

Chapter 1

The bus lurched, and Alana Lambright woke with a start. Her heart pounded from the unexpected jolt. Swiping her hand across her face and adjusting herself in the seat, she struggled to be fully awake. She'd been dreaming again. Taking a few deep breaths, Alana began to ponder. The frustrating thing about the dream was that it dealt with an event that really happened and one she was desperately trying to forget. If she was going to dream, why couldn't it be about something pleasant? She vividly remembered the details. She could smell the tang of the sweat-soaked horse as she held tightly to his harness. Ben, her boyfriend, had gone around the side of the horse to check for a rock in the back, right hoof. . .

"Hold him tight," Ben shouted. "I need to get a better look!"

Alana adjusted her grip as the horse began to shake his head and snort, sending droplets of horse saliva into her face. She let go, wiping the moisture from her eyes. The horse let out a piercing whinny as he jumped and kicked his back feet. Alana screamed, watching in horror as the horse's hoof made contact with Ben's ribs. The force of the kick sent Ben flying backwards several feet.

It was always the same; the dream ended with Ben lying on the ground, just as he had that day. Alana massaged the back of her neck. She allowed herself to recall the events that followed the incident. . .

Frozen in place, Alana debated what to do. Should I let go of the horse and help Ben? *She looked around, assessing her situation. If she let go, the horse might take off down the road, leaving her and Ben stranded. They were on a quiet county lane, and she hadn't seen any cars or other buggies. She spotted a fence post poking up among the tall weeds.* Maybe I should guide the horse and buggy over there. That might be the safe thing to do. But what if the horse spooks again? I am so afraid!

Alana glanced at Ben, still lying on the ground. He was beginning to stir, and she heard him groaning. No doubt he was in pain. Jumping up into the buggy and grabbing the reins, she guided the horse to the fence post and tied him in place. Running back to Ben, she fell to her knees beside him. "Ben! Ben! Wake up!" She gently patted his face as he slowly opened his eyes. "Are you okay?"

"What do you think?" he ground out through teeth clenched tightly. "I think I have a broken rib or two. I thought I told you to hold on to the horse! Why did you let go? This wouldn't have happened if you'd done what I told you to do."

"Seriously?" Alana, shaken by the tongue-lashing Ben gave her, rose slowly from the ground. "I'm sorry. I thought I had a good hold on him, but then he started to throw a fit. When he sprayed me with his saliva, I let go to wipe my face so I could see."

Ben grimaced as he tried to sit up.

"Remain still, Ben," Alana urged. "I'll use my cell phone to call 911 for help."

"I wish you'd give that phone up and prepare to join the church," Ben admonished from his place on the ground.

"This phone will bring help to you right now, and I'm glad I have it!"

After Alana made the call, she joined Ben on the ground. "Help is on the way. Ben, I'm sorry, but I wish you had tied the horse to the post instead of asking me to hold it. You know I'm not comfortable around horses. I don't trust them."

"Don't blame me for this, Alana." Ben's voice raised a notch. "This is your fault because of your ridiculous fear of horses. How will you ever manage when you join the church, get married, and have your own household to run? You can't always rely on others to make life easy for you. Give someone a call and have them pick you up, and find someone to get my horse and buggy. I sure don't trust you to get him home safely."

Alana winced at Ben's comments. "I had planned to go with you in the ambulance." She shook her head in disbelief. "But I think that would be a mistake. In fact, I think dating you was a big mistake."

Sirens in the distance alerted Alana that help was nearby. She brushed the dirt from her skirt as she stood, hands on her hips. "Don't worry about me or your horse and buggy. I'll take care of it. I hope you'll be okay and heal quickly. I am truly sorry you were hurt. I wish you well, but I think it's best we don't see each other again."

Alana felt relief as the ambulance attendants came to Ben's aid. A police officer had also been sent, and as she told the officer what had happened, Alana began to shake. With his assistance, she made arrangements to have the horse and buggy driven back to Ben's home. The police officer kindly offered to give Alana a ride home.

Alana blinked as her thoughts returned to the present. She and thirty other passengers were heading south on a charter bus to Sarasota, Florida. The sun had just started to peek over the horizon, and Alana watched in wonder as the clouds began to glow a majestic shade of pink and orange. *I wish I could get to the art supplies in my luggage and capture this beauty*, she thought wistfully. *Oh well, in a few short hours, I'll arrive!*

Excitement bubbled up in Alana as she thought about how surprised Leora, her older sister, would be when she appeared at the bakery where Leora worked.

A week after the accident and subsequent break-up with Ben, Alana had decided she needed a change of environment. She knew Ben was right about a couple of things. She did let fear get the best of her, and it was time to make a decision about her future. With her parents' blessing, she'd decided to pack her art supplies and clothes and head to Florida to surprise Leora for her birthday. Alana made arrangements with Leora's husband, John, to meet her at the bus drop in Pinecraft. The plan was to take Alana's luggage to John and Leora's home and then surprise Leora at work.

Alana daydreamed about what their reunion would be like. It was nice to think about something other than the events of the past couple of weeks. Restless from hours of sitting, she got up from her seat and took a trip to the small restroom at the back of the bus. Alana wanted to freshen up a bit before the bus arrived. Returning to her seat, she felt annoyed when a small ball sailed past her and landed in her seat. *Seriously?* She took a deep breath and turned around to see a young Amish woman admonishing her little boy.

"Son, it isn't polite to throw your toys. You could have hit someone. Please apologize to that young woman," the frazzled-looking mother scolded.

The boy walked cautiously up the aisle and shyly mumbled an apology in Pennsylvania Dutch to Alana.

"*Danki* for your apology," she replied as she knelt to his level. "It's a long ride to Florida, isn't it? It feels good to stand up and stretch. I'm sure you're getting tired of sitting in one spot, aren't you, little guy? *Wie heescht du*?"

The boy's mother joined them in the aisle. "His name is Jonah, and I hope he apologized." She sighed and wearily rubbed the back of her neck.

"Oh yes, he sure did," Alana quickly assured her. "I was just telling him I understand how bored he must be feeling. This is quite a long journey, isn't it?"

The bus braked hard and Alana, Jonah, and his mother quickly grabbed hold of the seat backs on either side of the aisle. "We'd better take a seat," Alana said. "Would you like to sit next to me for a bit, Jonah?"

Jonah, eyes wide, nodded solemnly. "May I, *Mamma*?"

"We don't want to bother you," said his mother. "I'm sure you don't wish to share your seat with a five-year-old for any length of time."

"Oh, I'd love to have some company. I know a couple games we can play to entertain us on this last leg of the trip. My name's Alana Lambright, by the way." She reached out to shake the woman's hand.

"Oh goodness, I've forgotten my manners. I'm Mary King, and of course you've met my son, Jonah. I suppose, if you're sure it doesn't bother you, Jonah can sit with you for a bit."

Alana smiled. "It won't be a bother at all."

Mary, stifling a yawn, turned and hurried back to her seat a few rows behind Alana.

The next few hours passed quickly as Jonah and Alana played games like Rock, Paper, Scissors, and I Spy. When Jonah started to fidget, Alana took out a small notepad and showed him how to draw some simple animals.

Jonah squealed in delight when Alana drew a funny picture of a rabbit and pig. "Are you ready to join your *mamm*?" Alana asked the boy as she turned around to see that Mary was now awake from the nap she'd taken while Jonah was occupied.

"*Jah*," Jonah said with a dimpled smile.

Alana took his hand and led him back to where his mother sat. Jonah crawled up into his mother's lap and whispered in her ear.

Mary laughed and nodded. "Jah, Jonah, Alana has very pretty eyes. They are nearly the color of the Gulf of Mexico."

"Thank you, Jonah." Alana blushed as she fidgeted with the ties of her *kapp*. "I've never seen the Gulf before, but I will soon. Danki for keeping me company."

Mary reached for Alana's hand and gave it a squeeze. "Thank you for entertaining my son so I could rest for a bit. I hope you'll enjoy Florida as much as we do. Maybe we'll see you at some of the community events in Pinecraft." Mary smiled and pointed out the window. "It looks like we're coming into Pinecraft now."

Alana nodded and returned to her seat. She placed a hand on her stomach to still the feeling of butterflies as the bus pulled into the lot. Alana picked up her purse and backpack and headed down the aisle toward the exit. She took a deep breath as she stepped off the bus into the sultry, warm air.

Chapter 2

Pinecraft

Alana stretched to her full height of five feet three inches, searching for her brother-in-law John. Rising on her tiptoes, she spotted him working his way through the crowd.

"John!" She waved enthusiastically.

"Alana, you made it!" John pulled her in for a quick hug. "Your sister's going to be over the moon when she sees you."

"Was it hard keeping this secret from her?" Alana asked as she reached for her luggage from underneath the bus.

"Not really. Leora's been so busy at the bakery lately, I don't think she noticed me getting the guest room ready, and she probably thought I was tidying up the kitchen this morning as part of her birthday gift." John laughed as he took the large suitcase from Alana. "Did you bring your entire wardrobe? This suitcase weighs a ton."

"Most of the weight is from my art supplies." Alana grinned. "Since I don't know when or if I'll go back to Indiana, I didn't want to leave my materials at home and have to buy new supplies while I'm here."

"Makes sense to me." John guided Alana through the parking

lot where the crowd was beginning to disperse. "Follow me. Our house is a few blocks from Pinecraft, so we'll drop your luggage off there and then walk over to the bakery and surprise your sister."

~

The delightful fragrance of fresh-baked bread wafted through the entryway of Der Dutchman Restaurant and Bakery as John held the door for Alana. "Mmm. . .that bread smells *wunderbaar*," he exclaimed.

"It does smell wonderful. I didn't realize that I was so *hungerich* until I caught a whiff of the smorgasbord of food coming from the restaurant." Looking to the right, Alana spotted Leora working behind the counter at the bakery. "Look, there she is!" Alana started for the counter, stopping abruptly as John grabbed her arm.

"Hold on," he said. "Let's do this right. See how busy she is? She hasn't glanced up once since we walked in. Why don't you go up to the counter and tell her you'd like to order a birthday cake. She's so focused on her work, she won't even realize it's you she's taking an order from."

"Are you sure?" Alana asked doubtfully. "Won't she recognize my voice?"

"Trust me. I have experience with this." John chuckled.

Alana walked up to the counter and waited a moment. "I'll be right with you," Leora called without looking up as she quickly moved a tray of chocolate-covered doughnuts. She slid the tray into the refrigerated glass display cabinet. "What can I do for you?"

"I'd like to order a cake, please," Alana replied.

Leora turned to move a dozen whoopie pies into the display case. "What type of cake would you like to order?"

"I'd like a small birthday cake. It's for my sister, and she loves key lime flavor. Do you have that available?" Alana tried not to giggle as John poked her and nodded his head with a knowing expression.

Leora turned and searched the counter for an order pad and pencil. "Unfortunately, we don't have that flavor for any of our cakes. We have key lime pie, though."

"Okay, I'd like one key lime pie. Can you add a happy birthday message to the top of it with green frosting? It should say HAPPY BIRTHDAY, LEORA!"

Leora's head snapped up. "Alana!" She dropped the pencil and pad on the counter, hurried around the display case, and wrapped Alana in a welcoming hug. "You're here! I can't believe my eyes."

Alana returned her sister's hug. "I decided to take you up on your offer to visit. John and I have been planning this for a couple of weeks now." Alana winked at John, who grinned from ear to ear.

"Oh, you. . .you've known all along, and you didn't once let it slip!" Smiling, Leora shook her finger at John. "This is the best birthday surprise ever. Why don't the two of you go up to the gift shop and explore? I have another half hour before my shift ends. Then we can go into the restaurant and have a bite to eat."

"Sounds like a plan," John said. "We'll see you in a bit, birthday girl."

~

After lunch the trio strolled past Pinecraft, making their way to Leora and John's home. Alana admired the blooms of a large plant in the front yard of a home they passed. "Wow, what a beautiful bush. What is it?" she asked Leora.

"That's a bougainvillea. Yes, it's gorgeous, but it's covered in thorns. Our place had one when we first moved in, but after the thorns got me a few times, I asked John to take it out. There are many beautiful flowers that grow well in the warm Florida sunshine and are better suited for me. This type of bush grows fast and can take over a yard before long," Leora explained.

As they approached the house, Alana noticed a large garage next to the home. "What do you use your garage for?" she inquired.

"I keep roofing supplies and tools in it, as well as our bikes and beach equipment," John replied. "Say, we should plan a bike trip down the Legacy Trail soon. It's great exercise and a good way to explore the area."

"I think I'd prefer to explore on foot or by bus," Alana said firmly.

"Alana's not much of a bike rider, John," Leora explained as she linked arms with Alana, guiding her down the sidewalk to the front door. "She's had one too many bike accidents, I'm afraid."

Alana's cheeks heated at her sister's words.

Patting her shoulder, John said, "No worries, Alana. I'm sure we can show you around without the use of bikes. Let's go in and get you settled. We dropped Alana's bags off on the lanai after I met her at the bus," he informed his wife. "She hasn't even seen the inside of the house yet."

Leora led Alana into the entryway and gave a quick tour. "Our house is small but cozy and welcoming. So make yourself at home. Follow me, and I'll show you your room."

The two made their way down the hall, John following behind with Alana's luggage. "Here you go," he said as he set the bags inside the room. "You two catch up while I make a few work calls and finish some paperwork. Don't make any plans for tonight, though. The final part of your birthday surprise is coming." John gave Leora a mischievous wink as he turned and headed toward his office.

"Now"—Leora grabbed Alana's hands, squeezing them gently and pulling her down to sit next to her on the bed—"tell me what finally made you decide to come for a visit."

Alana returned the squeeze and sighed. "Where do I start? A

lot has happened recently."

"How about you start at the beginning?" Leora urged as Alana nervously played with the ties of her kapp. "I can tell something has you feeling on edge."

"You've always been so good at reading me. I don't know how you do that." Alana shook her head in amazement.

The two settled in as Alana shared about the unfortunate accident with the horse and her break-up with Ben. "So after a week of watching me mope around, Mom suggested I consider taking you up on your invite to come visit. Since your birthday was coming up, we thought it might be fun to surprise you."

Leora patted Alana's knee. "I can't think of a nicer surprise. I'm thrilled you're here, and I can't wait to show you around. How long can you stay?"

"Well, that's the thing. . . ," Alana began nervously. "I was hoping to stay for a while. But don't worry, I'm going to find a job and help around the house. I might even look for a room to rent, because I don't want to be a burden to you and John. I mean, you're still newlyweds." Alana rambled on. "I already talked to John about this, so he knows my stay is an extended one. I need a change of scenery and a change of pace. I don't think I can continue to live my life in Middlebury where I'm forced to deal with horses, bikes, and bad relationships. *Mamm* and *Daadi* agreed that this might be what I need. Even Francine and Violet were supportive, although Francine was surprised I was willing to try something new because she thinks I'm afraid of my own shadow. I'm not though—I'm fearful of things that have caused me pain," she finished emphatically.

"I agree with Mom and Dad too, but you do realize that the Amish here rely heavily on bikes for transportation, right?"

Alana nodded her head as Leora continued. "It is, however,

possible to walk and use the public bus system to get around. Drivers are also available for hire. As far as work, the restaurants in Pinecraft are always looking for help."

"Leora," Alana interrupted. "The other thing I need to tell you is that while I'm here, I hope to make a decision about my future—specifically about joining the church or not. I talked with our folks about it. They were supportive of Violet when she decided to go English, especially since she's settled down quite a bit. Anyway, I might not dress Amish while I'm here or work in a place in Pinecraft. I hope that doesn't upset you."

"Not at all. I'm glad you're sharing this with me. I'll be praying you find what you're looking for." Leora stood, pulling Alana up from the bed and giving her a warm hug. "In the meantime, let's get your things unpacked."

Chapter 3

Sarasota Bay

On the small viewing deck of the *Marina Jack II*, Alana breathed deeply of the salty sea air. The sun had just begun to set, and the sky was streaked with vivid shades of orange and pink. John had arranged a sunset dinner cruise as the final birthday surprise for Leora. Taking out her cell phone, Alana began snapping pictures of the brilliant sky as the clouds and light shifted with the sinking sun. "I need to take as many pictures as possible so I can so I can put this gorgeous sunset on a canvas later," she told her sister and brother-in-law as they stood watching the beauty unfold.

~

Twenty-two-year-old James Fisher gazed out the window on board the *Marina Jack II*. "Dude, this sunset is amazing! Your parents are awesome for giving us a pre-graduation dinner cruise celebration," he told his best friend and roommate, Brian.

Taking a bite of key lime pie, Brian nodded. "Yeah, my folks are pretty cool. Tonight's also a celebration of the two of us having fantastic job interviews today. I'm confident that we'll both get hired to teach at the Christian school here in Sarasota."

"Man, I sure hope so. I want to work in a place where I can inspire kids to become lifelong learners, but on a foundation of Christ." James paused to take a drink of his iced tea. "I feel super good about the teaching interview today. But if God has a different plan for me and the door shuts on this opportunity, I'll go where He leads. The lifeguard interview I had this morning went well too, considering they hired me on the spot."

Brian reached across the table and put his hand up for a high five. "Yeah, that's great! I'm glad I don't have to worry about a summer job. My folks said to take time this summer and give myself much-needed rest. I'm going to do whatever I want. No more early morning classes and late night study sessions. If I want to sleep till noon, I will."

"Hey, don't brag." James grimaced. "Some people have to work, you know. But I hear what you're saying. Downtime would be great. Here's my plan: during the week, I'll lifeguard, but the nights and weekends will be dedicated to having fun and hanging out with friends. The summer will go by too fast. Before you know it, we'll be busy being adults, working full-time jobs and paying rent." He groaned.

"Yeah, don't remind me," Brian said. "Hey, it looks like we're headed back to dry land. Once we dock, we can hurry and catch a movie if you want."

They stopped talking long enough to finish their pie as the boat slipped into its spot at the dock. As the other upper deck passengers stood to exit, James and Brian followed, making their way down the narrow staircase.

~

"What a fun evening it's been. Danki for making my birthday a memorable one," Leora exclaimed as the boat docked. "The food was wonderful, and seeing the beautiful homes along the waterfront was fascinating."

"I think I saw a few that need new roofs." John chuckled, wiggling his brows at Leora. "Maybe I'll hang my business card on the bulletin board at the marina if we have time. I don't want to make our driver wait for us." He rose from the table and gestured for the sisters to go in front of him as the passengers exited.

Halfway up the walkway, Alana stopped. "Wait! I need to go back! I left my phone on the table." Several passengers who'd been sitting on the upper deck were heading up the walkway. She moved to the side to allow them to pass, then made her way to the lower deck cabin. With a sigh of relief, Alana spotted her phone on the table where she'd been sitting. She snatched it up and hurried out of the cabin, nearly colliding with a tall young man. "Excuse me," she mumbled looking down in embarrassment as she swiftly made her way past.

Recovering quickly, she trekked up the ramp again, but not before another quick stop to capture one last picture of the lit-up boat and harbor at twilight. Searching the waiting area, she spotted Leora standing at the dock railing. "Sorry," she apologized. "I can't believe I did that. I captured some great pictures on this phone, which I need because I don't want to forget anything about this night."

"No worries," Leora said. "John went to find a bulletin board and hang his card. He said he'd meet us out front."

~

James halted after barely avoiding a collision with a young Amish woman who had exited the lower cabin. He watched as she hurried up the walkway, stopped suddenly, turned, held up her cell phone, and appeared to take pictures of the harbor and boat.

"Hey!" Brian's voice jolted him back to the moment. "Why are you stopping? Let's go!"

"Sorry. I almost got taken out by some Amish gal. Then I was watching her take a picture of the boat with her cell phone. It took me by surprise. I wasn't expecting to see any Amish on a boat cruise in Sarasota, Florida."

Brian shrugged. "Whatever. Let's get going so we make the show on time."

~

Sarasota

Saturday passed swiftly as Alana spent most of the day recreating Friday's magnificent sunset, and before she knew it, Leora was home from work and in the kitchen fixing a simple meal.

"What can I do to help?" Alana asked as she joined her sister at the counter.

"Grab the potato salad out of the fridge, please. I made it Thursday, so it'll really be flavorful today." Leora pulled two plates out of the cabinet, placing them alongside the ingredients for sub sandwiches. "After we eat, I thought we'd walk over to the community park in Pinecraft and listen to the yodelers perform. John's going to meet us there, and I believe he'll join the singers on his harmonica tonight. I think they're having a shuffleboard tournament and a volleyball game too."

"That sounds like fun." Alana assembled her sandwich, took her plate to the table, and sat down.

Leora joined her. "It'll give you an opportunity to meet some of the Amish young people who are here to work during the summer season."

~

Pinecraft Park

Standing on the path above the creek that ran behind the park, Alana watched a turtle make its way across the water and up the bank, where it settled in among the rocks. A cheerful yodeling tune floated through the air. *I'd better rejoin my sister.* She took a tissue from her pocket and dabbed at her nose. *Thankfully, the bleeding's stopped. I knew I shouldn't have tried to participate in the volleyball game. This was worse than the last time I played and jammed my finger. I'm so embarrassed. Now I'll be known as the poor girl who took a volleyball to the nose on the first serve of the game. What a great impression I made.*

When the sisters had arrived at the park, Leora had introduced Alana to Carlie and Sara, coworkers who waitressed at Der Dutchman. They'd introduced Alana to a group of young adults in attendance, then invited her to join the volleyball game. Alana, not wanting to seem rude, reluctantly agreed to play.

I should have trusted my gut. I knew it was a bad idea, she mused. *Okay, Alana. Pull yourself together now.* She took a deep breath, pulled her shoulders back, and held her head high as she rejoined Leora at the picnic table where she sat visiting with friends.

"Are you okay, Alana?" Leora scooted over to make room for Alana on the bench.

"I'm fine. . .just embarrassed. But that's nothing new for me, is it?"

Leora turned to examine Alana's nose. "Well, other than a little swelling, it doesn't look bad. I'll give you some Arnica gel to put on it when we get back to the house."

Just then Carlie and Sara appeared. "We brought you some ice cream and wanted to see how you're doing, Alana." Sara held out a small cup of soft-serve ice cream.

"Danki." Alana accepted the treat. "That's so nice of you. I'm fine. Please, join us." She gestured to the other side of the table.

The girls took a seat across from Alana. "Have you been to the beach, yet?" Carlie asked as they ate their ice cream.

Alana shook her head, explaining that she'd only arrived the day before. "I'm hoping to go soon, though. I've never been to an actual beach, except for the shoreline at the lake, which I'm sure doesn't begin to compare."

"Oh, I meant to ask if you'd like to go to Lido Beach tomorrow after church," Leora interjected. "On Sundays we often have a beach day. It's a wonderful way to relax and enjoy God's beautiful creation."

"I'd love to!" Alana clapped her hands. "Is it far?"

"It's only about a twenty-minute drive by car, depending on traffic," Sara explained. "It takes longer by bus because there are transfers along the route. That's why we usually ride our bikes if we are going out to Lido. It only takes us about forty-five minutes."

"I asked Violet to take us. It's been a while since you saw each other. She said she'd love to drive us and get in a little beach time," Leora told Alana.

"Who's Violet?" Carlie asked.

"She's our youngest sister, and she lives nearby," Alana explained.

"Is she Amish?" Sara inquired.

"No, she decided to live in the English world," Alana told the girls.

"Carlie and I haven't joined the church yet, but we will when we return home in the fall," Sara informed. "What about you, Alana?"

"I'm not sure what I'm going to do. It's one of the reasons I'm here. I'm hoping to find some clear direction for my life."

"Maybe we can help by showing you around," Carlie suggested. "We're planning a day trip to Venice soon. Caspersen Beach is one of our favorites. Do you want to come along?"

Alana looked at Leora, who nodded and smiled. "That's a wonderful idea, Alana."

"I'd love to. Thanks for inviting me," Alana said.

"I'm sure we'll see you around. We'll finalize our plans before then," Sara said as she and Carlie stood. The last volleyball match of the evening was beginning. "It was nice meeting you, Alana."

Alana waved. "Thanks! I feel the same."

Chapter 4

Sarasota

Alana stretched out on the lounge chair late Monday morning. John and Leora were at work, so she'd put on shorts and a tank top and begun to work on her tan in the backyard. Gazing up at the sky, she watched as the light breeze rustled the tall palm trees, and she studied the puffy white clouds as they passed in front of the sun. A sense of peace enveloped her as she closed her eyes and thought about yesterday's trip to the beach.

Alana couldn't believe the contrast between the white sand and the brilliant aquamarine hue of the water. She recalled what the little boy and his mother from the bus trip had said about her eyes being the same color as the Gulf waters. Reaching for her cell phone, she opened her camera app and took a close-up selfie. She studied her image. *My tan's coming along nicely. The bronze tone of my skin really makes my eyes stand out, and my freckles are kind of cute.* She'd always considered herself rather plain, especially compared to her sister Violet. Now, with her kapp off and her light brown hair piled on top of her head in a messy bun, she felt pretty.

Alana squinted as the sun broke through the clouds. She jumped up from the lounge chair and headed into the house for her sunglasses and a glass of iced tea. As she passed through the laundry room, she spotted the bag of seashells she'd collected during the trip to Lido Beach. *I need to clean and sort those. I can't believe how many shells I found in just a few minutes. I hope I find even more when I go with Violet to the beach at Siesta Key on Thursday.*

Grabbing an old plastic colander, along with her tea, shells, and sunglasses, she returned to the lanai, where she carefully dumped the shells into the colander. Alana gave the shells a good rinse at the outdoor sink and marveled at their varied colors. One by one she sorted them, laying them on a paper towel to dry. *I need to come up with a creative art project for these beach treasures.* She picked up a butter clamshell. *This seems so plain compared to the other shells I found—kind of like me, I guess. Maybe I can paint something pretty inside the shell.* "Hmm. . .I wonder. . ."

Hurrying into the house, she gathered her art supplies and rushed back out to the lanai. She laid a painting mat on the outdoor dining table and took a seat.

Opening the photo app on her phone, she scrolled through the recent pictures. She stopped at the picture she took of the *Marina Jack II. What a fun evening that was.* She zoomed in and noticed a tall, handsome man in the picture. *Hmm. I didn't realize there was anyone in the last picture I took of the boat and harbor.* She continued scrolling through her camera roll. "Ah, there it is." She studied the image of the Lido Beach sunset she'd taken the night before, then took up her brush, dipped it into the paint, and began recreating a miniature version of the sunset.

~

Thursday morning, Alana greeted Violet at the door. "Come in," she said. "I need to grab my beach bag and sunglasses."

Violet stepped into the living room. "Wow! That painting's gorgeous. Is it one of yours?" she asked, moving closer to study the landscape of Sarasota Bay at sunset, which hung on the wall.

"Yes, it is. Thanks for the compliment. I painted it Saturday morning after we watched the sunset on the dinner cruise where we celebrated Leora's birthday."

"John invited me to come too, but I had to work. It looks like I really missed out. It seems like I'm always working when the sun is setting. You really captured the beauty of a Sarasota sunset, though."

"Thanks, and I painted a sunset for you too." Alana handed Violet a small clamshell.

"I don't know how you captured a sunset on a little clamshell, but you did. It's gorgeous. Thank you, Sister. Are you ready?" Violet asked as she headed toward the front door.

Alana held up her bag and nodded. "Let's go!"

Siesta Key

Alana and Violet waited for the Siesta Key Breeze Trolley. They had just come off the beach and were ready for some shopping and lunch.

"I'm glad we found a parking spot by the beach access. We can leave the car there all day. Parking can be tricky in the village," Violet explained. "The free trolley is a great way to get around Siesta Key. Look, here it comes."

The girls entered the trolley and took a seat toward the back. All the windows were open, allowing for a fresh breeze to pass through as the bus moved down the road and toward the Siesta Key Village shopping area.

After lunch at an outdoor café, the sisters strolled through the village, stopping to browse at several shops. Alana noticed a HELP

WANTED sign hanging in the front window of the store they'd just entered.

"There's something for everyone in here," Alana remarked. The shop was full of unique items, including a section of local art.

"Yeah, this shop's one of my favorites. They have a nice selection of beachwear, as well as souvenirs and gift items. Did you notice they're hiring?" Violet nudged Alana.

"I did. Should I ask about the job?"

"Why not? You're planning to stay for a while. You'll need an income while you're here. I can picture you working in a place like this, and you have experience since you worked in a gift shop in Shipshewana. I say go for it!"

"We'll see." Alana spotted a sale rack toward the back of the store. She flipped through the hangers, stopping when she spotted a modest beach cover-up. She grabbed it from the rack and joined Violet in the next aisle. "I think I'll get this. I'll feel more comfortable strolling on the beach if I'm wearing a cover-up."

"Hey, that's a great price! Where'd you find it?" Violet examined the price tag.

"Right over there." Alana pointed to the sales rack.

"Excuse me, do you work here?" an older woman asked. "I'm looking for a large, brimmed beach hat. Do you have anything like that?"

"Oh, I'm sorry. I don't work here, but I can show you where the hat rack is." Alana directed the woman to the proper area.

"See, you're perfect for a job like this. Go buy your cover-up and ask about it." Violet turned Alana toward the checkout and gave her a little push.

Alana waited in line behind another customer, and when it was her turn, she placed the cover-up on the counter and smiled shyly at the cashier.

"Did you find what you were looking for today?" The middle-aged woman smiled in return.

"Almost. I wanted to ask you about the HELP WANTED sign I saw in the window."

"I'm glad you noticed. I watched you help that woman a few minutes ago. I'm desperate for help, and you seem perfect for this job. Would you like to fill out an application?" she asked, handing her the form and a pen.

"Umm. . .sure." She glanced sideways at Violet.

"Do it!" Violet mouthed.

"There's a table on the back porch of the shop. You can sit there to complete the application. By the way, my name's Patricia, and I own this shop," she said with a wink.

"Thank you, Patricia," Alana said appreciatively. Violet joined her as she headed toward the back door of the shop and stepped out on the porch.

"I think I'll run across the street and pick up a few things from the drugstore. I need new lip balm and toothpaste. How much time will you need to complete that?" Violet pointed to the application.

"Is half an hour okay? I don't want to make you late for work. If I get done earlier than that, I'll text you."

"Sounds like a plan," Violet called as she skipped down the steps.

Alana sat down and began filling in the application. Fifteen minutes later, she was ready to hand it to Patricia. She had to wait because a long line of people had formed at the checkout. *This store really does need help.*

When things slowed down, Alana approached Patricia. "Here you go. Let me know if you have any questions. I can be reached on my cell phone at any time."

"Do you mind if I look at this right now? There's a lull in customers," Patricia said as she began reading through the application. "This is great! You're perfect. I'd like to hire you. Can you start tomorrow?"

Alana's mouth dropped open. "Really? Don't you want to interview me?"

"Nope, I saw how you helped that customer, and I like what I see on your application. I have a good feeling about you. You've got experience, you're young, and you have energy." Patricia tapped her fingers on the counter, grinning at Alana. "What do you think?"

"Well. . .sure. I can start tomorrow. What time do you want me here, Patricia?"

"Please, call me Patti. We open at 10:00 a.m., but if you can be here by nine, that'll give me time to show you the ropes." She reached up to tuck her curly blond hair behind her ears. "Sound good?"

"That sounds great! Thanks Patti. See you in the morning." Alana felt like she was floating on air as she left the shop. She pulled out her phone to text Violet.

"Alana." Violet called, waving as she crossed the street. "I'm coming. Let's hurry to the trolley stop, and you can tell me everything on the way back to my car."

Alana filled Violet in as they made their way through the village and onto the trolley.

"That's awesome, Alana. I'm so happy for you!" Violet reached her arm around Alana and gave her a squeeze. "Maybe you can sell some of your artwork there. You should ask your new boss."

"Oh no!" Alana said suddenly. "I didn't ask what my schedule will be. What if she wants me to work on Sundays? And I have a trip to Venice coming up. What if I'm scheduled to work that day too?"

"Don't worry, Sis. That shop's closed on Sundays. As for your trip to Venice, I'm sure, if you explain to your boss, she'll understand and give you that day off."

Alana closed her eyes and said a quick prayer. *Lord, thanks for helping me find this job, and please help this to work out.*

Chapter 5

Lakeland, Florida

Monday morning, James glanced in the rearview mirror of his older model Jeep Wrangler, making sure the moving van his dad was driving still followed him. He felt on top of the world as he made his way down the freeway toward Sarasota, where he would start the next chapter of his life.

Turning up the volume on the radio, he tapped the steering wheel to the beat of the music and hummed along. He reflected on the words of 1 Chronicles 16:34: "Oh, give thanks to the Lord, for He is good! for His mercy endures forever." *I have so much to be thankful for: a place to live, a summertime job, and my very first teaching assignment! I'm blessed that my parents were here to see me graduate and help me move to my new place. And what would I do without Brian? He's the best friend a guy could have. Thanks, Lord!*

After a whirlwind weekend, James looked forward to having a few days to relax before starting his lifeguarding job on Friday. With the help of his folks and Brian, he'd be able to get moved in and settled quickly.

Brian's parents owned a dozen rentals in the Sarasota area, so when a two-bedroom bungalow became available, they offered it to

Brian and James at a discounted monthly rate. The only condition was that James and Brian would perform the landscape upkeep and any maintenance on it themselves. Still, Brian had a long list of activities for the summer and said he was going to make sure they both had time for fun and relaxing, even if they did have to work.

First on the list was a trip to Venice. Brian was part of the young adult group at his home church, and they'd planned an outing to Venice for Thursday. James looked forward to the day because he hadn't been shark tooth hunting in a couple of years. When he moved from Texas to Florida to attend college, he met Brian at the new student orientation. They hit it off immediately and were happy to find out they were roommates. For Christmas break that year, Brian invited James to come to his home in Sarasota. During the short break from school, Brian took him to Venice and taught him how to search for shark teeth. He loved being out in the surf searching for teeth. *Yep, I'm really looking forward to that. It'll be nice to connect with some other young adults that are believers too.*

Siesta Key Village

Alana climbed down the stepladder and stood back to check out her work. She'd arranged some artwork the shop had received last Friday. Monday seemed like a good day for cleaning and restocking the store. It wasn't as busy as it had been on Saturday, and since it was just her and the boss working, Alana was sure they'd have an easy day.

"I really like how you laid these out. You have quite an eye for design," Patti said, standing by Alana as she studied the layout. "I'm glad I hired you. You're an answer to prayer."

"Thanks, Patti. This job was an answer to my prayers too."

"Alana, I was wondering. . .are you a believer in Christ?"

"Oh yes, Patti. I believe in God and His Son, Jesus Christ." Alana placed a hand over her heart. "Sometimes, though, I wonder if He hears all my prayers."

"It appears that He heard both of our prayers this time. Sometimes when we pray and ask Him for something, we expect an answer quickly or we feel like He didn't hear our request, especially when the answer He gave was no. Some think that God is a genie, just here to grant our wishes. But He knows the plans He has for us, and He will guide us in paths of righteousness." Patti laughed. "My goodness, I think I just preached a sermon!" She placed her palms on her cheeks. "Sorry about that. I hope I didn't offend you."

Alana shook her head. "Oh no, Patti. I needed to hear that."

"Say, I know you're new to the area, but have you found a church to attend?"

"I've only been here a couple of weeks, and I went to church with my older sister and her husband. Right now I'm staying with them." Alana fidgeted with her braid. "There's something about me that you don't know."

"Oh?" Patti picked up her feather duster and dusted the hand-blown glass trinkets on the shelf.

Alana folded up the ladder. "I grew up Amish, and one of the reasons I came to Florida was to figure out what my future holds."

"Does your sister live in the Amish community of Pinecraft? I stop there sometimes to pick up some of that wonderful Amish baking."

"She lives just outside Pinecraft," Alana said as she turned to put the ladder in the storage closet. "She works in the bakery at Der Dutchman, though."

"That's a bit of a commute for you. How are you getting to Siesta Key each day?" Patti inquired.

"I've been taking the bus, but my younger sister, Violet, said she'd take me to work if I wanted. She's busy with her own life, though, so I don't want to impose. She didn't join the Amish church, which is why she has a car," Alana added.

"Oh, that's nice of her to offer. Well, I'd like to invite you to attend church with me sometime. I go to a small nondenominational church here in the village." The bell on the door of the shop tinkled, and Patti turned her head. "Looks like it's about to get busy in here. You ready?" She winked at Alana and held out the feather duster. "Do you want to dust while I tend the register?"

"No thanks, I'm good. I'll cover the register." Alana giggled as she headed down the aisle.

Sarasota

Wednesday afternoon, James drove his parents to the airport. The last two days had been spent cleaning the rental thoroughly, moving in the furniture, and sorting boxes.

James felt grateful for his parents' help. "Thanks for everything, Mom and Dad. I really appreciate your help with moving." He pulled into the passenger drop-off area, jumped out, opened the passenger door, and extended his hand to help his mom while his dad opened the back of the Jeep to pull out their luggage.

"Son, be sure to let us know if there's anything you need. And don't forget, we'll be back to see you at the beginning of August before you start your new teaching position. And you can come home to Texas for Thanksgiving or Christmas too," James' mom said as she hugged him tightly. "You'd think I'd be used to saying goodbye after having you away for the last four years."

James patted her on the back. "Don't worry, I'll call you at least once a week, and we can video call too. It won't feel any different than when I was at school."

"It might not feel different to you, but your mom is always a mess when she says goodbye to you." His dad smacked James on the back. "Come on, Ruth, we need to get checked into our flight and let our son get on with his life."

Mom fumbled in her purse for a tissue and dabbed at the tears in her eyes. "Okay, Tim. I'm ready. We love you, James," she called over her shoulder as the two headed into the airport.

James hopped back into his Jeep and turned up the volume on the radio. "Finally, I'm on my own. So let the adulting begin!"

Alana settled into her seat on the bus and let out a weary sigh. It had been another great day at work, but she was excited to have a day off. She'd worked five days and would get her first check on Friday. *I'm beat*, she thought as she stretched her legs and rotated her feet in small circles. She closed her eyes and went over the details for tomorrow's trip to Venice. She would meet Sara and Carlie at the bus stop in Pinecraft at 10:30 a.m. They told her to bring some snack foods, a beach towel, sunscreen, and money for dinner. *I'm really looking forward to exploring another beach!* Alana felt giddy with excitement.

Chapter 6

Venice—Caspersen Beach

Alana adjusted the towel, then reached into the bag to grab her hat, sunscreen, and sunglasses. She sighed as she stretched out in the warm sun.

"This feels wunderbaar." She placed her hat on her head. "I'd better put some sunscreen on before it's too late. Can you spray my back?" Alana asked Carlie.

"I'd be happy to if you'll help me with mine." Carlie took the sunscreen from Alana. "Stand up and turn around, please. You have a nice base tan coming along, but I brought a couple of rash guards for us later. We're going to be here all day, so that will protect us better than just the sunscreen, especially if we spend a lot of time in the water."

"Okay, my turn." Carlie handed the spray to Alana.

Once Alana finished helping Carlie with the sunscreen, she picked up her sunglasses and tied her sarong around her waist. "I'm going to the surf to look for shells."

"I'm going to lie here and relax. I'll join you later," Carlie murmured. "Have fun."

At the water's edge, Alana gasped when she saw the multitude of shells. *Wow! I thought the shells at Lido Beach were abundant. There's way more here.* Alana glanced up at the water. *What are those people doing out there?* She watched a man and young girl, standing thigh deep in the water, use a long-handled scoop to dig down into the sand near their feet. They dumped the scoop onto a floating screen and rummaged through the contents. *I'll have to ask the girls. I bet they'll know. Right now I have shells to find.* She walked slowly, head bowed, as she made her way down the beach in search of treasures.

~

James pulled the beach wagon down the ramp, following Brian and the other young adults. They'd taken James' Jeep while the others carpooled between two vehicles. James figured it was better to take his own rig. That way he could be home at a decent hour. Tomorrow was his first day lifeguarding, and he needed to report at 8:00 a.m.

"Let's get our spot set up. I want to start hunting for shark teeth," James told Brian as he shoved the beach umbrella into the sand.

"Dude, chill. We have all day. Let's set up the volleyball net first. It's easier if we work together." Brian grabbed the ball and practiced his set moves.

"Give me that ball then, and let's get to it!" James swiped the ball from Brian and laughed.

Ten minutes later, the net was in place and a game had started. "I'm going out to the surf," James called to Brian as he picked up his scoop and sieve.

"Okay, but you'd better come play with us later," Brian shouted back.

~

James kept his gaze on the water as he walked along the beach. *I need to find an area that's not overcrowded.* He was about to make his way into the water when his foot made contact with something hard, and he felt himself falling. *What's happening?* he thought as he landed on the wet sand. He was stunned to realize that next to him was the most beautiful girl he had ever seen. She was reaching for her hat and sunglasses lying haphazardly nearby.

"I. . .I'm so sorry," the girl stammered as she knelt by him. "I wasn't paying attention. I saw a small conch shell and bent down to pick it up and never saw you."

James sat staring at her with his mouth agape. "Wow! Your eyes are amazing! They're the same color as the water." Realizing that he must look ridiculous sprawled out on the sand and staring at her like that, he quickly jumped to his feet.

"Um. . .thanks." Her cheeks colored as she played with the light brown braid draped over her shoulder.

James offered her his hand. "Let me help you up."

The girl hesitated a moment before taking hold of his outstretched hand. As he pulled her up, he said, "I'm the one who wasn't watching where I was going. It's totally my fault. Are you all right?" He looked down and noticed he was still holding her hand. Recovering quickly, he shook her hand. "My name's James Fisher."

She returned the handshake. "I'm Alana Lambright, and I'm fine. Just embarrassed." She giggled as she released his hand.

"You have nothing to be embarrassed about. I, on the other hand, do. If I'd been paying attention to where I was going instead of scouting a place to hunt, I wouldn't have tripped over you."

"Hunt? What are you hunting for?" Alana asked as she brushed the sand from her sarong. "I noticed you have one of those scoops and floating screens." She pointed to the tools lying nearby. "I saw some people in the water with the same tools. What are they for? Oh my. I'm sorry. I ramble when I get embarrassed."

James chuckled. "No worries. I'm hunting for shark teeth, and these tools will help me find them." He bent down to pick up his scoop and sieve and then turned his attention back to Alana.

"Shark teeth?" Her aquamarine-colored eyes widened. "Are there a lot of sharks in the Gulf?"

"Since it's a saltwater body, yeah, I guess there are. I've never seen any or even heard of anyone having an encounter with a shark here in Venice. It's not likely that a dangerous shark would come this close to shore anyways. The teeth people search for here are fossilized. They say some are from prehistoric sharks."

"That's interesting. I bet it's fun searching for them."

"It's a blast, but it's also addictive. It's easy to lose track of time when you're out in the water searching. You can find some cool shells while you're looking for teeth too."

Alana put her hat on. "I love searching for shells."

Man, there's something about this girl. I want to spend a little more time with her. "Hey, do you want to look for teeth with me? I can show you the ropes, and maybe you'll find some shells for your collection." James pointed to the mesh bag lying by Alana's feet.

"I'd love to! Let me tell my friends so they won't worry about me. I'll be right back." Alana picked up her bag and turned to go.

"Wait up. I'll walk with you. You can introduce me to your friends. I don't want them to think some weird stranger grabbed you and made you look for shark teeth."

~~~

Alana watched as James swept a lock of brown hair out of his eyes, pulled a baseball cap from the back pocket of his swim trunks, and put it on his head. *He's handsome*, she thought as they walked to where her friends were napping in the sun.

Alana knelt on the towel and placed the bag of shells next to her beach tote. She cleared her throat, causing the girls to stir.
~~~

"Carlie, Sara. . .sorry to disturb you. I'm going to be in the water hunting for fossilized shark teeth. This is James Fisher. I met him down by the surf. James, these are my friends, Carlie and Sara."

The young women sat up. Carlie pulled off her sunglasses. "Hi, James. Nice to meet you. Are you here alone?"

"No, I'm with friends from church. We came down from Sarasota to spend the day in Venice," he replied.

"Us too." Alana grabbed a rash guard and quickly put it on over her one piece. She untied her sarong and placed it on the beach blanket. "Okay, I'm ready."

"Have fun," Carlie called as the two made their way to the water's edge.

~

Out in the surf, Alana concentrated on keeping her balance. She watched as James used his scoop to gather material from the seabed. He pulled it out of the water and dumped the contents on the floating sieve as Alana held it in place.

"Okay, now start looking for shark teeth," he instructed. "They can be hard to spot, but if you slowly move the rocks, shells, and sand around, you can find them."

"How big are they?" Alana bent closer to the sieve. "All I see is rocks and broken shells."

"Here's one." James placed it on his index finger and held it out to show Alana.

"It's so small. I'd never spot something that tiny."

"Don't give up. We may need to move a little deeper in the water. It's kind of sandy here. If there's more rock under our feet, we'll probably have better results." James took hold of Alana's arm and guided her to a new location.

They repeated the process of scooping, dumping, and sorting. "Oh! I didn't find a tooth, but I found a shark's eye shell. It's perfect!" Alana held it up for James to see.

"That's pretty," he agreed. "Here, you keep looking while I dig the next batch."

She moved the rocks back and forth across the sieve, as James had demonstrated.

"Look!" Alana gasped as she uncovered a thumb-sized, shiny black tooth. She plucked it off the sieve and held it in her palm to show James.

He took hold of her hand and examined her find. "That's a beautiful tooth. Now you're getting the hang of it." He winked at her as he let go of her hand and turned to dig once more.

Alana's heart pounded as she felt her cheeks flush. *Every time he touches me, it's like a bolt of lightning travels through me.* She dropped the tooth into the zippered pocket on her rash guard, bent her head, and began to search once more. *There's something about this guy.*

As they searched for teeth, James told Alana about his recent graduation from college and that he had just moved to Sarasota, where he was sharing a rental with his best friend, Brian. Alana listened as he explained that both he and Brian would begin their teaching careers, starting the second week of August, at a Christian school in Sarasota. But in the meantime, he'd keep busy as a lifeguard for Sarasota County.

When James asked Alana about herself, she told him that she was twenty years old and new to Sarasota. She explained how she came for an extended visit with her sister and brother-in-law and had recently started working at a gift shop in Siesta Key Village. She was about to tell him the reasons she left her home in Indiana when a jet boat passed by, creating big waves. Alana fought to keep her balance.

James grabbed her around the waist, keeping her from falling.

"You okay?" He loosened his grip but kept his arms around her.

"Thanks. I almost fell. I wasn't prepared for those waves." Her cheeks warmed even more. "Maybe it's time for a break."

"We've been out here awhile, and honestly, I'm getting kind of hungry," James said, keeping his arm around Alana's waist as he guided her out of the water.

Once on solid ground, James released Alana and the two trudged up the sand to where his friends were gathered.

"Hey, Brian, come over here and meet my new friend." James motioned to a young man playing volleyball with a group nearby.

"This is Alana," James said when his friend joined them. "We met down at the water's edge."

"Hi there." Brian appeared to look Alana up and down. "Not bad, dude." He punched James' arm.

"Cut it out, Brian." James tousled his friend's hair. "This is my best friend, Brian. He's the one I told you about."

"Nice to meet you, Brian," Alana said.

"Hey, you've been down there a couple of hours." Brian pointed at the surf.

"What? No way." James pulled his phone out of his backpack. "Guess you're right." He showed the time to Alana. "No wonder I'm hungry."

"We're going to Sharky's on the Pier to get something to eat," Brian told James.

"I think I'll head back to where my friends are," Alana said. "It was nice meeting you both. James, thanks for teaching me how to hunt for shark teeth." She waved and turned to go.

"Hold up a minute," James called after Alana. He turned to Brian. "I'm going to see if Alana and her friends want to join us."

"Whatever, James. Hurry up, though. We're all starving!" Brian walked toward the young adults, who were taking down the net and umbrellas.

James quickly caught up to Alana. "Hey, do you and your friends want to join us?"

"I'd really like that. Let me ask them. I feel bad. . . . I've kind of ignored them all day."

"Okay, I'll walk with you and see what they say."

Carlie and Sara agreed to accompany Alana and James, along with the young adult group to the pier. It worked out perfectly, because James offered to give them a ride, which meant they wouldn't have to wait for the bus or take all their beach bags into the restaurant.

After a late afternoon meal, the group decided to hang out on the beach near the pier for a couple more hours and wait for the sunset. Alana worried they might miss their bus, but Sara checked the schedule and saw that the bus route home would run until 9:00 p.m., so they'd have no problem getting back to Sarasota.

Alana enjoyed getting to know the young people from James' church. They laughed a lot and seemed to be good friends. The girls in the group made sure to include Alana, Sara, and Carlie in their conversation, helping them feel welcome. Now the girls sat on their blankets in the sand while the guys tossed a football around.

Alana watched Brian tackle James. She wasn't sure what to think of Brian. She could tell they were good friends, but Brian seemed immature compared to James. She had a hard time picturing Brian as a teacher. James, on the other hand, seemed like a natural. He'd been so patient as he taught her the art of shark tooth hunting. She watched James break free of Brian, catch the ball, and run down the beach. She laughed when Brian, in hot pursuit of James, tripped and rolled across the sand.

"Do you want to go back out and look for more teeth before

the sun sets?" James asked a few minutes later, joining her on a beach blanket. "I brought the scoop and sieve when I got the blankets from the Jeep."

"Sure! You're right—looking for shark teeth is addictive."

James stood and reached down to help Alana up.

~

Alana took a step back, as she dug the scoop into the seabed. Suddenly she felt a sharp pain in her foot. "Ouch!" She let go of the scoop and lifted her foot as close to the water's surface as she could, fighting for balance.

"What happened?" James abandoned his search for teeth and made his way closer to Alana.

"I cut my foot," she cried as blood swirled around her.

Chapter 7

"Put your arm around my shoulder, Alana. I'm going to carry you up to the blanket." James gathered her in his arms.

"What about the scoop and sieve?" she questioned as he made his way up the beach.

"I'll send Brian down to get them. We need to see how deep this cut is and slow the bleeding."

James sat Alana on the blanket as the others in the group hurried over. "I wish I'd thought to bring my first aid kit. I need something to help stop the bleeding," he called out.

Sara rummaged in her bag and pulled out a towel and unopened water bottle. "Here, will this do?"

"Thanks." James opened the water and carefully washed the sand away from the cut. After examining it, he applied pressure with the towel. "You need stitches, Alana."

"Oh no," she murmured. "Is it really that bad?"

"It's deep and about three inches long. Whatever you stepped on sliced your foot really good. There's an urgent care center close by. I'd better take you there and let them fix you up. They'll make sure it's cleaned thoroughly. You don't need an infection to go along with the cut."

"All right." Alana's teeth chattered. "I'm not feeling so well."

"You're showing some signs of shock. Let's get you wrapped up in one of the blankets. Carlie and Sara, can you help Alana get dried off and ready to go?"

The girls came to help, and within minutes James picked Alana up again and carried her to his Jeep, followed by Brian, Sara, and Carlie.

After he settled her in, he gave her arm a gentle squeeze. "Hang on, Alana. It's going to be all right."

"What about my friends? I don't want them to miss the bus."

"Don't worry. They'll catch the bus back to Sarasota as planned. Brian will ride home with someone from the church group, and I'll take care of you and get you home safely."

"I'd better give my sister a call so she knows what's happening and doesn't worry when I'm late." Alana closed her eyes and laid her head back on the seat, fighting waves of dizziness.

Sarasota

She stepped deeper into the water, feeling the broken shells and rocks between her toes. Water lapped at her thighs. Suddenly she spotted a fin slowly circling around her. A sharp pain tore through her foot. "It's got me!" she screamed.

"Alana! Wake up." Leora gently shook Alana by the shoulders.

Alana opened her eyes and slowly sat up. She trembled and cold beads of sweat dotted her forehead.

"It's okay. You had a bad dream. Take a few deep breaths, and when you're ready we can talk about it." Leora handed Alana a glass of water.

"Thanks. I dreamed that a shark attacked me. Guess my mind twisted the events of yesterday." She sighed and relaxed against the pillows. "What time is it?"

"It's 5:00 a.m. I was getting ready for work and heard you scream. Since you went right to bed after you came home last night, I'm glad we're both up and can chat before I leave. Do you want to tell me the rest of the story?" Leora settled in next to Alana on the bed.

"Sure. Maybe it will help me process everything that happened."

Alana told Leora all that happened before she cut her foot, including how taken she was with James.

"It sounds as if you really like this guy." Leora nudged Alana with her elbow.

"I do. I can't explain it, but there's something special about him. He's a Christian. He's so nice, funny, and smart, and such a good teacher. He's tall and handsome too. I've never felt this way about someone I just met. When he put his arm around me after I lost my balance in the surf, it felt like I was hit with a bolt of lightning. And he was so gentle and caring when I cut my foot."

Leora giggled. "I know what you mean. I felt the same way when John held my hand for the first time. Well, what are you going to do about it?"

"Nothing. I mean, we had a great time and had a lot to talk about. Even during the trip back to Sarasota, we never were at a loss for words." Alana picked at the edge of the comforter and shrugged. "Things changed when we pulled into the driveway, though."

"What do you mean?"

"Well, when John came out, James gasped and said, 'Your brother-in-law is Amish?' I said, 'Yes, my sister is too.' When I laughed, his reaction took me by surprise. I think he might have been offended that I laughed at his reaction, because he suddenly seemed really uncomfortable. I didn't even have time to thank him for such a fun day, for taking care of me, and for making sure I made it home safely. I'm not even sure he said goodbye before he peeled out of the driveway. It was so strange." Alana threw back the covers and cautiously stood, trying out her weight on her foot.

"Alana, what are you doing? I think you should stay in bed and let your foot heal," Leora admonished.

"I can't. I work this morning, starting at ten. I need to get ready."

"How on earth are you going to get to the bus stop? You can barely put weight on your foot. You should call in sick."

"I have a responsibility to my boss. I can't call in. I just started working there. I called Violet on my way home from Venice last night, and she said she'd give me a ride to work today and pick me up when I get off. I'll be fine. Don't worry."

"Sometimes you're so stubborn, Alana. Please, take it easy and stay off that foot as much as you can, okay?" Leora stood. "I need to leave for work. I'll be praying for you today."

Siesta Key Village

Alana sat behind the counter in the gift shop with her foot propped up. So far the store had been quiet, and Alana waited on customers without any problem. Thankfully, Patti was working, along with Tanya, one of the other employees. Patti, like Leora, had scolded Alana for coming to work instead of resting.

Alana explained to Patti that she couldn't turn her back on her responsibilities, even with an injured foot. Finally, Patti declared that Alana would spend the day at the cash register with her foot propped up as much as possible.

Alana's stomach growled. She looked at the time and was surprised to see it was almost two o'clock.

"Alana, it's time for your lunch break. Since it's slow, I'll leave Tanya in charge, and we can have lunch together. Let's go across the street to Gilligan's."

"Thanks, Patti. I'd like that." Alana stood slowly and limped through the store, following Patti.

Patti took hold of Alana's arm and helped her cross the street to the outdoor eating area of the restaurant.

The two ordered iced tea, burgers, and fries. As they waited for their food, Patti reached across the table and patted Alana's hand. "How are you doing, sweetie? You look pale. Is your foot hurting?"

"A little bit. I think the walk aggravated it." Alana reached into her purse and pulled out two small bottles of medicine. "It's time for my meds. I'm thankful I can sit and work behind the register today. Thank you, Patti. You're the best boss."

"How will you manage the trip to work each day on the bus while your foot heals?"

"My sister brought me today, but she works a morning shift tomorrow. I was thinking maybe I'd hire a driver." Alana reached for her iced tea and took a long drink, washing down the pain reliever that would help her get through the rest of the day, as well as an antibiotic that would help avoid any infection.

"I have an idea. I have a guest room. Maybe you could stay with me while your foot heals," Patti said. "Then you won't have to worry about getting to and from work. What do you think?"

"That's nice of you to offer. But I can't impose on you like that."

"Really, it isn't an imposition. I was planning to ask if you'd be interested in house-sitting for me next month anyway. Now with your injury, it makes sense to offer you my spare room. You're such a blessing to me at the store. You're a hard worker, with a good eye for design, and I'm glad I hired you."

"Where are you going next month?" Alana asked as the waitress brought their food.

"Each June I go visit my daughter and her family. School gets out at the end of May for my grandkids, and since June is usually a bit slower in the store, it works out perfectly."

"Oh, that's wonderful," Alana exclaimed. "You know, the more I think about this, the more it makes sense. I've thought about finding a room to rent because my sister and her husband are still basically newlyweds, and I don't want to wear out my welcome at their home. But if I stay with you, I insist on paying rent."

"If you house-sit for me in June, I can't very well have you paying rent. So how about I come up with a fair amount for rent for the remainder of this month, and then the first two weeks of June you stay rent free? When I return from my trip, you can start paying rent again."

Alana took a bite of her burger and chewed slowly as she thought the offer through.

After a minute, she nodded. "You've got yourself a deal, Patti." She reached her hand across the table so they could shake on it.

"Wonderful. How about I drive you to your sister's house after we close this evening? Then you can gather your things and we can get you moved in."

"I guess that would work. I hope my sister isn't upset when I tell her I'm moving out."

Sarasota

James entered the kitchen through the back door to find Brian standing there examining the contents of the pantry.

"Hey, man. How was your first day on the job?" Brian asked as James sank into a chair at the table.

"I'm exhausted."

Brian rummaged around the cabinet. "Thought I'd make dinner tonight. How's hot dogs and mac and cheese sound?"

"I'm not hungry. Go ahead and fix whatever you want."

"What? I've never heard you say those words before." Brian came behind James and touched his forehead. "Are you sick or something?" He laughed as he sat across the table from James.

"Nah, at least not that kind of sick. I'm just bummed out, I guess."

"What's the problem?" Brian asked.

"I feel like an idiot for the way I acted last night when I dropped Alana off at her sister's. I was planning to ask for her phone number and see if she wanted to go out with me. But when her brother-in-law came outside to help her into the house, I was shocked. I clammed up and hurried out of her driveway. I didn't even say goodbye."

"Why? Is her brother-in-law some big, intimidating dude?"

"No, smarty. He's Amish."

"What do you mean?" Brian's eyes narrowed as he tilted his head to one side.

"I just told you. He's Amish, which means so is Alana." James flexed his hands in frustration.

Brian got up and went to the fridge. He took out the hot dogs and put them on to boil. "She didn't look Amish. Do you think she is just because her brother-in-law is?"

"Well, think about it. If her brother-in-law is, then so is her sister, which means she is too."

"So what, man? She wasn't dressed Amish, and neither were her friends."

"Maybe she hasn't joined the church yet. It's not uncommon for Amish young people who haven't joined the church to dress English sometimes."

"I didn't know you knew so much about the Amish. But still, what's the problem? If she hasn't joined the church yet, why can't you ask her out?"

"Well if she's Amish, she won't want to have anything to do with me. Besides, I told you—I left in a hurry. I didn't get her phone number."

"Bummer, James. But there are other fish in the sea. Besides, you're going to be too busy working and having fun this summer to have time for a girlfriend." Brian came over and gave James' head a knuckle rub.

"Cut it out, Brian. Your food's going to burn if you don't watch it. I'm going to get ready for bed. I'm beat," James called over his shoulder as he made his way down the hall toward his bedroom.

He shut the door behind him, sank down on his bed, and cradled his head between his hands. *Dear Lord*, he prayed, *I need Your help. I feel bad about how I acted last night. I can't stop thinking about Alana. She's so beautiful and easy to talk to. I'm sure I hurt her feelings with the way I reacted when I saw her brother-in-law. If it's Your will for me to get to know Alana, please provide a way for us to see each other again. In Your name. Amen.*

Chapter 8

Siesta Key Beach

One week later

James walked along the shore, monitoring the water for signs of trouble. For a Friday, the day had been relatively peaceful. A couple of people had needed minor first aid treatment, but nothing he couldn't handle. Of course, he wasn't working alone. Four lifeguard towers stood on this stretch of the beach, and today he was working in the blue tower. His co-lifeguard was back at the tower keeping careful watch of the beach and shoreline too.

James reached the boundary of the blue tower area. As he began to walk back, he spotted a small conch shell and picked it up, thinking of Alana as he held it in his hand. *It's not as perfect as the one she found.* Turning it over, his thoughts scattered when his walkie-talkie went off.

His coworker, Paige, was letting him know she was going off radio for a ten-minute break. As James reached the tower, he saw her heading toward the restrooms. The previous Sunday, he'd met her at church. Monday morning, he was surprised when he found her in the tower, taking inventory of the first aid supplies.

Paige had seemed surprised to see him too. She'd told him that she heard she was getting a new partner but had no idea it would be him.

James climbed the steps of the tower, grabbed his binoculars, and sat in the lifeguard chair under the blue umbrella. It felt good to get into shade.

"The beach is pretty quiet for a Friday afternoon." Paige joined him on the deck.

"Yeah, it is," he agreed.

"Want me to put some sunscreen on your back? You're looking a little red."

"Nah, I'm good. It's my turn to watch from the tower, so I'll stay under the umbrella until my next patrol. Thanks, though," he said, scanning the shoreline with his binoculars.

"What are you doing after work?" Paige asked.

"Hadn't really thought about it."

"Some of the young adults from church are having a game night. I was thinking about going. Do you want to come?"

"Sounds like fun, but I work tomorrow at Manasota. I'd better not. Maybe some other time."

"Sure." Paige turned away from James, leaned against the deck rail, and hung her head.

"Brian and I are planning on going to the cook-off the young adult pastor is hosting Sunday evening."

Paige spun around quickly, giving James a wide smile. "Great, me too! Are you entering the competition?"

"Maybe, if I have time to put something together." He methodically scanned the beach.

"I guess my break's about over. My radio's on." She grabbed her rescue tube and hip bag. "When my patrol is over, you can take your break."

James watched Paige as she moved down the beach. *I hope I didn't hurt her feelings when I said no about tonight. Maybe I'll catch the sunset before I head home. I think it will be a spectacular show.*

Siesta Key Village

Alana turned the sign over so that it read CLOSED and locked the front door of the shop. She strolled up and down each aisle, double checking that everything was in order and the display lights were turned off. She glanced at her watch. *Good, I have some time before the sunset.*

She'd kept her eye on the sky all day. Tonight's sunset was going to be perfect for capturing on canvas. *I just need to lock the back door on my way out. Then I'll grab my art supplies and walk to Sunset Pier.*

Alana was thankful her foot was nearly healed. She could walk easily on it now, especially if she wore supportive shoes. Sunset Pier was several blocks away, but Alana was sure she was healed enough to handle the distance.

She opened the screen door to the covered porch and found Patti sitting in a wicker rocking chair.

Patti greeted her with a warm smile. "I made tea. Want some?"

"Thanks, but I'm going to gather my art supplies and walk to the pier to paint the sunset." Alana turned to enter the house.

"Are you ready for that long of a stroll?" Patti followed Alana inside.

"I think so. Guess there's only one way to find out. I'm not going to walk out in the sand, though. I'll set my easel up where the pavement ends and the beach begins."

"I don't mind driving you down to the beach," Patti said.

"I'm grateful, but I need to test my endurance. I'd better hurry or I'll miss the start of the sunset."

In her room, Alana rummaged around for the acrylic colors she'd need, along with an assortment of brushes. She grabbed a palette and an eight-by-ten canvas and dropped them into an oversized beach tote. Then she picked up the portable easel, slung it over her shoulder, and hurried out of the cottage.

~

James parked in front of a small cottage several blocks from the beach access. As was often the case around this time of day, parking was difficult to find. People were coming in to have dinner and watch the sunset.

He jumped out of his rig and proceeded down the street toward the old pier. He could already see the sky beginning to change as the sun sank toward the horizon. *I'd better hustle so I can soak it all in.*

As he grew closer to the pier, he noticed a crowd forming. *The sunset must be something else—so many people are gathering to see it.*

The crowd shifted, revealing a petite young woman standing in front of an easel, capturing the sunset as it happened. His heart sped up. *That's Alana!* Edging closer, he stood to the side and watched her work.

Finally, the crowd thinned out. Several people stopped to compliment Alana on her art. He watched her smile as she thanked them.

"I'd like to purchase your painting." James moved to stand behind her.

Alana kept her eyes on her work. "I'm sorry, this isn't for sale."

"Not even for a friend?"

Alana whipped around. "James! What are you doing here?" Her cheeks looked flushed, and her eyes seemed to sparkle.

"I came to watch the sunset. I had no idea that I'd be doubly blessed and get to watch you capture it so expertly. Wow, Alana, you're a very talented artist."

"Thanks, James. The real artist is God, though. What a splendid work of art the sunset was tonight."

"For sure. God is at work tonight, bringing us to the same beach to watch the same beautiful sunset. I prayed and asked Him to bring our paths together again if it was His will."

Alana began cleaning her art supplies. "You prayed you'd see me again?"

He nodded.

"Really? Why?"

"I wanted to apologize for the way I acted when I dropped you off at your sister's last Friday. But I didn't have your number or know where you worked. I thought we hit it off on the beach in Venice, and I wanted to get to know you better." He looked directly into her eyes.

Alana dropped her gaze, and her cheeks turned pink again. "I thought so too," she whispered.

"Do you want to join me for a bite to eat?"

"I'd like that. Let me gather my things. I need to be careful with the painting because it's still wet."

"I'll help you carry something. How were you planning to get all this back to your sister's house?" He cocked his eyebrow.

"I'm living here now. I was planning to carry it back to the cottage."

"How 'bout I carry your bag and easel, and you carry the painting?"

Alana nodded. "Thanks."

As they walked back to the cottage, Alana told James how her boss had offered her a room at the quaint cottage she owned behind the gift shop. "It's been a blessing. I don't have to feel like an imposition to my sister and her new husband, and it's helped me stay off my foot as it healed."

"Speaking of your foot"—James pointed to it as they walked—"how is it?"

"I get my stitches out on Monday. The walk to the pier and back tonight is the most I've been on it since I cut it. I'd probably better get off it soon."

"We can take my Jeep to find a place to eat if you'd like. Or I can just carry you again," he said with a chuckle.

"Your Jeep will be fine, and look"—she pointed ahead of them—"you're parked right in front of the cottage where I'm living."

"No way! God has such a sense of humor, doesn't He?" James laughed as the two climbed the steps to the porch.

~

Alana sat back in her chair and pushed her plate away. "That was delicious, but I'm stuffed!"

"Me too." James picked up his cola and took a drink. "Alana, I just realized that I haven't actually apologized to you. I'm so sorry for the way I left things last week."

"It's okay, James. I did think it was odd that you left in such a hurry, but since I was in a lot of pain, I thought I was probably misreading the situation."

"I'd like to explain. I was shocked when I realized your brother-in-law is Amish. I figured you must be too, and if I were to express an interest in getting to know you, you'd probably turn me down."

"Why did you think that?" Alana tipped her head.

"Well if you're Amish, you're not going to be interested in getting to know an outsider, right?"

"James, the Amish often have friendships with people outside of our faith. I did grow up Amish, but I haven't joined the church yet and don't know if I will."

"Really? Why's that?" James wiped the condensation from his glass.

"For a lot of reasons. For now, let's just say that I'm here to figure out what I'm going to do with my life." Alana tossed her braid over her shoulder.

James reached across the table and clasped her hand. "I want to get to know you better. You're easy to talk to, and I feel so comfortable around you." He gave her fingers a tender squeeze.

"I'd like that. I feel the same way." She squeezed his fingers back and let go gently.

As James paid the bill, Alana stood by, trying to calm the butterflies she'd felt when he'd held her hand. As they exited the restaurant, he placed his hand on her back, guiding her to his Jeep.

"Do you have plans on Sunday evening?" James asked as they began the short trip back to the cottage.

"Not so far. Why?"

"Our young adult pastor is hosting a cook-off, and I'd like to invite you to come. You can bring a favorite summertime dish to enter in the competition if you want. There'll be prizes, as well as a ton of food to eat, backyard games, and great fellowship." He pulled in front of the cottage.

Alana felt breathless at the thought of spending more time with James. "I'd love to come."

James grinned. "Awesome. I'll pick you up at four."

"That's perfect. See you then." She put her hand on the door handle, preparing to exit the Jeep.

"Wait there. I'll get your door and walk you to the house."

He's such a gentleman, Alana thought as she waited for him to come around.

He took her hand and helped her down. Keeping a firm hold

of her hand, James guided Alana up the porch steps. Her heartbeat increased as they grew closer to the front door. *Will he kiss me?*

James turned to face her. He cleared his throat, shuffled his feet, and ran his other hand through his hair. "Okay, then. Good night." He released her hand and practically leapt off the porch.

Alana felt puzzled as she turned to enter the house.

"Wait! I forgot to get your number." James bounded back up the steps, handing her his phone. Alana giggled as she added her number to his contact list.

"I'll text you tomorrow." He leaned in and gave her a quick peck on the cheek, then darted off the porch and into his Jeep.

Alana touched her cheek as he drove off. *That's not how I thought this day would end!*

Chapter 9

Sunday morning, Alana jumped out of bed, put on her robe, and headed to the kitchen to start a pot of coffee. She glanced out the window while she filled the pot with water. "Oh, no. It looks like a storm is coming."

"What was that?" asked a groggy voice.

"Good morning, Patti." Alana turned, greeting her with a smile. "Don't mind me. I was talking to myself."

"The weatherman said we'd be in for periodic showers and lightning this morning," Patti mumbled, covering a yawn. She shuffled to the table and eased herself into a chair.

Alana watched her, trying hard not to giggle. Patti was not a morning person. Her hair stuck up wildly on one side of her head, and her eyes looked puffy from sleep. This had become the routine over the past week since Alana moved in. Each morning, Alana bounced out of bed wide awake and ready to face the day. Patti, on the other hand, took a while to wake up enough to do anything. Alana was so grateful to Patti for offering her a room that she happily took on the responsibility of starting the coffee each morning.

She took out two mugs and poured the first cup for Patti, then carefully delivered it to her at the table. "There you go, Patti. The cream and sugar are out too."

"Thanks, sweetie. I don't know how I functioned in the morning before you moved in." Patti took a sip of coffee and sighed. "That's delicious. I guess I need to get myself moving if we're going to get to church on time."

"Thanks for inviting me to your church. I've never attended a church service that wasn't Amish before. I'm a little nervous."

"I'm sure it will be different than what you're used to, but we love the Lord and want to share His love with the community around us. We're a small but growing church—not only in numbers, but more importantly we're growing in our faith."

"That's good. I feel like my faith has become stagnant. I don't know what my purpose is, and I'm not sure what path to take."

Patti reached across the table and gave Alana's hand a gentle squeeze. "God will show you what He has in store for you. Have faith and remember what He said in Jeremiah 29:11.

" 'For I know the plans I have for you,' says the Lord. 'They are plans for good and not for disaster, to give you a future and a hope.' "

"Thanks, Patti. That verse has never spoken to me like it just did. It sounds so different in German. What version of the Bible was that?"

"I memorized it from the New Living Translation. It's the version we often use at church," Patti explained.

"Well, let's get moving. I can't wait to attend church!"

~

After church Alana bustled about the kitchen preparing a dish to take to the cook-off. She could hardly contain her excitement about seeing James in a couple of hours. She smiled, thinking about their conversation the night before. He'd texted her Saturday during her lunch break and then called her, just as he said he would. They'd talked for over an hour before they were interrupted by Brian.

She'd overheard Brian in the background teasing James about talking to "that Plain girl from the beach." James had told Brian to get lost and apologized to Alana for Brian's snide remark. He'd gone on to say what a good friend Brian had been to him at college and how he considered him to be his brother. Since James didn't have any siblings, he felt blessed to have Brian in his life, even though sometimes he acted immature. Alana told James she understood and shared a little about her relationship with her sisters.

She replayed the conversation in her mind:

~

"I love my sisters so much. They're always there for me. I'm very close with my oldest sister, Leora. But my second-oldest sister, Francine, and I clash sometimes. Still, I know she'd be there for me if I needed her."

"You mentioned you had a younger sister as well, right?" he asked.

"Yes, Violet. She lives in Sarasota too. In fact, she's the one who's taking me to get my stitches out Monday morning.

"Taking you? Do you mean she's going with you?"

Alana furrowed her brows, puzzled by James' question.

"No, I mean taking me. Violet has a car."

"But isn't she Amish?" James' voice seemed to raise a notch.

"No, she's not."

"I'm surprised. I know you said that you haven't joined the church yet, but I figured your whole family is Amish. That's unusual, isn't it?"

"Not really. It's more common these days, I think," Alana explained.

"That's interesting. And your family accepted your sister's decision?"

"Yes, of course. My parents hoped we'd all join the church and settle near them, but more importantly, they want us to follow the path God has for us, even if it means living differently than them or taking us far away," she said, fighting off a yawn.

"It's late. I'll let you go. I can't wait to see you tomorrow," he said before hanging up.

~

Alana pulled her mind back to the present, checked the time on the stove, finished mixing the ingredients for Marie's Homesteader Beans in the slow cooker, and set it to low before moving over to the sink to wash the dishes. *I need to clean up and start thinking about what to wear.*

~

Three hours later, Alana laughed as the wind whipped through her hair. James had arrived promptly at four. He'd removed the Jeep's hardtop, and now they traveled down the road toward Bradenton. Thankfully, the morning storms had cleared, and the sun shone brightly.

"Having fun?" James asked as they slowed for a red light.

"Yes! I've never ridden in a Jeep with the top off before. My hair must be a mess, though." She reached up to tuck her long locks behind her ear.

"Your hair looks nice like that," James said as he gazed into her eyes.

"Thank you."

He jerked at the loud blast of a car horn behind him. "Whoops!" James stepped on the gas. "I didn't notice the light change." He felt the heat of embarrassment creep up his neck. Alana didn't seem to notice. She was busy trying to keep the hair out of her eyes.

At the next red light, James reached under his seat, pulled out a baseball cap and handed it to Alana. "This will keep your hair out of your face."

Alana smiled as she placed it on her head. "How do I look?"

"Beautiful," James whispered.

"Uh, James? The light's green." Alana snickered as James accelerated through the intersection.

James and Alana carried their food into the house, following the sound of voices coming from the kitchen.

"James!" a pretty, brunette girl called as she came through the open patio doors and made her way toward him.

"Hi, Paige." James turned to the side as she moved to give him a hug. "Let me introduce you to Alana."

"I'm Paige. Cute hat." She pointed at it then turned to James. "I didn't know you were bringing a friend."

"Speaking of friends. . . Have you seen Brian?" James asked.

"Yeah, he's on the lanai filling the cooler with soda and water," Paige replied.

"Let's put our food on the table and find him, Alana. Then I'll introduce you to some others. I think a few people you met in Venice are here too." James smiled encouragingly as he guided Alana toward the food table. He wondered if she was bothered by the interaction between him and Paige. He watched as she shifted from one foot to the other.

"I think I'd like to freshen up a bit first, if that's okay." Alana placed a hand on his arm.

"Sure thing. The bathroom's down the hall." He pointed her in the right direction.

~

In the bathroom, Alana fussed with her hair, running her fingers through it to work out some of the tangles caused from the drive. "*Cute hat.*" She replayed Paige's words. *I wonder if that was a back-handed compliment.* It seemed obvious that Paige was disappointed to see James had brought Alana to this get-together. *He didn't correct her when she said she didn't know he was bringing "a friend" either. Maybe that's all I am, just a friend.*

With one last look at herself in the mirror, she gave her already flushed cheeks a quick pinch and tousled her hair again. *Good enough,* she thought as she took a deep breath, opened the door, and made her way to the kitchen, where James waited for her.

"Alana, this is the young adult pastor, Murray, and his wife, Jenny. This is Alana."

"Hi, Alana," said Murray. "We're glad you could join us this evening."

"Thank you. It's nice to meet you both," Alana said shyly.

"James told us you two met recently in Venice and that you just moved to Sarasota." Jenny smiled at Alana.

"That's right." Alana nodded.

"Well, make yourself at home and enjoy getting to know some wonderful young adults from our church." Murray guided them to the backyard, where others had gathered. "Would you care to participate in the horseshoe tournament?"

Alana looked at James to see if he was interested in joining.

"You bet! Alana?" James seemed excited about it.

"Sure, I'll play. I enjoy throwing horseshoes much better than I like putting them on a horse."

~

"That bean dish you brought tonight was delicious. Is it a family recipe?" James glanced over at Alana and watched as she reached up to adjust his baseball cap. They were traveling back to Siesta Key after a fun-filled evening.

"Yes, it's something my mom, Marie, makes for every big get-together back home. It's simple to make and perfect for backyard barbecues. I can't believe it won first place in the side-dish category. Now, your salmon? I'm not at all surprised it received the grand prize award. Talk about delicious." Alana licked her lips.

"Thanks! Tonight was full of wins for us, wasn't it? We won the horseshoe tournament, and we both won a door prize as well."

"Getting to know some other people was a win too," Alana added. "Your pastor and his wife were so welcoming, and your friends were nice to me."

"The biggest win for me was meeting you, Alana." James reached over and took her hand. Alana's skin felt soft, and her hand seemed to fit perfectly in his.

A few minutes later, James turned down the beach road that led to the cottage.

"I can't believe how fast this evening went. I don't want it to end, but I work tomorrow, and you have your appointment." James let go of her hand, shut off the Jeep, and turned in his seat to look at Alana. He took both of her hands in his and gazed at her intently. "When can I see you again?"

"Are you asking me on a date, James?" Alana tilted her head and smiled.

"I sure am!" He laughed as he reached out and touched the dimple in her cheek. "That's a pretty cute dimple you have, and you do look cute in my hat."

"Thank you." James felt the heat from Alana's cheeks, where his hand remained. She reached up to take off the hat.

"Hey, why don't you keep it? You never know when you're

going to need a hat, right?"

"Right," she murmured as James brought his lips to hers in the sweetest of kisses.

Chapter 10

Siesta Village

Monday morning, Alana peeked out the window, watching for Violet.

"I hope she didn't forget about my appointment." She paced the floor nervously. Her phone buzzed.

I'm on my way. Car troubles.

Alana read the text and plopped down on the sofa, blew out a sigh of relief, and picked up a clothing catalog from the coffee table.

I really need to go shopping for some new clothes. I'll mention it to Violet. Maybe we can go today. Alana flipped through the pages and thought about the styles she'd seen other young women her age wear since arriving in Sarasota. Violet wore skirts and plain tops, and sometimes if she went to the beach, she wore capris or modest shorts. The girls from James' church group wore jeans, capris, or shorts, and they all dressed modestly, except for Paige, who'd been wearing short shorts and a spaghetti-strap tank top the night before. *I'd never feel comfortable wearing something like that*, she mused. *But if I'm going to live in the English world, I need to figure out what my style is.*

Alana jumped when she heard the beep of a horn. She

grabbed her purse from the coatrack and turned to lock the door behind her.

She hurried to where Violet had double parked. "Thanks for taking me to get my stitches out, Violet. Having you there will help calm my nerves," she said as she settled into her seat and buckled her belt.

"You're nervous?" Violet seemed surprised. "Why? It won't hurt like it did when you had them put in, and besides, this isn't your first time. You've had more stitches than any of us!" She laughed as she put the car in gear and pulled out.

"Don't remind me," Alana mumbled. "I have the day off, so if you want, maybe we can go shopping after my appointment. I need some new clothes. We can get lunch too—my treat."

~

Alana dropped her purse and shopping bags on the floor of her bedroom and flopped onto the bed with a heavy sigh.

What am I going to say to James? While she was shopping with Violet, James had texted her and asked what she was doing tonight, and if she had no plans, wondered if she'd like to go bike riding with him around the village.

She'd texted back and told him she was out shopping with her sister, and she'd let him know when she got home. She really liked James and didn't want him to think she wasn't interested, but there was no way she was going to go bike riding with him, knowing how riding a bike usually turned out for her.

Alana rubbed her temples, feeling a headache coming on.

I guess I'll let James know I have a headache and don't feel up to a bike ride. It's true, and this way he won't know that I'm afraid to ride a bike.

She sent James a text, explaining. A few minutes later, he responded.

SORRY YOU HAVE A HEADACHE. NEED ANYTHING?

NO, THANKS. I JUST NEED TO REST.

I'LL BE PRAYING YOUR HEADACHE PASSES SOON.

Alana fidgeted with the bedspread as she read the text. *I really want to see James again. Maybe I can suggest we get together tomorrow after work. I don't want to be too forward.*

Taking a deep breath for courage, Alana texted James again.

ARE YOU FREE TOMORROW EVENING? WANT TO JOIN ME FOR A PICNIC DINNER ON THE BEACH?

YES! I'LL PICK YOU UP AT 6:45. Alana's heart sped up when she saw his reply.

PERFECT. I'LL TAKE CARE OF THE FOOD, she typed, adding a happy face emoji.

Alana felt better already, knowing that she'd see James tomorrow and the date wouldn't involve a bike. She relaxed against her pillows and soon drifted off to sleep.

Sarasota

James slid into the front seat of his rig. He was glad work was done and he could finally go home and relax. He'd worked the yellow tower at Lido Beach today, and it had been rough. They were shorthanded because several lifeguards had called out, which meant James had to cover a lot more area. When he finally got a break, he'd texted Alana and asked if she wanted to go biking. She told him she'd get back to him later, but he didn't get an answer for several hours, and he'd spent the time worrying that she might not want to go out with him.

When he was closing the lifeguard tower for the evening, his phone buzzed. He was disappointed when Alana turned him down saying she had a headache. His doubts about how she felt about him were growing. Maybe she didn't like him and the headache was an excuse.

When Alana texted him back a few minutes later and asked him to join her the next evening for a picnic on the beach, the doubts fled.

He began to relax. He started the Jeep and reached to turn up the radio when his phone buzzed. Looking down at the screen, he saw that it was his mother calling.

"Hi, Mom," he answered.

"Hello, Son. I hope I'm not catching you at a bad time."

"Nope. I'm just getting off work and was about to head home. Let me put you on speaker so we can talk as I drive."

"I don't want to distract you while you're driving."

"It's fine. I have a holder for my phone, so my hands are free," he explained. "How are you and Dad? I meant to call, but I've been busy."

"We're well, but I did want to check in and see how your job is going and give you some family news," Mom said.

"Today was tough, due to a shortage of lifeguards, but overall, it's a great summer job. I'm looking forward to school starting, though. I can't wait to meet my students."

James told his mom a little more about his job and some of the activities he'd participated in with the young adult group from church.

"Have you made any special friends yet?" she asked.

"Well, since you brought it up. . ." James explained about meeting Alana.

"Really? I was just teasing you, but I'm so happy!" Mom sounded excited.

"Mom, take it easy. It's a new friendship, and we've only had a couple of dates."

James gave his mother a few details about Alana. "She's a talented artist. She can capture a sunset on canvas as it's unfolding. She has a very sweet spirit about her, and she's beautiful, but she doesn't seem to know it. You know what I mean?"

"I think I do, James. Does she share your faith in the Lord?"

"To be honest, I didn't ask her. But I know she attends church, sometimes with her sister and brother-in-law, and sometimes with her boss." James hoped his mom wouldn't push the issue further. He didn't feel like getting into the part about Alana being from an Amish family.

"I know you're a grown man, but please listen. Before you get serious, make sure you're on the same page regarding your faith. It's important to be equally yoked."

"I know, Mom. Don't worry, I'll continue to seek God's will in my life." James tried not to let her know that he felt a little annoyed by the advice.

"Anyway, I have something to discuss with you." Mom sounded serious.

"What is it? You're freaking me out." James felt his heart rate increase, and he gripped the steering wheel tightly.

"Everything's fine, Son. It's just that the plans we made to visit you in August before school starts have changed."

"Oh?"

"We heard from your grandfather this weekend."

"I bet that was an enjoyable conversation."

"James, he's your only living grandfather and your dad's father. You need to be respectful, even if you don't have a great relationship with him." James felt his mother's admonishment through the phone.

"Sorry, Mom. You're right, and it's true. I don't have a great relationship with him and doubt I ever will. He's so angry and bitter all the time. After the last visit we had, I really dread seeing him."

"I understand. But when he called, he sounded different. He told us that he's planning a surprise birthday trip for your grandmother in early July. She's always wanted to visit Sarasota, so he thought that since you're living there now and we were planning to come visit you in August, maybe we'd change our trip and join in on the surprise."

"I can't believe he wanted to do something for Grandma for a change. Usually, she's the one bending over backward for him." James blew out a breath. "But I'm all for surprising Grandma for her birthday, and I'll try to set aside my feelings about Grandpa while they're here."

"Thank you, James. This visit is very important. They aren't getting any younger."

"I know, Mom." James pulled into the carport. "I'm home."

"All right. I'll let you go. Let's try to visit more often, okay? I want to hear more about how your new friendship with Alana is going."

"Will do, Mom. Thanks for calling. Tell Dad I said hi, and remember, I love you both."

"We love you too, James."

James hit the DISCONNECT button and sat back in his seat. He ran his hands through his hair and across his face. *Great. . .just great. If my relationship is progressing with Alana by the time they all come to visit, Mom is going to want to meet her, and how am I going to explain the situation with my grandparents to Alana?* James felt overwhelmed.

Bowing his head, he prayed. *Lord, help me deal with my negative attitude toward my grandfather. Help me find the right opportunity to explain my relationship with him to Alana. Speaking of Alana, please help her headache to ease. Bless our relationship, and if it's Your will, help it to grow into something that will last a lifetime. Thank You, Lord, for Your faithfulness.*

Chapter 11

SIESTA KEY VILLAGE

Three weeks later

Alana settled in the rocking chair on the front porch of Patti's cottage with a cup of coffee and her phone. It was just after 8:30 on Tuesday morning and time for her weekly call with her mother. She knew it must be hard on Mom having three of her daughters living far from home.

She opened her contacts list. As she scanned it, she spotted James' phone number. *I hope I hear from him today.* She smiled at the thought and then hit the icon for her parents' phone number.

"Hello?"

"Mom! I'm glad you remembered our weekly phone check in."

"Of course." Mom laughed. "Just to be safe, I wrote it on my calendar. I didn't want to miss our call. It's always so good to hear your voice."

Alana's mother spent the next few minutes catching her up on the news from home. She was glad to hear that her parents and her sister Francine were all in good health.

"How's your job?" Mom asked.

"I love it. Patti, my boss and landlord, asked if I'd like to sell some of my artwork in the shop."

"That's wonderful, Alana. God has blessed you with this talent, and I'm happy you can use it to help make a living. Have you sold anything yet?"

"Yes. I sold a landscape of the sunset over the Gulf. I also painted some beachscapes on clamshells, and several of those sold too."

Alana told her mom that Patti had left on a trip a week ago, leaving Alana to house-sit, as well as manage the store.

"That's a lot of responsibility. Are you up for that?"

"Of course, *Mamm*. You and *Daed* raised me to be responsible. I have it under control. I'm working every day except Sundays while Patti is gone. It's only for a couple of weeks, so I know I can do it." Alana felt a little annoyed by her mom's questions.

"I'm glad to hear the confidence in your voice. You're right, we raised you to be responsible."

Alana's heart softened a bit at her mother's words. "I am wondering how I'm going to have time to see James as much as I have the last couple of weeks. Things have been going so well."

"I was going to ask you about that. You said he acted strange when he found out your family is Amish. How does he feel about it now?"

"What do you mean?" Alana tapped her foot on the porch. "He doesn't seem to have an issue with it. Besides, I told him I was here in Sarasota to get away from home and figure out what my future holds. He's been supportive of that and hasn't pushed me one way or the other toward a decision."

"I'm sorry if my question made you feel defensive. I just don't want to see you get hurt again. Has he met your sisters?"

"No, not yet. But we have plans to join Leora, John, and Violet at the beach on Sunday."

"That's a great idea. It'll be good for your sisters to get to know your friend."

"You're right, Mom," Alana agreed. "I need to finish getting ready for work. I'll talk to you again next Tuesday, same time. Okay?"

"Looking forward to it. Remember that I'm praying for you and asking the Lord to show you the path He has for you. I love you, Alana."

"Thanks, Mom. Love you too." Alana hung up and sighed as she rose from the rocking chair. *I need to hurry, or I'll be late.*

~

A steady stream of customers kept Alana busy at the cash register. Her coworker Tanya stocked shelves and tidied up the store while she waited on customers. Finally, it slowed down enough for Alana to replenish the change in the cash register. She knelt behind the counter to get into the cash box for some small bills and coins.

"Excuse me," said a deep voice.

Alana popped up from behind the counter, bumping her head as she did. "James!" She rubbed her forehead.

"Are you okay, Alana? I didn't mean to startle you." James reached across the counter and touched the red mark on her forehead.

"I'm fine—just embarrassed." She giggled. "What are you doing here? I thought you were at Lido Beach today."

"They were shorthanded at Crescent Beach, so I volunteered to come out here," James explained. "I'm on my lunch break. Want to join me?"

She glanced at the clock on the register. "Sure! Let me tell my coworker so she can cover the register."

A few minutes later, James and Alana sat at an outside table at a nearby deli.

"I can't believe it's the second week of June already. Time

flies when you're having fun." James picked up Alana's hand and stroked it gently with his thumb.

"Are you having fun, James?"

"Spending time with you is always fun." He grinned and wiggled his eyebrows at her. "I've enjoyed our time together, but there's a lot I don't know about you." He paused and took a drink of his cola.

"What do you want to know?"

"Hmm. . . Let's see. I don't know your favorite type of ice cream, what foods you dislike, what your favorite season is, or even what your favorite color is."

Alana held up her hand, pointing to each finger as she responded. "First, I like most flavors of ice cream, but it's better if it has chocolate in it. Second, I don't like sushi or shellfish. Third, I like the warmer seasons, which is why I enjoy it here so much. Fourth, I don't have a favorite color. To me, they're all beautiful."

James nodded. "Just like you."

Alana pulled her hair forward and hid behind it as she blushed hotly. "You're the only one who's ever said that about me, James."

Reaching over, he pushed the hair away from Alana's face. "It's true. You're beautiful, on the inside as well as the outside."

"Thank you." Alana took a deep breath and looked James in the eyes. "Okay, now that I'm really embarrassed, it's your turn. How would you answer the questions you asked me?"

"Okay, but first I have one more question. I think I already know the answer, but I want to make sure."

"You sound serious, James." Alana fidgeted with her straw.

"Well, it's a serious question. Do you know Jesus as your personal Savior?"

"Yes, I do, and I'm so thankful that God sent His only Son to die on the cross, taking my sin and the sins of the whole world upon Himself. I believe He died and rose again so that anyone who believes in His name can live with Him forever." Alana took a deep breath. "Sorry. I guess I could have just answered yes." She laughed.

"I knew you were a believer. Your sweet spirit is a testimony of your faith." James sat back in his chair and gazed at her.

"There are a lot of things in my life that I'm unsure about, but my salvation isn't one of them. Sometimes, though, I feel that God is probably too busy helping others to be concerned about my problems, and I'm not always sure I know what His will is for me." Alana shrugged.

"I've felt that way before too. I'm glad we're both on the same page about our faith, Alana. We have a lot in common." James pointed to his fingers and counted as he told her, "I also prefer ice cream with chocolate, and warm seasons are my favorite too. As for my least favorite food, I'd have to say liver and onions. My grandfather used to make me eat it when I visited him—so nasty. My favorite color's blue, specifically the color of the Gulf of Mexico. . .and the color of your beautiful eyes."

Alana blushed again. "Your eyes are a nice shade of blue too." She glanced at the time on her phone. "Uh. . .I need to get back to the shop, and I'm sure you need to return to work. Shall we?"

The two stood and cleared their table. James reached down and took Alana's hand as they began the walk back to the shop.

"Hey, we should rent bikes soon and tour the area." James pointed to the rental business across the street from the deli.

"James, I need to tell you something." Alana stopped abruptly, letting go of his hand.

"Okay, Alana. You can tell me anything." James' eyebrows furrowed.

"I hate riding bikes." Alana folded her arms across her chest.

"You do? Why?"

"It's a long story. Maybe tonight we can talk on the phone, and I'll tell you about it." Alana turned and began walking again.

James hurried to catch up, took her hand, and said, "It's a date."

Sarasota

James hit the DISCONNECT button on his phone. He'd talked to Alana for an hour. He'd been sitting in the backyard as they visited because Brian was in the house watching baseball on television, and he'd wanted to be able to talk to Alana in private. Brian seemed a little bent out of shape because they hadn't been hanging out as much as they'd planned.

He rose from the lounge chair and stretched. *I'd better go watch the game with Brian. I don't want him to feel neglected.*

James was surprised to see that although Brian sat in the living room, he wasn't really watching the game. He seemed consumed with his phone.

"What's the score? Are you even watching the game?" James grabbed a pillow off the love seat and threw it at Brian.

"Cut it out, man! I'm watching it, but I'm also in the middle of a conversation with someone—someone who happens to be watching it too, and someone who's not you."

"Wait, you're watching the game with someone who's not here and discussing it by text? That's weird." He chuckled. "Hey, I'm sorry, Brian. I know I've let you down a lot lately, but I'm here now. Let's watch the rest together."

"Yeah, you have let me down. We were supposed to be making this summer about us and just having fun. All you do is work, see Alana, or spend hours talking to her."

"You're right. I've been working a lot. They're understaffed for lifeguards at the beaches. And I know I spend a lot of time with

Alana. I really like her and want to see where this relationship is heading." James trailed off when Brian seemed to be ignoring him.

"Whatever, James." Brian picked up the remote and turned off the television. "I'm going to bed."

"Brian, wait. Do you want to go fishing Saturday morning? I don't work until noon."

"I don't know. I'll think about it," Brian said as he headed down the hall.

James picked up the remote and turned the game back on. *Oh boy. I'd better set some time aside for Brian. It's a good thing Alana's busy with work and watching her boss's house. I'm sure she'll understand if I don't spend as much time with her this week. I'll call her every night, and I'll see her on Sunday, although truthfully, I'm not looking forward to hanging out with her Amish family.*

Chapter 12

Pinecraft Village

The following week, Alana slid into the booth at Der Dutchman. Her boss had returned, and Alana had the day off. She was meeting Leora for lunch. It had been awhile since she'd had one-on-one time with her sister. At the beach on Sunday, she hadn't been able to visit much with her sisters, thanks to the weird mood James seemed to be in all day. He'd been quiet and withdrawn, hardly saying two words to anybody except Alana. Even then he wasn't his usual upbeat self. She wondered if he was uncomfortable because he felt he had to act a certain way around her Amish family. Then she thought his attitude might have to do with her.

After they'd eaten lunch, James suggested they go play in the water. As soon as he mentioned it, Alana felt apprehensive. The thought of stepping foot in the surf brought back all the pain and suffering she'd experienced at Venice when she'd cut her foot.

Now she let her mind drift back to that moment between them.

~

"Come on, Alana. It'll be fun and will feel so good to cool off."

James stood and reached to help Alana up from the blanket where she sat.

"I told you, James. I don't feel like going in the water. Can't we just walk along the shore and look for shells?"

"Why don't you want to go in the water?" James shrugged his shoulders and pointed to the surf. "It's not too crowded, and the water's calm."

"I don't enjoy being in the water, and I'm not going to do it." She heaved a sigh of frustration, lowered her head, scooped up a handful of sand, and slowly released it through her fingers.

"Fine then. You sit here while I go cool off." James sprinted toward the water, leaving Alana sitting by herself in the hot sun.

~~~

"Sorry I'm late." Leora sat down across from Alana. "Hey! Earth to Alana!" Leora snapped her fingers in front of Alana's face, bringing her abruptly back to the present.

"Sorry, Leora. I was deep in thought."

"Is everything okay? Do you want to talk about it?"

"I was thinking about Sunday. James acted so strange, and the day didn't go the way I thought it would."

"He seemed a little uncomfortable," Leora remarked. "Maybe he has a hard time in new situations with new people."

"Maybe." Alana shrugged. "Want to get the buffet for lunch? I'm treating today."

"I always enjoy eating from the buffet." Leora rose from the booth. "Come on, Sis. Let's get our food, and then we can get caught up with each other."
~~~

~

Tuesday, after work, James opened the browser on his laptop and searched for local businesses that offered horseback riding. He felt terrible about the way he'd acted on Sunday, first toward Alana's family, and then toward Alana. He knew that some of his attitude had to do with the upcoming visit with his own family. He dreaded the reunion that was quickly approaching.

When Alana had refused to go in the water, he'd wondered if she was trying to get even with him for being distant all day. *That isn't fair*, he told himself as he clicked on the first horseback-riding business that came up. *Alana's never shown that sort of "get even" behavior before. She's too sweet to do that.* But he did get the feeling that something deeper was going on with Alana and was surprised by her stubborn response.

James knew he'd handled the whole situation badly. He was determined to make it up to Alana and decided to surprise her with a fun date. Her boss was back and had given her a couple of extra days off for the week. Since he was also off on Thursday, they could spend the whole day together.

Yesterday, while James was working, he'd spent some time thinking about the perfect date. He wanted it to be something that Alana would really enjoy and was familiar with. He knew how she felt about riding bikes, so that idea was out. As he'd sat on the deck of the lifeguard tower, he'd seen a couple of people on horses coming down the beach. *Horses! That's perfect. I'll research it tomorrow*, he'd thought.

He clicked on the description of the sunset trail ride at Myakka River Trail Rides. *Man, that's expensive. I'd better see if there is something a little more affordable.* Scrolling down, he spotted a one-hour ride. *That's better. It's still expensive, but Alana's worth it.* He clicked the link for reservations. *She's going to be so surprised!*

~

Thursday morning, on his way to pick up Alana, James stopped for coffee and doughnuts. He was excited to see her reaction to the day he'd planned. He'd told her not to eat breakfast and suggested she wear jeans and tennis shoes. Other than that, he didn't give her any clues as to where they were going or what they'd be doing.

Now they drove down the road, sipping their coffee and munching on the delicious doughnuts. Alana was quiet beside him, and he reached over and wrapped his fingers gently around hers.

"I'm glad we both had the day off. I wanted to make up for my foul mood on Sunday," he explained.

"I noticed something was up with you," she replied. "Do you want to talk about it?"

"Not really, but I do owe you an explanation. For now, I'll just tell you that my family is coming for a visit soon, and I'm feeling stressed about it."

"I'm sorry you're feeling that way. I hope I get a chance to meet your parents while they're here—that is, if you want me to."

"I know my mom and dad would love to meet you. I'm not sure I want to put you through meeting my grandparents, though. Especially my grandfather."

Alana lifted her eyebrows. "Why?"

"Let's just say he can be difficult and leave it at that." James turned down a narrow road. "Alana, cover your eyes and don't look until I tell you to, please."

"You're really going to keep this date a secret, aren't you?" Alana snickered and covered her eyes.

"No peeking, okay? We're almost there." He pulled into a parking spot and put the Jeep into PARK. He hopped out, came around to the passenger side of the vehicle, and opened the door.

"Okay, give me your other hand, but keep those eyes covered. I'll lead you to our adventure."

~

Myakka City

Alana let James guide her across the dirt parking lot. She took a deep breath and wrinkled her nose at the smell. "Where are we—Indiana?" she joked. "It smells like home."

James chuckled. "Are you ready? Uncover your eyes."

Removing her hand, Alana looked around. The first thing she saw was a hitching post with six saddled horses. Her eyes darted around, taking in as much information as her brain would allow. To the left of the hitching post was a covered area where a dozen ATVs were parked. She glanced back at the horses, who danced and snorted where they stood.

"Are we going to ride the ATVs, James?"

"Not today, Alana. We're going on a trail ride by horseback!" He grinned.

"Seriously?" Alana felt the blood drain from her face, and she sank slowly to the ground.

"Alana, what is it?" James knelt beside her, gently rubbing her back.

She put her head down between her knees and tried to get her breathing under control. She felt cold and clammy and was seeing spots.

After a few minutes, she found her voice. "I'm okay, but if you think I'm getting anywhere near a horse, you can think again!"

~

James was shocked at Alana's reaction. He couldn't believe she'd freaked out like that. He left her sitting at a picnic table, sipping water, while he went over to the office to see about a refund. He'd asked Alana if she'd rather take the ATV tour, and she'd told him that someday she would—just not today. In fact, she'd asked him to take her back home.

He felt annoyed during the drive back, which seemed to take forever. Alana sat silently beside him. He wasn't sure what to say, so he turned up the radio. *Man, what a wasted day.* He gripped the steering wheel tightly. He'd spent hard-earned money on gas and food, not to mention the trail ride. He couldn't get a refund, but he was able to get a voucher so that he could come back another day. *Maybe I'll see if Brian wants to go with me.*

James pulled up in front of the cottage and turned off his rig. He looked over at Alana and waited.

Alana stared down at her hands, tightly clasped in her lap. He saw tears on her cheeks and reached out to wipe away the moisture.

"I'm sorry," she whispered. "I ruined the day and all because I didn't tell you about my fear of horses." Alana reached up to wipe her nose with a tissue she'd pulled from her purse.

"It's all right Alana. But I get the feeling you struggle with fear about many things. Am I correct?" he asked gently.

Alana buried her face in her hands and sobbed.

James reached over and pulled Alana to him. He stroked her back, trying to soothe away her tears. "I shouldn't have planned such an extravagant date without talking to you about it first. I assumed you'd be comfortable around horses because of your Amish background, and that's my fault. When you're feeling up to it, maybe you can tell me why you're afraid of horses."

Alana nodded. "Okay, James. I'd better go. My head hurts, and I need to lie down."

James walked her to the front door and gave her a tender kiss on the forehead. "Feel better." He hurried back to the Jeep, then turned and called, "I'll check on you later."

Chapter 13

Siesta Key Village

The two weeks following the disastrous date had been busy for Alana. Not only had the shop been filled with tourists, but the demand for her artwork had increased. Each evening she could be found on the porch painting sunsets on canvas or seascapes on clamshells. She appreciated the extra income her artwork was bringing in, but she had to admit, she missed spending time with James.

Now she was once again on the porch. She'd been scrolling through the many sunset pictures she'd taken since arriving in Sarasota, looking for inspiration, when she came to the pictures from her first day in Sarasota. As she scanned the pictures, she stopped abruptly at the last picture she'd taken that day. It was a picture of the *Marina Jack II* and the harbor. She remembered being annoyed that she'd captured people in it, but now her heart sped up as she realized who was in the picture. *It's James! Our paths crossed on my very first day here. I can't wait to show him this picture. I'll send it to him as soon as I hear from him.*

James had also been busy, picking up double shifts so that he could attend a weekend retreat right before his family arrived.

He'd told Alana that he'd heard about the retreat from Murray, the young adult pastor at church. Alana thought back to a conversation they'd had the week before.

James had confided in Alana that he was struggling with his attitude toward his grandfather. He'd shared that growing up, his grandfather seemed bitter and angry toward him whenever he'd visit over the summer. As he grew, nothing he did could please his grandpa. Finally, when James turned eighteen, he'd told his grandparents that since he was heading to college, he wouldn't be spending any more time visiting them. The last time he'd seen them was four years ago.

Alana had suggested he speak with Murray and see if he had any wise words of advice on getting through the visit. Murray did have some advice for James, and one of his suggestions was to attend the retreat with him, which would focus on the topic of dealing with bitterness and anger. She remembered exactly how the conversation went.

"I think that's a wonderful idea, James. I'm happy you felt comfortable sharing with me about the relationship between you and your grandfather."

"*And I appreciate you opening up to me about some of the fears you have*," James said.

In an earlier conversation, Alana had told James about her fear of horses, bikes, bad relationships, and her newest fear of wading in the surf. His reaction wasn't what she thought it would be. She'd figured he would react like her last boyfriend had—calling her fears "ridiculous" and telling her to "get over it." Instead, James had listened with quiet sympathy. He'd told Alana he'd be praying that God would help her overcome her fears. After they'd hung up, James had texted her a scripture that spoke about fear. He'd also sent her a couple of links to Christian songs that talked about overcoming fear.

Alana clicked on one of the links and listened as the song played. She picked up the paintbrush and began to blend the colors of a beautiful Gulf sunset, moving the brush across the canvas in time to the music. Her phone vibrated, and she set the brush in a jar of water to soak. She picked it up and read the message from James:

I made it to the retreat.

I'm glad! I hope you find some answers.

Thanks. Hey, they want us to put our phones away so we're not distracted while we're here. I'll text you when it's over on Sunday.

Sounds good. Are we still going to the sunset-watching beach party with the young adult group, Sunday evening?

Planning on it! He signed off with a heart emoji.

Alana resumed her painting, humming along to the song James had sent her.

Later Alana remembered the picture she'd captured of James on the *Marina Jack II*. *I'll send it to him now even though his phone is turned off. It'll be the first thing he sees when he turns it back on.*

Tampa, Florida

James closed the texting app on his phone, preparing to shut it off for the next few days while he focused on his spiritual life. Before he could, he received another text, this one from Paige.

Hi, James. Did you make it to the retreat?

Yup, I did.

Cool. You left your work bag in the tower.

I did? Can you grab it for me?

Sure thing.

Thanks. I've got to go.

No problem! Looking forward to seeing you on Sunday at the young adult beach party.

James turned off his phone, tossed it toward his bag, and hurried out the door. It was time for the first session, and he was eager to see what the speaker had to say about dealing with bitter and angry people.

Sunday morning, James sat next to Murray in the final session of the retreat. He felt like he'd been on an emotional roller coaster. The weekend had done little to show him how to deal with his grandfather's bitterness. Instead, it had revealed to James his own anger and bitterness that he felt toward his grandfather.

James opened his New Living Translation Bible and read Ephesians 4:31–32: "Get rid of all bitterness, rage, anger, harsh words, and slander, as well as all types of evil behavior. Instead, be kind to each other, tenderhearted, forgiving one another, just as God through Christ has forgiven you."

He listened as the speaker reminded them that the world is full of sin, which causes plenty of situations in life that produce feelings of bitterness, anger, and even hatred.

"No one is immune to these situations. We're all sinners, and every one of us will experience a time when someone does something to us that will cause us to feel bitter. We like to use it as an excuse for our own behavior; we break relationships and refuse to forgive. But at the root of it all is pride. What would happen, if instead of holding on to those nasty, bitter feelings, we asked the Lord to help us overcome the anger and bitterness we feel? What would happen if our first response was love?"

James swallowed the lump that seemed to engulf his throat.

I've been holding on to the pain I felt, and I allowed bitterness to grow in my own heart. I haven't tried to show love to either of my grandparents, especially my grandfather. Please forgive me, Jesus, for letting bitterness and anger fill my heart. Help me to make things right with Grandpa and help him to find a way to overcome his own bitterness. Help us to set aside our pride, and please bring healing to our hearts.

Siesta Key Village

Sunday afternoon, Alana sat on the porch with her Bible. God had been speaking to her all week through the scriptures and songs James had shared with her and through the sermon at church that morning.

The pastor preached about emotions and why they matter. Alana had never really thought about how God, Creator of all things, also created emotions. As she listened to the message, she began to realize that God created emotions for a reason, but when one focuses too much on the negative aspects of an emotion, it can cause problems that will last a lifetime. *That's what I've been doing—focusing on the negative aspects of fear.* She recalled the pastor's words.

"Fear can be a good thing. It's a powerful emotion that everyone experiences at some point in their life. But when fear takes over and becomes what drives our thoughts, decisions, and actions, that's when we have a problem. The best way to protect ourselves from this is by building a strong foundation on the Lord. Let our relationship with God be what drives us in our thoughts, decisions, and actions."

Alana opened her Bible to 2 Timothy 1:7 and read, "For God has not given us a spirit of fear and timidity, but of power, love, and self-discipline."

That's right. This negative spirit of fear and timidity is not from the

Lord! He has given me power and love, and I can be self-disciplined in learning how to deal with the things that have caused me pain. I don't need to let fear prevent me from doing things that I might enjoy—like playing in the surf or riding bikes.

Alana checked the time on her phone. The young adult beach party would be starting in a couple of hours. "It's time to tackle my fears and get back on the bike," she said out loud as she headed into the house to get ready.

Crescent Beach

The sun was making its descent when Alana arrived at the beach. She pulled into the parking lot and rode up to the bike rack. Her eyes scanned the parking lot for James' Jeep as she securely locked the bike she'd borrowed from Patti.

She saw a group of young adults gathered around the picnic table area watching the setting sun. She spotted a tall man with his back to her wearing a hooded sweatshirt that had the name Fisher across the back.

"James." Alana began making her way toward him.

Just then she saw Paige approach, reach her arms around his neck, and pull him in for a kiss. Alana covered her mouth with her hand and gasped as she watched him bend down and return the kiss.

Chapter 14

Alana fumbled with the bike lock with one hand while she wiped tears away with her other. As soon as the bike was free of the rack, she hopped on and rode away from the scene on the beach without looking back.

At Patti's cottage, she took a few deep breaths as she put the bike in the storage shed. *Pull it together, Alana*, she thought as she headed into the house.

"Back already?" Patti asked from the recliner, where she browsed through a magazine. "Alana, what's wrong? You look upset." Patti stood and moved toward Alana.

Alana reached for Patti and fell into her arms with a sob. "I can't believe it! I thought James was different and that he cared for me."

"Take some deep breaths and tell me what happened," Patti coaxed as she led Alana to the couch.

Alana replayed the events for Patti as she began to calm down.

"I'm sorry, Alana. But maybe there's a reasonable explanation for what happened."

"But I saw him return Paige's kiss. He's never kissed me that passionately before. I still can't believe it, but I saw it, so I know it's true. That explains why I didn't hear from him today. I bet he's been flirting with both of us, and he's too much of a coward to tell me he likes someone else," Alana huffed.

"I don't know, Alana. From what I know of James, that doesn't sound like him at all. One thing I do know is that while tonight's events are certainly upsetting for you, you have a reason to rejoice. You were able to let go of your fear of riding a bike. That's cause for celebration, don't you think?" Patti rubbed Alana's back.

Alana nodded slowly. "I guess so."

"Why don't you take the day off tomorrow and go visit your sister Leora? I know you're close with her, and that might make you feel better."

"Okay, and thank you Patti. You've been a big support to me these last couple of months." Alana rose from the couch.

"You're welcome, sweetie. Try to get some rest. I'll be praying that you sleep well tonight."

Sarasota

James had felt such a pressing need to make things right between his grandfather and himself that as soon as the retreat was over, he'd grabbed his overnight bag and jumped into his rig for the hour-long drive back to Sarasota. He had to stop at his place to find the address of the vacation rental where his family would be staying for the next week.

Now James tossed his bag on the bed and unzipped it to pull out his cell phone. He hadn't bothered to get it out of his bag after the retreat. He had only one thing on his mind at the time. But then he remembered that he'd promised Alana that they'd go to the beach party tonight, and he needed to cancel.

After a few minutes of digging around, he dumped the entire bag out on the bed.

"Where are you, phone?" he said, searching through the pile

of clothes. "Ugh! Don't tell me I left it there."

James recalled turning it off and tossing it toward his bag the first night of the retreat. *I bet it missed the bag and fell behind the bed. That's just great. I don't have time to deal with that now. I've got to go see my family. Alana will understand, I'm sure.*

Pinecraft

James hurried up the walkway to the house and knocked on the door. He felt nervous but knew what he needed to do.

"Guder owed, Grossvadder." James greeted the elderly Amish man who'd opened the door.

"James! Good evening to you," said the man, pulling James in for a hug.

"I'm so glad you're here," they both said at the same time.

"Come in. I have much to say to you. Let's sit here." Grandpa motioned to the kitchen table.

"Grandpa, I need to say some things to you too. Please, let me go first." James took a deep breath. "I want to ask for your forgiveness. I realized that I've been carrying a lot of bitterness and anger toward you. The Lord showed me that I have let bitterness take root in my heart and have held on to it out of pride. Please forgive me for my attitude, and especially for the awful things I said to you the last time I saw you." James cleared his throat, feeling tears well in his eyes as he watched the expression on his grandfather's face.

"Oh, James, that's why we are here. The Lord showed me the same things about myself. I know I have been nothing but bitter and angry for years. It was how I dealt with my feelings when your daed told me he was leaving home and not joining the church. I couldn't believe my only child would leave the faith or his family.

What I didn't understand is that God had called your daed to a ministry that he never would have been a part of if he'd stayed. He'd never have been able to be a teacher at a school for students with disabilities. But God knew. He also knew that growing up on a horse-breeding farm would equip your dad with skills he could use with his students."

James sank into a chair at the kitchen table as his parents and grandmother came into the kitchen.

"I was just telling James how the Lord has taken hold of my heart and shown me my sin," Grandpa told the family as he joined James at the table. "James, I've already made things right between me and your daed, but now I need to make things right with you. You see, when you were born, I hoped that someday you'd take over my business for me. But as you grew older, I saw so much of your father in you. You had such a natural gift for nurturing others, and you didn't seem interested in the Plain life. It frustrated me, so instead of encouraging you, I grew even more bitter and angry, which led to me distancing myself from you. Please forgive me and know that I love you, Grandson. I'm so pleased with your accomplishments."

"I forgive you, Grandpa. Will you forgive me?" James reached his hand out to his grandpa.

Grandpa grasped James' hand tightly and pulled him in for another hug. "I forgive you."

James rubbed the moisture from his cheeks and glanced around the table at each member of his family. "I love you all so much!"

~

Patti was right, Alana thought. *Taking the day off from work and visiting Leora was just what I needed.* Alana had spent time lying in the sun on the lanai while she told Leora about her weekend, from the wonderful healing of her fears to the awful realization that James didn't feel the same way about her as she felt about him. Leora had listened with sympathy and rejoiced with Alana over her freedom from fear.

Now the two sisters were riding bikes to the corner ice cream shop in Pinecraft.

As they grew closer, Alana drew in a sharp breath. "Seriously?"

"What?" Leora glanced over as they rode side by side.

"I think I see James. But what would he be doing in Pinecraft, and why would he be with that older Amish couple?" She pointed as she slowed her bike to a stop.

"I'm sure it's not him. Come on, Alana," Leora urged, as she started moving her bike again.

"And I'm sure it is!" Alana quickly turned her bike and peddled back in the direction they'd come.

"Alana!" A deep male voice called her name as she sped down the street.

"Wait," Leora huffed as she caught up to Alana. "James was calling for you. You should at least hear what he has to say for himself. Let's go back."

"No way! It's too late now," Alana said as she peddled faster.

Siesta Key Beach, Sunset Pier

Three days later, James strolled along the water's edge. He'd finally managed to get his phone back, and now he looked through the missed messages from the past five days. "Nothing from Alana," he said out loud.

She must be so mad because I didn't tell her about my own Amish heritage. I bet she feels like I lied to her. In a way, I guess I did. I should've been willing to share all the details about my relationship with my grandpa. Now I might not get to tell her how the Lord has worked in our lives. Maybe I'll give Alana some time, and if I don't hear from her soon, I'll call. But wait. Why should I have to do that? If she's so mad at me that she can't forgive me, then maybe we don't belong together. James argued with himself as he wandered aimlessly along the beach.

~

It was almost closing time when Alana heard the bell ring on the shop door. She hurried to the front to greet the customer and stopped midway when she spotted Paige and Brian.

"Alana! We missed you at the beach party the other night," Paige greeted with a friendly smile.

"I came, but then I left." Alana shrugged her shoulders, turned on her heel, and stepped behind the register. "Is there something I can help you with?"

"Yeah." Brian smacked his hand on the counter. "You can tell me why you're giving James the cold shoulder!"

"What do you mean? James made things very clear to me when I saw him kissing you." She pointed a finger at Paige.

"What?" Paige's eyes grew round, and she blinked rapidly. "James has never kissed me. Why would you say such a thing? Brian is my boyfriend." She quickly put an arm around Brian's waist.

"But I saw you two at the beach party. I saw you reach up and put your arms around James' neck and pull him in for a kiss, and then I saw him kiss you back."

"Uh. . .I think I know what happened," Brian said. "That night I was wearing James' hooded sweatshirt. I bet you saw his last name on the back and thought it was him."

Alana slapped her hand against her forehead. "Oh no! But then why didn't he call me?"

"Well," Paige began. "He lost his phone behind the bed at the retreat and didn't realize it. He only got it back today. He thinks you're mad at him because he didn't tell you about his Amish family."

"His *what*?" Alana's voice raised an octave.

"Look, you probably need to discuss this with each other. I think there's been a big misunderstanding."

"Do you know where he is?" Alana glanced at her watch and began shutting down the register.

"He's at Sunset Pier," Brian said.

"Okay. Thanks for coming in and setting me straight. I'll close and go find him. Oh, and congratulations on your new relationship." Alana ushered them to the front door, locked it behind them, and turned the sign in the window to CLOSED.

~

As soon as Alana arrived at the pier, she spotted James. He sat on an old piece of concrete, staring off at the horizon.

"Is this seat taken?" Alana sank down next to him.

"Alana! What are you doing here? I didn't think you'd ever speak to me again."

"Well, me neither, but then I found out that there was a big misunderstanding between us, and I wanted to make it right."

"I know, and it was all my fault. I should have told you about my Amish family. I'm sure you were shocked when you saw us in Pinecraft getting ice cream."

"I was shocked, but not because of that. You see, the night before, I rode Patti's bike to the beach party, and when I got there, I saw you—well, I thought it was you—kissing Paige." She hesitated as she put her hands on her flaming hot cheeks. "Turns out, what I saw was Brian wearing a sweatshirt with your name on it kissing Paige." She fidgeted with her hair.

"Wait, you rode a bike?" James took Alana's hands in his and grinned.

"That's the part you're going to focus on?" Alana laughed

and squeezed James' hands.

"I'm sorry I ignored you in Pinecraft on Monday. I felt so hurt by what I saw."

"Alana, surely you must know how I feel about you." James let go of her hands and reached up to gently touch her cheek as he gazed into her eyes.

"I think I might need you to tell me, just so I can be sure." Alana lowered her eyes.

"Every day when I wake up, you're the first thing on my mind. All day long, I think about you and can't wait to see you or talk to you again. At the end of the day, after I thank the Lord for bringing you into my life. . ." James stopped. He reached out his hand and lifted Alana's chin so she was looking at him once more. "I love you, Alana."

Alana's chin trembled, and she blinked away the tears quickly forming in her eyes. "Oh, James, I love you too."

James drew Alana close and kissed her tenderly.

When the kiss ended, Alana pulled away and looked up at James. "What did you think about the picture I sent you?"

"What picture?" James scratched his head.

"Friday night, I was looking at pictures I took since I came to Sarasota. There was this picture I took my first night in Sarasota, and you are in it."

"No way. I never saw the picture on my phone."

"Maybe it never went through."

"Where was I?" With raised eyebrows, he tilted his head.

"On the *Marina Jack II* sunset dinner cruise." Alana pulled out her phone, found the picture, and showed him. "Our paths crossed from the moment I arrived, and I believe God brought us together for a reason."

James pulled Alana in for another kiss. "I know He did."

Alana pulled away and gazed into James' eyes. "I have a lot to tell you about how the Lord worked in my life over the past weekend. And if I'm not mistaken, I bet you have a story to tell, as well."

"I sure do. And we have some time before the sun sets." James pulled Alana to her feet and kissed her once more.

Epilogue

Caspersen Beach

April 21

Alana stretched out on the beach blanket next to her sisters and mom. It was Leora's birthday, and the whole family had come to celebrate. It was the first time their parents had visited Florida, and they were having a wonderful time together.

Alana shielded the sun from her eyes as she scanned the shoreline for James, who'd been looking for shark teeth in the surf with her dad and Leora's husband, John.

Just then she spotted him coming toward her.

"Alana, come join me. I found a great spot to hunt before the sun sets."

"I don't know, James. The last time I looked for shark teeth at sunset, I ended up getting stitches."

"And that's why you'll put your water shoes on. Besides, you've been in the surf many times since then, and you've been fine," James reasoned.

"I know. I'm just teasing you. I'm coming."

Alana followed James to his hunting spot, and the two began

scooping, dumping, and sorting through the sandy debris.

"Alana, look. There's a pod of dolphins!" James pointed toward the horizon.

Alana glanced up. "I don't see anything."

"Hmm, I thought for sure I saw some. Weird." James shrugged as he pulled up another scoop from the ocean floor. "Can you look through the sieve before I dump this next load?" he asked.

Alana bent her head to examine the contents of the sieve, running her hand slowly back and forth. "What on earth?" She stopped abruptly as her hand uncovered a sparkling diamond ring. Her head snapped up, and she gasped as she watched James pick up the ring then kneel in the shallow water.

"Alana, you're the woman God had planned for me. I love you. Will you marry me?"

Dropping her scoop and sieve, Alana threw her arms around his neck. "Yes, James! I will marry you!" She let go and held her hand out as James stood and slipped the ring onto her finger.

Alana heard cheering coming from the beach, where her family stood watching as James bent down and kissed her.

"God has been faithful to help you overcome your struggle with fear, and He's healed my feelings of bitterness. Just like the sun will rise and set each day, God will go before us in all we do," James said as they turned and watched the glorious display of the setting sun.

Marie's Homesteader Beans

Mix together in large pot:

1 large can pork and beans
1 or 2 cans drained kidney beans
1 can drained lima beans
1 pound cooked ground beef
½ pound cooked and chopped bacon

Mix in bowl:

½ onion, chopped
¼ cup barbecue sauce
¼ cup ketchup
½ cup brown sugar
1 tablespoon mustard

Stir mixture into beans and heat through on stove. Optionally, mix beans in slow cooker and heat.

Lorine Brunstetter Van Corbach became interested in the Plain people's culture as a young child after visiting the Lancaster Amish with her parents. Lorine is a music teacher and lives in southwest Idaho with her husband, Bil. They have three daughters and two grandchildren. Lorine enjoys playing the piano, singing, writing, gardening, cooking, and traveling.

Brides of the Big Valley

In an area of Pennsylvania called The Big Valley, a uniquely blended Amish community thrives in which three distinct groups of Amish identify themselves by the colors of their buggies' tops—white, black, or yellow. Three young women search for faith and love within this special place. Deanna is a widow who sees her second chance of love slipping away. Rose Mary is at a point in life where she must choose the path of her faith and the right man to walk with her on it. Leila is burdened with family responsibilities and wonders when she will ever start a family of her own.

Paperback / 978-1-68322-886-8

Return to the Big Valley

Return with the bestselling Brunstetter authors to an area of Pennsylvania called The Big Valley. Three young women put romance on hold as life throws heartache their way. Wilma calls off the wedding when Israel's life takes an unplanned turn. Martha breaks off with Glen when he talks of leaving the Amish faith. Recently widowed, Alma has unexpected news and returns to Kentucky just as an old romance was being renewed with Elias.

Paperback / 978-1-64352-871-7